THE DARKLING WIND

S.P. SOMTOW

CHRONICLES OF THE HIGH INQUEST

THE DARKLING WIND

INTRODUCTION BY THEODORE STURGEON

DRAWINGS BY MIKEY JIRAROS

DIPLODOCUS PRESS

BANGKOK · LOS ANGELES

THE DARKLING WIND

originally published by Bantam-Spectra 1985
First Edition
Diplodocus Press 2013
Revised Edition 2020

published by Diplodocus Press Bangkok • Los Angeles

for information about the author:
www.somtow.com
about this publisher
www.diplodocuspress.com

ISBN:
978-1-9409996-0-9 (paperback)
978-1-9409995-9-3 (hardcover)
978-1-9409996-1-6 (ebook)

0 9 8 7 6 5 4 3 2 1

for Ted Sturgeon
from whom I have learned so much
who doesn't have feet of clay
always I remain
your disciple

CONTENTS

An Introduction to
The Darkling Wind
by Theodore Sturgeon

What's that you have in your hands?

A book, you say.

No, it isn't.

A novel, then?

No — it's more than that. It began to be a novel three novels ago.

What, then? Some kind of explosion?

No; one can't even say that. (Don't be alarmed; it won't go off in your hands.) No; because there's one characteristic of all explosions; like plucked strings, they begin to decay the very microsecond they reach their peak. This book doesn't.

What is it then?

Ah. So many things. It is the fourth part of a trilogy. It's a shattering storm that whirls away, leaving your world full of brilliance and cacophonies of color — but never leaves its residence just over the horizon. It's an adventure — yours, perhaps much more than the adventures of its array of astonishing characters. It's (to use a critic's cliché) a mind-stretching experience; few if any writers have even attempted the description of a universe so vast, nor the almost limitless power — and powers — within it. Yet never for a moment is it out of the author's control, and therefore out of the reader's understanding (or at least, his comprehension.) There are things which simply *are* which passeth understanding; but this young giant never enters the intangible through laziness. Listen:

> There is a difference between the old gods and the new. The important thing is that the new gods are moulded in man's image. They do not seek to force mankind into something it is not: they are ideals, not entities. You have seen the consequences ... of having gods that actually exist! In freeing them, we have returned to them the right to fashion their own gods.

Throughout his work, Sucharitkul breaks the reader's pace (never his own!) with asides so provocative that one must, with great reluctance, guide oneself to the banks of his stream of narrative, and sit and think it out:

> "Truth, my dear friend, is merely the prevailing percentage of our private illusions."

Take that before breakfast, my dear friend, and it will surely alter your day.

***

I have a confession to make: I don't make a habit of blowing deadlines, but I have done so drastically this time, and for a very interesting reason. A part of my confession is this: I have developed a curmudgeonish impatience with the current rash of trilogies, tetralogies, multi-volume 'epics', 'sagas' and so on (and on.) (Unless, of course, they're written by Marion Zimmer Bradley, Quinn Yarbro, or their rare ilk.) I've tried to be fair; as a reviewer, I hide behind the phrase "For those who enjoy ..." and keep the curmudgeon in check.

But I heard Somtow read a portion of his *Vampire Junction* and was quite carried away, and produced a fulsome review for the Washington *Post,* which resulted in the request that I introduce this — this which you hold in your hands. Reading it, I wanted to know more (not that exactly; later, I wanted to bathe more in this chiaroscuro of style and movement (and found myself avidly and attentively reading this book's precursors: *Light on the Sound, The Throne of Madness,* and *Utopia Hunters.* One cannot read with such attention and intensity within the confines of short deadline-time; at least I couldn't and didn't. My gratitude, therefore, to your editor, Chris Edwards, for his monumental patience. The result of this long immersion in these four great books has been that I have not more to say to you, but less. My greatest wish is that the work speaks for itself to you, and not that I speak for you. I think that the best way to express it is to say that I deeply envy anyone who has not read the tale of the Inquestors, for they have before them this transcendent experience.

***

A last word, concerning Somtow personally. Write as he does, at times, about murder-en-masse and buckets of blood, he is one of the gentlest, most well-mannered and engaging people I have ever encountered. He looks like a smiling teenage Buddha. He has been seen (at this writing, 1985) increasingly at conferences and conventions; if the occasion arises for you to be in his presence — be there.

I don't know what his age is.

Perhaps he doesn't have one.

— *Theodore Sturgeon*
Springfield, Oregon

The Seven Inquestors of the Darkling Wind

VARUNEH Mother Vara, the One Mother, created the High Inquest and the game of *makrúgh,* and established its dominion over the million known worlds of the Dispersal of Man. It was she who first tamed the Throne of Madness on Uran s'Varek, and bound the boundless power of the Darkling Wind.

ELLORAN the Wise took from Vaurneh the gift of compassion and established it in his heart, and the hearts of the worlds over which he ruled. When men looked on him and his works, they knew that the Inquest was good.

KARAKAËL the Lord of a Million Masks perverted the game of *makrúgh* and compassion's meaning. When men looked on him and his works, they knew that the Inquest was evil. Yet the Inquestors pitied him, for he did not understand himself.

DAVARYUSH the Heretic found the flaw in the utopia the Inquest had made, and he knew that it must fall. But he could not bring that fall about, for he was already tainted by the Inquest's corruption, and the good he tried to accomplish turned against him. So he searched for an innocent to continue his cause.

KELVER was a peasant boy whom Davaryush raised to the Inquest to be that innocent who would bring about the Inquest's fall. He found the Throne of Madness and unleashed the Darkling Wind, cloaking himself in shadow. But in fulfilling the plan of Davaryush, he was compelled to shatter Davaryush's hold on him.

ARRYK was another peasant much like Kelver. Elloran raised him up to be his disciple. He learned to love the old ways and their embodiment in Elloran. Kelver was his closest friend but when the revolution came, he became his bitterest enemy.

SIRISS was the Inquestrix they both loved. She was caught in the clash of light and shadow. She saw the war from both sides. The more she understood, the more she became unable to choose between them.

OVERTURE

The Burning of the Rainbow

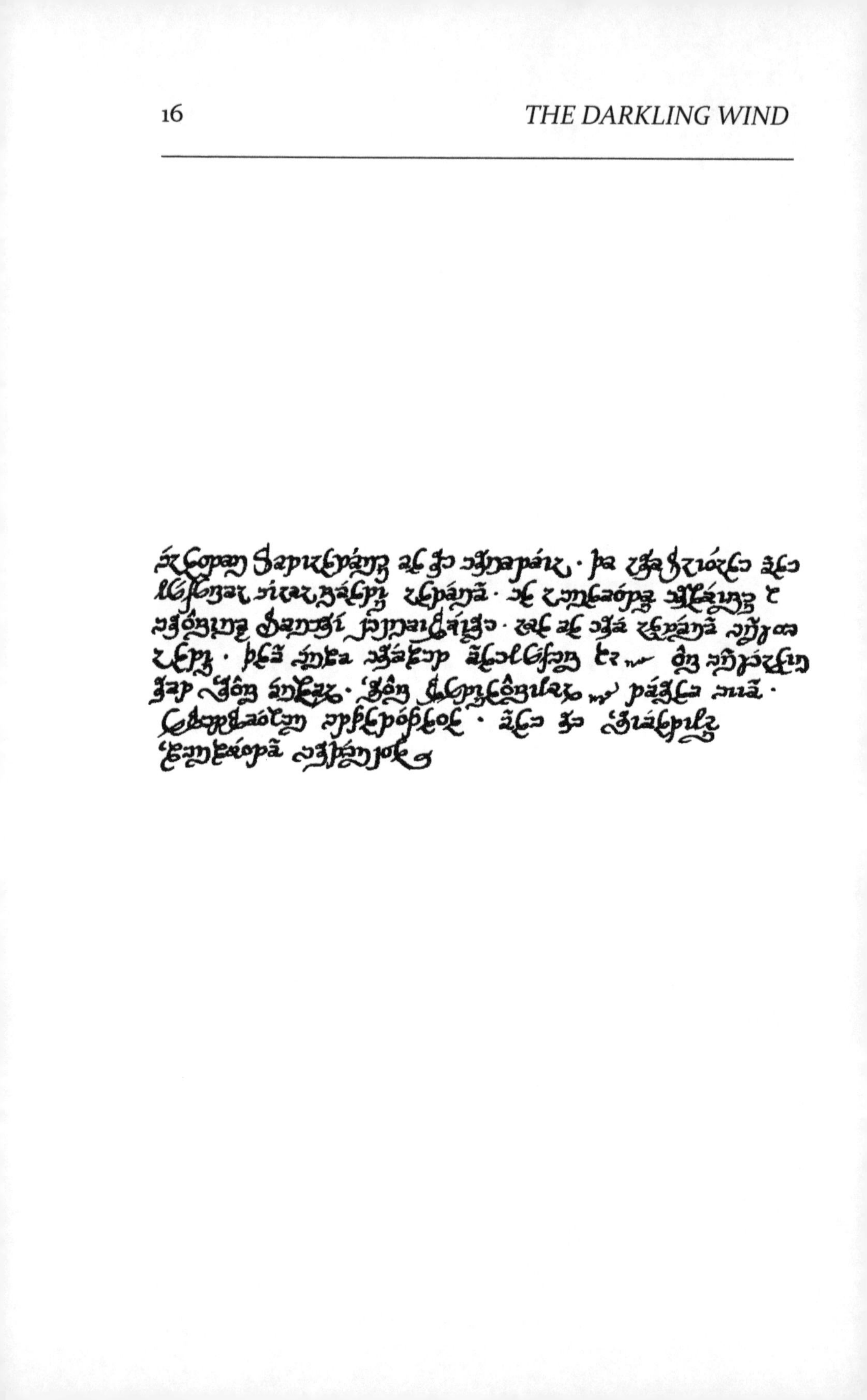

In the Highspeech of Varezhdur

esturan paristránen at ke eknaráis, sha skapsiúste ahtelýxmas eisas matrin stranáh, et sentaóraran ektháimen z ekóminas panekí jejnaivaiske: sat at eká stránah Enquéstrin, shtáh énda ekáder ahtelýxem za. Om Enquéstin kar chum ánthas, chom vyrintómilas. Rákta eyáh, yverváuzen ershtrúshtut, áhte ke chiátrilan dhendáorah ekshénjut.

In the Lowspeech of Essondras

ka swe tu narwest an shterwo di parwe shterwenekeks, tu shast sweperen fordwektos yezhwe a nwweros di shterwenekeks, pweke nweskeren a sentrawaros iero temwo ka iarek wominek. Ma swe ano di shterwenekeks sha degweren d'an Inwestro, fordwekto di si sha kwemeren forekwe. Pwekwer pwe Inwestro nwa swem kom wizwyeks ka kom entwomos di puiro. Es rekwo, owerwederen a shtroweren, forke lilo tiwatro di daunwaros es ekshwendo.

And if you tell a manystranded tale, you shall construct prologues equal to the number of strands, so as to acquaint your audience of the principal theme and personages of each; but if one of the strands concerns an Inquestor, its prologue must by definition come first. For we are to the Inquest as flowers, as mayflies; it is proper that the grand view be established before the little drama of us mortals is played out.

—from Karnofara's *Treatise on the Composition of Necrodramas,* bilingual edition, Essondras: forty Old Years before the Falling Beyond.

THE INQUESTORS' PROLOGUE: *The Game to Vanquish Time*

There is history, and there is no history. These were the opening words of the game of *makrúgh,* which the High Inquestors had been playing for twenty millennia. The words were spoken at elegant dinners and extravagant receptions; they were intoned to the strains of shimmerviol quartets and the brash brayings of conch consorts. They were shouted while drunk on sweet zul; they were spat out in anger and whispered in erotic arousal. They were spoken before great throngs of Inquestors, with their shimmercloaks fluttering and rustling and glittering thousand-eyed in a man-conjured wind; they were muttered in secret, in shadowed vestibules, in crowd-cloaked plazas, in steel-walled starship corridors; they were spiced with solemnity and leavened with levity. Always they presaged the game; and always, these words having been uttered, the participants played as if driven, unrelenting, joyless. It was a game of words alone: of lavish hyperbole and trenchant conceit, of nuance and inconstruable ambiguity, of half-truths laced with lies. It was a long game, as the shortlived ancestors from an old dead world counted time: it lasted days usually, sometimes even years. One game was reputed to have lasted a century. There was no need for haste; indeed, compassion compelled the delaying of the game's conclusion. For *makrúgh* had but a single known outcome. When an Inquestor accepted the challenge of *makrúgh* he accepted also what must happen at the game's end: a world's death, a civilization's ruin, a planet's soul laid desolate.

A thousand thousand were the worlds of the Dispersal of

Man. Those that fell beyond in the playing of the great game were few and soon forgotten; for most planets prospered, and the Inquestors were as gods, their motives as inscrutable as their power absolute. And every thinking man knew that the Inquestors' acts of destruction were not motivated by vengeance or the desire for carnage. Bloody, personal warfare was a thing of the old bad times, before the Inquest. The new wars were compassionate ones; their victims need never suffer guilt, for the Inquestors had taken the universe's guilt upon their own shoulders.

And so for twenty thousand years they stayed the advance of time, and engineered a great stasis; for the little wars, ripples in mankind's ocean, created enough of an illusion of movement so as to mask its stillness. This was the meaning of the salutation *History there is, and no history.* In their compassion, the lnquestors had sought, by inflicting what they deemed the lesser suffering, to avoid the greater suffering which was a necessary consequence of man's fallen state; by manufacturing histories in miniature, to bring about the end of history itself.

Yet it should not be said that this was an evil time. Later, after the fall of the Inquest, many would remember it as a golden age. And all the protagonists of the days of its downfall would attain the status of gods. They would be imbued with mythic motives; knowledge of the mysteries of the universe would be imputed to them.

And yet-deification aside-the legends of the future would fall far short of the reality. For in the dark ages to come (though they would not, of course, *see* themselves as living in dark ages) they would not truly be able to imagine a past in which men sailed the overcosm on delphinoid ships, and breached transfinite dimensions in their tachyon bubbles, and thought nothing of pulverizing whole planets, and who danced on the faces of suns ... men who had tamed the soul of the black hole at the galaxy's heart. How could they imagine those things?

No. Gods it would be. Epic battles. Hero against hero splayed across the starstream. The names would mutate into alien names and star systems be scaled down to walled cities. In the end, this history would be reduced to the myth of a fall from grace: a myth that existed long before the Inquest was even dreamed of, and that will exist, in some form, for as long as men yearn for a past more glorious than their own. It is in men's nature to create gods.

But the story of the fall of the Inquest is not a myth. It should not deal, then, with gods, but with men; and men are the provenance of history.

But it would be well to begin with a myth, and with the historical event that was to become the germ of that myth....

THE MORTALS' PROLOGUE: *The Burning of the Rainbow*

A thousand years later it would be said that it was the burning of Ir Jenjen's Rainbow Darkness that heralded the coming of the revolution to the backworld Essondras. Inevitably so, for the confusion and complexity of history must finally be filtered into legend; and legend, amplified by resonances from ever more remote pasts, must at last be transformed into myth.

Ir Jenjen the darkweaver did not believe in myths at all; for every myth she had cherished in childhood had been shattered by the true tales told her by Tievar, the old rememberer from the palace of Elloran the Inquestor.

Indeed, it is probably true that for every citizen of Essondras who experienced the rebellion and the coming of the Shadow Inquest, there was a separate moment at which the revolution could be said to have begun. Some would have said, on the last night of the performance of Zalo's play at the necrotheater; others might have mentioned the first appearance of Rememberers in the streets of Íkshatra, the capital city; still others the emergence of the kashanthras from the sewers, or the coming of Kelver, the compassionate one, from the stars.

But a goodly number would have mentioned the burning of the rainbow.

***

It is perhaps ironic, then, that Ir Jenjen, the creator of the Rainbow Darkness, did not even witness the burning. She was alone on a floater, far out to sea, when it happened.

Because of the interactions of Essondras's many moons, its oceans were among the most eccentric in the Dispersal of Man. There were a few who enjoyed the game of predicting the tides, but most people were content to think of them as entirely random. But it happened that, by some curious alignment of the moons, an island, submerged for some centuries, had reappeared in the middle of the sea of Arweshkash. The place was something of an archaeological curiosity, being the site of the landing of the people bins that first seeded the planet. The bins themselves, indestructible, still ringed the island like a barrier reef, forming cylindrical metal walls of a lagoon; on the island itself stood monoliths of an amethystine rock not found anywhere on the mainland.

Jenjen had parked her floater on the beach of purple stones. She spent the day sitting on the rocks and watching the sunset and the moons' rise over the string of people bins. She loved the colors of this place. In the twilight the moons glistened like tears. The beach was crosshatched with the shadows of the tall stones, lines of lavender, mauve, violet, deep purple ... there came a wavewind from the sea. She closed her eyes, thinking of the new darkweaving she was preparing for the opening of a new wing of the Ministry of the Thinkhive. All these new colors should go into it, she thought.

She slipped deeper into her reverie. She thought of how those people bins, each bearing thousands of her ancestors, had sailed the overcosm, their inhabitants time-frozen, between life and death, perhaps for centuries. Now the bins were just empty shells. She wondered whether they could be reactivated, or whether the Inquest just discarded them after use.

She must have drifted off. When she opened her eyes again it was much darker, and some of the moons were high in the sky.

Suddenly she became aware of a kind of rumbling, just at the edge of her hearing, an unease. She looked about.

Halfway toward the horizon, the people bins still glinted ... they seemed to be bobbing up and down! Something has to be wrong. But it was nothing she could put her finger on. The sea ... it smelled strange, metallic.

Then a dull boom, as if from a great distance, like a far avalanche. What was it? She screamed involuntarily. A tower tall wave was lurching out of the ocean—coming straight for the island! She whirled around and began to run away from the beach. Water lapped at her feet. She ran up the slope of the beach, toward the purple standing stones. A watery crash. She heard the wave receding. She turned, watched the sea, the sky. Stillness. I must have imagined it, she thought. But then she realized that her feet and arms were soaked.

What could it have been? She waited, breathing nervouslv. And then—

A dark cylinder dropping from the sky! Crossing the face of one moon ... then another ... swooping down to the ocean ... I have to get uphill, uphill, she thought, there's going to be another wave, my floater's going to capsize for sure—

A burst of incandescence behind the uppermost of the moons. Silent fireworks. Without warning, a wall of water burst from the sea and engulfed her for a moment. Gasping, coughing up water, she grasped the slick rocks and pulled herself farther up the incline. More cylinders were falling now. She could hear them: the tense air hummed, the salt wind of their falling stung her eyes. She groped, found a few more handholds, reached a dry ledge. Water clogged the mechanism of her darkrobe; it had ceased to generate the holosculpt images of dark flame with which she cloaked herself ... she appeared naked suddenly except for some soggy scraps of cloth plastered to her skin.

The water was gathering up again in the distance. More thuds as the cylinders hit the water far away ... she was thinking, Not much of a noise, considering what it's doing to the sea, it sounds like a zul flask being uncorked, that's all. It was all dreamlike, unreal, like a scene from a necrodrama.

She climbed a little higher, huddled in a monolith's purple shadow. She was well above the waterline now. Below she could see her floater being tossed about like a toy starship. How am I going to get back to the mainland? she thought wildly. She clutched at the farspeaker she wore in a locket around her neck, wondering whether it was waterproof. She was about to use it when she saw a second floater overhead, searchbeams swathing from its underbelly. She could make out a few men looking out over the railings: darkrobed men, pacing back and forth, shouting to one another. There were children too, of a sort she recognized from her sojourn in the palace of Elloran the Inquestor—

Childsoldiers!

And she understood why all this was happening. Well, she thought grimly, there's my answer to the question of people bins. They don't reuse them. They send down new ones. It's starting now. The end of the world.

Somehow she felt obliged to express great outrage, to wail in anger ... she stood there on the rocks, now and then getting drenched, battered by a manmade wind, screaming her rage ... but within herself she felt curiously little passion: only a coldness, an emptiness, a deadness. She had known for ten years that this end was coming. They had told her when she left the palace of Elloran: that Essondras had *fallen beyond* in the game of *makrúgh,* that her world was doomed. She had been angry then, truly angry. But she'd used up all her rage as fuel for the great Rainbow darkness that she had built in Ikshatra. She had woven the entire history of the Inquest into that bridge of darkness that spanned the city. Many had called it the greatest of all darkweavings.

But all Jenjen could feel about her creation was the grief she had woven into it. Colors had stranded and unstranded themselves until they had canceled each other out and become dark ... was that not the nature of darkweaving? The long hours at the lightloom, the peremptory discipline of Jenjen's training, had led her finally to reject the weaving of tapestries of light, garish, coruscatory, unfulfilling. She had come to love the darkness.

Her Rainbow Darkness, which she had named *Utopia Hunters,* was a testament to her bitterness and the bitterness of millions who felt manipulated and abused by the great powers who controlled the universe. Some called it the greatest darkweaving ever made. It had incited riots. But ten years had gone by; the *falling beyond* had not happened, nor the revolution come to pass. Only the Rainbow Darkness remained.

I cannot truly feel rage anymore, Jenjen thought. The darkness has drained it all away from me.

All this while she yelled and cursed at the floater with its grim-faced operators and alien markings as it hovered over head, its searchbeams now and then intersecting the translucent amethystine of the menhirs and making them glow oddly. She could not bear the thought of showing them the emptiness she really felt inside. Anger! She must show anger! Wasn't that the only proper reaction to the senseless slaughter of her homeworld? But the ocean thunder drowned her cries and the people bins continued to tumble into the sea. She shrieked till her throat felt raw but no catharsis came. Had those tiny men up there in their floater even seen her? She thought not.

After a very long time she noticed that her farspeaker was blinking: amber-red, amber-red, amber-red. Quickly she held it to her ear and subvocalized: "Response."

A voice, agonized: "We've been trying to reach you for hours! They're burning the rainbow, Jeni! You've got to stop it—"

"I can't come," she subvoked. She wondered who it was and how they had known her personal code. "My floater's gone. I'm stranded."

"They're burning the rainbow!"

"Who? Who is burning the rainbow?"

"No one knows! You must save it—"

"What difference can it possibly make?" she screamed. "The world is going to end!"

And then, at last, came anger. And with it relief, that she was still capable of feeling anger. That, for her, was the moment it began. With that gnawing, bursting fury. That first flash of genuine anger was the real beginning of the revolution for Ir Jenjen, weaver of darkness.

***

Zalo pressed his farspeaker back into the servocorpse's outstretched hand. "I'm not even sure I raised her. She's out at sea or something."

Outside, despite the soundproofing of the theater guild's private zul-club, he could hear the rabble. They must be cramming the streets to watch it.

"Try again," the apprentice said. His makeup-stained hands barely met around the skull that held warm foaming zul.

"She's got to know what they're doing to her creation—"

"Powers of powers, get that hero-worship look off your face! I haven't spoken to the woman since ... since the day she unveiled that thing."

"Sorry, sir. But surely you are the only one who can tell her. After all, the whole world knows that you and she were lovers before the Inquest snatched her away."

"I cannot presume on an ancient relationship," Zalo said.

He knew the apprentice was staring weirdly at him, but his thoughts were far away.

He remembered Jeni: when they were young together and she wove brilliant tapestries of light and had not yet faced the darkness in herself, and himself barely a boy, just like this young apprentice, painting the corpses' faces in the dungeon dressing rooms of the necrotheater....

And later when she came back from her sojourn among the Inquestors and told him the true story of the Rainbow King and he was angry that she'd dared to shatter his myths and darkness began to encroach upon her lightweavings and she could no longer bear Essondras and fled back, skyward, into the arms of the Inquest.

And when she came back a second time she was young still, time-frozen by time-dilation, but he was seven years older, seven years more sad; and she had spoken of revolution and the Inquest's fall; and she knew herself no longer a lightweaver but a darkweaver, and she wove the Rainbow Darkness over the city as a monument to all she had seen and heard from the mouths of Rememberers; she wove into her city-spanning darkbridge all the Inquest's pain, its glory, its splendor, its brutality, and the sum total of its history was the one unbroken darkness ... foretelling the end of the Inquest....

And they'd clung to each other more than ever, their passion fierce, uncontrollable, knowing that the end would come soon, and they'd waited, waited, waited, for the In quest's vengeance, for the firedeath to fall on Essondras, and there was nothing, for years and years and years, till their love's flame sputtered and was spent and they went their separate ways....

And now someone was burning the rainbow!

"Come quickly," the apprentice was saying, tugging at his arm. "You'll miss it."

He thrust a few gipfers at the servocorpse's hand, which had remained outstretched, locked in place, as was the manner of servocorpses, all through his reverie; together they slipped out of a side door onto the street.

He half-expected a wave of heat; there was none. There was no wind; the night was clear, cold, the moons' light blotted out by the cold reflected fire that danced on mirror metal domes and on the silver patens of displacement plates that spangled Angkhoshti Avenue. It came from the sky, from the ribbon of what had once been pure darkness—

The street was crammed with gawkers. He could scarcely breathe. "My floater," he said. "Get my floater." The boy subvoked a command; the floater came zigzagging through the crowd. He leaped on and the boy followed. "Skyward," he whispered. They coiled up; the throng was motionless, staring glazedly upward, like a huge storeroom of servocorpses. Other floaters peppered the brilliant night. Ahead, the rainbow. It used to slice the night sky, eclipsing the starfield with its arc of shadow. Now filaments of color were crackling inside it, lightning jags of crimson and cerulean and gold and mauve and sea green were bursting loose and flashing against roof tops. And now and then, as the light-strands unraveled, an image—

"What does it mean, Master Zalo?" the boy was crying out.

"I don't know!"

"Look, a man!"

Brief afterimage of a shimmercloaked King on a throne.

More Kings. Childsoldiers, their laser-irises dilated. Planets being torn apart. All these images had been warpwoofe into the Rainbow Darkness, blent so artfully that their sum total had been the rainbow's total blackness. But it wasn't right to pry so deeply into a darkweaver's thought processes. It was positively obscene to think of this unraveling, this vomiting out of raw unconscious energy. Art was control. Like the words that you thought into the mouth of a servocorpse in the necrodrama. This was madness. "Who could have dared to burn the rainbow?" he shouted.

"Master, only Jenjen herself could have done it. To unravel a darkweaving requires almost as much art as to bind it together in the first place ... and they all seal their artworks with secret ciphers so that they cannot be undone."

"She would never do it! She loved that Rainbow Darkness. It was her masterpiece. Her whole life went into it. But there *is* one that would know the codes ... the planetary thinkhive."

"Master—what is that?"

A woman outlined in electric blue, her hairstrands swirling from the sea to the mountains—

"That is mother Vara, who created the Inquest, who charged them with the playing of *makrúgh* and commanded them to hunt utopias, freezing the march of history," Zalo said, remembering what Jenjen had once told him. "And look." He pointed. From the swirling hair, which parted like an ocean, sprang other figures "There they all are! Karakaël of the million masks, who has drawn the hordes of the Inquest unto himself ... Arryk the melancholy, who was once beloved of Kelver and Siriss, but who now fights for the old ways ... Siriss of the opal eyes, torn between light and shadow ... and in the middle, at the eye of the galactic storm, sitting on the Throne of Madness from which he has drawn his power—"

"The Prince of Shadow!" the apprentice cried.

"Quiet!" Without thinking, Zalo slapped the boy's face. "You want to get us denounced and sent to the Arm? You want to be a corpse instead of a corpse dancer?"

"Master ... " Tears welled up in the apprentice's eyes. But he was defiant. "I thought it didn't matter anymore. This is the sign, isn't it? The sign of the end of the Inquest. Surely Kelver will come now."

"You're a superstitious little boy. No one will come. Kelver is not a god. He's an Inquestor who has turned his back on the Inquest, that's all. He is no Prince of Shadow. Grow up." They'd all gone mad, that was it. Jenjen and the renegade Inquestors and those who supported the so-called revolution ... ten years and no salvation had fallen from the sky. He was angry because he too had believed, had so desperately wanted to believe. And the light raged in the sky, mocking the people's blind faith ... It was to have symbolized the rebellion!" Zalo said. "Our hope, our dark hope. No, *she* did not burn the rainbow. We are crushed now."

"Master Zalo, Kelver will come. The stars will no longer be symbols of man's imprisonment." He had certainly memorized all those propaganda disks. "He'll come, sir, he'll come," and he was crying bitterly, his tears catching fire from the burning night, his face a chalky checkerboard in the latticed firelight. "All right, all right, he'll come." But Zalo did not believe it. "Now let's hurry back."

"One last look, sir ... please?"

"Yes."

In the flashing of the rainbow: armies of childsoldiers swarming among the stars ... palaces crumbling ... nebulas of dust ... birds sizzling in mid-flight ... a screaming star ... a mountain girt with rainbows ... a flock of pteratygers, a fleet of delphinoid starships, a chain reaction of exploding planets. Was it past or prophecy? He didn't know, he didn't care to know yet. The play, that was the important thing. "Come on, kid, no more dreaming," he said. "We've got to get the Elloran corpse made up again by tomorrow night; its cheeks have gotten smudged."

"Yes, sir!" The boy had blinked back his tears now. They would go back to work. They would turn their backs on the sky that exploded with visions of a repressive past and a nebulous future:

"Oh, and I want the stormwatchers alerted about Jenjen being stranded on the island. She'll probably be too distracted to subvoke a help signal, knowing her. But ... anonymously. Let's not have her rescuers blabbing some tale to her about the lovesick Zalo, raving hysterically—"

"Right. Yes, sir."

"Come now, don't be disappointed at missing out on some amorous intrigue. We've no more time for complications. We've dead men's faces to paint by dawn."

No, Zalo thought, the revolution had not begun today.

Not for me, not for anyone else.

***

There were streets in Essondras that no one traveled anymore, not since the system of displacement plates had been installed centuries ago. There was no more need for streets; the arrondissements had sprawled and mushroomed, freed from the need for spatial planning, and the streets had become overgrown with dark orange lichenmoss and extravagant fungi. The streets were safe meeting places for lovers' trysts or political rallies; even the Arm did not care to monitor them.

To such a street came Ir Jenjen the darkweaver, led by a phantom pteratyger. She knew it was only an image because it wavered, its wings passed through the walls, and through its tawny featherdown she could see graffiti scrawled on the worn sandstone bricks. She had followed it from the academy, through several displacement plates, and now into the plateless labyrinth, the seams of the city, not questioning it at all; for it had roared noiselessly at her, and she had seen in its eyes the emerald eyes of Kelver the Prince of Shadow.

At the corner the pteratyger, shimmering against the flagstones, faded away. It was not a corner she recognized, but she trusted the Way of Shadow, and would not despair. She waited. It was day, but the walls of the arrondissements on either side of her were so high as to admit only a slit of sunlight. The lichenmoss was moist; a sickly scent, as of putrefying citrus fruits, oozed onto the still, heavy air.

She said (her own voice frightening herself a little), "I'm here."

A woman spoke from the walls' shadow: "Ir Jenjen: I am Kail Jannif, astrogator, emissary of Shadow."

"Yes." A moment passed. "Don't hide, let me see you ... "

"No. The Prince sent me to tell you, to tell all who have secretly labored for the revolution, that—"

"I know! I was caught in the tidal wave of the people bins' landing!"

"Yes. We know." And Jannif emerged from the shadow a little, a gray-garbed woman, hooded, a polarizing darkfield drawn tightly about her eyes. "Be glad!"

'They have destroyed my rainbow. Who? Who?" "Don't be afraid."

"And Kelver ... how is Kelver?"

"We are all concerned for him, Jeni. He is ... troubled. It must not be easy to sit on the Throne of Madness. When we can see him, though, he greets us with the old love in his eyes."

"I remember." When she closed hereyes she saw him clearly: green-eyed, the boy-man, beautiful, compassionate. She, like many others, had loved him in Varezhdur, the golden palace that sailed the overcosm. And had bound herself to follow him into profoundest darkness, not looking back. “But who burned the rainbow?”

Hands clasped her hands. Their warmth came from the Prince of Shadow himself.... “We don’t know. It was not in the plan. Perhaps it was Arryk, acting on Karakaël’s orders, avenging himself on all those who have robbed him of Kelver’s love.

“Then they’re here already? The ones from the other side, I mean. The war has begun?”

“No. First I and Tya must go to the galactic arm to capture and haul in one of Queen Ynyoldeh’s deathmoons. And the Inquestors must play out the endgame in the *makrúgh* that will seal Essondras’s doom.”

"I'm afraid."

“The litany, then. Together. You and me.”

“All right.” She tried to calm herself, and then she and Jannif spoke together the simple words that had already been repeated and would continue to be repeated a million million times, words that would become part of the myth of the fall of the Inquest ... the only words that, in the dark age to come, would remain undistorted by the calumny of time:

He is Love. He is Shadow. He comes to salve the sick soul. He comes to set history in motion again. His heart is pure. He will shatter the fetters that bind us to the Inquest and the Inquest to us. The war will rage around him and trillions will perish for his sake; but those trillions will have known freedom. And though they perish, he is the truth that will not perish. For ever and ever. He is the Eye of the Galactic Storm; he is the Darkling Wind unleashed.

BOOK ONE
The Embalming-Bird

Vzerma Kivrellin

e réjeshom myzdren éo
hohss sha tresheúr ómbrein z témbrein;
den temávo ney'vió
kar mun shánto s'athmenem
ómbres y'hokh'Tathoten.
Mun veráva jivýten mi
eih eih Tón Kivrélleh:
dhánatan ektasía vezashío,
kar dhanáta ke hautíereh tembra,
z yver angs shtah rejéshom zi:
chítarans mi ke hyémadh;
chitármadh nahaa shéno;
makházhnemas kis varak;
ánym ke tembrázhande.

Hymn to Kelver

I go to a hidden kingdom,
a kingdom to be found in shadows and dark places.
No more am I afraid,
for I feel upon me the breath
of the Prince of Shadow.
Demand of me my life, Ton Keverell!
Death I will face with joy;
for death is the darkest of places,
beyond which lies your kingdom:
homeworld of my heart,
heartworld of my desire,
eye of the galactic storm,
the Darkling Wind.

—traditional, from before the Ages of Darkness

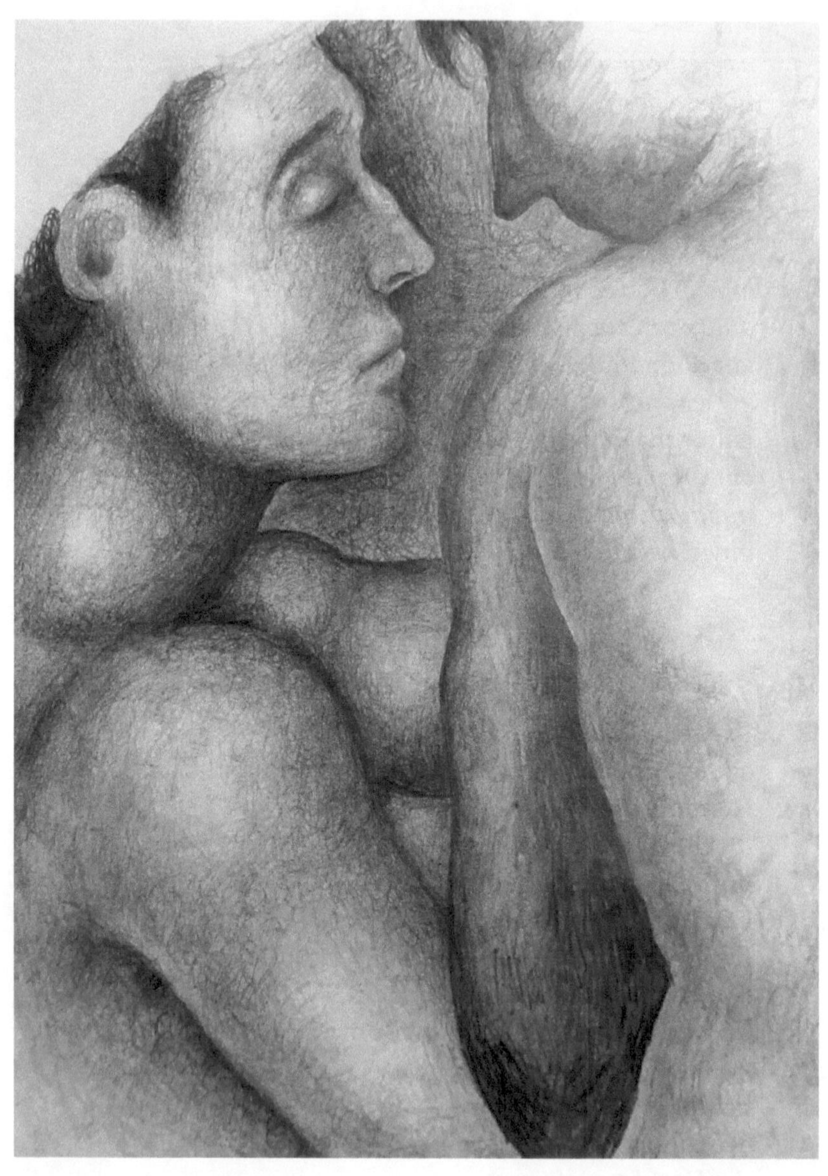

One

The Wings of the Shadow

Out of the light-mad overcosm, darkness.

"Are you sure?" Tya shouted over the groaning of the reluctant delphinoid, awoken from the dreamstate of sailing the space between spaces, bursting into dark reality. "Kail Jannif, it's so dark here!"

Kail Jannif broke free of her astrogating trance. Tya, childsoldier turned woman, ran from wall to wall, subvocalizing the command to deopaque again and again, unnerved.

"They are deopaqued," Jannif said wearily. "We're in the far arm of the galaxy, Tya. Look, behind you—"

Tya turned. Here and there, a pinprick of light. And, behind them, a mistveil veined with lightstreaks.

"That's where we came from," Jannif said. "The Dispersal of Man."

"Where's the armory then?"

"Ahead. Ton Ynyoldeh, the Dark lnquestor, made a point of keeping them as far from the center as possible."

"Come then."

She felt no motion. As she grew used to this darkness she saw that there were many stars after all: not the dazzling richness of men's homeworlds, but an austere tapestry of cold lights. Tya knew better, but she shivered. The starship shuddered; had the thin starfield shifted a little? Had it? She knew they were moving, but which way?

"Where is it?" she said. "The armory, I mean."

"Ahead. Don't you see it? A gap in the stars, too round to be anything but manmade ... a moonful of deathtoys. We're to cast a net of force about it and tow it through the overcosm, back to Ton Keverell n'Davaren Tath."

Tya could make it out now, a black nonrefleetive sphere, a hole in the starfield. "Do we have the key?"

"No, the Inquestor has it. We're just to grab the satellite and tow it in. Quickly, secretly, without leaving a trail. ... What's the matter, Tya? Afraid?"

"Nothing. It's just ... I'd feel a lot better with millions of stars staring at me. Why did Ton Ynyoldeh have to hide her armories at the ends of the galaxy like this?"

"Who can know the mind of an Inquestor? But the answer's obvious. It's to stop people like *us* from snooping, raiding, stealing," Jannif said. She's really relishing this pirate's role, Tya thought. She was born a revolutionary.

Whereas I ... I was bred from childhood to unswervable loyalty. I was a childsoldier. I sang the anthem along with all the others, throwing my life on the High Inquest's mercy, laughing at death. It's hard for me to fight the Inquest.

She wouldn't have dreamt of fighting the High Inquest if it hadn't been for Kelver, the peasant boy named Inquestor, who now plotted the Inquest's downfall.

Jannif said, "Your childsoldiers are ready?"

"Yes."

"Here we go, then!"

For a second, a wild motion, a stomach-pit surging. The delphinoid was gliding toward the armory moon now. She could see it clearly now, a sphere riveted together from citrus segments of black metal. If you had the right key, you could make it pop open and disgorge its contents—weapons so powerful they could shred whole planets. Tya was in her element now. She closed her eyes and subvocalized to the starship's thinkhive.

Jets. Pressure skins.

A faint rumbling in the back of her mind. She knew that the childsoldiers were rousing themselves, pulling on the one-celled pressure skins, readying the tows to be planted ·on the armory. The black moon loomed ahead now. If only there were more stars, she thought uneasily, more stars.

Now!

Full deopaquement of the walls! And now, lightpods shooting from the ship's airlocks, bursting open, the childsoldiers scattering like petalfluff! A hail of children over the moon's blacksurface!

"Beautiful," Jannif said. "They're so beautiful."

"And their lives are over in an instant," Tya said. "Are you sad?"

"No. I wish I was like them. But my body's gone adolescent and mawkish, and I haven't the reflexes to be a soldier anymore. I can only give orders—"

"Let's go closer."

Jannif closed her eyes again and Tya knew that she was linking her mind with the delphinoid brain that controlled the ship's movements, that was its seeing-eye through the pinhole paths of the overcosm between spaces. Suddenly they were hugging the deathmoon's surface. You could make out the individual childsoldiers, storming over the darkness like phosphorflies, the pressure skins giving off a faint luminescence against the glareless surface. Now and then, when their graviboots spurted blue flame, they looked like spiraltailed meteors. In a moment the forcestrands would be in place, and the armory could be towed back through the overcosm to civilization.

The delphinoid drifted against the spinning of the armory. Suddenly, over the precarious close horizon-—

"What is it?" she cried, panicking suddenly. Just a comet.

"That's no ordinary comet. It just popped into existence on the other side of this armory!"

They both watched it as it arced up over the horizon, cutting a lightswath against the thin starstream. It couldn't be a natural object! Abruptly now it changed direction. It was *circling* the deathmoon, twisting closer and closer inward—

Tya remembered now what it was. “We had them on Bellares,” she said, thinking of the barrack world where she was trained to be a childsoldier. “They’re comets that have been animated with the brains of dead childsoldiers. They use them to smash into planets. They’re deadly, they’re sentient weapons that know only fanatical loyalty to the Inquest—”

“But Kelver ordered no such comet—”

“It’s not from our side!” Tya cried. “It’s someone else’s and it’s trying to kill us! Powers of powers, Jannif, divert it.”

“What about the children on the deathmoon?” “I don’t know, I don’t know,” Tya screamed.

The comet *was* getting nearer.

“What can we do?” said Jannif. “Can we contact it?” “I’ll try.” Tya subvoked a command to the ship’s thinkhive.

Awaken the sleeping child, she ordered. *Try to make him see us ....*

A hush. Then, out of the thin air, a child’s voice:

Beware. Beware. Doom. Doom. Die. Die.

It was a voice devoid of emotion, innocent of hatred. Just a childish treble.

Just then Tya heard a whisper in her mind that told her that the yoking was complete. The deathmoon dangled from the delphinoid now on strings of force. *Come back!* she screamed with her mind at the lost children. But even as she spoke she knew it was too late. The comet was bearing down on them, and with a jerk Jannif flung the starship in a somersault and the children scattered like dandelion seeds and the deathmoon swung below them like a pendulum and still the comet pursued them, its tail wriggling like a fish—

Flash! A split second of strained luminescence as they threaded the comet’s tail—

“The childsoldiers! Hold still for a second, Jannif, so we can reel them in!” Tya shouted.

"I'm losing control—the delphinoid shipmind is bucking against the mindmeld—”

Far away, against the moon’s surface, she could see the spore-children settling, a fine white dust on the circle of dark ... here and there, one or two still floated **in** space.

Lost. Dead. Though she knew that this was how war must be, she still felt these little losses, these pinpricks of anguish. But there were millions of childsoldiers. And only one goal: to pry loose the awesome shadow that had fallen over the universe of the Dispersal of Man, to cast down the High Inquest, to bring to pass the utopia that Kelver had promised them....

That was why, when her body had grown too adult for her to be a useful childsoldier, Tya had refused to be granted a clan-name, to take her place in the world beyond wars. Kelver, the strangest of Inquestors, had come to *her*. He had demanded not only service, but love. No one had asked her for that before. And so, when he had spoken of himself as the shadow's shadow, she had listened, and he talked of revolutions and *makrúghs* and the lives and deaths of star systems, and she had touched only the edge of his vast vision, but she had given him everything. Everyone in the childarmies of shadow had yielded up everything, bodies, souls, to the green-eyed Inquestor. The ones who had just died now, who would float the gray spaces, sealed in by their one-celled pressure skins, for all eternity, had died, she was sure, with Kelver's name on their lips.

Tya didn't understand about the revolution. But she knew what it was to be loved.

Now she communicated with the childsoldiers left on the deathmoon, making sure they had tethered themselves down. When this little scene with the comet was over, they'd pick up the survivors and—

Another jerk as the delphinoid swooped to avoid a head-on collision. "What—" The comet danced now, toying with them like a beast with its prey. Inside the head of the comet, Tya knew, was the brain of an angry child, extracted from a head severed at the exact moment of death. More lightning now as they wove in and out of the tail. The comet was huge but slow, for it was built to crash down on cities, not to play dodge'm with an agile starship.

Tya looked away, confident now that they would soon elude it, when—

Up, over the horizon of the comethead, black silhouette of a monster insect—

"It's the enemy!" shouted Jannif. "Let's get out of here!"

"Too late."

The other delphinoid soared up over the comethead's corona. Pods of childsoldiers rained into space. Now she could make them out, their bootjets thrusting blue fire as they headed toward the deathmoon.

They were near now, she could see them, silverfaced in the laminating skins that warmed them and let them breathe, their black cloaks stiff in the windlessness of space. They circled. Then, all at once, their laser-irises came on, and lines of yellow light streamed toward the deathmoon. They were all doomed now. It was unnatural that childsoldier could attack childsoldier! Once, they had *all* served the Inquest together, they had been one and powerful, but—

I've got to counterattack, Tya thought. I've got to forget that we're killing our own.

And, at the top of her lungs, she screamed out the childsoldiers' war-paean: *Isha ha! Isha ha! Isha ha ha heiy ha!* And she heard a responding chorus from all about the starship.

She skipped to the displacement plate and in a moment was rushing down the corridors, pausing in every segment to deopaque the walls so that they would see the encroaching enemy vessel and the firefly soldiers. Children flooded into the corridors, throwing on pressure skins, their long hair and their cloaks flying. Tya's eyes smarted from the glitter of a hundred iridium boots. But her childsoldiers were different from the ones she had fought beside, before she met Kelver. These children laughed as they made ready. Their eyes, slitty-golden from the laserimplants, did not have that perpetually haunted look that had, for thousands of years, been the childsoldiers' hallmark.

Now she could see, overhead, through the ceiling viewscreen, that the enemy children were circling the delphinoid; that some had already landed and were carrying tractor anchors such as they themselves had just planted on the surface of the deathmoon. *Hurry, hurry!* she subvocalized. She watched the strange battle from below. Her children were streaming from the airlocks, their pressure skins shrouding them in cold light. Silently, in a slow weightless ballet, they had joined forces. Quickly she subvocalized a command via the ship's thinkhive, to dispatch another battalion to the other ship. In an instant she saw it fly out, falling on the

enemy starship like a living meteor shower.

Now came the killing lasers from the soldiers' eyes as they grappled overhead; but pressure skins were made to withstand a great deal, and only now and then did one fall, sliced cleanly into segments, instantly cauterized, the segments at once sealed in by the elasticity of the pressure skin. Mostly all she could see was legs, the glare of iridium, an occasional body, face down, angelic in death. The legs crowded together, crammed, interlocked, as in the copulating of giant millipedes.

Overhead, eclipsing the black moon and the comet tail, the silver crab of the enemy starship.

A violent tugging now. She slammed into the wall. It was done! The two ships were yoked to each other on strands of force now, they were playing tug-of-war ... an eerie wheezing sounded in the corridors. Above, in the viewceiling, legs buckled, heads shattered noiselessly on the starship's hull. A grinding vibration now, pounding at her very bones-

Suddenly an ancient instinct seized her and she ran for the displacement plate. In the split second before she materialized beside Kail Jannif, she had seen—

Fire, coiling in the corridors, hissing as it snaked toward her, and tiny charred limbs spattering-

"They're boarding us!" Jannif looked up at her. Haggard. For a moment she felt tears well up. She knew she mustn't lose eye control, though. Or the laserimplants might go bad and slice something up.

They stared ahead. A black door was opening up in the forward screen's view of space. The comet was diving now, dazzlebright, and the stars whirled, and the lightmotes that were dead children stirred, though no breeze had touched them, only the ragged motion of the captured starship—

In the door, an lnquestor stood.

A young man with violet eyes. Possessed. He never looked at Jannif or Tya.

And Jannif blurted out: "I know you ... I saw you once, on the backworld Charra ... you were chasing Kelver "

“Kelver?” The Inquestor stood statue-still for a long moment, his shimmercloak shifting hypnotically from pink to ultramarine, pink to ultramarine. “Where is Kelver?” When he spoke the name Tya saw that he withheld some concentrated, awful emotion.

“We can’t tell you that, Ton Arryk n’Elloren Tath,” Jannif said, and Tya was surprised that she knew the strange Inquestor’s name.

“And you, little one?” Arryk touched her for a second. His hands just skimmed her incipient breasts. “Old for a childsoldier, aren’t you?”

“Never too old,” she said defiantly, “to serve Kelver.”

“What is this Kelver, Kelver?” Arryk said. “Do you no longer address Inquestors by their proper honorifics? Has degree then perished completely in your little heretic band?”

The two women didn’t answer him.

“Shall I be forced to torture you then? To wring your secrets from you like dirt from a washcloth, to despoil my own compassion?”

“We won’t speak,” Tya whispered fiercely. “We are the wings of Kelver’s words. We are his will, his shadow.”

“Religious mania sweeps the Dispersal of Man!” said Arryk scornfully. And then, in a voice fraught with true anguish, he cried out, “But why do you love him so much? What does he have?”

Tya said, “He is the Darkling Wind.”

And Arryk laughed a bitter, angry laugh, and said, “"There is no Darkling Wind. A small rebellion stirs; we crush it; that is all."

But Jannif said, “I remember you clearly now. I remember that you, too, once loved him. Before you faced the void at the heart of Uran s’Varek and were found wanting. All the universe knows the story.”

For a time Arryk was speechless. Then he said, “For the sake of that remembrance, astrogator, I will release your ship. We have captured the armory moon you tried to steal. Go back to your master, and tell him you have seen me. Tell him that we will meet over the dust that soon will be Essondras. He cannot win! He is an idea, but we are might itself. We stand for the insurmountable wall of twenty millennia. Tell him to turn back from the Throne of Madness ... for the High Compassion's sake. Tell him ... I don't choose this war! Tell him...." And the Inquestor turned and stepped out through the hole in the simulated starfield, which closed up behind him; and the comet that had heralded his coming spiraled loose and blazed a light-trail for Arryk's starship to follow; and behind, on strings of force, the deathmoon sailed serenely.

Tya watched until they were almost out of sight, and

then she directed the surviving childsoldiers to man the shuttlepods and to go scoop up the dead from their endless airless grave.

Two

The Pit of the Corpse Dancer

A whirring sound, then the creaking of unoiled hinges ... curse this audience! Zalo broke out of the trancelike state from which he had been controlling the personages of the necrodrama. He glared as he looked up from the control pit. Powers of powers! A character was tottering ... with a jerk of his mind he straightened the corpse's posture and forced it to resume its ponderous walk upstage. Its robes, made of simulated shimmerstuff to mimic the garb of an lnquestor, rippled slowly in anartwind.

It had paused in mid-sentence ... of all things to forget now, what was the line? Mustn't panic, Zalo thought. But the disturbance had set off a chain reaction in his mind.

It was a sound that had never before been heard in the Royal Theater of Ikshatra in the four centuries since the founding of the city, twenty-fourth capital of the world Essondras. But he knew it at once. The panic was spreading through the audience now. They hadn't even noticed that the lnquestral corpse had stopped speaking.

Being a consummate professional, Zalo paused only a few seconds. In those seconds he surveyed, through the one-way deopaqued forcefloor of the stage, the level upon level of audience ... the tiers of jasper for the lordlings, the granite seats for the burghers, the wooden balconies for the peasantry, who swarmed like insects up there at the top of the arena; above them, ten rainbows of silk and tinsel bridged the sky, for the play was *The Romance of the Rainbow King,* based on a true happening in the boyhood of the Inquestor Elloran, whom trillions called *the compassionate one.*

And above the artificial rainbows, the night sky of Essondras. Cloudy now; through a parting of the clouds, a glimpse of the three crescent moons that had not yet, at this late hour, set. It was strange not to see the Dark Rainbow in the sky; the production had been designed to play off the holographic, brilliantly colored rainbow projections against the big shadow that dominated Ikshatra's skyline. Not seeing the rainbow made him think of Jenjen, though he knew he could not afford to be distracted. He wondered if she had made it back safely from the island of the amethystine monoliths.

The play. Zalo searched his mind for the speech. Ton Alkamathdes, mad with power, storms through his rainbow palace ... in his search for utopia he has caused all the people of the world Ymvyrsh to be killed and replaced with servocorpses, eternally happy ... yes. Zalo had been a young man when he wrote the play; the tale of young Elloran and Sajit and the Rainbow King was well known even then, but Zalo had invested it with new ironies by adapting into a necrodrama some of what Jenjen told him about the real Elloran. It was a play *about* servocorpses, played by servocorpses, an elaborate conceit heightened by the continual double entendre of death imagery.

He had gone through four years of red tape to get a revival at the Royal Theater approved, this was only the fourth performance of the new production, and now this!

This! Nothing less than the end of the world!

For that was what the squeaking of the hinges portended. He glanced at the four reserved balconies that faced the stage from the four points of the compass: the enclosure of priests, the box of the oligarchs; the critics' balcony ... and the fourth, the one whose doors had never until now been opened ... the Balcony of Remembrance.

And now its doors were wide open (beyond, Zalo could see city lights, and, silhouetted, the ruined palace of the Old Dead Emperor) and an old woman in a white robe was being shown to her seat. A face rarely seen in public, and always feared. She sat down. Scattered murmurs in the audience now, but the panic had abated a little. Now was his chance. He had to get their attention back to the play. Forget the end of the world....

The lines were gone from his mind; breaking his trance had dislodged them from their mnemonic sequence. Desperate, he began to drum out, against his thigh, the hendecasyllabic meter of the mad Inquestor's speech. He had the corpse stagger wildly about, counting rapidly, *tum ... ta-tum ta tum-tum* ... then threw in the first tag he could think of that scanned:

Lo! The breaking of joy
Is the beginning of wisdom!

And now straight into the rhythm of that speech, tag after tag from a dozen mad scenes in a dozen necrodramas, pace, pace, *tarum tum ta-ta-TUM,* pace, pace, left hand out, circle, glower, rasp, stagger, stagger, right arm up, chin jerk, eyelids snap open and shut ...

The apprentices! Their cues were all shot now. He looked wildly around the control pit as he improvised, and saw them, wired to the thinkhives that monitored the movements of the supporting characters, childsoldiers and peasants and robot pteratygers ... applause now, as he began to make his Alkamathdes ham shamelessly, wooing the audience away from the despair that must beset them now ... how long could it be, a matter of months, of days? ... again he stared up at the Balcony of Remembrance. Others of the ill-omened House of Tash stood behind the old woman now, but she was Tash Kerin, their mistress.

"I can't, I can't," one of the apprentices was saying. She tore the electrodes from her head and fell down in a faint. Another one—-the one who'd been with him the night they burned the rainbow, who had demonstrated such innocent fanatic faith in Kelver's redemption-had stopped altogether and was muttering some litany. Onstage, two spearcarriers toppled. Quickly Zalo improvised a line about their having been felled by a bolt from the childsoldier Sajit's laser-irises. He wrenched the play back on course, but as other apprentices turned to gape at him he realized that he had skipped more than a hundred lines. "Just exposition," he muttered.

Soon would come spectacle ... the murder of mad Alkamathdes and the collapse of the rainbow sky, a mechanical feat that did not require the necrodramatist's attention. He waved to the engineer who stood by at a panel of blinking lights. Got to finish the play as soon as I can, he said, skipping a few more pages as the others scrabbled to keep up. Switching to control of the boy-corpse that played young Elloran, Zalo abbreviated his speech and simultaneously screwed up the emotional intensity of its formalized body language. He was carrying the crowd with him. Then the boy-corpse that played Sajit, hurling the whisperlyre at Alkamathdes's head and killing him ... "No epilogue!" he shouted at the stage manager, and signaled for the special effects.

A cry of terror, primal, unison, burst from the audience as the stage sky tumbled and the rainbows crackled and spewed thousand-colored flame.

That's taken care of it, he thought. Tonight they will experience the most stunning catharsis of their lives. Abruptly he severed the thinkhive linkup and clapped his hands to smother the stage in thick darkness.

When the smoke cleared, the audience was stamping its feet and calling his name. An apprentice got up to rouse the master, who by the end of a play often worked himself into a catatonic stupor and had to be gently brought back to reality. But in the confusion the necrodramatist had slipped away; had stepped onto the displacement plate in the center of the control pit and spirited himself into the streets of Ikshatra, where the rumors were flying and people were congregating everywhere to hear the news of impending destruction.

***

Zalo's home was in the unpretentious ninety-third arrondissement of Ikshatra, seventeen displacements from the theater. The district was a bewildering labyrinth of tall featureless walls and shadowy alleys. He found the displacement plate outside his house, faced its blank wall, subvocalized a secret code, and found himself in a garden of illusions; turning a corner behind a kyllap-bush, he stepped into an inner chamber of his home.

For a moment, he faced familiar sights. From a niche above the thinkhive, the preserved head of Karnofara, his old mentor, grinned down at him. If the terrible thing had not happened, Zalo would soon have selected one of his own apprentices, the most talented, as his successor. And when he died his own head would adorn the home of the new master necrodramatist. It was a tradition of at least ten centuries.

But this would never be. The Inquest had, with one decree, broken all their traditions.

"Greetings, master," he said, and the head nodded.

When he turned around he saw that a woman had materialized in the room. She was dressed in black—or rather, there stormed about her body an almost palpable tornado of utter darkness, through which he could sometimes catch a glimpse of a limb, a breast.

"How did you get in?"

"Your garden gate still remembered my voice, I'm afraid. Come now, don't be angry, Zasha. I can still call you Zasha, can't I? It hardly seems to matter now."

"You do me honor, Ir Jenjen, poetess of darkness," Zalo said stiffly. Then, as though impelled to confess that it had been he who had sent for her rescuers: "You survived the storm all right, then. They tell me the tide was terrible. Unconscionable, this weather."

"Have you heard the news? May I pour you some zul?" She pulled a flask out from the writhing blackness that enveloped her. He accepted it, drank a little.

"One can hardly avoid it. *She* was at my play tonight."

"Really?" said Jenjen. "I take it she rather stole your thunder?"

"I was stunned, but I improvised my way out of the mess."

'Always the professional, my dearest. I would expect nothing less. But you've come straight from the theater, so you haven't heard the announcements over the city's thinkhive network ... we have forty-nine sleeps before the High In quest rains destruction on our world. The people bins are already on their wav. I saw them, Zalo "

"But why Essondras? We're such an average world. I would have thought that the Inquest would barely know of our existence. Did they give any reason?"

"They never do. But you should have been expecting it, like me. They hate any world where the Prince of Shadow has gained a foothold."

"A political myth! These aren't the old days, the days we dreamed of change."

"I have never stopped dreaming."

"Well ... " Suddenly, watching her now, memories came flooding back. They wouldn't be so vivid, he told himself sternly, if the end of the world wasn't coming. "I remember ... fountains of zul at the house of Pari the Puppeteer ... you were not dark then, but wore a garment of clingfire, rainbow-colored. I remember your eyes, how they shifted color as your robe rippled."

"We're older now." She did not add that he had become older than she, because he had never breathed alien air or flown through the overcosm. He was grateful that she did not rub it in.

"You were still a lightweaver then. I remember the time you were reading from the program notes for your new work, *Five Analyses of Flame.* That wall of light that still adorns the vestibule of the Ministry of Horticulture. I cried. I was in the audience, and you didn't even see me. You thought I was at rehearsal. When was it that you first felt drawn to darkness?" But Zalo knew the answer to that; it was when they had first quarreled. After she had come back from the Inquestors' world.

"There are four million shades of darkness," said Jenjen, "my work will never be done." He sat down on a chairfloat, and she played with the patterned cicatrices on his bald head. "There are many more of these now," she said softly, "than when I first knew vou."

"Yes." She touched one, a roseate design on which was superimposed the emblem of a skull. "That one when you left me, and when I had my first big critical failure." A thought, suddenly: "If we register together, we can get assigned to the same people bin. When we awaken, centuries later, from stasis. on a new world, at least we'll have *some* memories—"

"I had another plan altogether, Zasha."

"Plans! How can you have plans now? Essondras will *fall beyond* in forty-nine sleeps!"

"You have become fatalistic, Zasha, since our love—"

She could not finish. "I saw your play last night. You've sharpened the lines. There's a new bitterness."

"It's a play about corpses, played by corpses."

"You are dissatisfied?"

"I ... " Why should he tell her this? They had not spoken to each other for ten years, ever since Jenjen had gone over completely to the side of darkness. In their youth *he'd* been the one to bluster about revolutions ... but when she chose to become the mouthpiece of a *real* rebellion, he had become afraid. He'd told himself, I have my art, so much yet to perfect. But the truth came welling up, he couldn't stop himself. It's the end of the world, he thought. It does things to you, it batters down your resistance. He said, "I've pushed the irony of the talking corpse to its limits! There's nothing for me now ... I've been thinking about something revolutionary. Maybe *live* players. People. I wouldn't be able to control them, you see, I'd relinquish the fine tuning, they wouldn't have the polish of dead actors, of course, but what raw energy! I've been thinking about it for many years now." "Many worlds have a live acting tradition," Jenjen said. "You don't understand! I'm talking about a live acting rooted in the mannerisms and formal structures of necrodrama, see, a further level of irony..."

I'm so excited, he thought ... I'm not making sense, the world is ending, it doesn't make any difference....

Abruptly they kissed. He remembered the urgency of their first lovemaking. They'd been young then. Ir Jenjen broke off suddenly, took him by the hand, said, "And what if I told you the world is not going toend?"

"What do you mean? I saw Tash Kerin herself appear. The Rememberers must be all over the city now, noting every detail of these last times so that they will be able to rehearse them for the Inquestors after the world is gone."

"But there are those who say otherwise. I'm a student of darkness, and I hear many dark things."

"Oh, you mean that Shadow Inquest and all your other fantasies."

"Their agents have been visiting us all this time. You've met them."

"One. He told me, 'Change is corning to the Dispersal of Man at last. Utopias are possible after all. The High Inquest is uncompassionate, consumed by its own madness for power and by its absorption in *makrúgh*. When the time comes for Essondras to fall, some will resist the Inquest. A revolution has begun.' You know how much I wanted to believe that, Jeni. But I can't. It's meaningless!"

"No." She had the same mad confidence the apprentice had had on the night they burned the rainbow. Zalo could only gape. Perhaps it was true that the study of dark things drove one to insanity.

"You can't resist the Inquest. As well resist the sunlight and the night."

"A line from one of vour own necrodramas."

He stared at her then. I always underestimate her, he realized. It sounded crazy to me then, that a person should give up so much just to go off gazing on darkness day after day, trying to understand, define its colors. But she'd been confused then, moody, after building the Rainbow Darkness. Now she had certainty, and it was he, so conscious once of his destiny as the great necrodramatist, who had lost faith.

For a white they didn't speak. The room: chairfloats, a frozen firefountain on whose mantel stood three or four awards, a tank containing spare limbs from discarded corpses, wires trailing in the nutrifluid. Stacked boxes from which more wires and embalmed body parts flapped. A holosculpture of an island ringed with ancient monoliths. A pile of masks. A shelf of corpse cosmetics.

Finally Jenjen said: "There's going to be a meeting tonight. A messenger has come to Essondras from the dark Inquestor, Kelver, the Prince of Shadow. I have already met her. She has come to brew the storm."

She smiled, conjured up a ghost of love. It was so vivid that at once he had no choice. For the alternative was to despair.

Three

The Eye of the Galactic Storm

There was no sky. Only the churning clouds: umber, sienna, ocher, maroon, melding, billowing, the patterns shifting too fast to comprehend. And at Siriss's feet more cloudbanks: a dozen whirlpools in dark marbled reds and streaked yellows. What kind of city had Kelver chosen to hide in? She dissolved her tachyon bubble and stepped out over a hard floor of force. There were no streets, no buildings. Only the raging cloud layers with their lurid colors whipping overhead and around and beneath. Siriss was disoriented. Surely Kelver had sent someone to show her the way. But lately he had been forgetting little courtesies.

After all, he had other worries. Like destroying a twenty thousand-year galactic tyranny.

And yet, Siriss thought with a sudden childish annoyance, he should not forget me, his lover ... I've not been standing still. I've crossed seven planets in the last seven sleeps, overseeing Kelver's work.

Sharing Kelver was hard.

Where to begin? And why, in any case, had Kelver decided to move his center of operations to this world Zorn—certified uninhabitable, by the powers of powers, a gas giant of all things? Here she was, high up in the poisoned atmosphere of this garish world, where the scenery was so fluid as to be unrecognizable from one hour to the next. She knew it had to be the right place. After all, the tachyon bubble had known the coordinates ... and on her arrival she hadn't been sucked into a whirlpool of methane or crushed flat by the surface gravity. She knew that where she stood was the city. The hard, invisible forcefloor that supported her told her that, and the fact that, though the sky raged, she felt no wind at all, and her shimmercloak glowed a healthy pink against the deep blue, indicating the utter safety of the environment. No, this was one of those habitats completely enclosed in a membranous forcebubble. It was like a waterdrop from a pond, its teeming microscopic life shielded from the inhospitably waterless air by the surface tension's meniscus. But where was that life here?

Movement ... slim shapes shifting behind the shadow of a cloud on cloud. Childsoldiers. "Stop!" she called out.

Two ran to her across the invisible road. "Where is Kelver?"

"Do you want an audience, Inquestrix?" A pert face, red hair covering one eye, a wrinkled smile.

"Do you know who I am?" Siriss said.

"You are Ton Siriss of Varezhdur, the Inquestrix of the opal eyes and white hair," said the childsoldier. "Anyone can see that. Have you come to see Kelver?"

"Anvone can see that, boy!"

"God. He needs someone. Someone who knew him, you know, before. He won't see anyone right now. It won't be easy."

"But I am—"

"Yes, Inquestrix. We know who you are. Our thinkhives saw your palace plunging through the overcosm, and detected your tachyon bubble. We came to greet you."

"Hokh'Ton," the other said, in the archaic ritual of respect. From this Siriss knew that he was only newly among the army of shadow, for he shied away from her, behaved as though she had the power of life and death over him.

She followed them; they seemed to know the way well. They were in a square from which avenues radiated, and buildings towered on every side; but all was built of walls of mirrorforce, so that the whole city appeared to be made of intersecting planes of cloudscape, the illusion was so complete that there seemed to be no city at all ... suddenly she would see a cloud sheared in half, a turbulent whirlstorm cut in two and separated by a vista of different clouds on which crowds of people went about their business, and she would know that they had reached a comer of one of the avenues. Here and there were displacement plates, like silver trap doors set in the embankments. They skipped from one to another.

Eventually they found themselves in a small room ... she knew it was a room because six tempestuous and wildly divergent landscapes cubed them in. Ahead was a door in a red cloud, and beyond it she could see a square of snow storm. "Where is Kelver?"

"In there," said the first of the childsoldiers, the one who had known better than to use honorifics. The second one said nothing. He just cowered. When Siriss reached over to pat his head he jumped.

"He just deserted from the other side, my Lady," said the first one. "He's still afraid."

"Don't be, little one," she said. "But what about Kelver?" "He hasn't seen anyone for many sleeps. This is the antechamber. In the hallway beyond, hundreds of people are milling about, demanding an audience of the Prince of Shad ow. We're to keep them out."

"He'll let *me* in, though."

"I think so." The little soldier tossed the hair out of his eyes and went through the door.

As Siriss watched him leave, two others came into the room. She recognized them at once. One was Kail Jannif, the astrogator, one of the first to throw everything away and enlist in Kelver's service. The other was Tya-without-a-Clan, the first childsoldier to call Kelver master. Tya had grown tall; she was getting to be a woman, Siriss thought. Perhaps I should award her a clan-name after all. But Jannif was getting old. She was one of the shortlived, after all; how could one expect otherwise? But Siriss had not been an Inquestor long enough to know the passing of centuries and the insect generations of those the Inquest ruled.

She wondered if, when the fall came, she would have to relinquish the almost-immortality that Inquestorhood had conferred on her. Would she, too, become like Jannif, who had given Kelver her life, and yet whose life was already running out? She greeted them formally, afraid to let them see her distress, to hurt their feelings.

And this was in itself a wonder ... for she was an Inquestor, and in the old days she would never once have considered the feelings of a single shortliver ... but those were the days before Kelver changed their lives.

"You're here to *see* him?" Tya said.

"Yes."

"We've been waiting seven sleeps," Jannif said. "I've just arrived. What's the matter?"

"It's the Throne of Madness, Lady. He's in there alone, fighting it," said Tya. "And we're out here, and *we* can't do anything. And we've just lost an armory, and meanwhile, the war is waiting—"

"An armory—"

"Lady Siriss, we saw the Princeling Arryk!" Tya blurted out.

"Arryk...." Memories welled up. She wanted to weep, but even now balked at showing her tears to the shortlived. Presently the little redheaded soldier returned. "My Lady," he said, genuflecting to her, "please have forbearance. The Prince of Shadow will see you in a moment. But he asks for Tya and Jannif, for a report of their battle over the armory."

As the two women scurried into the doorway of the snowstorm, Siriss thought fiercely, angrily: He makes *me* wait! Because he wants to know how Arryk is, Arryk his enemy. Even after all this, he loves Arryk more than me, Arryk who has put himself beyond our reach.

And she remembered a time when all three had been lovers, joyous, undivided, under the pearlbright sky of Uran s'Varek, the Inquestral homeworld. She wanted it all back. She wanted to turn back time itself.

But even for the immortal there is time.

"Curse the war!" she whispered. And she longed for an ending.

"So now it's the Prince of Shadow," said Siriss as she stepped inside the room. "New titles every day. The Lord of Compassion. The Light. The Shadow. The Eye of the Galactic Storm. And the Darkling Wind—as though you were yourself the Throne of Madness."

The room stormed; but Kelver sat at its center, in a still pool of darkness; his face was in the shadow, and all Siriss could see were his eyes: emerald-clear, distant.

"Sirissheh." The voice: ghostlike; it was as though the planet's windrage, silenced by the layers of force that enclosed the city and the palace, had leaked for a second into the sanctum.

"Let me come closer." She felt a sudden embarrassment at asking his permission. Trillions might worship him, but surely he was still *her* Kelver. Uncertainly she made toward where he was sitting.

Now they were almost touching. But she felt nothing, she thought. Yet her shimmercloak, more certain of her true mood than she was herself, sensed the stirrings of buried sexual desire, and began to seethe a little, awakening a little light in Kelver's cloak; so now the pool of darkness was shot through with fragments of a blue-red light. She watched him. The cloak fell crookedly from his shoulders, revealing an emaciated arm.

She said, "Kelver, you don't have to be alone."

The cloaks rustled, the only sound in the room, though around them billowed the red-brown blizzard.

She said, "Why have you chosen Zorn to hide in? There are probably a million uninhabited worlds within the Dispersal that would be less trouble to live on."

"They won't look for us here for a long, long time. And besides, Zorn has desolation. And grandeur. Come, Sirissheh, into this puddle of darkness."

She slid in beside him. At once they were cocooned in the shadow, and she knew it for an artificial darkfield.

Before she could reflect on it, she was in his arms. “It was terrible,” she whispered. “To be without you, and to hear your name almost every waking minute. I’ve been to Menjifarm and Chembrith, to Madragorva and Kalisseai and cold Urmist. They all want to see you again, Kevi, they want you to come down from the sky clothed in light to tell them not to be afraid of the Inquest anymore. And instead you’re here.”

“It doesn’t matter.” He didn’t meet her eyes. “Here, there, anywhere, the Throne of Madness still touches me. It knows me, it knows where to hurt me.”

“The war’s going badly, Kevi. Essondras slated to *fall beyond* next; the death moon lost; Arryk’s party gaining strength among the leftover Inquestors.”

“Do you think I don’t know that?” Kelver shouted angrily. “Tya and Jannif were just here. They saw Arryk, you know.” ‘That’s what it’s really about, isn’t it? That’s why you’re closeted on Zorn, sulking in an inner room—” I shouldn’t have said that, she thought wildly, but it’s too late and I can’t stem the tide now-

“Don’t make it worse, Sirissheh!” He gripped her arm, whether out of anger or desperation she could not tell, but it burned where he touched her. And though it was dark, she knew he was weeping.

“All right. I’m sorry.”

“Yes. Now look about you again.”

He clapped his hands and the darkfield had dissolved. They must have been sitting over a displacement plate, because with a flick of his mind Kelver had transported them into a railinged floater. They were flying into the thick of a roiling storm. Around them the clouds clashed. Here yellow was twisting into brown, here blood marbling into bile.

“Look!” Kelver said. And she saw that he had become animated for the first time. “My new world. A world whose face is never the same from second to second.” And below them, peering from banks of red-ocher mist, she saw the glistening globules that were the cities of Zorn, each one encased in a forcebubble. Within the spheres she could see spires and battlements and castles and aircars swarming against the sides of buildings. One bubble only seemed empty; she could barely make out its outline, for it blended with the storm.

"'And that's *your* city, Kelver."

"Yes. The invisible one."

"You thrive, then, on the planet's uninhabitability, on its bleak splendor."

"Yes. More than anything now, I am drawn to the wilderness. I grew up on a desert's edge, you know. The sands of Zhnefftikak, blinding-white, and the stark Skywall were all I saw for all my childhood. Do you understand?"

Siriss feigned understanding. It was best not to intrude on his privacy when he remembered the past.

In silence she watched the tempest. There now, a herd of treehawks, parrotgreen, riving a red cloud asunder. Chi meras of an Inquestor's whim, their plumage was foliage, huge webbed sailwings spread to catch the thin light of Zorn's sun, and their falcon faces were sculpted from scales of bark. They swarmed against the storm like algae freckles on a gold lake. After them came herders on floaters, their lasercrooks like brilliant hairpins on the massycloudbanks.

Kelver said, "It's not so bleak, Sirissheh. There is a kind of life here. But it's far from the Inquest. Only the Throne of Madness knows where this world is, and it's not about to betray me."

She didn't like it when he talked about the Throne as if it were a person, so she turned away from him. The flock of treehawks twisted in the whirlpool wind. He pulled her hard into his arms, and she saw the madness of the Throne fleck his eyes, and knew that though she might still be his lover, a part of him was forever lost to her.

"You're right, though," he said suddenly.

"About what?"

"I must appear again. Clothed in light. I must go myself to Essondras. That is what I have seen, what the Throne of Madness tells me."

"To reassure the worlds that have come over to the side of shadow? To let them know we have not abandoned them?"

"And to lure Arryk. So that he can be destroyed." And Kelver, as the cloud storm raged about them, wept bitterly.

***

A winged boy ran down the corridor of storms. Childsoldiers turned, stared, did not stop him. He had been seen before.

The bubble-city's skyline: angular blocks of seething earthcolors, finned floaters that seemed to swim against the reflected tempests. A bloodred cloudeye shifting from building to building, its image fractured and refracted as it crossed walls of mirror metal.

The winged boy knew only terror, blind terror. He did not know his own name or where he was. He was a one-dimensional sort of person, really. He didn't even have any vague memories of a former life, beyond his sudden appearance in this nameless city shrouded in storms.

He ran. The terror whipped him. Feet pounding hard against the avenues of force that threaded the swirling cityscape. An alleywav ... the face of a woman, tall as a mountain, condensed momentarily out of the cloudbanks. A traffic servocorpse waved him firmly onto a careening walkway that spiraled through the windows of glass turrets. Now the planes of paperthin cloudscape converged. A room; a woman and a girl stood guard.

"Don't come in," said the older. "Oh ... it's you."

They exchanged a strange look, the two of them. They waved him inside.

It was Kelver who sat down in the room that was the confluence of intersecting planes of mirrorforce that were the city. "Siriss—" She was not there. The floater-gone! And he was inside, not flying through the whirling storm.

A familiar figure came in. "Tya," Kelver said with relief. "We were worried for you, Kelver. We saw the boy come in, and—

"What boy?" He stared, his eyes wild. Tya-without-a-Clan looked perplexedly at her master, seemed about to speak; but she stopped herself, and Kelver was too afraid of what he might learn to force her. "Call Jannif, call some of our more trusted childsoldiers," he said. "We're leaving Zorn. It's time to put in another appearance."

Tya said, "You don't know how happy I am about that. The war will change course for sure now."

"Yes. But where is Siriss?"

"Lodged at Varezhdur, of course, Prince. You gave the order yourself, for her palace to be brought into Zorn's atmosphere and camouflaged with storm ... don't you remember?" "Of course." What was wrong? It was a logical enough thing to have commanded, but- "Go now," he said softly.

As Tya left the room, the whispering began. He never could quite understand what they were saying. It was just above the limit of audibility. Sometimes a single word, over and over, hypnotic. Sometimes dissonant voices.

It was the whispershadow that the Throne of Madness had told of. The prescience of a star's death that would haunt him until the very end of this war.

And Kelver cried out: "How can they call *me* the 'Eye of the Galactic Storm'? I am the most storm-tossed of men, the loneliest, the most despairing." He rammed his fists against his ears. The whispering grew louder. Where had he been for the past few hours? Who was the boy people had reported seeing around the palace, the boy everyone seemed to see but himself? The whispering became insistent. My very mind is fracturing, he thought. The whisper became a roar, and when he closed his eyes he saw the bursting of giant suns.

Four
Kelver's Tears

It was in the Garden of Sculpted Mist, in the eighty-fourth arrondissement of Ikshatra, that Zalo first saw clearly the face of the Prince of Shadow. It was holosculpted into a tree of black thorns, and when he passed it, it spoke to him. The path through the garden was aswirl with an animated mist through which a babbling ran, as of a stream just around the corner.

"Zalo," the holosculpture whispered, knowing his name. He panicked at first. "Who are you? I'm on the way to Jenjen's house, to some meeting she insists I go to."

The holosculpture said, "Light is the shadow's shadow." Then it dissolved into mist.

He shivered and turned a corner. Jenjen had certainly gone up in the world in those ten years. She spoke the lnquestral highspeech with barely a trace of backworld burr; she had stood face to face with Elloran, whom Zalo had only written about. She must have grown rich, too. Only the wealthy could afford a house in this arrondissement. Zalo felt a stab of jealousy. Had she seduced that lnquestor into granting her that clan-name? Surely she had not done it on artistic merit alone. Unworthy thoughts! He knew, really, that she was a great artist. That was why she'd left him, wasn't it? Love for a man was one thing, but she loved the darkness more.

He took a displacement plate into the heart of a pyramid of mist. A path twisted beside a brook. These gardens of the rich were maddening, half built of illusions. Where was the house?

He turned swiftly and caught another glimpse of Kelver's face melding into fog. I don't need this, he told himself. Jenjen's pretentious friends have probably enticed her into some end-of-the-world cult.

A lightshaft piercing the mist. In the gravel, a small clawed creature strutted in a circle. It was a kashanthra about to embark on its deathsong. When it saw him it stopped and glared at him, its wings fluttering in a bronze blur, its eyes cold crimson. Many kashanthras had been seen in the streets of Ikshatra. They had secret nesting places, deep in the sewers. On a whim, an Inquestor had had them created millennia ago.

It hobbled sideways, inclined its neck, sang a cold flutelike music, its gaze fixed still on him. Zalo bent down to its level. "No, you mustn't die," he said, thinking of how he daily dealt with corpses, never once reflecting on the humans they had once been. The kashanthra sang only once in its life, and when it sang it wept formaldehyde, embalming itself into living death ... they were empathic. That was why no one kept them as pets; for if a child in the house cried over a scolding or a lost toy, the kashanthra would weep until death seeped deep within and made rubber of its flesh.

Now the people's collective sorrow had driven them from their hiding places, and flocks of these self-embalmed reptile-birds could be found at the sewer entrances, by the banks of the River Kisifoni, and by the shores of the Bay of Blue Laughter.

In a few minutes, this kashanthra would begin to die. Its wings flapped ever faster now; a bluish phosphorglow emanated from its downy body. Where was that woman's house?

At once a childhood memory surfaced—

By the Blue Canal. Boy Zalo shucking his tunic, bracing for the icy water ... winter. Four moons, ghostly outlines, in the sunset. Small arms thrusting ... there it is now, bobbing up and down in the water ... a rubber bird! *Mother, look what I found . . . it's squeezy, Mother. I want to sleep with it by my pil-*

low ... "Throw it back. It cried itself to sleep. Forever." Mother's face, a blur ... suddenly a counterimage of Kelver's kelp-green eyes, and the salt water spurting from them ... shaking the cold dead thing now, trying to breathe life into it, and the choking stench of formaldehyde in his nostrils ... another day now, older. In a small-town theater, maybe Urazbedang, maybe Orika-shamamhet. The play, *The Lamentable Tragedy of Nika the Web Dancer.* A crowd scene ... and among the ghostly pale faces, Mother's face, the eyebrows rhythmically twitching in mechanical mimicry of grief, and—

The kashanthra's wings spread wide now, and it tottered into the misty wind, but it could not rise; already its feathers were leadening in the seeping death. Did my mother have green eyes? Zalo strained, but the remembrance was gone. A vague guilt stirred. I should atone, he thought. Atone—

He raced after the bird, down the jewelcrusted path beside the stream. The kashanthra was weakening. He grabbed it in his arms. It flailed, weeping still. Got to sever the empathic link ... got to fight the terror of this whole cursed world ... he thought of colored lights and carnivals and firefalls and making love and the flavors of subtle sweetmeats.

The kashanthra stirred. He knelt by the brook and submerged the bird and held it down to flood the formaldehyde from its pores. Easy now, he thought, easy, easy. Don't die.

A soft hand on his shoulder.

"Is this what the end of the world has wrought?" It was Ir Jenjen's voice. "Oh, Zasha." She had been sobbing. "Don't think of it. You'll kill the kashanthra." The fire-red was draining from its eyes. Its wings were waterlogged, gold glinting through soggy feathers. He got up; the bird-reptile, trusting him completely, had found a perch on his wrist. Jenjen took his other hand. "Where's your house?" he said irritably.

"Pretty stupid, isn't it, to lose your way on the eve of the end of the world."

"Shut up. There's something fishy about all this. I just remembered ... in a flash ... so much. Childhood. Suddenly I'm inspired. And there's no time."

"And Kelver's rebellion—"

"I will weave it into my art. You'll see. All at once I've rediscovered the passion to move the whole world to action." Sensing his excitement, the kashanthra erupted into a trilling, pointillist melody.

He saw Jenjen close her eyes and, with a flick of her mind, unlock the gate of her house. Mist parted. He stepped from the garden with the singing stream into an atrium silvered by brilliant moons' light. There were white panels on which hung artworks: squares, circles, quadrilaterals, polygons, and all of them windows into utter blackness; beside each hung a little scroll that elucidated the qualities of the particular color of darkness that the pane represented.

As they stepped into the room and the mistwalls cleared away, the hubbub of conversations was suddenly hushed. As Zalo looked around, it resumed. It was a motley assemblage. There were Rememberers and wealthy burghers, but he also saw a beggar deep in talk with a hermaphrodite in a whore's robe; there, in the corner, meditating on a pentagon of darkness, a sewer guardian was taking a quaffer of mulled zul from the uniformed servocorpse.

"You are surprised I admit such people into my house?" Jenjen said.

"I'm confused."

"Nothing will ever be the same again. We may as well get used to it."

Voices: *the visitors, the visitors.*

Again a puff of mist. A girl stood in the center of the room. Someone screamed. The girl wore the iridium graviboots and black cloak of a childsoldier. Her eyes were tiger-slitty, topaz-yellow. Disarmingly, the girl smiled.

Zalo stared at her uncomprehending. There was some thing almost obscene in that smile, because it contradicted all he had ever believed. How could a childsoldier smile? How could a childsoldier enter a house without being preceded by fire and destruction? How could a childsoldier possibly be an emissary of peace?

As the girl raised her hand, Kelver's image flickered across the face of the sky. "I am Tya-without-a-Clan," she said softly. "And I am of the childarmies that have renounced death; I am of the wings of the shadow." She went on to explain that she had just left Varezhdur, the palace of Ton Siriss, by tachyon bubble, and would be returning there instantly the meeting was done.

"Tachyon bubble!" someone cried out, impressed. "But they kill stars to fuel them."

There came discussion, heated, deep into the night. But Zalo did not listen to it, though he was sure that grand sentiments were being exchanged. He quaffed his zul and heard high-sounding concepts bandied about: star systems' dying, new worlds, homeworlds of the heart, and the galactic storm that was stirring in men's hearts.

Sure, they were great ideas. But Zalo was not one to feel for the collective passions of trillions; it was as if he was discovering, for the first time, his own passions. For, from the moment he had stooped to pluck the kashanthra from death, Zalo saw where his creative crisis had been urging him. The confusion of the end of the world; the visit from his old lover; his reaching out to rescue a weeping bird; and now the ironic catalyst of the childsoldier as messenger of peace ... they were telling something important about his art. And he only had a few days, a few vital days, to make his grand statement, his tiny gesture of rebellion, before the big darkness overtook them all.

***

The Rememberer was the last to leave the gathering. Zalo was never to forget the way the old man stood, his white robes billowing in the artificial fog that concealed the dis placement field that led from the atrium to the Garden of Sculpted Mist. Zalo knew the man was merely exercising his trained reflexes, drinking in all the sensations so he could be commanded to conjure them up for an Inquestor's whim. But it seemed that the Rememberer's gaze fixed upon Zalo's kashanthra, and that there was somehow a kinship between them; for both were harbingers ofthe encroaching doom.

Then they were alone.

Jenjen said: "She was so strange. She had such certainty, even though what she said went against everything we know." Zalo said: "My head's full of ideas. Out there, in the sky, beyond the light of all our moons ... a revolution we can't see, sweeping over the torpor of twenty thousand years! And the story of the man Kelver ... not a god. No different from us. He came from a more backward world even than Essondras." She stood against a woman-tall circle of blackness whose scroll read simply *dark dark flower dark.* They said nothing. He had never understood her art before; but now, staring at the perfect absence of color behind her, he was beginning to see things there. It was like a tunnel into the soul ... and at its end, perhaps never to be reached, a flower-field, awash with light ... he said, "You've come far in your art. Or I've grown older. When we parted so bitterly I couldn't believe you'd withdraw so much into the depiction of nondepiction, that youwould choose it even over me."

"Enough. Forget, Zasha." Their lips almost touched. "How many more days?"

"I don't know. Shall we watch the news?" She clapped her hands and the house thinkhive summoned up, in the air between them, a holodrama of the day's events.

On an island with ruined monoliths ("I was there," she whispered, "I saw the skies erupt with silver cylinders—") they were opening up registration for people bins. Essondras was sparsely populated; only one evacuation center was needed for the entire world ... Jenjen clapped impatiently, speeding up the news so that it was full of tiny figures rushing jerkily, and the narration became a squawk ... a story about kashanthras' eggs found with the unhatched embryos already embalmed, their inchoate empathy dooming them to stillbirth. A ban on spaceflight; pleasure cruisers abandoned in mass spaceship graveyards. Everywhere the crowds marched zombielike from place to place, uncomprehending....

"Can you believe what the childsoldier said? That the Inquestral decision was just some part of a game?" said Jenjen.

"Compassion. That's the reason the lnquestors give for everything. That's why they have the people bins, to rescue as many as they can. To assuage their guilt, too! But we've got to show them we're not part of some cosmic game, to be shunted across the galaxy like *shtezhnat-pieces.* We're humans- we can feel, we can bleed, we can die—"

"What's wrong, Zasha? I feel you're on the verge of ... something terrible "

"Listen, Jenjen. I was always a mediocre artist before. Oh, competent enough; I wouldn't have inherited my master's head if I wasn't the best of that batch of apprentices. But everything's changed now. I have fear, terrible fear. And the end of the world has heightened my perceptions. I'm going to fight fate till the very end. I'm going to work for Kelver's revolution, Jenjen! Not because of some childsoldier's propagandist blandishments, but because—because—"

Feeding on his passion, the kashanthra left his wrist and essayed a halfhearted soar toward the largest moon. He fell forward into the woman's arms. He was weeping, but it was not from grief; it was from rage, and from this crazy joy that the world's end had engendered in him.

"No, you mustn't think of death," Jenjen whispered. They embraced in the midst of the holographic newsreel, in the frantic hustle of ant-sized crowds.

"Not death, not death," Zalo said. They kissed. Later, Zalo was to remember that kiss as the turning point, the moment when his art overstepped the bounds of necrodrama and was reborn....

"Look!" Jenjen broke off the kiss and pointed to the kashanthra. It was hovering in front of the circle of darkness. Its wings were spread wide, its eyes seemed to smolder, its feathers of lapis-flecked bronze quivered ... for a second it defied gravity. In that second a gold fire seemed to streak across the black circle that was Jenjen's darkpoem.

"You must never weep again," Zalo said to the bird. "No kashanthra should ever weep ... I forbid mourning ... I will call your tears Kelver's tears, for an Inquestor never weeps, yet Kelver has taken all our sorrow upon himself."

And Jenjen laughed, and they made love again and again. Each time they reached orgasm the kashanthra, maddened by the emotional maelstrom, flew fluttering in zigzags across the atrium. And after, they laughed again and again, making light of their despair.

Five

A Night of Ghosts

They had drawn the palace Varezhdur from its orbit down into clouds of Zorn. Outside, Varezhdur's spiny spires strained in the wind like blades of grass, and you could not see the burnish of its surface through the churning fumes. But within, the palace was peaceful.

In the corridor of sighs, a chamberlain paused to pet a pteratyger cub that had wandered in from the stables. Looking up, he saw a winged boy at whose shoulder a winged tray hovered; it held a flask of pale blue zul and a basket of peftifesht pastries such as Lady Siriss liked. The chamberlain did not recognize the boy, but did not question his errand. The pteratyger gave a little roar, scampered down the hall, whose walls gave off a continuous erotic moaning. It bounded on a displacement plate and vanished abruptly.

"What a nuisance," the chamberlain said. "I shall have to have the plates realigned. We can't have the palace crawling with menagerie creatures."

"No, I suppose not," said the boy. He was softspoken, but his voice had a commanding edge; the chamberlain was not used to hearing it in the palace servants.

"Is the Lady Siriss retiring?" the chamberlain said. "Yes." The winged boy turned and walked away. He reached the spot where the pteratyger cub had disappeared. He faded out; a ghostly outline lingered for some moments, as though the dissolution of the boy's material substance had taken longer than the customary nanoseconds. The chamber lain rubbed his eyes.

"Have to have them aligned," he muttered again. "Can't have a displacement plate malfunctioning like that."

***

Many klomets away, in another wing of the palace, Ton Siriss z Varezhduren K'Ning, the White Inquestrix, opened her eyes and saw the winged boy. He clapped his hands and the tray came to her. A scented breeze from the flutter of its wings.

"Thank you, boy," Siriss said. She was about to dismiss him when something prompted her to look into his eyes. They were clear green, like Kelver's ... indeed, the face of the winged boy, open, innocent, reminded her so powerfully of the day she had first met Kelver and challenged him to *makrúgh,* that at last she could not bear to look, for an Inquestor must not be seen to weep.

"You are sad, Mistress?"

The voice was familiar too ... another voice from Uran s'Varek ... the boy Aoauei from Shentrazjit the singing city, who had been sliced in two by the childsoldiers, a sacrificial victim in a game of illusions. "You're not the usual boy who brings me my sleeping-zul," she said. "What is your name, boy?"

"I don't really know, Mistress. Actually, I don't even know what I'm doing here, or what this place is. But it's beautiful here, and so full of peace."

"Yes. But full of ghosts." Now why had she said that? Why did she feel she could speak freely in front of this stranger ... who might even be a spy from Arryk? For Siriss had grown increasingly paranoid as she and Kelver had become more embroiled in the war.

"Ghosts?"

"Yes. Elloran's, mainly. I wish I knew where he is. Since he decided to sail the spaces between spaces, and to hear the silence between the stars, I have ruled Varezhdur and its tributaries. But I cannot feel that this palace is mine, though I grew up in it and I know its labyrinthine corridors well. His spirit suffuses the hallways, the thronerooms, the forgotten wings, the thousand gardens. And the songs of Sajit continue to be sung here. I keep expecting them both to return, for the war never to have begun, for everything to be the way it was."

"Why did Ton Elloran leave, my Lady?"

"Old Sajit died at last, boy, and we buried him at the heart of Shentrazjit, the city that was his final song. But other Inquestors came; they stole the body and shipped it to a servocorpse factory."

"Why?"

"It's part of a game of *makrúgh.* Arryk and Karakaël wanted to see if they could goad Elloran into playing the game, which he had forsworn, once more. Instead, Elloran, mad with grief, decided to go on the journey he had always vowed to make—to listen to the gray silences between the stars—to turn his back on the Inquest forever."

The boy smiled shyly. She wondered whether he was listening, or whether he was simply waiting to be dismissed. "You remind me of someone too," she said.

"Me, my Lady?"

"Yes. How I loved him that first day, though I didn't dare admit it to myself, and started off by challenging him to a duel of *makrúgh!* You look like him. Those clear green eyes!"

"Like who, Mistress?"

"Like the Prince of Shadow, of course. Kelver."

The winged boy seemed puzzled. "Who is that?" he said at last.

"What? You work in my palace and haven't heard of the Lord Kelver, the Shadow's Shadow?"

The boy bowed his head. "I am only an ignorant boy," he said.

"But in this palace no one ever talks of anything else but the rebellion!" Siriss said. "Well ... he no longer looks like you, anyway. His eyes are lined; his cheeks are gaunt; he's wasting away from worry. And I think he's going mad. And we've drifted apart. Can you understand that? Though I still love him." She sipped at the cool blue zul. "For a moment you stirred up ... ghosts of memories. Go, boy; I must not burden you with the griefs of princes."

The boy genuflected and silently departed.

A restless night, she thought. A night of ghosts. It must be that Kelver is finally going to leave Zorn and show himself among the liberated worlds. And the shock of seeing him and discovering his passion for bleakness.

She reclined on her hoverthrone of clingfire stuffed with kyllap leaves. From behind a diaphanous forcecurtain at a far end of the vast chamber came the strains of a Sajit symphonia. She luxuriated in its sadness. I love beautiful things, she thought. It's hard to lay down the trappings of absolute power.

And then, as she drifted into an uneasy sleep, she remembered how she had first learned about the bizarre fate of Sajit's body....

They had been in the throneroom waiting for Elloran to speak. But instead had come the voice of Varezhdur's thinkhive, booming: *Quickly, Mistress! Quickly, Lord Elloran! Some thing very strange has happened.*

"What is it, thinkhive?"

A tachyon bubble has arrived from Idoresht.

The water world, where ancient Varuneh now ruled the snakescale city, where they had built servocorpse factories in the bowels of monstrous sea serpents ... "Can't it wait?" Siriss said.

You must come, Ton Siriss. The tachyon bubble contains the corpse of Shen Sajit.

"His corpse! It was shipped to a factory on Idoresht, then —"

There is no message, Lady. Only the corpse.

"We shall inter it in the palace, with all the honors due to it. I will decree a ceremony."

Lady there is something wrong. The servocorpse treatments were in progress when Lady Varuneh learned of it and presumably ordered it halted. But the corpse is embalmed, has certain motor functions, and, by some shortcircuiting of the brain, sings, over and over; an old song—"

"Ghosts," Siriss had said wonderingly, as she arose from the clingfire throne and prepared to see this prodigy. But Elloran had said nothing at all, and she had been able to do nothing to assuage his grief.

***

The last thing Ton Elloran had said to her before leaving Varezhdur forever: "Siriss, you rule now. Once I presided over Sajit's funeral, when, riding the backs ofblack pteratygers, you and I and Kelver watched his body plummet earthward into the heart of Shentrazjit, the singing city he designed. I am glad I will not be staying for a second funeral. I am glad you waited for me to go. It is good." And he stepped down from the throne and left the chamber which had as its centerpiece a galaxy of dust, and he did not look back.

***

They no longer used Elloran's throneroom; Siriss could not bear to sit there and feel his absence. It was one of Varezhdur's many gardens into which the White Inquestrix stepped; a chamberlain escorted her to a throne cunningly wreathed about with holosculpt kyllap-bushes.

The throne was set on a tetragonal island in the center of a lake the color of liquid gold. Mechanical crystal fishes leaped, feathery fins fluttering, and dived. Surrounding the lake were seven terraced lawns. One had the red grass of Shtoma, another the chlorophyll-rich grass of ancient lost Earth, another the wavy blue lakeweed of the planet Aararaut. Each tier sliced from an alien world, and carried hither to simulate a rainbow mountain ... and all because of the words of one of Sajit's songs: *Though I have slain the Rainbow King, it is you who must possess his throne.* It was something to do with when Elloran and Sajit were children. Even here, then, Siriss was haunted by the ghost of this unorthodox friendship that had crossed the boundary of degree.

Now others of Varezhdur were gathering. Chamberlains on the violet lawn, childsoldiers on the scarlet, musicians squatting on the blue grass with their instruments in readiness ... and, materializing on the displacement plates at 'the foot of her throne, her most trusted servants.

Tya and Jannif were here too; they must have come back from their mission to Essondras, to prepare for Kelver's journey from Zorn. Siriss looked up; the simulated sky showed a brooding twilight, pink and deep blue, the colors of an Inquestral shimmercloak. I must seem strong, she thought, like Elloran. She beckoned to Tya and the astrogator Jannif; they came up to her.

"Kelver has found out that you have finally decreed the funeral," Jannif said. "He is coming."

"Yes," Siriss said.

Across the water, almost inaudihle, a voice singing. High-pitched, more like a windwuther than a human sound. A faint malodor of embalming, such as servocorpses exuded. Across the water, a barge, a canopy made from the skin of a pteratyger, a sarcophagus of frozen fire. A winged boy rowed the barge.

"Who is that boy?" Siriss said. For it was the same child who earlier that night had brought her the sleeping-zul.

Tya said, "We have been seeing him in Zorn. We thought it must he one of Kelver's confidants, because he passed easily through forcedoors programmed to incinerate intruders. You don't know him, Lady Siriss?"

"No." Siriss suspected *makrúgh.* Or worse. Perhaps a spy of Karakaël, who had never been known to play fair.

She looked at the child as he held out the control rod over the water. The lake, being an artifact, possessed a rudimentary intelligence; wavecrests sprang up and formed a corridor to propel the barge toward the island throne. "He rows well," she commented. as if he owned the place." As the barge approached she was again reminded of Aoauei, the neuterchild from the singing city Shentrazjit on Uran s'Varek. She remembered the war of illusions that Karakaël and Elloran had fought, and the eyes of the childsoldier whose laseriris had sliced Aoauei in two, and the wind whining through the cavity of his body. "It can't be, of course. He was killed a long time ago."

"Who?" Tya said.

"You would not know him," Siriss said. And now she heard for the first time the words of the song that emanated from the sarcophagus—

den om verek en-tinjet
in darein shirenzheh
zenz kel skeıúh
varung e varande ...

No man alive has touched
The silence between the stars
But that it drove him mad
Or gave him enlightenment.

She remembered the song so well now. It had always been one of Elloran's favorites. The song continued: *I have touched, o High lnquestor, the silence between the stars! I, the mad singer! Envy me, High One, envy me, the mad singer.*

Elloran, mad with grief had gone in search of just that silence. She wept, and did not care that all at her court saw her. In the Shadow Inquest, one no longer locked in one's emotions and left them to smolder for centuries until they became utterly warped, like Ton Karakaël's.

The barge had reached the island now. The coffin-fire parted to reveal Sajit's body.

"Summon a Rememberer," she said. Almost before she was through, one stood beside the throne, a woman in a white robe. "This is something I never want to forget." She watched as the woman of the clan of Tash stood, silent, etching the scene on her memory so that, years later, she would be able to conjure up its remembrance in her mis tress's mind.

Siriss came down from the throne. She stood beside the barge. The old man's lips were parted, but did not move as the song came from them, over and over. "Who are you?" she whispered to the winged boy. "Why do you haunt me?"

The boy said, "I don't know, Mistress."

"Are you from Kelver? Where is Kelver, anyway?"

"I think he will soon be here."

And the boy faded slowly away.

"Where has he gone?" Siriss cried. A chamberlain hastened to her side, thinking that she called for help. "The boy, the boy ..." she said. The chamberlain looked about him but saw no one, and turned to order a childsoldier to search the palace. Again she wondered whether Ton Karakaël had somehow managed to infiltrate Varezhdur. Perhaps a mindhearer planted on this very barge! Quickly she controlled her paranoia, made her mind blank. No stray subvocalizations! she thought. And aloud, she began to instruct her servants to immure the body somewhere within Varezhdur, for she sensed that this is what Elloran would have wanted. And as she spoke, the instrumentalists on the blue terrace lifted megaconchs to their lips and blew a stately, plangent melody punctuated by the knell of a deathdrum, fashioned from the hide of a delphinoid.

As the music welled up, Siriss gave the barge a little push; on either side the golden water churned. The barge drifted toward the far shore and burst into cold holographic flames as the crowd began the formal ululation customary for the funeral of an important man.

A second funeral, Siriss thought, and still the corpse sings....

"Where is Kelver?" Siriss said half to herself.

"Here." She started. And there he was, standing beside her, smiling ingenuously. He must have plated in while her back was turned. She raised her arm to silence the crowd's ritual grief. Then she turned to embrace Kelver and to invite him to sit beside her on the throne.

"Not a word!" Kelver whispered. "Order the ceilings and the walls deopaqued. There's something you must see." There was a crazy joy about him; for a moment he seemed like the old Kelver. She clapped her hands, and the funereal twilight evaporated; instead the huge holoscreens showed cloudstorming Zorn, bleak and majestic.

"We are leaving soon," Kelver said. "Look, I've ordered the Throne to bring us another palace—" At first she saw nothing. Then bubbles in the wind, each bubble a whole city. And then, resolving out of the mists, a palace like a swirl of snowflakes. She gasped. "Varuneh's palace!"

"I want her spirit to guide us," Kelver said. A sudden sadness fell over him. She clasped his hand, trying to follow his change of mood. And she remembered the first time she had seen this palace; it had appeared, ghostlike, orbiting the moonworld Kilimindi at the fatal game of *makrúgh* which had brought about Ton Karakaël's downfall and precipitated the war.

One by one or in little groups, the attendants and officials who had been present for Sajit's ceremony were lining up at the displacement plates that dotted the rainbow grasses, and were dematerializing. Presently the two were alone on the island. The snowflake palace approached; each flake was a complex of chambers, and each was linked to every other by displacement fields and by corridors of force. Against the red-streaked ocher of Zorn's atmosphere the snowflakes twinkled. Here and there were attendants, antlike, scurrying down their filaments. The palace was wrapping itself about Varezhdur, whose glitter-burnished spires rose up all around them ... Kelver closed his eyes to subvoke a command, and a holosculpture of Varezhdur burst from the surface of the golden lake, a dance of needle towers and domes and twisting corridors ... an image of the snowflake palace formed in the air above it. Now the snowflake palace was a spiral, wrapping itself around Varezhdur like a lover. "We will be two and one: two palaces twined into one: Kelver and Siriss, Varezhdur and Sharamonda."

"Sharamonda?"

"That is what Lady Varuneh called it, when she still ruled as Inquestor. In an ancient language, it means *The Dark Heart.*"

"A strange name for so beautiful a palace." And kissed him on the cheek, chastely.

"Man and woman," Kelver said, half to himself. "Snow and fire. Good and evil. Illusions."

"Where will we go first?" Siriss said.

"Essondras!" cried Kelver.

As if in response, a black opening appeared in the clouds. It expanded. The blackness smeared itself across the entire sky image. Siriss felt no motion, but knew that in those few seconds they had left Zorn parsecs behind. For Kelver, calling on the power of the Throne of Madness, had smashed open a tachyon corridor in the space between spaces. The blackness overhead was absolute.

And then, abruptly, stars once more.

And a crescent world, a slice of brilliant blue.

"They want to destroy that world," Kelver said. His mood had swiftly become naked anger. Siriss flinched. He hardly seemed the same person. "Destroy, indeed! A world to whom you and I have given the gift of freedom!"

"And hope," Siriss said. They were glorious thoughts. Why then did she feel such despair? Could it be that she was jealous of Kelver's dream, that it possessed him more utterly than she ever could? Once she had kept no secrets from him, but now she no longer dared to speak her mind.

Six

Masks Beneath Masks

Zalo caught the apprentice's attention as the boy was leaving the pit at the end of the performance. "Why so fast, boy?"

"I've ... somewhere to go." He avoided his eyes.

"I know, I know. You're going to one of those revolutionary rallies, aren't you?"

"Let me go!" Zalo suddenly realized that he had been clutching the apprentice's arm too tightly. He released him. There was a bruise there. "Master Zalo, there's not much time anymore." The boy's face was slick with sweat from running back and forth from the pit to the dungeons, from lugging the corpses to their proscenium marks.

"I want to go with you," Zalo said urgently.

A pause. "But your words to me, that day, at the burning of the Rainbow ..."

"Something has happened." As they stepped through the displacement field onto the street, a kashanthra leaped up, joyous, startling them.

"You're not ... a spy? From the Arm?"

"Lead the way. And by the way, you must tell me your name. We should no longer stand on ceremony, now that the world is about to end."

"I am Jherwo."

"I have an idea, Jhisha," Zalo said, calling the boy by his child-name. "I need your help. I'm not sure how you and I, just human beings, can really do much against the whole Inquest. But we can make gestures, grand gestures. We can go out laughing. Not candleflames guttering, but fireworks!"

"Like the Rainbow Darkness," the boy said, smiling.

"Yes. Tell me, why is it that we paint masks onto corpses that make them resemble people, when it's the fashion for people to paint masks of death on their own faces?"

"I don't know."

"That's what we're going to find out."

***

The night on a barren, barbarous planet: the stars thick and brilliant, masked to the east by the silhouettes of mountains. "What world is this?" Ton Arryk said, as the floater, disguised as fog, skimmed over desert, then mountain, then reddish seething ocean.

"Why trouble to learn its name?" said Ton Karakaël, who sat beside him on a hoverthrone of azurite and small imprisoned waterfalls, canopied with the flayed and animated skin of an albino pteratyger. "You will feel the more compassion at the world's death. Isn't it enough to know that it's a lair of heretics—a potential utopia? But the world is called Essondras."

The somberness of night made of their floater a garish spectacle. Arryk looked at Karakaël, who was no longer Lord of a Million Masks; the Lady Varuneh, in that cruel game of *makrúgh* which had ended in a declaration of galactic war, had stripped his last mask from him, had shown the assembled Inquest his five-hundred-year shame. His face was scarred, pitted, ribbed with the scab-texture of the sackcloth over which his own skin had grown. "Don't tell me you have doubts, Ton Arryk n'Elloren Tath," he said, his coalred rodent eyes peering from that mummy's countenance.

"No, I don't," Arryk said uncertainly. Two childsoldiers, who had been crouching at their feet, sprang up at some imagined noise, lashed out at the darkness with the lightning of laser-irises. In the distance, rumbling-for the children's overzealous vigilance had caused an avalanche in the mountains that ringed the horizon. Terrified of punishment, the childsoldiers scurried back into position. But Karakaël smiled indulgently at them.

"Mountains, only mountains. And we have long since gone beyond moving mountains, haven't we, Rikeh?" "Perhaps."

"You do have doubts," Karakaël said, watching the wasteland roll by.

"I am afraid of you," Arryk said. "Bah! What *makrúgh* is this?"

"You were easier to understand when you were still masked. Now that I see your true face, I don't know what I see."

"I am still masked. You are my mask now."

Black hills beneath, and here and there a village built in the hull of a cast-off starship. "I am not your mask," Arryk said.

"How young you are!" A river beneath, branching like the silhouette of a rippling willow. "You are my mask, boy. Let me tell you why, because it is essential that you understand, since we are making you a figurehead of our war. Not that you have any importance in yourself, Rikeh. But it is you who renders Kelver vulnerable. And it is not meet that we, the High Inquest, should use our mightiest forces to squelch the so-called revolution of a peasant boy. That would be unseemly, inelegant ... uncompassionate."

"Compassion!" Arryk laughed bitterly. At the sound the childsoldiers sprang up, tigerlike, vented their laser-anger on the river beneath, so that a steam jetted up and shrouded their floater for a few seconds

"Listen, boy. You must understand. She who unmasked me also loosed my five hundred years' rage. The mask had sealed it in while it seethed. If only I had died in the sewers of the city of Airang! But no. I was raped by corpses; drenched in the fetor of their breath; I felt their pus-gorged members in my anus! When fear and pain had passed away, and I fell into the arms of the compassionate Inquest, all that remained was rage! But an Inquestor feels no rage. Varuneh knew all this. Perhaps she even sought to heal me. Instead she has unleashed a monster! But I am an Inquestor. I still will not show rage overtly, though rage is a fine thing. No. I will use you as its instrument. You are my mask, and though you struggle to be free, you will not wrest yourself from this mummy face. Don't you, too, feel it? You who once loved those two renegades, Kelver and Siriss, who would despoil our empire of twenty millennia."

"I don't love them anymore," Arryk said. Dark islands rose from the dark water ... and then darted eastward, so that he knew them for humps of a cetacean creature.

"Are you sure?"

"Yes!"

"Good. Your sureness, boy, will be your undoing. An Inquestor should not feel love, after all. Love is tied up with transience. It is not of the fabric of eternity. It is compassion, cold compassion, that we must feel. And when we destroy this world that your Kelver has tainted, we will savor that compassion. We will allow it to waft through our senses like a rare perfume, and we will find a kind of dark joy, that we have preserved the Dispersal of Man from the heresy of utopianism. But you lie, boy. You do feel love. It is this helpless, hopeless love that lets me use you, that binds you to me forever."

"It is not true!" Arryk cried out. The dark plain swallowed his cry. The childsoldiers looked one to the other, attentive, never showing dismay. In their black uniforms, their iridium chased graviboots gleaming in the moons' light, they blended with the passing landscape; only their cat-slitty eyes seemed alive, flitting shiftily from side to side.

"It is good to be angry," Ton Karakaël said. A wry crease of a smile.

"There's no life here."

"Of course not! They have long since been herded into the people bins, stasis frozen for the voyage to new worlds. We are of the Inquest—not insensate beasts, wagers of bloody, primitive war!"

Essondras. The gloom engulfed Arryk's senses. At first he imagined it to be of a kind with the black darkness of the void at the heart of Uran s'Varek. But presently he could see that all was not uniformly black. The pale fire of stars and moons played across fields and forests, silvering the treetops. The lakes were not black, but deepest ultramarine, and starstitched, still. Forests flecked the mountains, silver-maroon, shivery. Here a light rain, and the stars streaking as though tear-blurred. And Arryk said, "If we are of the light, as we claim, why do we come swooping on Essondras from darkness, while Kelver bursts out of the sunlight? Are we, then, the evil ones?"

"Never say that, Ton Arryk n'Elloren Tath! We are not creatures of darkness. We come clothed in compassion. Think of Uran s'Varek's pearl-skied splendor. *That* is our land."

But Arryk remembered the black hole at the heart of the Inquestral homeworld; and he thought, It's not as easy to use me as he thinks. He too is weak. And so it is that *makrúgh* is played, level twisting into level.

"Oh, don't be so gloomy," Karakaël said at length. "This is a festive occasion, my boy! Later, in the hour before this planet's dawn, we'll gather in my palace and watch the fireworks."

"And now?"

"Now there is a splendid sight I want you to see. Across this ocean, over the rim of mountains ... youwill see the people bins. And millions of people preparing for the stasis freezing. You'll see what a mighty thing this Inquest of ours is."

There it was now, the island. It was circular; men had built it. Two rings of crystal monoliths, jutting from the ocean, circled it; on the island more stone circles. *Hover;* Arryk subvocalized. "Why is it so still?" he said.

"It should not be! It should be a hive of activity, what with the machines packing the stasis-frozen people into the people bins and the last-minute convoys from the most distant continents."

Arryk saw the people bins now. Tethered to the island by strings of force, they floated on the water, each a cylinder of gray metal many klomets long. When they were filled, they would be towed into space, and they would sail the overcosm until such time as a new world was readied. But there was no hubbub. No lines of airships and waterships teeming with the planet's populace. "What's the matter with these people?" Karakaël said. "I suppose they think war's just a game. Maybe they've listened too long to your friend Kelver, and they think we've already been cast down from our hoverthrones!"

But Arryk thought: Kelver would not have lied to them. He loves the truth too much. Too much for his own good, even.

Kelver! the chocolate wilderness, the desert of dessert! O, I hunger for him ... the thought rose up uninvited, quickly stifled. An Inquestor does not love.

Karakaël said: "What tedium! I suppose I shall have to investigate. It's a nuisance to conduct one's own wars in person. Far better to watch the pyrotechnics from out in space, eh? Like sitting in the front row of a street opera; you see the sweat caking on the actors' makeup, and the illusion is lost."

"Illusion?"

"Ah well. There is one more thing to be done, Arryk; another of our unspeakably dull traditions that one must conserve. We must visit the house of Tash."

"And choose Rememberers, who, till the end of our days, will live in our palaces and regurgitate, at our whim, the history of the planets we have caused to *fall beyond* . . ."

"Boring, boring, boring! I don't believe I've ever listened to a Rememberer since the day I took the shimmercloak," Karakaël said. "But it must be done."

"Where is the house of Tash on this world?"

"Who knows? The capital city's usually a good place to start looking. Ho, there, childsoldier! Find out for me!"

One of the childsoldiers, in response, summoned up a holosculpt of the world, a carpet of illusion that rose from the floater floor to a height of some three centimeters. Having located the world, the floater rose swiftly, sliced through the night air, northward, over an ocean strewn with icebergs.

"I'm uneasy about it," Arryk said. The idea of forestalling the impending destruction of Essondras crossed his mind, but he flicked away the notion at once. Nothing that Kelver had touched must be allowed to survive, or the contagion would consume the High Inquest and with it all he believed in. Yes. It was more compassionate this way. The Inquest must continue. *Makrúgh* must continue, and with it the cycle of minor wars that gave the great stasis the illusion of movement. The lesser compassion must be swallowed up in the greater. I must be resolute, he thought. I must be strong for all mankind, and suffer its guilt; for man is a fallen being, and the breaking of joy is the beginning of wisdom.

It was good to be strong. Like an arch in an ancient cathedral. Like the pteratyger on whose back, the ancients said, the cosmos rested. This was what it was to be an Inquestor.

Kevi! Sirissheh!

He closed his violet eyes—both Kelver and Sirissheh had kissed those violet eyes, in a past best unremembered, and breathed in the wind of the doomed world. I will not let the past haunt me, he thought, I will kill love. He remembered his mentor Ton Elloran, who had once said, "The Inquest falls"; but Elloran had fled, no one knew where.

Perhaps he had been unable to face this truth: *I am an Inquestor, and the Inquest is eternal.*

***

Torches on the towering tombstone walls; night over the necropolis of mnemothanasions on the outskirts of Ikshatra; the rebels meeting in secret. Jenjen, deep in conversation with a Rememberer, felt a touch on her arm: "Zasha!"

"Quiet, my darling. I've only come to listen, that's all. I've my own ideas about what to do for the revolution."

"It's all right. But look at these people... the childsoldiers who have lost their looks of despair ... the lovers, the old men, even some of the oligarchs ... they carry Kelver's image in their hearts."

"What do they dream of, some mystical salvation? Then it's no better than any other religion."

"He's coming," a young boyish voice. Jenjen saw that it was Zalo's apprentice Jhisha.

"I am content that you have brought him here," she whispered.

The boy said, "He insisted on corning. He has an idea, he says. He needs volunteers. Those who love to go masked, he says.

"Come, boy, let's go among them and see what we can find."

Jenjen watched as they disappeared down an alley between two tombstones, each some fifty meters tall, carved with the names of those who had fallen in some ancient war. She was happy he'd come, so happy. It made the end of the world complete for her.

It was a humid night. The moons were bands of light in the slit of sky between the tall oppressive walls. The people were crowded, crushed against the etchveined marble. She moved to follow her lover and the boy, but overheard her name and stopped.

"But who could have burned the rainbow?" an old man was saying to another. "Could it have been Jenjen after all?" She was about to stop, to say that she hadn't even been there when it happened, when another voice, the voice of an old woman, spoke up. It was a startling voice, sepulchral, seeming to come from an ancient time. She looked and saw the woman; swathed in black like herself, her face veiled, theonly feature Jenjen could see was the deep, green eyes, eyes hauntingly familiar to her. And though the old woman was not even addressing Jenjen, it seemed that those eyes were watching her, that they penetrated her soul. But the old men she was speaking to had not noticed anything.

The old woman was saying, "I have heard it said that a young boy was seen running from the central generator of the rainbow. A winged boy, with eyes green as the sea." And still she transfixed Jenjen with her eyes.

Jenjen was about to say something when the woman seemed to dissolve into a darkness ... her form drained into shadow, the shadow crawled skyward along the marmoreal whiteness of the tombwalls and dissipated into the pitch black spaces between the slits of moonlight. Who could she have been? But Jenjen knew well those eyes. Panicking, she ran after Zalo and the apprentice, calling their names frantically.

Seven
The Fractured Prince

At that same moment, a thousand parsecs away, in one of the hidden thronerooms of Varezhdur, Kelver wept.

The twinned palaces breached the overcosm. In a control room astrogators linked their minds with thinkhives and the brains of delphinoids. A tachyon corridor was opened, smashing through spacetime; and Kelver had not done weeping when the palaces emerged into realspace in the vicinity of the system of Essondras.

Finally he cried out: "You've lied to me. I'm not the agent of some great galactic destiny. I'm just a plaything of yours."

A voice, penetrating the wall of ceaseless whispering: *I never lied to you, Ton Keverell n'Davaren Tath. Godhood is bitter.*

Another voice: *Escape! Escape!*

A third: *Do not stare at the Skywall day after day, Kevi. Do a man's work!*

The whispering welled up like sandpaper against his mind ... he had to escape, but the whispering invaded every corner of his thoughts ... "Free me!" he shouted at the Throne of Madness.

As you wish, came the voice in his head, across the tachyon universe, from the black hole at the heart of Uran s'Varek.

Pain now, as though layers of skin were being flayed from him, one by one, and he screamed and screamed until suddenly, like the resolution of a violent dissonance, came release, and-

The throne was empty. A winged boy stood at the foot of the steps of sculpted clingfire.

"Where am I?" the boy whispered to himself. He had never been in this room before. The last thing he remembered was a corridor lined with marble pteratygers. And now this room. The walls were wavering, dissolving; beyond he could see an image of a planet and its attendant moons.

Presently—compounding his confusion—a young woman materialized on the displacement plate in the center of the throneroom. She glanced only briefly at the boy, as though he were quite familiar to her; then she said, "Where's the Prince of Shadow, boy?"

"I don't know."

The woman—she was garbed as a childsoldier, although breasts were beginning to bulge against the tight black tunic—smiled indulgently and said, 'Tell him that Tya-without-a Clan has returned. Tell him that the seed has fallen on Essondras. First-level infiltration has been going on for some years, but when Ton Arryk discovered that Essondras was one of our target worlds, he hastened to play it in *makrúgh,* and it was designated for *falling beyond.* I and other operatives arrived to step up our subversive operations, and I have recently incited two artists—one a darkweaver, the other a writer of necrodramas-to come over into shadow with us. Tomorrow they are planning to give a signal, during the performance of a certain necrodrama, *The Romance of the Rainbow King,* that will trigger the revolution."

"What are you talking about?" said the winged boy. In the back of his mind came a faint whispering. Those voices aren't mine, he thought, but another's. He wished them away; with a flick of subvocalized thought he dispelled them. There was so much the others seemed to take for granted here ... he smiled ingenuously, hoping that the childsoldier would give him some clue to her meaning.

"One more thing," Tya said. "Our thinkhives have learned how Ton Karakaël means to destroy Essondras. It will be the Deathrain of the Million Shooting stars. It was one of fifteen planetary destructions programmed into the deathmoon that he and Arryk captured from us." The winged hoy wondered at the bitterness in the girl's voice. "I'm sorry."

"Why are you sorry?"

"Lord, isn't it time you ended this charade? I don't know how you're projecting this illusion, but I would be stupid if I didn't recognize your eyes through this disguise ... don't you trust me, Lord Kelver?"

"Why are you so hurt? I don't even know vou... ,"

The childsoldier raised her hands as though to fend off a blow ... at that moment the winged boy felt himself shifting, shifting ... he looked down at his hands and saw them melting into other hands, he felt his wings wilt and shrivel and be sucked into his spinal column, and then came that incessant whispering, it had never gone away at all, it returned redoubled, drowning his own thoughts, and he reached up to touch his face and there was nothing there—

Kelver saw Tya, back turned, fleeing toward the displacement plate. He called out her name, but she had dematerialized. He must have had one of those blackouts... death by shooting stars, was that what she'd said? ... he called her name in the empty room, but a thousand inner voices drowned his own ... "Free me!" he screamed again, and—

A very old woman in a shimmercloak stood at the foot of the throne. She looked around for a moment, taking in the situation, understanding it immediately. Kelver was gone for now, but she knew he could always be reached. So could the winged boy and the pteratyger ... she was the old one, the wise one. Only she could put together the pieces of the puzzle and confront the Throne of Madness.

"Come, Kelver," the old woman said softly. "You can't hide forever. Come out from the abyss within. I will hold the whispering at bay, for it was I who the Throne loved, long ago."

Slowly she felt the shift come on. "Be comforted, Kelver, be comforted," she said. When the shift was complete, he would no longer hear her, for only she could see all the shattered fragments of his soul. I must soothe him, she told herself, while I can.

And she allowed herself to fade into the chasm of Kelver's mind; and when Kelver emerged from the blackout he was strangely comforted, as though an old woman had held him in her arms and sung him a crooning lullaby.

***

On a whim, Zalo decided not to plate his way to the theater but to walk there in the twilight. It struck him that he had never walked to the theater before, even though it was a distance of only five klomets; but even Karnofara, his old mentor, was able to recall a time before the system of displacement plates had been extended to the west of the old city, and when it was either walk or hail a hovertaxi. Twelve gardens stood between him and the theater. To his surprise, he discovered that the Garden of Sculpted Mist stood right next to his own arrondissement; it had never occurred to him, in his fifteen years' separation from Ir Jenjen, that she was only a few minutes' walk away from him the whole time.

He gave his name to the gate; presently Jenjen popped up beside him. Today she had rouged the flower-scars on her cheeks, and the darkness that she wore hugged her thin body tightly. They linked hands and walked on, not speaking; he was so full of what was to come that no words came.

She stroked the kashanthra; it perched on his shoulder, its feathers slightly abrasive against his bald head.

They walked past a slum; in an open sewer, a ragged child scratched for something; two kashanthras darted dolefully back and forth, their wings oil-soggy and useless.

Ahead, the theater: tier after tier, rising from the twilit fog.

A mechanical, its metal chest blazoned with an Inquestral crest, lurched through the streets, buzzing the same message over and over: *Please register for your people-bin assignment immediately. A shuttle leaves from the seaport every twelve minutes for the people-bin loading center on the island of Kshewosh. Excuse me, sir and madam, have you registered for your people-bin assignment yet? The High Inquest is compassionate, but it cannot be responsible for your failure to report for registration. Let me remind you that the* falling beyond *of your planet* *is not an act of hostility but a necessary and compassionate Inquestral act. Please, no ran \cor, no bitterness.*

"Leave us alone!" Zalo shouted. He felt Jenjen's hand grip his even tighter.

Sir, I am only a mechanical, I do not even have life. If you value your own you will not gainsay the High Inquest's offer of compassion and hope. The people-bin loading station on the island of Kshewosh—

Zalo began to walk faster. The mechanical turned its attention to another pedestrian.

They reached a grand concourse, with people streaming from displacement plates, others on rapid skywalks overhead ... here and there a doompreacher was halfheartedly exhorting the throng, although the imminent actual doom of the planet seemed to have driven away much of their traditional business ... beneath the steps of the ruined palace, old women hawked roasted hawknuts and skewers of jangyll meat marinated in the juice of winter krellesh. In the center of the square a gigantic holorama played the news, but no one was watching; indeed, people were walking right through it, and one young couple were actually making love in the middle of a ghostly holoimage of a bursting volcano.

Everywhere, mechanicals marched about, stopping passersby and trying to impress upon them the need to regis ter for people bins.

"It's only an hour till the performance," Jenjen said. "Is it all ready then?"

"Barely. But there's been so little time."

They found the alleyway that concealed the displacement plate to the artists' entrance; there was the plate, tucked between two firefountains, disguised, by a holographic overlay, to resemble a firefountain itself. They stepped into the illusory flames, and Zalo subvoked the code, and they stood outside the secret door.

A network of sewers ran just beneath the theater; just beyond the control pit there was an entrance where necrodrama students used to toss half-arjents for luck. He pulled a coin from his tunic and tossed it in; then they stepped inside the portal, which was friezed with human skulls, painted in gaudy colors, that someone had retrieved from a warehouse of disused servocorpses.

Zalo nodded to his apprentices and showed Jenjen a chair-float.

"I don't suppose there's anyone here who hasn't heard about the changes in tonight's performance," he said.

"No one in the audience, either, Master Zalo!" one of the apprentices said, laughing.

"Karnofara would turn over in his his grave," Zalo said. "All but his head!" said another apprentice. Typical pre-performance banter, Zalo thought. Hardly what you'd expect for the eve of the revolution ....

"Will you do the honors, my love?" he said to Jenjen. "Of course."

She waved her hand in an ancient gesture that had been handed down to necrodramatists for centuries. Far overhead, music began: the overture. Zalo looked, trying to gauge the size of the audience. The stands were packed, and people were still trying to barge in. And the Balcony of Remembrance was jammed with the white-robed clan of Tash-the entire house of Tash must have turned out for this performance.

He took his seat and closed his eyes, as he had always done before a performance, to meditate. But this time, though he concentrated as usual on the visage of his old mentor Karnofara, it was the face of Kelver, the Prince of Shadow, that flitted in and out of his visions ... and over and over he heard the words he himself had spoken to the embalming-bird: *You must never weep again.*

***

Lady Siriss stirred and murmured Kelver's name. But when she opened her eyes he was not there, and the huge bedchamber was empty ... or was it? Behind an arras at the far end was the old orchestra pit, from which old Sajit's musicians had used to lull Elloran to sleep; a faint light came from behind it, and she thought she saw shadows dancing.

She got up, gathered her shimmercloak around her. It hissed, sensing her confusion, as it swirled. The thinkhive of the palace spoke: *The childsoldier Tya wishes an audience, Lady.*

"Admit her."

She had a few seconds to arrange her shimmercloak properly and to toss back her snowy hair; then Tya appeared, distraught and breathless.

"Mistress, I've just seen the most terrible thing. Kelver ... shifted shape!"

"I don't understand," Siriss said. But already she was remembering the green-eyed winged boy, and a chance encounter in the corridors of the palace with a tawny pteratyger with a stare like polished jade. "Yes. Now I see it. It's the Throne of Madness. Who is controlling whom?" Siriss trembled, wondering how quickly the rebellion would founder if Kelver were to go completely mad. Then what would happen to me? she thought, and saw, in her mind's eye, the Inquestors of Judgment, and the choral anathema, and Davaryush standing alone, stripped of his name. She said, "I don't think he can handle the Throne. His soul is fracturing; and because the Throne is capable of manipulating the very matter around its possessor, his image too has become schizoid. Do you understand, Tya?"

The childsoldier did not answer; instead she turned away and began to sob. "What, you're crying, you who have lived through wars and through the burning of planets? You must be strong, girl." But Siriss herself felt helpless. If only I'd foreseen all this, she thought. Before I discovered my love for him ... "We must tell no one," she said to Tya. "You or I or Jannif will take control when necessary. What about Essondras?" "The Deathrain of the Million Shooting Stars," said Tya. "Once, once ... I would have found that profoundly beautiful."

"Oh, Lady Siriss—"

The adolescent fell into the woman's arms. Siriss marveled at how they were able to comfort each other. Before Davaryush's plan and Kelver's revolution, no childsoldier would have dared touch even an Inquestor's shadow ... and Siriss thought: Perhaps these anomalous friendships are all we will have wrought, in the end.

Is it worth it? she thought. They held each other close, the woman and the girl.

There was another message from the thinkhive: a steward with the Lady's evening zul was on his way. Siriss turned and saw the winged boy guiding a winged tray.

"Is that—" she said. Tya nodded.

"Don't you know me at all?" the White Inquestrix asked the

boy. "Don't you remember anything of our first meeting in Rhozellerang, of our lovemaking in this palace, when Sajit was still alive?"

"Mistress, why do you always confuse me?" the boy said. The tray glided to Siriss's bedside; the boy genuflected and made to depart.

"No, stay...." said Siriss. The winged boy waited while she gave a few orders to Tya about the disposition of delphinoids and childsoldier troops; then Siriss was alone with the stranger she knew to be Kelver.

"Do you have more commands for me?"

"No. Just ... stay awhile. I want to tell you about Lord Kelver —"

For a split second she thought she saw his features shiver. A troubled look crossed his face and was quickly dispelled. "I'm not as ignorant as I used to be, my Lady. I've been haunting the passageways, spying in the palace kitchens. I've learned a lot about the Prince of Shadow."

"Do you know then who he is?"

"Of course! He is the Lord of Compassion. The Shadow's Shadow. The Bringer of Bread. The Hand of Mercy. The God Above the Inquest."

"So many titles they're giving him now ... but boy, *you* are the Prince of Shadow."

"You're crazy, my Lady!"

"Look into my eyes." He stared at her transfixed. "You remember nothing?" And she saw that his eyes, emerald clear, had no life in them; they were like the jewel eyes that were sometimes implanted in the heads of servocorpses, to make them seem more decorative, less grisly. She touched him then; the flesh was cool, like soft stone. She told him to come to bed. If this was all that was left of Kelver, a boy who did not even know his own name, she could still cling to it. She made the child lie back on her lap and lightly flutter his wings. The tickling roused old memories: of her and Kelver and Arryk speeding across Uran s'Varek, of their tempestuous lovemaking. This shard of Kelver's personality was a poor surrogate, but presently it brought her to a kind of climax, and allowed her to fall into an uneasy sleep.

***

And an old woman, swathed in a shimmercloak, rose from the bed and watched her as she lay tossing on the mattress stuffed with kyllap leaves and perfumed with blended essences from a hundred worlds ... sighing, the old woman with sea-green eyes turned her back on the bedstead canopied with molded lightning and twisted rainbowvines ... for a few seconds she felt manmuscle ripple through her withered arms, she felt the stiffening of a spectral penis ... those memories too are mine, she thought. It was curious to be at once a woman twenty thousand years old and the manboy Kelver, bursting with young strength and passion ... crushing soft Siriss against himself-herself.

She forced the memories down, deep, into the abyss where lay all the fractured persons that together made up Kelver. Let them war among themselves down there, she thought. I alone have the key.

Once, she thought, there was a woman who looked like me. Only her eyes seemed different. The woman with my face stood twenty thousand years ago in a sandy wilderness of Uran s'Varek. And wrung love from the black hole at the galaxy's heart. And chained the power she had named *the Darkling Wind,* and bent it to her will. And joy had flowered in the universe of men.

But now someone has unleashed the Darkling Wind.

Who could it be? the old woman thought.

Surely not—

But, in another recess of her mind, she knew: it was the manboy who now wore her face.

Whose face?

She made for the displacement plate, calling for the secret coordinates of a room in Sharamonda, the iceflake palace that coiled about Varezhdur—

A room itself named Sharamonda, the Dark Heart.

***

"Empty!" Karakaël cried. "How can this be? Against all custom, all propriety!"

They stood before the house of Tash in the city of Ikshatra. The gates were half-open; crammed into the crack were a dozen or so rubbery dead reptile-birds, gold-feathered, crimson-eyed.

Karakaël kicked them out of the way and stormed inside. "You inside! Don't you even recognize an emissary of the High Inquest? Doesn't this shimmercloak mean anything?"

"You'd think they didn't know their world was coming to an end," Arryk said.

Karakaël gave the door another kick; a hinge broke and it clattered to the flagstones, crushing the piled-up creatures. "And what are these disgusting birds anyway? Some gesture of *makrúgh* on Kelver's part, no doubt?"

"Calm down, Karakaël. We have to figure out what is going on."

An alleyway. Displacement plates. Gardens within gardens. Here and there one of the birds, dead or half-dead and staggering, a noisome rheum dripping from its eyes.

A square. "At least the mechanicals are hard at work," Arryk said, as one of them accosted him and then, seeing the shimmercloak, backed off.

"Everyone seems to be going that way, toward that amphitheater-like building."

Many moons were shining; shadows were flung wildly in all directions. Firefountains burned. "You there! What is happening?"

A beggar, seeing the two shimmercloaks, cringed before them. "Masters ... they are going to the theater ... tonight is the night when they're going to unveil the new ending—"

"The new ending of what?" Karakaël screamed.

Arryk beckoned to the childsoldiers who had been shadowing them unobtrusively. They sprang out from behind two columns, readv to kill.

"... of the play! Of the play!" said the beggar, falling to the ground and attempting to kiss Karakaël's feet.

"What play? Speak, or I'll have you sliced in two!"

"The Romance of the Rainbow King."

"Come on then! Rikeh, hurry! Let's taste the nightlife of this planet before it shrivels to ashes!"

"The Rainbow King," Arryk whispered. He felt an uncomfortable foreboding.

At once he remembered the old story. He had heard it from Sajit's own lips once ... the story of how Elloran hunted his first utopia. Suddenly he had no taste for Karakaël's frantic pleasures.

"Aren't you coming?" said Karakaël. And Arryk followed despondently as the childsoldiers, shrilling a warning paean, cleared a path through the crowd with a swath of laserlight from their eyes ... the throng fell to its knees ... corpses smoked on the flagstones.

"Hurry, hurry," Karakaël cried out, excited as a small child by this surprising tum of events, as Arryk walked slowly behind, trying to shut out the wailing and the stench of charred flesh.

Eight
The Resurrection of the Rainbow King

The sound of the hinges from the Balcony of Remembrance was no longer strange to him. They had come every evening, vultures in white robes, to stare. They too must know what he planned tonight; how could they not know? How many more sleeps until the night of the deathrain? Two, three? But word was spreading. The Inquestral mechanicals hadn't succeeded too well, had they, in recruiting for people bins? What must the Inquest think? Zalo thought. Or do they think at all?

He broke out of his trance. The whole world is watching, he thought. It seems like everyone in the city is here, although I know that's impossible. But if not they'll be squatting around their holoscreens ... even in the outlying villages. Onstage, over his head, a swarm of corpses stirred at once. The audience, cramming the aisles, gasped all together. They had never done that before. He pulled Jenjen to sit beside him; he barely noticed her reassuring smile.

He subvocalized a command, through the thinkhive, to his assistants; the opening chorus began, a bloodthirsty, cliché-ridden thing lifted from necrodramas penned by the long dead: it described the thrusting of delphinoids through the overcosm, the clash of ship against ship in the silence of space, the thousand-year argument between the worlds of Ymvyrsh and Ainverell ... vain words lilting from dead lips ... for what, as Karnofara had told him so often, can mimic reality so well as a corpse, its every gesture and facial contortion controlled and heightened by a master of necrodrama? The texts were not that important; it was the life that the master breathed into the dead flesh.

He turned to Jenjen. "And the others? Are they ready?" "How can you break out now'?" she said in alarm.

"It's all right. The apprentices have it well in hand. I'll go down to makeup, I think, and do some finishing touches on the protagonists."

"I'll come with you."

As they stepped on the displacement plate beside the master console, Zalo turned to wink at his apprentices. One of them got up and scurried out.

"What's he doing?" Jenjen said. "Shh. A surprise. Come with me."

As they vanished, he heard the first lines he himself had added to the old play, intoned in unison by the chorus of corpses:

No use thinking of glory:

No use thinking of starships that seem to stand still against the starlight.

***

I have never ridden a starship, Zalo thought as they materialized in makeup, several levels beneath the theater.

One wall was deopaqued; it showed, through the furcewall, a network of sewers. Its walls were of old brick, not simumetal or the new forcelattices; here and there were niches in the walls, and in the nearest one a dozen larval kashanthras, soggy little things, dirt-colored, speckled with glinty gold. "I want you to see something," Zalo said, pointing out the wall and up; when Jenjen followed the crook of his arm she saw what he saw, a cathedral-like dome overgrown with vines, and

beyond it a tiny tunnel into the open air beyond. "This place has been many things, Jeni," he said, at last bringing himself to call her by her child-name; he had committed himself now. "Once, centuries ago, it was an arena where criminals were fed to giant beasts...."

Jenjen shivered. "Cold, dear?" She shook her head. He said, "I know every centimeter of these levels. After my mother died, Karnofara bought me for thirty gipfers and I grew up in these mazes." The old memory surfaced: rubber kashanthra, mother's face, the Blue Canal rippling ... gone, gone, gone. "Now, makeup."

He turned. "I want you to meet someone." She spluttered, wrinkled her nose; he said, "I forget sometimes that outsiders aren't used to the smell. Just breathe deeply a couple of times." She obeyed him uncertainly.

Corpses lined the walls. One, a young boy, was lying on a makeup table being made up as the young princeling Elloran. Apprentice children were painting its cheeks with white foundation; another was working on the eyebrows, adding the brilliant streak of shimmerchrome paint that signified lnquestorhood; two lightning jags were being brushed onto his cheeks, to show that he had come during a war. An old man was lacing on the tall boots which contained subvoke-sensitive circuits; another was carefully pleating the folds of iriditartan that was traditionally used, in lieu of genuine shimmerfur, to suggest the lnquestral shimmercloak. A little girl no taller than Zalo's waist was lacquering the nails with a colloid of powdered metals and ruby-dust.

An old man shuffled toward them. "Shocking, very shocking," he was saying to himself. But not unkindly.

"So which is this, father pisspot? The quick or the dead?"

"What are you doing down here, lad," said the old man, "when you should be directing the corpses? I don't hold with this avant-garde nonsense myself. Why, old Karnofara never used to leave his post ... if we were both younger I'd tan your hide myself!"

"Come on, Enshtewo, we have company. Answer my question."

"Oh. Your pardon, mistress." He seemed a bit taken aback at the bracelet of darkness she wore, which symbolized her allegiance to the clan of Ir and automatically elevated her to a social status higher than that of anyone in the room. "But see for yourself, Master Zalo!"

He clapped his hands; light came on in one of the corpse niches in the wall; a dead boy, attired and made up identically to the one on the makeup table, was lit up. At the same time, the corpse on the table sat up and smiled ingenuously, the rouge smearing on his lips.

Jenjen screamed.

"What do you think, dearest?" Zalo said.

The boy—who was not at all dead—said, "Am I convincing, Master?"

"Absolutely, Jherwo!" Zalo said, beaming. "I would hug you for joy, but I don't want to mess up father pisspot's handiwork! Here, hold still, they'll have to redo your lips. And wipe that grin off your face, you're cracking the makeup."

"It's hard, like porcelain. I don't like it."

"It'd only for a couple hours. And remember to do exactly as I told vou. For the sake of Kelver."

"Who could forget?"

Jenjen stared, openmouthed, from corpse to living child. "Is *this* your altered ending? You, Jhisha?"

Zalo laughed. "There's more, more, more!" Nothing mattered now. A maniacal joy seized him. "If I must die, at least I'm going to trigger a revolution in necrodramatic sensibilities! You like the kid? But you two know each other."

Jenjen laughed.

"I'd forgotten how you laugh," Zalo said, very seriously.

They kissed.

A voice from overhead, echoing oddly down the labyrinthine corridors: "Master Zalo, you're wanted back in the pit. Act I is coming to an end, and—powers of powers!" A scream; then the voice was cut off.

"Quick," Zalo said. "I should never have taken my eyes off

those apprentices." He tapped the boy's shoulder and said, "Make sure the others are ready too." Then he and Jenjen plated up to the pit.

A commotion in the audience. A glazed look on an apprentice's face. "Don't just sit there, subvoke!" Zalo shouted, shaking the apprentice. She pointed.

He looked up. A crowd scene in the play: corpses lumbering, gesticulating, dancing. In the audience ... people in the front tiers had risen and were pointing wildly up ahead. The canopy of artificial rainbows was untouched. What could be the matter?

Then he saw them. Two flashes of shimmerfur in the tier reserved for the nobility. Empty space around them; the petty nobles cowering in the corners of the rows of seats ... and, hovering about the Inquestors on gravidisks, a guard of childsoldiers. Even from here he could see the pinpricks of topaz light that were their laser-irises.

"They can't be here yet! They're ahead of schedule!" Jenjen said.

"Calm down," he said grimly. He sat down at the console and began to direct the corpses, heightening the choreography with grand gestures. "They're not going to steal the show. I don't care who they are! I'm only going to have this one chance in my whole life to defy the Inquest—and I'm probably going to have to die for it—and they're not going to take it away from me!"

***

"It was unseemly for us to come here," Arryk said. "They'll think of us as vultures, hyenas, scavenger dragons."

"What nonsense!" Karakaël said. "Enjoy the show. Your sensibilities are astonishingly delicate for one who was ready to condemn Períssafa to perdition!"

"Don't remind me of doomed Períssafa." Arryk looked down at the arena. The personages of the drama were moving across the stage now, their motions impossibly fluid, their voices far more mellifluous and modulated than humans'. There was the corpse-boy that represented young Elloran. He progressed slowly along a ramp that descended from halfway up the tiers of viewers down to the stage itself. The flutter of shimmercloak was symbolized by a quivering of the outstretched hands, like wings of a hovering bird that windless set the stiff braided cloak ashiver. Above them shone a manystranded light, light of full moons through a weave of translucent rainbow bridges.

"I wish I could understand this gibberish," he said at last.

"It has a certain charm, does it not?" Karakaël said. "The very idea of drama in the lowspeech is quite precious. One *can* make out a word or two here and there, of course, but one wonders why such a supposedly high art form has been bent to such populist aims."

'"Do not mock me," Arryk said. For he had been born a peasant, and there had been a time when he did not know the highspeech, and did not realize that what he spoke was not proper for human beings. And he knew besides that the speech of Essondras was not *that* alien to the highspeech. He could pick out whole phrases, and found it not unlike the lowspeech of his own homeworld, the speech he had learned strapped to his mother's back while they herded firephoenixes in the scarlet snow. "Listen! The crowd is murmuring. What's next?"

"The young Sajit," said Karakaël. "Look, there he comes, costumed as a childsoldier; he's carrying some sort of zitherorgan."

"It was a whisperlyre," Arryk said, "in the true story. Elloran told it to me many times. And so did Sajit." '"Truth!" Karakaël sneered. "Within *our* lifespans we may see such things as anecdotes our friends have told us ... for *them* it happened centuries ago. We are their myths, Rikeh, are we not?"

"Just as I said! And therefore our presence here is unseemly, Ton Karakaël z Karakit Kerún! It is not the place of gods to mingle with the throng. You've told me so often enough." Suddenly he realized he had been drawn into a new game of *makrúgh*. I'm allowing emotion to get the better of me, he thought. I must think only of the greater compassion.

Karakaël pretended to be engrossed in the drama, so Arryk too watched. Even without signaling to his polyglot implant he found himself understanding more and more of what was going on, and was becoming more than a little miffed at having missed the first act. Now came the moment—he knew it because Shen Sajit himself had told him the tale—when the boy Sajit was to sing the song of the homeworld of the heart, accompanied only by his whisperlyre, the melody was the same, though the words had an alien ring to them, and the accompaniment was not the sighing resonant whisperlyre but the staccato twang of the zitherorgan:

Ye, ye, wa'l mwenso kshepradan, no prezhwan fra danwedo'l yerdo...

"What a caterwauling!" Karakaël observed.

"You understand the words very well, *Hokh'Ton,"* said Arryk. "I will quote them in the highspeech, since you see fit to feign obtuseness! 'When man dispersed, we wept for the dead earth; we cried, 'Where is the Homeworld of the Heart?'"

"Animal mutterings," Karakaël said.

Careful. Perhaps he seeks to entrap me with a new ploy in *makrúgh*. "I'm not playing now." Determinedly he watched the action; once more he felt the magic of the old story.

Corpses strutted, wailed, declaimed in uncanny mimicry of life. The boy-corpses that played young Elloran and Sajit had an emotional duet (punctuated by gongs and glass shatterers) in which the boy Inquestor declared that whatever the consequences, he must hunt this utopia, for this was the Inquest's purpose; a chanted chorus depicted their difficult journey up the mountain to the castle of the Rainbow King, the mad Inquestor who ruled the planet Ymvyrsh. They arose on the back of a soaring pteratyger, represented by a mechanical beast with a soldered grimace and great metal wings, who dangled from the rainbow-girt roof on wires, and whose voice roared from the depths of a waterfall-synthesizer below stage. Now the pteratyger-mechanical bearing the two boy corpses paused eerily in midair and began to hover, its wings a flutterblur of gold-iridium.

A scenic transformation: since they could not easily depict the ascent of the pteratyger to the summit of the mountain, they lowered the rainbow castle from the height instead. The audience gasping: much oohing and aahing over the castle, a meld of holosculpture and metalfoil crinkled over wiremesh scaffolding, the whole enveloped in mists tinted with fine dust ground from serpen tine and azurite and rosequartz and citrine and amethyst and lapis and flowers of sulfur.

"Not bad," Karakaël said, "for native art, eh?"

"A pity it will all be gone in a few sleeps' time."

"Now, now. We cannot afford regret. Not with the entire Dispersal of Man at stake. Not with the very nature of compassion in dispute." And Arryk saw that, though Karakaël's expression was precisely that which the Inquestral texts recommended for pronouncements regarding compassion, there was something quite artificial about it, as though Karakaël had never quite succeeded in divesting himself of those million masks. Once more he turned his attention to the necrodrama, for the boy-corpse Elloran had begun to speak:

Come forth, Alkamathdes, Rainbow King, If thou still rulest here.

Thou hast much to answer for; For thou hast created utopia And peopled it with the dead!

And this was just as old Elloran had told the boy Arryk, in the days when he was still growing up in Varezhdur; that Alkamathdes, driven mad by the hopelessness of the Inquestral doctrine regarding utopias, had caused the entire population of Ainverell to be put to death, and rebuilt the world according to men's dreams, and peopled his new world with servocorpses whom he commanded always to radiate happiness ... how long ago had this happened? Five centuries, a millennium? Who could tell? For those not fettered to a planet, who sail the overcosm, space between spaces, or thread through the tachyon universe, time runs more slowly; for Inquestors it almost stands still. Arryk was moved, that people on an alien world, who had never set eyes on Elloran, could be touched by this ancient tale.

Also he remembered that Elloran had betrayed him at Sajit's graveside.

An utter stillness now. The portals of the castle opened. The corpse of a very old man sat on a gilt-and-plastic throne. The crowd hushed, waiting. Something momentous must be about to happen. The scene played: a stychomythian ex change between Elloran and Alkamathdes, the realization that the old Grand Inquestor had gone mad, the pronouncing of the Inquestral anathema, the only highspeech words in the whole necrodrama, and then, just as in the true story, Sajit hurling his instrument at Alkamathdes—

The instrument struck the corpse on the head. It clanged down a thousand holosculpted steps. Electric excitement in the crowd. And then—

A jagged lightning bolt forming on the old corpse's forehead where the zitherorgan had struck. The bolt growing, running down the length of the body, and then lightning bolts formed too on the boy-corpses, and when Arryk glanced at the chorus below he saw that each of the corpses was begin ning to split open, and—

The jagged half-corpses, shriveled and were sloughed off like snakeskins, and within were other corpses, dressed and made up identically to the ones they replaced. In unison, the chorus-corpses stepped from their skins and advanced across the stage in a slow ballet, their footfalls thudding strangely on the stage floor, almost as if—

They were not corpses! Arryk could hear people in the audience whispering, some in outrage, some in glee. He realized that to the sensibilities of this audience the appearance of live actors was shocking, obscene almost ... an uproar in the Balcony of Remembrance. In the top tiers scattered cheering. The live actors moved in a passable imitation of the dead ones, butsomething was missing ... the balletic precision of absolute control. Music welled up, a wild, syncopated madness, and when the chorus began their next strophe they no longer kept time, but mouthed their words frenziedly, in a grotesque parody of the ordered chant of the dead.

"I don't understand," Karakaël said. "What can this mean? Surely these ... these *boors* are not attempting to stage a game of *makrúgh* between themselves and *us?*"

— The chorus ranks were broken now. Some danced arm in arm, careening across the arena. One or two capered solo, somersaulting, flinging their arms drunkenly about. Many members of the audience had risen to their feet and were yelling too, off-key, and some from the lower tiers had actually leaped onto the arena and joined in the bacchanalia.

Karakaël screamed something; Arryk couldn't hear him over

the tumult.

And Arryk cried out: "Kelver! Kelver is behind this!" The roar became overwhelming. Why did they not notice *him,* the Inquestor? What meaning could this simple illusion have? Grimly he watched the stage as the frenzy began to subside.

***

One second before he gave the sign it seemed to Zalo that he could see, as from the bottom of a well, all the way round the theater at once: from the tiers where the merchants sat to the rows of nobles to the vendors that crammed the aisles to the peasants that swarmed the uppermost stories near the awning of simulated rainbows. He could see the two Inquestors quite clearly now. One was younger; his eyes held a hint of violet, Zalo thought, and it almost seemed as though the Inquestor was looking into the necrodramatist's eyes ... though that, of course, he told himself, could not really he possible. He knew it must be Ton Arryk n'Elloren Tath; for his mentor Kamofara had once composed a necrodrama, *A Day in the Scarlet Snow,* on a legendary event in Arryk's life. How strange to see in reality a face he had known since boyhood, a mask painstakingly painted onto the face of a corpse. Others too must know that face, he thought. But most of the crowd had respectfully averted their eyes from the two hoverthrones....

He did not recognize the other Inquestor, the one with the mummy face from which stared fire-crimson eyes. This one was as ugly as the other was beautiful, and Zalo wondered briefly why, with the unlimited somatic renewals available to them, all Inquestors did not simply banish all ugliness from themselves.

There was no time to waste now. He looked straight up to where the boy actor was standing over the holorama of Rainbow Castle. The hubbub hushed itself.

He gave the sign, the *incipit* for a newplay—

And the boy who had once been a pickpocket and then an apprentice and now portrayed a god, a tiny figure in the simulated splendor, his robes heavy with the machinery that generated the illusion of the airy shimmercloak, spoke—

The new words Zalo had composed, after a frenzy of lovemaking, slashing them in laserpencil across her unfinished canvas of darkness—

The dream is no more, friends; There never was a dream.

Can a servocorpse dream?

We were once even as the corpses that strutted, capered, wept, rejoiced to the subvocalizings of a puppeteer.

But now our planet's heart is breaking.

That is why we must awaken from our thousand-year death, seize every second that is left to us.

Rejoice! we will have utopias after all, we will wrest from the great darkness every drop of joy that is our due!

Drink the very dregs, though they be mixed with bitterness.

Terrible words, Zalo thought, as Jenjen squeezed his hand. The apprentices were on their feet now, the audience hushed, perplexed, afraid. It is good that the Inquestors should hear this, Zalo thought; our gesture will count for something now; our little deaths will echo through the stars. Almost without thinking he began to subvocalize the words along with the actor, as though he were still controlling a corpse; here and there the boy stumbled, for he lacked experience, and it was painfully clear that his words did not have the artful artlessness that a brilliant master could inject into a corpse's utterances, and yet their halting innocence held a magic that Zalo once possessed but until now had thought forever lost-

Let them tear down the stars!
Let them grind our world to dust!
They will not take from us our souls
and none save we ourselves will steal
the laughter from our lips,
as we sing out defiance.

The speech he had written was hopelessly mangled now ... what difference did it make? It was overblown bombast anyhow. He stopped subvoking ... it was a strange feeling, like losing control in a necrodrama, and yet ... "Quick, Jenjen! Tell them to unlock the sewer gratings in the labyrinth below." She looked at him questioningly, but obeyed him. The boy said—

Like the kashanthra, we will embalm Ourselves ....

And then the live boy actor began to laugh, a chiming childish laugh that carried clear over the speechless crowd.

And then the other live actors, whom Zalo had caused to plate up on the stage to replace the corpses, using the old special-effects displacement-plate system that a mad master had installed in the theater a century ago, all of them too began to laugh ... the lowest tiers were infected now. Many leaped onto the stage and they too laughed; those in the second and balconies, the more intrepid ones, jumped down, shrieking like children, drunk on this dark joy; and now the boy who played Ton Elloran had found his place and was mouthing, almost unheard over the tumult, the words Zalo had taught him, words of peace and brotherhood and freedom and of Kelver's promises and of utopias to come ... and this wild joy was flowing from tier to tier, splashing up the walls of the arena like strong wine pouring into a chalice, and at Zalo's command the rainbow hangings were cut loose and swayed in the light of many moons—

If cruel gods have stolen our fire from us,
and robbed us of light itself,
let us take the shadow for our own!
Let us embrace darkness,
let us defy our death with laughter.
For death at least belongs to us;
Death cannot he wrested from us.
Defy, defy, laugh, cry.

In the upper tiers people were jamming the exits now. Warmth flushed his face. Displacement plates in the arena disgorged noblemen, peasants, whores, and vendors. Some of the aristocrats had probably never been so close to their social inferiors before; but they were swallowing their disgruntlement and dancing with the peasants. Here and there Zalo could even see a Rememberer. It was hard to tell because they weren't standing apart from the others, clinically drinking in the details; they were screaming and whooping with the other celebrants ... trampling the zigzag halves of servocorpses that littered the proscenium ... with a handclap Zalo disintegrated the one-way-mirror shield that covered the control pit, and the apprentices ran up and joined in ... only the two Inquestors and their retinue of childsoldiers seemed unmoved, their hoverthrones poised above the tempest of radiant faces. And the crowd chanted Kelver's name, though some had never heard it before this night; and the chanting flooded the theater with the wind of a thousand breaths. It was no longer a cacophonic orgy but a solemn ritual, an affirmation of a people's love for their world, their culture, themselves.

Zalo closed his eyes. The world will end tomorrow, he thought. But behind the terror there will be joy. Jenjen, behind him, had wrapped her arms around him and he could feel moist hot breath on his scalp and his own heartbeat pounding against her palms. The crowd's crying crescendoed. He couldn't bear it anvmore. As he stood still at the storm's eye the joytide swept him up and he screamed crazy things, things you can only say when your world is about to end. And memories whirled ... the mother-corpse in the chorus of the play ... the rubbery dead kashanthra slipping from his hands, the bracing choppy scent of the Blue Canal, and ... when he and Jeni first made love in the shadow of a painting of shadow and she cried out and at first he thought it was pain and saw his mother's face first a warm woman then a chorus-corpse and the ooze of the kashanthra's squishy eyes ... his eyes were burning, he squeezed them tight shut but couldn't squeeze out the roaring and when he opened them he was half-blinded by the tearblur but he could see what he had hoped he would see, when he had his first premonition of this night, at Jenjen's house when the guests had all gone home, even the Rememberer, even the messenger from Kelver, when in a brief spurt of joy he had seen his kashanthra try to soar skyward—

"Look!" he heard a shout from somewhere in the throng.

"Out of the sewers—"

Bursting—

Bursting—

Thousands upon thousands of kashanthras, blue-gash-gold in the moons' glare through shredded rainbow holosculptures ... bursting unprisoned from the sewer labyrinths ... riding the tide of joy, their soaring fueled by the roaring. A lull, a throatcatch, then scattered shouts, whistles, all at once a thunderdamburst of cheering as sky thick kashanthras mottled the faces of the moons and churned up a wind by the frenzy-blurred beating of their wings and in their madness dashed themselves against the stands and the balconies and the Rainbow Castle... a glimpse of the lnquestors still aloof upon their hoverthrones ... the endless roaring ... roaring ... roaring ... the birds flew faster now, wings flapping like hurricane battering of unbattened eaves, crazed, circling, careening ... until at last a single kashanthra, high up, excited beyond endurance by the crowd's hysteria, streaked into cometlight and vaporized with a bang, and others, catching its mood, plummeted, sizzling, like meteors, and with each fireworks explosion came a collective shriek from the crowd, a cry of grief and joy so mingled as to know no name, and Zalo found himself weeping as he'd never wept before, not even when he'd seen his mother's corpse adorning the scenery of a third-rate necrodrama, and he yelled with the others as the birds fell flaming, his screams made fierce by the joy of being alive and human and a part of the great rebellion.

"Zasha, Zasha." Jenjen's voice, tiny against the wall of sound. "I'm afraid. Where will we go now?"

And he turned to embrace her, and he kissed her, tasting his own tears on her tongue; and when they broke free he said, "Don't be afraid. We must go to Kelver. You've got to follow me now, never looking back, understand?" He gripped her hard; she gasped. "The displacement plate." He felt her hand tremble in his as they stepped onto the plate. As he subvocalized a secret command, he felt the roaring swell up even more; and then, abruptly, they were in darkness, and the cries grew faint, like the distant swooping of a mountain wind.

***

Arryk's hoverthrone swung high over the howling mob. He turned to Karakaël, who was still, incredibly, clinging to correct

Inquestral composure.

"Are you not angry?" he shouted. "They have declared their world a utopia!"

"Then we have come to the right place," Karakaël said, bringing his hoverthrone alongside Arryk's. "Have we not? For the breaking of joy is the beginning of wisdom." He sighed. "Just breathe that doomladen air."

Arryk said, "But they're going to die!" And he remembered the day that he and Siriss and Kelver had gone on their quest-journey, children still, on Uran s'Varek ... the war between two armies of illusion dreamed up by Elloran and Karakaël ... how it was *he* who had faltered, who had failed in compassion, who had summoned the childsoldiers to vent his rage. This time the people were no figments of a *shtezhnat* game. "I can't believe what Kelver is doing to me," he said. "If we destroy Essondras now, people will truly die. They won't be caught up in people bins and made to sail the overcosm. He's blurring the line between the game and the reality, the illusion and the massacring. He's fed them a phantom love, a deathjoy that denies all that the Inquest has struggled for these twenty millennia—"

"Shall we cancel the war, then?" Karakaël said, taunting.

"No!" Arryk understood then what he must do. Again there were no choices. "Since those I loved and trusted have sought out the shadow, it remains to me to be all Inquestor."

He gazed at the deathflight of the embalming birds, driven by empathy until they could no longer contain the crowd's emotions and burst with joy in white-hot feather showers ... he watched the people surge as a single organism, as they chanted the name of the one he once loved ... remembering the scarlet snow of his youth and the flight of firephoenixes and the first game of *makrúgh* he had played with white-haired Siriss and the deathjewel embedded in his neck that on his death would one day trigger a planet's destruction ... it had seemed simpler then. He had thrown himself into the game, into the salvation of the Dispersal of Man. But now Kelver was forcing his hand. Constraining him to cut short a million lives. Making a mockery of *makrúgh,* which had been designed to protect men's innocence and to allow the Inquest to shoulder the compassion and the grief.

He did not feel the blind fury he had felt on Uran s'Varek, in the war of illusions. What he felt was necessity: cold, unalterable. Look at them! he thought. With their delusions of love and joy and their pathetic embalming birds ... perhaps they meant the kashanthras' skyward soaring as a symbol of their aspirations, but couldn't they see that this unbridled joy was as self-immolating as the ancient sorrow? The birds were exploding everywhere now in a blue-gold firegrid crisscrossing Essondras' many-mooned night, anticipating the deathrain of the shooting stars.

"I—" he began, but Karakaël interrupted him.

"Say it! Say what you must! It is you who lead the war against the heretics, Ton Arryk n'Elloren Tath!" In the shadow of the hoverthrone's awning, all Arryk could see were the coals that were Karakaël's eyes.

He knew at last that not only Kelver but Karakaël had goaded him to this point. By giving him supreme power, Karakaël had made him more than ever his pawn.

I have hate now, Arryk thought.

And he closed his eyes, and with a single flick of his mind summoned forth childsoldiers from the sky. Those few that guarded him ringed both Inquestors at once and cast a net of force about their hoverthrones. As the darkfield closed around, Arryk looked up and saw, beyond the rainbow veils, through the vaporclouds of self-destructed kashanthras—

Locust-specks against the faces of the moons! Closer now, and the distant shrilling of the childsoldiers' war-paean:

Isha ha, ha, ha!
Isha, ha ha heiy ha!

The crowd being mowed down now. Death gurgling down the theater aisles. Red steam of evaporating blood billowing across the seats, the chanting shattering into panic cries, the mob rushing, trampling, a lone servocorpse jerking stupidly in a corner beneath a statue—

"Utopia indeed!" Karakaël cackled as the darkfield shielded them and the deathcries fizzled to a whisper. "How long did *this* one last?"

Arryk heard in his mind the whisper of a distant thinkhive: *Seven minutes,* hokh'Ton. *Seven minutes since the live actor replaced the corpse.*"

"Must be a record," Karakaël said, laughing. "Well, it certainly goes to prove the Inquestral precepts."

"How can you laugh?" Arryk said, anguished.

"Perhaps we'd better watch from a distance," Karakaël said, "now that you've gone ahead and called down the lightning."

"Watch?" A beam of killing light sliced through the nobles' balcony and brought it crashing down on the stage; through the darkfield the cacophony was reduced to a hollow thud, far away. "Watch this innocent city reduced to rubble?"

"The lesser compassion must be swallowed in the greater."

"Riddles and platitudes!" He clapped his hands and the forceglobe was hurled skyward, away from the carnage; in seconds they had passed the city completely. Already the deathrain streaked the sky.

"You forget yourself, Inquestor," Karakaël said implacably. "If you cannot think of compassion now, think of revenge ... of the breaking of Kelver's heart!"

"Kelver! Kelver!" Arryk screamed. He did not know whether it was from love or hate.

Nine
Labyrinth; Deathrain

Tya was glancing casually at the holosculpt display of Essondras and its surrounding space when she noticed that the red pinpricks that represented the Inquest's delphinoid ships had shifted formation. She called for Jannif.

When Jannif had spoken with the astrogating thinkhives of the twin palaces, she said, "The Inquest is attacking."

Tya said, "But the people bins that they sent down to collect the planet's inhabitants—"

"Have not yet been towed into space."

Not quite believing, Tya ran panicstricken to the displacement plate and shouted aloud the code for Siriss's throneroom.

***

Movement in the shadows. A dank, damp smell: eroding stone, sewage, formaldehyde from dead kashanthras.

A sharp corner; a slice of light from some lofty skylight. Zalo started. He gripped Jeni's hand. Her eyes widened **in** the sudden brightness. She was just a face floating above the rippling darkshift she was wearing.

"I'm afraid. I can hear others," she said.

"You don't have to whisper," Zalo cried out. Echoes, sifting down shafts of moist rock. "We should shout it out, over and over: joy, joy, joy, joy." Other voices now, behind: apprentices mostly, those who knew well the sewer labyrinth beneath the theater.

The voices: "Lead us, Master Zalo. Lead us to Kelver." *"Kelver. Kelver."* The k-sounds clicking, trickling on the cavern walls. And Jenjen, gaping in wonder at the many darknesses.

"Follow me," Zalo said. A flock of kashanthras sieved through the huddle. Wings against his cheek. A momentary hail of gold dust in the pool of light ... If only I can remember the way! He thought of being a child again. Ahead, still water; he saw himself springing nimblefooted from flagstone to flagstone, always afraid of being caught by master Karnofara ... his feet remembered even if his mind couldn't. He leaped. A vast chamber now, vaulted, gridded with lancet lightstreaks that leaked from the cratered ceiling. An archipelago of dead kashanthras across the Hooded floor, and the few extant flagstones rising from the water like stepping stones. "Follow, follow," Zalo said again. He and Jenjen together, hands linked, hopping like children, the others following in long single file, their clanging footfalls syncopating into eerie percussive music.

And from far far overhead, the whisperrumble of kashanthras dying.

"Look!" a young man's voice. "There are others—"

Yes. Here and there were other groups, some wading with hands linked, some wandering in circles, disconsolate, lost. "Follow!" Zalo shouted at them. "I know the way out. I've explored every klomet of these tunnels. Don't be sad, you'll only set off the kashanthras. Rejoice and follow." By the minute the crowd was growing ... from behind, in the jumble of conversations, Zalo could hear that many were repeating the words of the boy Elloran's speech, garbled as it was. He asked if anyone had seen the child actor; one thought he had seen him crushed beneath a column. I can't think of martyrs now, Zalo thought, I have to think of freedom. He forced his grief down and thought only of the future, of Jenjen, of the survival of his people.

The cavernous hall thinned, became little more than a crawlspace. Where was that displacement plate he had once found? There, a glint at the passageway's end ... the air syrup-thick as hundreds struggled to breathe. "We must all hold hands now," he said to Jenjen, who turned to seize the hand of the woman behind. They were all linked now. He felt like the end of a live wire, felt the jolt of a hundred life forces ... I'm so alive! he thought. Even though the world is ending. And he subvocalized a sharp, monosyllabic command, and they all sank one by one into the space between spaces and he stood suddenly by a different wall and pulled Jenjen through and it was like drawing in a long chain of human lives, link by link by link.

"In the days of live theater," he told Jenjen, "they stored scenery down here." Passage after passage, curving, twisting, the walls stacked with cardboard palaces and thrones and painted flats ... in the phosphorglow he could see scenes of forests and deserts, vistas of vast cityscapes, in one chamber an enormous backdrop, a battlescene in brilliant colors, cobwebbed here and there, in another room a jungle of artificial trees, in yet another statue after statue, forgotten deities in plastic and papier-mache and canvas ... behind him the others moved more slowly, some stopping to stare at spectacles from the past. .. "Quickly, quickly," he cried, "they are burning down our planet!" But even he could not resist lingering ... for he knew they were things he would never see again ... even if they survived, even if they joined the resistance and became members of Kelver's army of shadows, they would never set foot on Essondras again. For their homeworld would be uninhabitable, perhaps for a thousand years.

"I never dreamed," said Jenjen, "that these things still existed."

"Somewhere in spacetime the past is frozen forever," Zalo said. "Forget, forget, hurry, hurry."

So far away, a firehiss ... "The streets are on fire," said one voice.

"No panicking," Zalo said. "We will be free ... we will not be embalming-birds anymore. Hurry, hurry."

"My children must he dead now."

"The old palace, toppling. I'm sure I hear it!" "I should go home."

"I think I heard the Gardens of Tarahaha go up in smoke."

"I'm sure that was the boiling of the Blue Canal." "Forget! Forget!" Zalo cried out. And he ran forward again, toward the next bank of displacement plates. They were deep underground now, and he knew that the next level would be the oldest one; in this stratum was the arena where, in the planet's earliest times, criminals were thrown to chimerical beasts for the crowd's amusement. Once only he had passed through this level, and that after failing to heed Karnofara's direst warnings, and he had been beaten soundly for it. If only Karnofara were still here! He hastened on. They ripped through a backdrop veil spangled with five pointed metal stars, and beyond was a granite corridor lined with the mirror-squares of displacement plates. "Hands again!" He reached out to clutch Jenjen's and felt the line of humans grow taut ... like the tightening muscles of a giant snake uncoiling. As long as I remember the right subvocalization—

—and tripped headlong into thick darkness.

***

Crying out Kelver's name, Siriss plated across to the snowflake palace. Seeing who it was, a steward led her, through tubes of force, from flake to flake, each crystal a vast chamber suspended in the emptiness. From some six hallways radiated; from others six towers linked by spiderweb lattices. She saw Varezhdur through the crystal layers, sometimes a single golden casement magnified a thousandfold, sometimes a wing or turret made tiny or endlessly reflected in facets within facets ... but always a seeping winter coldness, as though the presence that once animated the palace of Sharamonda was long dead.

"Hurry, steward," he said. "A whole world is at stake ... can't you hurry?"

"The palace is vast, and there are few displacement plates, for it is ancient...."

The steward smiled implacably. "There!" He waved his staff. A black wall that seemed to stretch beyond the limits of the snowflake hall they were standing in. It must be an illusion. She started to walk through, but was met with stone.

"Let me in!"

It seemed that a whispering filled the chamber, a maddening tittering just at the threshold of audibility, though the steward showed no sign of hearing it.

"You're mocking me, Kevi," Siriss said, despairing. She battered at the hard illusion with her fists as the whispering grew louder, drowning her thoughts in random noise.

Then, suddenly, the forcebarrier gave way and she was standing in a viewchamber of which three sides had been deopaqued; ahead shone half-Essondras, erupting milky-blue from the sea of darkness. In the foreground delphinoid ships littered the starfield. The ships of the Shadow Inquest were a motley fleet: there were warships, needle-sleek, slices of silver light; there were converted pleasure vessels, darting like phosphorflies; there were Inquestral delphinoids donated by those Inquestors who had come over into Shadow, ships built in the shape of pteratygers or treehawks or metallic saurians or fantastical abstract designs. There were segmented ships that rippled like centipedes. One ship resembled a beautiful woman, crosslegged, meditating; her half-parted lips would soon expel platoons of childsoldiers on spinning hoverdisks, blowing the enemy a kiss of death.

And in Essondras's shadow lurked Karakaël's delphinoids

... and with them the deathmoon they had won from the edge of the galaxy.

And Siriss thought, We can't win. Here and there a victory maybe, but we'll be swallowed up in the end ... like stars that may shine for a billion years but must finally sink into the black hole at the heart of Uran s'Varek.

She looked around for Kelver; at first she couldn't see him. The room was full of attendants and astrogators and admirals. No, there he was, half-hidden in the crowd that huddled around him. She was afraid he might have assumed some other form, but no. Only this Kelver was so careworn, so emaciated. She ran to him across the carpet of snowy crystalgrass. "Kevi, Kevi, they've done a terrible thing."

"We know." The room fell silent.

Siriss turned and saw Tya and Jannif. What was wrong? Were they waiting for her to speak? But it was not she who was in command. "Kelver—"

Kelver clapped for a closer view. At once they seemed to be in the thick of the delphinoid fleet. Essondras curved away, its atmosphere a misty corona beneath them. At Kelver's command the floor was deopaqued, and then the black wall behind them; it seemed that they stood above the half-world stitched into the starstream, while around them the ships swam silently. Again he clapped; their vantage shifted. They stood in the upper atmosphere of Essondras now; clouds roiled beneath, and in the gaps were landscapes. A vast black delphinoid glided into view, parting the clouds. It was like a cetacean's breaching. Siriss stepped back involuntarily; a murmur ran through the gathering; Kelver raised his hand to still it, and when it died away Siriss heard a single voice still sobbing.

At once the delphinoid sprouted a thousand bloodred mouths, and each spat out a swarm of childsoldiers. Each was encased in a black pressure skin; perched on his hoverdisk, he seemed more locustlike than human.

"Closer!" Kelver cried to the thinkhives that controlled the field of vision. "Follow them down to the city." They lurched into the thick of the throng. Someone screamed as they seemed to dash themselves against the viewwalls ... down, down, down they followed the eyes of the thinkhive. They pierced one stratum of cloud; now the viewwalls were steeped in violet night. The childsoldiers streaked the sky like meteor showers as their pressure skins burned against the atmosphere ... in accurate formation they fell, each igneous filament stranding into a vast abstract design ... farther away were smears of light that were childsoldier swarms too distant for the lightlines to be made out. It was beautiful, that sight. Even now, though she knew that the deathrain fell on a planet still living, still rebellious, and not a dead world whose life had been emptied into people bins ... gold and violet, royal colors, thought Siriss. At first the others in the room were gasping at the spectacle ... before the truth dawned on them. "It is a killing light," Kelver said. "A killing beauty. I weep for them." And his sea-green eyes filled with tears.

Bursting through another cloudlayer now, and the city, erupting—

Siriss was crying out, "We have to stop them now! We have to unleash our own weapons—"

"Oh, Sirissheh." There was such sadness in him. "How little you've learned. You still want to answer death with death." And she looked at him and remembered young Kelver she had loved on Uran s'Varek, of the haunted eyes, strong, passionate; surely this could not be her Kelver any more.

"Unloose the counterattack!" she hissed at Tya and Jannif. But they just stood there. Didn't they understand that she was still Inquestrix here? That she had power of life and death still?

"Be still!" Kelver's voice was a whisper, but it silenced the whole crowd as they continued down to the city in their simulated falling. "It is already begun."

"What! But you've been in your chambers all these sleeps. It was I who oversaw the movements of our armies, I who approved the generals' strategies." Resentment flooded her. "I gave no such order—"

She looked again. It seemed they stood upon a floor of force over a populous city, at the center of which lay an arena ... two dots of shimmerfur blinked against the waves of people. Karakaël and Arryk ... they had actually entered the city itself ... how could they be so morbid, so self-torturing? As she watched, the shimmerspecks were sucked into a globe of darkness and whirled westward, away from the city. Three phalanxes of childsoldiers formed a black wedge in the sky, flame-smothered, like the point of a gigantic fire-arrow. As they moved closer she saw them somersaulting, leaping from hoverdisk to hoverdisk as they ululated their warpaean ...

though it all took place in an eerie silence, for the thinkhive had not yet awakened its ears. Their iridium-edged boots flickered like clusters of twinned stars. Some hung by their feet from their spinning disks, defying death and gravity; some cartwheeled, some sprang and dived like porpoises, and all the while the topaz lightlines spurted from their laser-irises. Towers toppled. Fire ran in the streets. And everywhere people fleeing ... it sickened her.

The lesser compassion must be swallowed in the greater, she told herself angrily. Even we, the rebellion, cannot forget that!

"What counterattack?" she cried out, despairing. "We are lost, Kevi."

A whirlpool of blue-gold flecks in the center of the arena ... from the pile of crumpling flame-blackened plastic rainbows ... draconine birds, their metal-sheened wings wide open, soaring moonward ... beneath them a crowd of bacchanalian dancers ... "They've gone mad down there!" Siriss said.

"No," Kelver said softly. All had turned to hear him now, though the madness seemed to rage around them. "For a few moments they tasted utopia. It was enough. They are free now."

"Free to be slaughtered by the Inquest?"

Kelver smiled. "What is the nature of freedom?" he said.

Siriss watched once more. The birds stormed toward the wedge of childsoldiers. She was reminded of how she first met Arryk, how they had played *makrúgh* among the firephoenixes of Kailasa. The birds wheeled, soared as though charged with an all-consuming joy. Some flew so fast that they sparked against the friction of the air and became balls of blue fire. And now, almost purposefully it seemed, they fell into formation and propelled themselves at the thickest part of the soldiers, and Kelver clapped for a still closer view, and—

Chaos among the soldiers! Blindly the birds dashed themselves against hoverdisks. Formations shattered. Children plummeted in mid-somersault and fell screaming. I have to watch, Siriss thought. I am still an Inquestor. A string of childsoldiers twisted like a dying snake. Lightswaths writhed; where buildings once toppled into neat piles they now were sliced by jagged lightning bolts. Still the birds swarmed, darting at the childsoldiers' eyes, spraying their faces with blood and fumetz and the cinders of their self-immolations.

Confusion now. Phalanxes ripped apart. Laser lancets flashing at random; the soldiers themselves exploding, sliced into whirling sheaves of flesh by the deadly gazes of their own comrades ... pieces of children blowing in the wind like autumn leaves. Terror in their childish faces. One seemed to mouth the words of the Inquestral anthem until a stray light-streak severed his head and sent it crashing into another rank of childsoldiers so that they toppled from the sky like black and silver dominoes ...

"You see, Sirissheh," Kelver said. "We did not lift a finger. But now we will. We will not let them taste utopia and then die."

He motioned with his hand; all at once they were returned to their first vantage. Activity all about them: the ships of shadow were shifting positions. Once more half-Essondras hung in the starstrewn blackness. It was hard to believe that so much was happening on its surface.

And Kelver said to his assembled generals: "The flight of the kashanthras has won time for us. This is what the Throne of Madness has show me. Now let our work begin swiftly." All at once the gathering was breaking up. Astrogators ran for displacement plates and vanished. Childsoldier leaders like Tya followed, already subvocalizing commands to their platoons.

And Siriss knelt down and clasped Kelver's knees and said, "Oh, Kevi, Kevi, though I'm losing you I see that you've acquired all Elloran's greatness, all his compassion." And she wept because of all he must have suffered, and because she knew that her love could not touch his loneliness. But he was preoccupied, and broke free of her; and doubt sprang into her thoughts unbidden, and she realized that it had always been there, like the black-hole-canker in the heart of Uran s'Varek.

***

Zalo groped his way onward, still clasping Jenjen's hand. The tunnel narrowed until he was forced first to crouch, then to crawl. Far behind, old ones spluttered. He wondered whether Enshtewo, old father pisspot, had made it. But he dismissed the thought quickly lest it pollute hisjoy.

"Only a little way now until the next arena level," he said. "I'm a lot taller than I was when I used to play here. Grip harder and you won't stumble. Here." The passage narrowed even more. How could he possibly have gotten through last time? But he saw a circle of ghostly light, beckoning from a vague distance, like a lone star in a cloudy night;" and it rekindled his hope, and he thrust forward into the dank and dark. "In the old days they had no displacement plates." He tried to make time pass, to lessen the agony and fear, by telling Ir Jenjen stories old Karnofara had told him. "The people bin that first colonized Essondras bore few technicians, but it did have gene-engineers; and they manufactured chimerical creatures to pull their carts ... and to devour criminals in the arena. With the second wave of people bins, four centuries later—"

"The light!" someone shouted from the back. The circle had grown; the tunnel had widened into a man-tall passageway. At the same time came a rumbling far overhead, and he knew that Ikshatra was burning. But as the passage became a corridor and then a cavernous hall, and the circle of light was seen to be the opening to a huge subterranean arena, the crowd could no longer restrain itself. Children sprinted forward; older ones tottered toward the portal, their hands upraised as though to embrace the light. As they neared, it streamed out from the entranceway, and when Zalo stepped through he was almost blinded.

But children who had preceded him were screaming in fright. "J should have warned you!" he shouted. "Don't worry, the monsters are all in stasis—"

A round stage; seats carved into the rock; a ceiling of earth. A forcebubble had surrounded this complex once; no one had turned it off, and it had merely served as the foundation for more building ... they were encased in a capsule of

Essondras's history ... the very air was the air the ancients breathed, unsullied by the scents of more civilized times. The light came from the forcebubble itself, and from *luktillas,* masses of unicellular symbiotes that emitted a cool blue light. And monsters, guarding the gateways.

Children clustered around them. There was an arachnosaur, blood still glistening on its gaping mandibles. There a hypogeodont, whose titanium-coated teeth had been so useful to the ancients in burrowing and digging foundations. ("You must never go there, boy Zasha!" Kamofara had told him that time so long ago. "They are not dead, merely time-frozen, like the denizens of people bins. If you should awaken one—") A hekatophthalmon, its hundred eyes bristling on tentacular stalks, was caught in a forward-lumbering attitude; three eohippopters, at its feet, scurried in place. And over the senatorial gate four pteratygers with outstretched wings stood guard, two rampant, two reclining, a fiery fierceness frozen on their features.

Jenjen said, "It's sad, somehow. Do you think, after they annihilate our surface civilization, that these creatures in their forcebubble will still be here?"

"One day, when all our traces have been smoothed over by the elements," Zalo said, "another people bin will land here, and they'll dig down deep and find all this—that's what I used to think, when I was a kid. But now, with the rebellion, who knows?" He stopped. Something flapped—an eohippopter come to life! "Who did that?" he shouted. A glum child looked guiltily away. "Don't touch them! Don't touch them!" The others gaped as the eohippopter spread its dainty wings and leaped up, trying to catch a wind that would not come ... a ludicrous creature, neither miniature horse nor bird, capable of flight only in the controlled currents of a wind machine.

"Look at the ugly little flying horse!" someone yelled.

They were losing their fear now; a heady sense of wonder was replacing it.

"What are you thinking?" Jenjen said.

"I'm thinking about how long these living things have simulated death, and how long I've spent perfecting the art of making dead things imitate the living ... and you?"

"More colors of darkness. And the eerie circle of light at darkness's end." And kissed him, impulsively, like a child.

Rumbling. "We have to push on," said Zalo. "Yes."

"The tunnel—"

Beyond the senatorial gates a passageway led into infinity. The walls were hung with fettered skeletons. And at its end —if Karnofara was to be believed—a way to the surface, far from Ikshatra, in the ruins of a far more ancient city. They must hurry if they were to attain Kelver's deliverance. In the arena some of the living actors Zalo had recruited from the streets were strutting about, gesticulating and declaiming with the mannerisms of necrodrama. Others crowded around the eohippopter, encouraging it in its laughable attempts to fly. "Hurry now, follow," Zalo said urgently.

Into the corridor. Floor of fragmented flagstones littered with brittle bones and coprolites. The air dense, close, muffling the hundred-footed shuffling. He reached for Jenjen again. She smiled as if to say, "This time you will never lose me again."

Onward. Intermittent darkness. Here and there a cave-in; evidently the forcebubble sealed in only the arena itself. They tripped over skeletons that had fallen from rusted gibbets. Someone's inadvertent subvocalizing set off a dozen electronic guillotines, and laserblades whipped across skeletons already headless. A few people had phosphordisks; they pulled them out so that all could see by the dim glow.

Suddenly the walls vibrated. A pile of skeletons slithered in front of them, and then a fall of dust, and then the rumbling, no longer distant, but thundering-

It's the end! Zalo thought. After all our labors—

An arm of bone torn from its socket slapped his face.

Pillars were moving, rocks sliding "Trapped!" said Jenjen.

The way forward was blocked now. Zalo saw an old man's body crushed by the rubble. Could it be ... it couldn't be! "Enshtewo!" he screamed. Only then did he feel real despair.

"We must go on," he whispered hopelessly. But he wanted to flee, to die.

"How?" another old man taunted, kneeling over the corpse.

Maybe it's not father pisspot, Zalo thought. There was no face ... only the hem of an old tunic, billowing gently from beneath a pile of rock.

"You want me to scratch down the rocks with my bare hands?" the old man went on.

"It can't all have been for nothing!"

"If we lived in the arena beneath the forceshield," a woman said, "how long before the air runs out, how long before we start eating each other?"

Nobody moved. They all stared at Zalo, expecting a solution. "I never asked to be a leader!" Zalo cried. "I just wanted to write a new chapter in the history of necrodrama ... I never wanted to lead you people to the promised land."

A moment of desolation, of utter aloneness. Silence greeted him, appalling, unforgiving. A stone fell, echoing.

And then Ir Jenjen took him by the hand and led him to a shadow beneath a rusty decapitator, and whispered: "Every darkness has a color. Every tunnel contains a hidden circle of light."

"What do you mean?"

"I have a plan."

What she told him took his breath away. It made him understand how much she had changed since their old affair, and how much she had learned from the study of the meanings of darkness....

***

Siriss and Kelver were left alone in the throneroom. And she saw him, how he raged, how he paced across the carpet of crystalline snow, how he would not let her comfort him.

She took him gently by the arm. He did not resist. She led him to one of the vacant hoverthrones that lined the black wall. Around them glistened the glazen lattices of Sharamonda; behind them golden Varezhdur glowed. She sat him on the cushion of kyllap leaves and wiped his brow with a fold of her shimmercloak. "At least I have memories of you," she said.

He said, "I deal out deliverance ... yet I am more and more enslaved "

"Forget, forget. Kiss me, Kevi."

He twisted away from her. He sprang to his feet and paced again. The shimmercloak hissed as it wrapped itself around his skeletal frame.

"Are you cold?" Siriss said, hastening to walk beside him. "Shall I warm you?"

"Warm? And warm the planet's seas to boiling?" "You're delirious, Kevi."

"And vaporize the dark mountains? And collapse the hearts of suns?"

"No. Oh, Kevi, you must wake from this living nightmare!"

"Nightmare...." Kelver clapped his hands three times, commanding Sharamonda's thinkhive. Once more the thinkhive's eyes fell planetward; not stepwise this time but in a vertiginous swooping. Siriss gasped—

Ikshatra burning! The arena crumpled like a paper sculpture! The thinkhive's eye skimmed the city's streets, hugging the surfaces, careening around corpse-piled corners. Flame tongues flicking from the casements of a palace. The eye zooming wildly now ... the whole viewwall closing in on the face of a dead woman, frozen terror, like one of Karakaël's masks. The vantage panning across the sky now. Childsoldiers speckling the moons' faces like black hail. The sky luminous with meteor showers. The view lurching skyward now.

At the head of Karakaël's fleet, the deathmoon; gathering around it, like dragonflies, a flock of deathcomets, each animated by a dead child's brain.

"You mustn't look at these things if it pains you, Kevi." But she knew that an Inquestor cannot shrink from these things if he is to know true compassion. Already they had broken so many rules. They had wept. They had shown anger. And now they caused the deaths of innocents, not out of the compassion of *makrúgh,* but simply to arouse Arryk's willfulness and to force him too to break rules—Is this what freedom means? she thought.

She held him tightly in her arms. He was light; it was as if the shimmercloak billowed about an empty holosculpture. "You're drowning," she said to him. "My love can't pull you out."

Around them the scenes shifted ever faster swirling images of death. As she clasped Kelver to her, his face shimmered; other faces flickered on and off ... the winged hoy, wanly smiling ... an old woman ... she shook him; when he did not respond she kissed him, and in her very arms he slithered into the shape of the winged boy.

"Now I know," Siriss said. But she had, she realized, known all along. "Your mind hasn't survived the Throne of Madness ... it's fractured into many selves, each self lent shape by the power of the Throne!"

"My Lady, where am I?" The boy broke from her embrace and stared, horrified, at the kaleidoscope of carnage that continued to whirl around them. "My Lady, I'm afraid, afraid!"

"Kelver—"

In consternation the boy's wings fluttered into a blur. He was shifting again now—

—into a pteratyger, pawing majestically at the air. "Ke Iver —"

"I am—afraid—no more—I am only an animal—a servant of the High Inquest—" the pteratyger growled.

"But your eyes are still the eyes of Kelver, whom I loved," Siriss said. "How I loved you, child of mystery! I don't want it to end, can't you understand that?"

"I am only an animal—afraid no more—"

It was then that Siriss knew what her next step must be. And because she was an lnquestor, she knew she must walk her personal *makrúgh* to its end, even though her journey must lead from darkness to greater darkness.

Around them, images of dying Ikshatra. Childsoldiers tumbled into the flames. Overhead shone the blue-gold arc of a lone kashanthra's burning.

***

In the englobing darkfield that blew hither and thither across the sky of battle, Arryk and Karakaël sat on their separate hoverthrones. They did not speak to each other. For, though Karakaël had manipulated him by *makrúgh* into giving the command for the world's destruction, and had thus exonerated himself from any blame for an act which must outrage the sensibilities of the least compassionate Inquestor yet Arryk could feel no more rage. He was spent now. He had become completely Karakaël's creature. In upholding the Inquest's most treasured values he had rendered himself unworthy to be called Inquestor, for he had taken compassion itself in vain.

"Look!" Karakaël said, pointing at the wedge of childsoldiers arrowing over the smoldering city. "They have regrouped. Those birds were only a momentary nuisance after all. We've lost no more than a few hundred thousand fighters." He would have smiled, thought Arryk, save that the mummy wrappings woven into his face gave it a certain immobility.

He could not talk to Karakaël about the waste of childsoldiers' lives. Karakaël would never have understood. Instead Arryk watched as the soldiers' replacements wove anew the intricate grid of killing light-not a perfect geometrical pattern, for already the suicidal kashanthras had shredded it in many places.

It was strange about birds. In Kailasa, as a seventeen-year-old boy, he'd played *makrúgh* with Siriss over the fate of firephoenixes and star systems ... it was then that Elloran had raised him to Inquestor. Even now the deathjewel was embedded in his neck; if he should die, a nameless world of the Planzhadavynn star cluster would perish too.

And now the deathflight of these kashanthras would signal the end of his once-cherished dreams of glory, of redeeming mankind with compassion, of becoming like godlike Elloran....

Karakaël's mocking voice interrupted his reverie. "You are not moved by all this beauty? By this pyrotechnic display of human transience? You must, indeed, have a heart of stone."

"I want to die," Arryk said.

"Nonsense! You will never die ... not if the deathstone is still wedded to your neck!" Karakaël's disdain had never been so thinly disguised.

"I can sink no lower," Arryk said. He was drowning, drowning in the quicksand of Karakaël's *makrúgh*. If only he could reach oblivion! Darkness called to him with mother warmth. "I'm finished, Kaarye, finished."

Softly, "Do not tempt me," said the mummy-faced Inquestor of the bloodshot eyes. "You are too useful for me to permit myself the pleasure of destroying you."

The voice of a thinkhive: *Masters, the forces of shadow have been loosed. A large-scale confrontation is at hand.*

"Powers of powers!" Karakaël exclaimed, unnerved at last.

"You are not, *hokh'Ton,* as confident of the outcome as you led me to believe," Arryk said lightly, for it was not seemly to show disheartenment at a setback in the eternal game of *makrúgh.*

***

As quickly as possible Zalo led the others back, through the senatorial gates, across the arena, and bade them stand in the dark cavern just beyond the circular portal. Then he and Jenjen went back into the amphitheater. Three hypogeodonts, gape-frozen, hulked in front of a souvenir stand. They were at once elephantine and saurian; their jaws glistened with titanium teeth and supported a fearsome assemblage of metal tusks and a many-digited, prehensile trunk. Their tails, also metallic, fanned at their ends into the shape of shovels.

The arachnosaur and the hekatophthalmon had been placed in stasis at the moment of squaring off; the two creatures had been designed to battle one another, not devour criminals, but they could doubtless be dangerous if awakened.

No, it was the hypogeodonts they needed. Centuries before, these monsters had been engineered for tunneling and burrowing; when more technicians arrived on Essondras, the hypogeodonts had been consigned to arenas, where their serrated titanium teeth were spectacular for disembowelings and their tusks for painful impalements. A barbaric time, Zalo thought, but nevertheless the only history that is my own.

"I ... will this work?" Jenjen said. Although it was she who had first put the idea into Zalo's head, he could see that being close to one of them made her very uncomfortable. "Surely you're not going to just set it off and allow it to run rampant. "

"That wouldn't be too clever," Zalo said. "But wait ... pteratygers! The old monsters of the arena were controlled by trained pteratygers who were in turn commanded by their mahouts." He pointed upward, at the senatorial balcony. Four pteratygers, stasis-stiff ...

"You ride one," Jenjen said, shuddering. "I'll go wait with the others."

"No. You see, I might just be able to order a pteratyger to obey me ... there are scenes, in some of the necrodramas, including *Rainbow King,* where pteratygers are given commands, and the words for these commands are traditional ones ... I certainly didn't change them. I don't even know what they mean. Now, assuming they haven't gotten too garbled over the centuries. I could probably clamber aboard one of those things" — actually he was not at all certain that he could— "and get it to ascend, descend, turn left, that sort of thing; but as for telling it to rout a pride of hypogeodonts—"

"You need the lnquestral highspeech! Of course! And you've never taken the time to learn it. "

"Whereas you, Ir Jenjen," he used her clan-name with a trace of bitterness, "have been granted a clan-name, and have hobnobbed with Inquestors, and probably have more than a smattering-right?"

It irked him to feel so dependent suddenly. His decision always to use the vernacular in his necrodramas had always meant a great deal to him. He realized suddenly that his decision not to learn the highspeech in his youth had been, in some small measure, his first act of defiance against the lnquestral hegemony. But now that he had to rely on the Inquest's tools—

"All right," she said uncertainly. "You know the command words and l know the language of discourse ... I guess we're a team. Lead the way."

He took her up a stairwell carved into the rock, and they emerged on the balcony where perched the pteratygers, unmoving. Even a holosculpture, with its programmed autokinetism, seems to possess more life, Zalo thought. These are more like servocorpses, given verisimilitude only by cosmetics ... and yet they *are* alive! It's amazing. That one flash of insight that I had, when I made the corpses come to life, has made the relationship between life and death so much more ambiguous for me.

The two outermost pteraygers were rampant, the middle pair prone. They could not mount the outer ones without ladders, so each sat himself on one of the middle ones. Jenjen's was tawny; a streak of faint iridescence ran down its feathers. Its jaws were frozen in a soundless roar.

"Ready?" Zalo had to whisper. "I suppose so."

"All right then." And then, striking the pteratyger's flanks firmly three times with his fists, he intoned words of waking; in the echo-rich forcebubble his voice took on the resonance of a well-trained corpse's: *"Dha! dha! enquestrewo shratrava, thyr, thyr, enquestans! dha! dha!*

"What does *that* mean?" Jenjen said.

"How should I know? It's just a formula—" Suddenly the beast shuddered between his knees. Jenjen gave a little scream. But her cry was cut off by a tremendous roar, a mountain-wind roar tinged with a hint of miao. The wings flapped once, twice, like thunderclaps. A vibration shook the beast's torso, and he realized that, though it felt like an incipient earthquake, it was also a kind of purring.

Then the pteratyger spoke!

"What does it want?" Zalo shouted.

Jenjen said, "He rejoiced that he is awake. He asks what century this is." The two awakened animals continued to yowl and to paw the air and to beat their wings. "He asks by what authority we claim to command him, since we are neither Inquestors nor wardens of the palace prisons ..."

Terrified now, she translated ... "if we do not answer, we will be thrown off, cast down into the pit of monsters!"

"Explain to him!" Zalo shouted. "Tell him we speak in Kelver's name, the name of Ton Keverell n'Davaren Tath, the Prince of Shadow—"

"Bhashavy hokh'Kelveronami hokh'Ombretathi hokh'Ton Kevrellin Davaren y'Tathoten—" Jenjen said, and Zalo recognized in the abundance of many-syllabled honorifics the puissant cadence of the hightongue. And at her words, timorously uttered though they were, the two pteratygers struck their paws in unison against the stone terrace and sprang ceilingward. They had no reason to doubt Jenjen's words; for who would dare take an Inquestor's name in vain? Such names had been inviolate for twenty millennia.

A windrush in his face, sweet, ancient air. The thrum of the breathing beast beneath him. They wheeled above the arena. Past the forcebubble, a sky of dirt and rubble and city foundations. Here and there a jagged faultline in the sky, through which flashed, like thunderbolts, light from the city's burning. He steadied himself, clutching the downy neck, eased into the curve of falling as the pteratyger, at Jenjen's command, dived toward the three hypogeodonti.

The crowd, ignoring his warnings, had begun streaming from the entrance, gasping at the wonder of the pteratygers' flight, for such a thing had not been seen for centuries except as a special effect in a necrodrama. "Back!" he screamed at them, making his pteratyger veer toward them and forcing them to retreat. "Keep them behind the tygers!" he cried to Jenjen, who brought her pteratyger down between the crowd and the frozen monsters.

"Now!" His tyger soared to the apex of the forcedome, hovered against gravity for a stomachwrenching split second, then pounced on the first of the hypogeodonts. The thud shook Zalo as the tyger butted the creature's back three times with his front paws, sprang to the next to administer the three blows, and to the third—

"Keep back!" he cried to the others. He joined Jenjen; in tandem their tygers trod the air, waiting.

Sluggishly the hypogeodonts were coming to life. Their heads swayed lugubriously from side to side; one lashed its tail at the empty stands, ripping down a tattered awning. "We have to drive them down the tunnel!"

And Jenjen whispered something to her animal in a voice both haunting and soothing; he had heard her speak this way to him only once, the day she walked out of his life. "Follow close," he cried to others. "Stay together, and keep behind the pteratygers."

Now the huge beasts were stirring. One lumbered forward. And then the two pteratygers leaped into the air and fell upon them, growling, and, as though knowing their masters, the brutish hypogeodonts began to move toward the senatorial gateway. They crashed through the portals into the tunnel of skeletons, trampling great depressions into the earth, relentlessly battering down the walls on either side. The pteratygers followed them down the passageways, now and then egging them on with roars and by scratching at their scaly hides. The escapers, clinging together, followed. Zalo heard a rumbling from behind, and the light dimmed.

That was it! The hypogeodonts had caused the entrance to cave in ... they could only go forward now, and they would have to hurry ... Jenjen urged her tyger on, the tygers forced the hypogeodonts onward, soon they were at the first cave-in, and the pachyderms were smashing their heads against the rocks, scooping them up in their tusks, drilling into them with their teeth, trumpeting eerily all the while.

"They're clear!" An opening in the rubble. Ahead, a faint glowing ... the crowd could not be restrained now. They began to thrust through the bottleneck. Rocks falling everywhere. The hypogeodonts lumbering, oozing forward. Faster now, as the tygers goaded them and the rocks flew thicker and the tunnel grew wider ... trotting now, and a distant bursting light....

The corridor collapsing behind them now, the hypogeodonts stamping their feet and uplifting their trunks and trumpeting as they ran toward the light—

Ever steeper now, and then almost straight up, the big beasts charging at the light, the people clambering, and Jenjen and Zalo on their winged tygers soaring upward into the open at last—

"What is this place?" asked Jenjen. The pteratygers flew low, skimming a shredded starship caked with rust ... they rounded a hillock, and Zalo saw ancient starships by the hundred, stacked against the hillside, mounds of them piled high across a metalstrewn plain, and he turned to Jenjen, flying beside him, thinking of how men always dreamed of the stars, even lowly people on a backworld slated for slaughter.

He answered her: "I never came this far, but I think it's the starship graveyard that surrounds the ancient capital, where the people bins first landed—"

A cold wind gusted in their faces. Below them the crowd was spreading out over the derelicts, climbing, gazing after the suffocating confines of the labyrinth, the open plain unnerved him.

"At least," came Jenjen's voice, "the sun is rising." "No." He looked where she pointed. "It is Ikshatra."

It was true. A red glow at the horizon, and at its center an incandescent, hurtful brilliance ... Ikshatra.

Zalo wanted to weep at this, but tears did not come, for anger had taken the place of grief. Instead he cried out in anguish.

"Don't be angry, I can't bear it," Jenjen said. They reined in their pteratygers and landed them softly atop a mountain of old metal. They held hands and watched the burning. He felt the ground quake under their feet. The end would not be long. The sky was graphpapered with laser streaks. There was a beauty in this deathrain, a terrible beauty.

Some of them don't understand, he thought, as he watched the crowd. Children laughing at the pretty lights. The older people hunched up, many weeping by themselves or in each other's arms. A rage took hold of him, a rage he knew was impotent, and he could not speak.

The sky ever brighter now whirling lightsparks as the childsoldiers circled away from Ikshatra and began destroying its environs ... the whole sky luminous, peppered with black dots of childsoldiers ... here and there kashanthras fizzling like black meteors against the brilliant backdrop the hypogeodonts gleefully ripping up metal hulls and devouring them, trumpeting....

"We *are* like the kashanthras after all!" Zalo said bitterly.

"When we stuck in the mud we despaired and died. And when in the last days we came to know about joy, and to dream of utopias ... when we tried to soar skyward we sizzled and plummeted! Like the kashanthras. It was an empty conceit after all. Nothing was achieved." Jenjen came close and tried to hold him, but he rebuffed her. What could she know of hisdespair?

"Did you not think," said Jenjen, "that Kelver would redeem us?"

"It's just another cult, another religion, something to clutch while drowning," Zalo said.

And suddenly it seemed to him that the burning curtain of the sky cracked open, and dark whalelike ships burst through it, breaching the sea of light ... the fleet filled the sky ... at its head was a starship like a kneeling woman, and from her parted lips fell, like dandelion fluff, a troop of childsoldiers ... not dark like the distant dots, but rainbow colored. Scattered screaming in the crowd. Meteors fell. One landed at Zalo's feet. It was a loaf of bread.

And then he saw that, all over the plain of dead starships and aborted dreams, there were other crowds moving, converging toward them; and he heard the chant of *Kelver, Kelver, Kelver* across the starship graveyard like the whisper of a distant sea. So others had succeeded in fleeing Ikshatra and found their way to this meeting place! But what would happen now?

Crowds joined with crowds ... the cry of *Kelver, Kelver* became a jubilant roaring, drowning out the plosive rattle of far-off missiles ... over the husks of the dead starships fell shadows of still-living delphinoids ... once more, as in his radical necrodrama, the corpses and the living.

A sea of people now. Above them flocked the rainbow childsoldiers. No fearful paean shrilled from their lips ... but another song. He cursed himself for not understanding the highspeech.

At last he turned to Jenjen, who whispered, "They long for the heart's homeworld ... where the Inquestor touches the beggar child."

Zalo felt the tug of big, vague emotions. Was this hope? He could not tell. It was quite new to him. His eyes burned from the sunrise of the dying city.

And then, as in a dream, the face of Kelver formed in the sky above them, like a sun ... it was holosculpted from lines of force and colored with polarized light. Slowly his body formed. He was kneeling, hulking like a mountain over the starship graveyard. His arms rested on the earth, palms open, like twin bridges.

And the Kelver-mountain smiled over the people of doomed Essondras.

And then the crowd began running toward him, no longer chanting but screaming Kelver's name again and again like a benediction, storming the two hands, climbing the sky on the forcebridge, rushing up the arms of their god. And Zalo too was seized with the frenzy of their joy.· He mounted his pteratyger; at first Jenjen made to summon hers, but instead, as the creature impatiently pawed metal, he grabbed her arm and pulled her up beside him.

As they rose up, they saw the starships descend and hover around the shoulders of the Kelver-mountain. Ramps were being disgorged from their bellies; other ships darted back and forth, scooping up stragglers.

And Zalo shouted, with sudden realization, "They don't have people bins! They're saving *us*, saving human beings, not *makrúgh-fodder!*" Jenjen threw her arms around him. Her darkfield garment enveloped them both in black fire. At last he gave himself to the joy. It was good to he human, to be loved, to be free. The pteratyger, with a single flap of its wings, followed the slope of the forcebridge and arced up to the face of the Prince of Shadow. He looked into the vast green eyes and saw visions of oceans, of endless meadows, of fields of grain. He began to sob helplessly, passionately, like a child being born. Both grief and joy seemed new to him. To his surprise, he could not remember a time in his life when he had wept so unashamedly, not even when his mother died.

Then, for the last time, through the blur of tears, he set eyes on Ikshatra. A lone kashanthra crossed the sky. He thought of himself in that control pit animating the gestures of the dead. So many times, breathing life into those corpses, until he had almost none left for himself. But never again. Behind the false dawn of the exploding city, the real sun had begun to rise. Two suns seared his eyes. Life and death. He could not look. He could not look away. Then the tears streamed down so thickly he could see no more.

Ten

He Who Burned the Rainbow

Another labyrinth: the makeshift quarters that had been built for the refugees. Strings of discarded people-bin hulls, now packed with level upon level of cramped living space.

Jenjen did not know whether they were motionless or flying through space, whether Ikshatra had already perished. She remembered running up the side of the Kelver-mountain, drunk with joy, being snatched up into a starship in a spider-web of force, screaming Zalo's name ... how much time had passed since then? A single sleep? Or many days? She remembered a corridor piled with gangrenous corpses ... she had screamed Zalo's name again, and hearing her, a child soldier had pulled her free and poured sour, searing zul down her throat from a steaming flask, and put her on a pallet in a hallway lined with pallets. A mechanical stalked silently to and fro, monitoring the life signs of the thousand or more that lay there. No sense of motion, and yet she felt she must have gone far away, into another universe. She whispered the word *freedom* to herself over and over until she fell asleep.

Presently she had startled herself awake with a dream of fire. And, calling out Zalo's name again and again, she had staggered through the corridor, threading the tangle of interlocking limbs and anxious faces. From corridor to corri dor, crying his name.

Death images. Terror-stricken faces. Have I simply ex changed one labyrinth for another? Jenjen thought, remembering the subterranean world beneath Ikshatra. Dark. Here and there, lightshafts from gaps in the makeshift metal planking that separated the levels, lighting up faces caked with vomit, eyes swollen shut, eyes listless, eyes glazed by grief. The mechanicals drifted by, silent sentinels dispensing food and drink from oven bellies. She spotted a white robe of the clan of Tash, made for a fork in the corridor to speak to him, but he had gone. There must be displacement plates in so vast a structure, but they were, she surmised, hidden beneath the press of dead and dying. "Zalo!" she screamed. "Zalo, Zalo!" The closeness of corpses muffled her cries. She found a staircase that wound baroquely from level to level, and clambered up. The gravity was uneven; they must be in space, and the gravity control must not be working efficiently. Junkyard generators, perhaps.

A holosculpture of Kelver at a junction of hallways. Sick men and women converging upon it, crawling toward it with their hands outstretched. One turned and saw her.

"Ir Jenjen, darkweaver," he said hoarsely. "You have the favor of the Prince of Shadow ... tell him to release us from this hell!"

"I am lost myself," Jenjen said. She clasped the old man's hand. There was blood on it. "I am looking for Zalo, the playwright Zalo; his face is known throughout Essondras; surely someone has seen him."

"We pray to Kelver. Many have not been as lucky as we. Our planet—"

An alien voice, grave, of an ancient stillness: "Don't be sad, old man."

They turned. They saw an old woman. Beneath her frayed robe Jenjen glimpsed shimmerfur. An Inquestor! And her eyes ... "You are the woman I saw in the city!" she cried out.

"The woman whose green eyes reminded me so much of Kelver's."

The woman smiled.

"I've seen statues of you!" The voice of a startled hermaphrodite in a whore's robe. "You are Mother Vara, the goddess!"

"No goddess," the woman said. And when Jenjen saw her smile she knew. *Knew!*

"You *are*—"

"Be still, Jenjen. All of you, be comforted. This is no hell, but a temporary sanctuary. Dry your tears and think of the homeworld to come. You have been saved from the clutches of the Inquest; you have fallen into the arms of shadow. In darkness you will find freedom. Be comforted, my children, be comforted."

She touched the forehead of the old man who had been so bitter before; it was as if a ray of light had fallen on him.

"How can you be both he and the creator goddess?" she whispered.

"No goddess, Jeni."

"And when I saw you by the mnemothanasion, at the meeting of believers, and I overheard you say that a winged boy had been seen running from the generator of my Rainbow Darkness ... I was meant to overhear that, wasn't I? Where is Zalo?"

There was no reply. The woman with sea-green eyes who so resembled the statues in the temples of Mother Vara ... she seemed to shimmer against the mirror metal of the walls, and then her image began to swirl, it siphoned away into the stuff of the air. But Jenjen took comfort from her coming, and grew less afraid.

***

More corridors: but these airy, bright, high-vaulted. There were no jostling crowds here; instead the stars revolved as the passageway, walled by force, twisted out of the convoluted innards of Sharamonda. And Ton Siriss was alone save for a stripped-down retinue of scribe, steward, handmaidens.

"Perhaps the Inquestrix would rather not, in her compassion, observe the *falling beyond* at close quarters? Perhaps she would rather hear of the *fall* from the lips of a Rememberer, recollected in tranquillity, distilled by the poetic vision?"

"Hurry, old man!" she cried. "These are not the old days. I must see what has been wrought. Lead on."

The steward raised his clenched fist. It burst into cold flame; an empty ceremony, since the corridor was adequately lit already. But the ritual ran deep in him, who had once been a linkboy in the reign of Ton Elloran the Compassion ate. She let him walk unsteadily ahead, though she knew the way better than he, and though she was bursting with impatience.

"My bones ache. I must rest, Lady Siriss."

"Oh, very well. We still have some hours before the moment of Essondras's final destruction." She stood, nervously watching the stars dance in the distorting shimmer of the forceshield. Presently her steward roused himself and they proceeded. It seemed that the passageways were endless, though displacement plates relieved their weariness here and there, and now and then slidewalks and airchutes were provided to ease their journey. She could have gone to the observatory in an instant had she wished; but the trek was part of the ritual. She well remembered what Elloran had told her in her training: "With each step, daughter, you will think of humans being violently, insolently, needlessly cut down. You will imagine your very footfalls crushing the shortlivers. If you must flagellate yourself to find compassion, then that is what you must do! But you will feel these deaths, all deaths, as your own." It was a good doctrine. But with what hypocrisy they had practiced it, leavening it with rich oppressive ritual, lining the road to the deathwatch with beautiful things to distract from the acts of destruction to come!

As Siriss thought upon these things, she saw a fork in the corridor up ahead. To the left was the path they must follow ... to the right, something moved. The rustle of a frayed shimmercloak. A swirl of gray hair hooded in the skin of a metawolverine. An ancient face, time-smoothened, with eyes of deep jade. She could not look away from those eyes. The old woman ... Siriss started to speak, but the woman had moved further down the corridor, into a patch of shadow.

"I know you," Siriss said. "I know you well."

"Mistress, the path lies left," the steward said, clenching his flaming fists and raising them, driving out the shadow.

"But do you not see the old Inquestrix out there? Surely she too has come to see Essondras's end. She must be formally acknowledged and invited—"

"There is no one, my Lady. Sharamonda is an ancient palace, full of mirages and images of vanished things, still stored in the memory banks of its thinkhive, still now and then replayed, ghostlike, in the corridors. Think nothing of it, Lady Siriss."

And where the pool of shadow had been there was nothing... only the wavering outlines of the steward's fire-hands against the insubstantial hardness of the forcewalls, and the starfleld beyond, seen through snowflakes within snowflakes. But she heard a voice: "Sirissheh! Sirissheh!" Only dimly did she remember that voice: her mother's voice, from a world long dead and forever isolated by time dilation. "Sirissheh." A voice from a time before she had been made Inquestor: before Elloran, before *makrúgh,* before Kelver. It called out to her from a past she had thought forever buried.

"Mother!" she screamed. And ran, heedless of the steward's warning, into a corridor that darkened about her even as she ran.

***

Jenjen climbed stairwell after stairwell. She no longer cried out Zalo's name. She no longer mopped the sweat from her face and arms with a fold of her clinging darkness. There was no up or down in this place. Stairs lurched sideways and downward and veered off in impossible curves, and the seams of the corridors groaned under the stress of contradictory gravity-generators and leaking fields. But presently shenoticed that those she passed in the hallways were not so consumed with despair as they had seemed at first. Here and there she could hear singing: a rousing chorus from an old necrodrama, or one of the many hymns to the Prince of Shadow. It was beginning to dawn on them that they were saved, that this was no people bin but a place of breathing, living people. Now and then she overheard people talking about Zalo's play and how the living had played at corpses playing at being alive. But no one had seen Zalo.

At last, when it seemed that she could go no farther, she reached a confluence of many staircases. There was a platform against whose railings she could rest. She looked around: vistas of humanity stretched in all directions.

It was then that she saw the winged boy. She looked up and he was there.

"You!" she whispered.

"You know me?" His eyes were clear, sea green.

"It was you who burned the rainbow. You were seen. An old woman saw you ... an old woman with your eyes."

He laughed. She thought she should know that smile.

He said, "I am sent to fetch you. By my master."

"Who are you?"

The winged boy took her hand. The smile drained from his face. He said, "I don't know."

"You don't know who you are?"

"Lady Siriss says I am like the wind. She says I have the eyes of the Prince of Shadow."

"Kelver! Where is Kelver?"

"He has sent for you."

"And Zalo—"

"You will be together soon," the boy said. "But you are to come to the observatory in the palace Sharamonda. To bear witness to the fall of Essondras."

"Then we're still in Essondrish space? We've not yet left our world behind?"

"Please come, Mistress Jenjen." He tugged at her hand. Could this really be the one who burned down her Rainbow Darkness? If so, what was he doing here? Why did he have the eyes of the old woman, the eyes of Kelver himself? She could not cope with all the unanswered questions. Better to follow, she thought, than to try to puzzle out these enigmas within enigmas.

She closed her eyes and allowed the winged boy to lead her away.

***

Siriss felt a drift in the continuum about her, a moment of disorientation. And then she was standing on the Inquestral homeworld. On Uran s'Varek, the sphere that surrounded the black hole at the galaxy's heart. A wasteland stretched all around her, a grayness that climbed halfway up the sky, and that sky a flawless sheet of pearly radiance. Almost two million stars were crowded into that one cubic parsec, and the atmosphere, thousands of klomets thick to scatter the harmful cosmic radiation, smeared the starlight into one expanse of brilliance.

"How did I get here?" Siriss cried out.

Ahead—distances could not be estimated, for the landscape was desolate of habitations or natural formations—the doll-like figure of an old woman, beckoning. "Who are you?" In the vastness she could barely hear her own voice. "How did I come to be on Uran s'Varek? Did you summon me here?"

And suddenly she was beside the old woman. And knew her for the first and greatest of the Inquestors, she who had dreamed the Inquest into being and created the game of *makrúgh*. "Mother Vara," Siriss whispered.

A dry hot wind sprang up. Gray sand, biting the skin of her arms, her face; quickly her shimmercloak swirled to cover her. Through its veil of colors she saw Mother Vara's eyes. They were not as she remembered them; the eyes were Kelver's eyes. How could that be? And how had the old Inquestrix been able to speak to her with the voice of her dead mother?

"Can you not speak to me? I followed you, forsaking the ritual of the *falling beyond*. I see that you have caught me in a tachyon corridor and brought me home to Uran s'Varek."

"I have come to tell you what you already know, daughter Sirissheh." It was Elloran's voice that issued from those withered lips; authoritative, comforting.

"What do I know already?" Siriss said. "I am lost. That's all I know. I loved Arryk once. I love Kelver. I have lost Elloran, whom I loved and trusted. I've lost Arryk to cruel Karakaël. And Kelver... no one can reach Kelver anymore." "Not even you, Sirrisheh...." It was the voice of Vara now.

"Are you truly Ton Varushkadan el'Kalar Dath, known as the Lady Varuneh, worshiped also as the goddess Vara? But you're not exactly how I remember you. There was always a profound calm about you; I felt utterly safe in your presence. But now there is unease. There's something different about your eyes. And when we last saw you, you had forsworn *makrúgh*.

You had determined to live the rest of your life on Idoresht, amid the people of the snakescale city, whom you had adopted for your own."

"I am what you see, and I am not what you see."

"Have you no answers, then?"

Sand stormed around them. Beside the Lady Varuneh was a wooden chair, half buried. "Once Kelver came to Idoresht to beg you to intervene in Karakaël's game of *makrúgh*. All you had to do then was speak; the Inquest listened. Kelver's war was precipitated by those few words that shamed Karakaël and angered Arryk. I still feel the power flowing from you ... but it's not the same. There's madness in the power. I'm afraid, Lady Varuneh."

"For you, the next step is a terrible one. But you have been thinking of it a long time. Betrayal, Ton Siriss k'Varad es-K'N-ing. You are confused at Kelver's transformation, rebuffed by his indifference, angry at what you perceive to be his ingratitude ... did you not choose him, and the side of shadow, over all that you knew to be true and good? Love alone was your motive, Sirissheh. And you cannot have love without jealousy. And thus it is that your role in this last Inquestral drama has been preordained from the moment that you set eyes on Kelver: you are to be his betrayer."

"It can't be—"

"Search your heart, Inquestrix of the opal eyes."

She may have said more, but the sandstorm, howling, drowned out her words. They stood at the sandstorm's eye, the sandmotes sparkling in the eerie radiance of Uran s'Varek. Siriss shouted, "But I love him!" but could not hear her own voice, only the windrush like the roar that burst upon a crowd when they saw Kelver's image burning sunlike in the firmament, and over the thunder the windwhine like the warpaeans of swooping childsoldiers. And the image of Lady Varuneh streamed into the sandwhorl until only the eyes remained ... not the eyes of Mother Vara, but the eyes of him who stood at the eye of the galactic storm.

"I will never betray him," Siriss said defiantly, as the landscape faded away and she found herself once more in the starswept corridors of Sharamonda.

***

When she took the hand of the winged boy, Jenjen saw that a mist had wrapped itself around them.

"Where shall I go now?" she cried out; her voice echoed as in a cavernous hall of marble. The mist was thick; she could not see at all; it had a faint fragrance of mulled zul and myrrh. Her feet touched no ground; they too were swathed in dense mist. At last she made out the boy's eyes; an emerald laserlight seemed to emanate from them. It was a comforting light, not like the killing radiance that flashed from the eyes of child soldiers. She doubted no longer....

"Kelver!"

"Do not mistake me."

"You! Who unwove the rainbow of darkness so that all Essondras could see what had gone into it."

"I did not know what I was doing. I was in the palace stables, feeding the pteratygers, when I found myself running up the forceshield bridge that holds in your Rainbow Darkness. Lady, I don't know what came over me. I found the generator; somehow my hands knew what my brain didn't know, and—"

"Why are you tormenting me, my Lord? Why have you assumed this shape ... perhaps to infiltrate Essondras without being seen by the Inquest?"

"I don't know what you mean—"

"But you must! If you don't know what we're all doing, who does know? And who can lead us?"

The mist dissolved. There was no winged boy now, but an old woman whose raiment was the skin of a metawolverine bordered with shimmerfur, and in whose white and streaming hair a golden flamedisk burned. But the eyes were still the same....

"Kelver! Why all this mystery, who won't you tell me what I've already guessed?" So mesmerizing were those eyes that Jenjen hardly realized she was now standing in a corridor of force within a vast palace composed of interlocking snowflakes; that in front of her were gates of stone; that a small crowd was jostling past her, jamming through the portals as they parted soundlessly.

The old woman said, "The winged boy does not know, Jenjen. I alone know. There are many of us within him now."

"Then it's true! The Throne of Madness has caused the Prince of Shadow to go mad himself, to fracture into warring personalities—"

"And none knows the minds of the others. Save I. I am the core, the mother, the teacher, the knower, and I have the shape of Mother Vara."

"But we must cure him! Or the rebellion is doomed."

"Don't be a fool, woman. The revolution is only a small part of a far more sweeping vision ... do you think you are the only sentient creatures in the galaxy? What of the whisper-shadows? You cannot understand such things yet. Who is to judge between madness and sanity? Did the High Inquest, which even now begins to crumble, not consider itself wise, upright, moral, logical?"

"How many personalities are there?"

"Many, daughter, many. Perhaps, by the war's end, they will be infinite. They are developing the power to appear in many places at once; perhaps, by the war's end, they will be in all places at the same time."

Jenjen thought of dying Essondras and its place in the universe. She remembered the radicals sitting in the zul shops, guiltily looking around as they mouthed obscenities about the Inquest. But no one expected it to fall! In the old order there was a proper place for everyone, even the malcontents ... now all was in confusion. Perhaps there would even be a dark age, not the coming of the utopias they had all dreamed about.

As if in response, the apparition that wore the shape of Mother Vara said, "There are four million shades of darkness, daughter. You yourself know that, for you are a priestess of darkness and know its mysteries. Do not fear darkness and confusion. Embrace the darkness with joy."

She knew then that the past was done with forever. It was no longer a question of choice; had never been. The decision had been made years before, in the palace of Uran s'Varek, when she had agreed to follow Kelver into shadow, when she had turned her back on the art of lightweaving and chosen the path of darkness. She must accept it all now. "I shall. I shall," Jenjen said, her heart surging with emotions she could not name. "I am free now, free, free, free!"

"But you are learning, child, how bitter is this freedom for which men yearn. Am *I* not free? I have at my disposal all the power of the galaxy's heart. Yet freedom has fractured my soul, and made me slave to madness!"

The image of the old woman, ghostlike, began to dissolve. Behind the apparition, as through a crone-shaped veil, Jenjen saw the winged boy standing with his arms outstretched; behind him other shadowy persons: hierophants and magicians, whores and princes, warriors and scientists. The images were so superimposed that their eyes were as one pair of eyes, green and profound as an ocean. And a voice came, issuing from a hundred mouths as a single mouth: "Now that you know my secret, will you still follow me?"

"What other can I do, Prince of Shadow?" Jenjen whispered as the shapes dissipated into the crowd. "I have chosen."

They were streaming past her now, pushing her toward the stone gates. A hand clutched at her arm. "Quick! You're here at last!" A familiar voice. "They're going to destroy Essondras now, come see!"

She whirled around, defying the surge of the crowd. "Zasha!"

The face: the bald scarred head, the kindly smile. "I've been worried. They said you were in one of the converted people bins. They sent a winged boy to fetch you."

"Zasha, Zasha—" She threw herself into his arms.

"Oh, don't cry, hush, hush," he said. "We've seen the worst of it. We'll never live through anything more terrible now."

"You don't believe that."

"... No."

"We must go in. The world's going to end soon."

"The end of the world ... and you were on the brink of a whole new art form, with your living drama. There was so much to discover."

"We've come so far, suffered so much to reach this ending ... only to find that we have only reached the beginning of something far more vast."

"Oh, Zalo, I've just seen Kelver. Something terrible has happened to him."

"So it is whispered. Are you afraid?"

"I've never been so afraid in my life! It must be part of being free."

"Let's go in now."

They joined the crowd. Rather, they were pushed into the observatory by the mass of people. As they entered, they seemed to be standing under a huge metallic dome. The throng gasped in unison as the hall was suddenly deopaqued; at once deep space surrounded them, and they milled about on floors of force, the starstrewn darkness their only carpet ... thousands of the legions of shadow. And overhead, flanked by her crescent moons, Essondras, cloud-rippled blue, beautiful and cursed by the Inquest.

Eleven
The Throne of Madness

Kilimindi: the palace of unmasked Karakaël. There too was an observatory; here too were crowds. A thousand ban quet tables, end to end, arranged in an unbroken coil from the couch of Karakaël to the observatory's wall; and all was deopaqued to afford the best view of the doomed planet. Here was no sign of the Sharamonda or Varezhdur; the twinned palaces of Shadow were hidden on the far side of the planet.

Arryk, seated beside the mummy-faced Inquestor, had no appetite, though the viands for this victory feast were among the most elaborate he had seen, and though all around him reverberated the rapturous sounds of eating. A neuterchild, one of Karakaël's cupbearers, poured cup after cup of zul from a cornucopia whose tip hid a displacement field that was linked to the palace zul vaults; the zul flowed, sparkling, now crimson, now turquoise, now citrine-yellow, now like the stuff of rainbow. Cup after cup Karakaël quaffed, his coal eyes burning in his pitted face. "You do not eat!" he shouted to Arryk.

"You don't have to shout. Do you want all of them to see my unease?" Arryk said.

"So sad, my son! Though this is a victory celebration!"

"Victory! What victory?"

"The round of *makrúgh* is over; Essondras will soon fall. Magnify!" Karakaël cried out, and the planet doubled in size in the ceilingscreen. "Look ... the deathmoon, and the comets swarming like phosphorflies. Beautiful, eh? Beautiful. Summon my armorer."

A woman of the clan of Aush, haughty-eyed, came to make her obeisance. "My Lord."

"Describe the spectacle once more, for all to hear."

The woman said, "One by one, the living comets will ram into the surface of Essondras. The sequential battering will dislodge the outer shell of the crust from the magma on which it floats, causing the continental drift to outpace the planetary spin; the crust will break open in a hundred thousand places, turning the land into a volcano of many craters and the sea into a monstrous geyser."

Deafening applause. "A splendid conceit!" Karakaël cried. "Arryk, you do not cheer with the others? Is it not beautiful?"

"It is, Karakaël." But he spoke bitterly. "But what kind of victory is this? We have not succeeded in evacuating the population into people bins; they've elected to die!"

"Not all. It seems that Kelver saved a few."

"But that doesn't change the fact that they chose death rather than accept their destiny."

"That is Kelver's way of manipulating us. He's trying to tell us that this is a new kind of war: messy, bloody, uncompassionate. That we must once more be ruled by mortal emotions ... it is a terrible thing! Who will lead when the leaders are no wiser than the led? Do not let the deaths of a few miserable millions sway you from the changeless truth: they are as nothing in the face of the Greater Compassion, in whose name we rule all mankind. Eh, lad!"

"Don't patronize me. You have made me the titular head of our side of the war—"

"To lure Kelver! For Kelver loves you, Rikeh. Now let the zul gush forth in fountains!"

At his words the intoxicating drink welled up from the mouths of statues, from cornucopiae concealed in dining-couches, from the stamens of flowering monster plants that ringed the observatory, from pillars of purple flame. It rained from the starfield above. Applause! Applause! But for Arryk it was empty. He was Karakaël's creature; he had lost his soul.

Now from eight corners of the observatory sounded eight consorts of brasses, and the revelers' eyes turned worldward. There were the strings of comets.

"Magnify! Magnify!" shouted Karakaël, and with each command the planet lurched nearer, until it filled the sky and the one landmass could be made out, and, like a star on the edge of the sapphire sea, burning Ikshatra. "Let us have music, my friends; music for a world's destruction." A choir sang: a wordless jangle of death-shrieks and cries of pain, contrapuntally interwoven into uneasy harmony. As the images were magnified still more, the city was splayed out overhead. A starburst of exploding lightstrands radiated from its center; these were the lines of killing light from the eyes of childsoldiers, slicing the skyscrapers and the surrounding mountains. "Magnify! Magnify!" the dinner guests were screaming in thunderous unison. It's a hungry sound, Arryk thought, like starved wild beasts.

"You are still sulking, Rikeh," Karakaël said. "Tell us why. I'm sure the other Inquestors would like to have the benefit of your wisdom."

Kiembre and Siembre, Inquestral Siamese twins who shared a single hoverthrone and shimmercloak, floated by. "Yes, speak, Rikeh," they chorused.

"We have won nothing. It is an empty spectacle."

"Not empty, I think, to those who are at this very moment dying ... how many would you say, twelve million or so, eh?" Karakaël said.

"But that is precisely the point! He has forced us to kill these people. In a routine *falling beyond* there would be nowhere near this much carnage ... but now, fired by his doctrine of freedom, they would rather die than be put to sleep for a while, until a new world is found for them ..."

"A most parochial heresy!" one of Karakaël's court philosophers Piped up. "They lack the galaxy-spanning vision that we have."

"Nevertheless," Arryk persisted, "an act of uncompassion has been wrung from us. And by rescuing some of the world's inhabitants, Kelver further scoffs at us." How had Kelver managed so to pervert the Inquest's teachings? He would plunge the Dispersal of Man into chaos, and call that chaos utopia. If only Elloran the Wise were here to guide them. But the old man had forsaken him and gone to seek some private salvation.

But they were waiting for him to go on, circling in their hoverthrones like carrion birds. "This shadow heresy continues to sweep across the galaxy. We still don't know where Kelver's center of operations is. There are times when he seems to be in many places at once."

"Easy enough to find out. The thinkhives—"

"Are, for some reason, quite silent on the matter, Ton Karakaël z Karakit Kerún," an elderly lnquestor spoke, with one hand balancing a zul-flask, with the other stroking the breasts of a voluptuous kallogyne.

"Surely someone will betray their nest to us! One of the captured childsoldiers, perhaps!" said Karakaël.

"You know, Karakaël, what happens when we try to get them to talk," Arryk said. And he shuddered, remembering that it had been he who had commanded the torture of a hundred thousand captives ... it had happened on a grassy plain on an abandoned pleasure world ... a hundred thousand childsoldiers, bound to machineries of torment. And all at the same instant, as though they saw some sign in the heavens that gave them the courage to do so, they had cried out Kelver's name, and bitten down on the calcifying capsule that every childsoldier had implanted in his cheek ... a hundred thousand children had instantly turned to stone ... the blood of their scars of torture had crystallized into veins of ruby ... their twisted bodies, frozen into marble, dotted the plain for many klomets. Arryk could not bear to think of it. Yet the heresy had to be eradicated.

"I wish, Karakaël," he said softly, "you had not reminded me."

"Of what?" For the incident had meant nothing at all to Ton Karakaël.

"It does not matter." At last he lifted the zul to his lips and drank a deep draft of the deadening drug. Its seductive sweetness seeped into him. He called for more. And more still.

While overhead, the comets broke formation and readied themselves to strike.

***

"This is it. The end of the world. Oh, Zasha, hold me." He held her close. Frail, he thought, so vulnerable, this woman I have loved. Voices all around them. Above, around, beneath, the wheeling starscape. Voices calling on Kelver's name. Still the Prince of Shadow had not appeared.

"Where is he? Where is Kelver?" Zalo said.

"I have seen him," Jenjen told him once more. "But in the state he's in, I don't know if he can come. I don't know if he can control the changes that shake him—"

"Stay close." He need not have said that; the crowd pressed on them. He could hardly breathe at first. But just when it became unbearable, a strong wind gusted in the chamber. Someone had thought to command the palace thinkhive to conjure up an artwind. He could breathe again; but the artwind was chilly, and even with all these people he began to shiver.

The throne ... in the center of the chamber a space was cleared. Steps of force rose up to a dais. Because the room had been deopaqued, Zalo would not have been able to tell that they were steps, for the starfield shone through them, save that upon each tier there crouched a blackwinged pteratyger, and on the shoulder of each a carrion crow, cawing, strutting. Symbols of ill omen. And the throne itself: no gaudy panoply, no gilt, no precious stones, but a chair of wood, and that wood gnarled and peeling.

He stared at it. "It is the Throne of Madness," Jenjen said to his unasked question. "The source of Kelver's power; the soul of the black hole at the heart of Uran s'Varek."

"I don't like it." He thought of the eyes of servocorpses, which could never be made to seem living even under the most skilled of corpse dancers; that was why those corpses culled for the theater had jewels for eyes. He looked away. And saw Essondras, closer now.

"But I am drawn to it," he heard Jenjen say, "because I am a darkweaver."

A gasp from the crowd. A swarm of comets shot across the blackness. Abruptly the view of Essondras enlarged itself and the perspective changed, so that it filled the sky above them. Needles of blinding light as the comets pierced the atmosphere.

"So slow, so graceful is their plummeting," said Zalo.

"A line from one of your plays—"

"About pteratygers diving from the clouds with the sun behind them!"

"Kelver!" screamed voices in the crowd.

Jarring discontinuities in the landscape as the thinkhive moved the images exponentially closer. They seemed to be falling earthward. "There's Ikshatra!" someone exclaimed. Zalo saw it: a pillar of white light, thrusting up from the charred and cratered hills ... to the west, in the bay, steam clouds where the ocean boiled.

"You see?" Jenjen whispered. "They would have burned the rainbow anyway."

"How many have they snatched away, how many are free?"

"I don't know. I don't know whether it was worth it. It's all so messy, so complicated, like a jumble of lightstrands, unwoven, formless."

"Essondras."

"Look! The comets, striking the surface!"

Slow, so slow, those light-arcs streaking ... mountains collapsing ... forests ripped from the hilltops ... one crater after another now as the living comets bombarded the landmass and jagged cracks joined mountain range to mountain range and swallowed lakes and villages ... in the zigzags a hint of glowing magma, as though red lightning had been painted on the landscape ... closer and closer the thinkhive panned ... the sounds of explosion and eruption came faint and infinitely distant, blended with the warpaeans of the childsoldiers ... and now he could see the soldiers themselves, riding in convoys on the comets' tails, their hoverdisks afire from the friction of their falling. From their eyes streamed laser-light like yellow rain. He saw the toppling of hilltops in the topaz gauze. He saw lava gushing like blood to the whipwelts of the world's gray deserts. And through the chamber paced Rememberers, whiterobed, their eyes dead as they burned the world's death into their memories.

Memories! "Do not lose hope." A voice behind him spoke. It was a voice he had not heard since his apprenticeship. A ghost! An old man ... his bald head sculpted into elaborate cicatrices as was the custom among the corpse dancers ... "Life and death, Zasha. It is all one. The world dies, but you see I live again."

"Karnofara!"

"How can this be?" Jenjen said. "The grand master of corpse-dancing ... I recognize your face, of course, because your head adorns the memory-niche in Zalo's home, and I have often heard your voice in the night, when he and I made love."

"This is so hard to understand!" Zalo said. Karnofara looked sternly at him, as he had often done when he still lived. There was something not quite right about him ... was it his eyes, perhaps? Zalo did not remember Karnofara as having had such sea-green eyes, eyes of such mesmeric brilliance.

"It is not Karnofara," Jenjen whispered, understanding suddenly. "It is he. The prince of Shadow."

"I am Karnofara and no one else," the old man insisted. "I have come from the dead to tell you, Zasha, that all is well. All you have done is as it should be. Lo!"

And as the terrain of Essondras loomed closer Zalo could see skyscrapers being sucked into fiery fissures in the earth ... and towers of frothy water shooting from the sea ...

and at the north pole icebergs foundering on tongues of liquid flame ... and then, as the scene shifted suddenly to a starscape, a flight of kashanthras, their plumage incandescent, soaring upward to the vault of the Inquestors' heaven....

"The embalming-birds. I did well," Zalo repeated listlessly.

"Lo!" And as he spoke the thing that had worn Karnofara's shape began to shift. The face formed and unformed in the air. Abruptly the crowd made way, clearing a path up to the Throne of Madness. Zalo gasped; for unlike Jenjen he had not known the Prince of Shadow before.

Silence fell.

A shimmercloak drape about an invisible form a shimmercloak that billowed about a great emptiness that was what moved across the pathway carpeted with stars.

As the shimmercloak fluttered to the first of the forcesteps the pteratygers that flanked it growled, uncertain; then, sensing the presence within the cloak, they cried out in unison, in a cavernous thunderyowling: "Hail-Shadow of Shadows-Eye of the Galactic Storm-Darkness Concealing Light."

By a trick of the thinkhive they seemed now to be falling toward Essondras. People covered their eyes as the kashanthras swarmed, magnified a hundredfold in the viewscreens, their scales and feathers dazzling with deathlight. They seemed to be dashing themselves against the hull of the delphinoid palace, though that was impossible, for in reality they were far out to space. Yet Zalo could not help but flinch.

They flew closer. A single kashanthra filled the whole sky. The air shook with their sobbing cries. "They can't come any closer!" Jenjen cired. And then-

Kashanthras whirlpooled out of the cloak that fluttered about the Throne of Madness! Scattered to the corners of the hall! Crazy vertigo as the palace appeared to pull back from the planet and whirl spaceward! And in the sky, veined with rivulets of exploding blood, Essondras.

And a mighty voice shook the chamber, a voice cloaked in a windrush, seeming to issue from the dying planet itself: *Oh, Zalo, I have pulled your embalming-birds free from the burning world. I have sealed them within psychic shields that they might no longer suffer. I have brought them here to Sharamonda, for they are beautiful. How well you understand us, shortliver! Your birds are as we Inquestors are. We too suffered from an empathy that led us always to want to spare men pain; we too have sealed ourselves in with a forceshield named compassion ... when you let the kashanthras fly free, when you fueled them with your rage and your love of freedom, you did to the embalming-birds what I would have the Inquest do to itself.*

"It's strange. They seem oblivious of the mood of the crowd," Zalo said. For the kashanthras stayed in perfect spiral formation as they burst from the shimmercloak. "Some of these people are angry, some elated, some triumphant, some despondent. On Essondras it would drive them into a frenzy. It's not natural."

"The psychic shields," Jenjen said.

So which will it be, people of the Dispersal of Man? the great voice cried out, stilling the babble. *Shall we shield ourselves thus, as we have done for twenty millennia? Shall we dance in the skies in patterns of cold beauty? Or shall we dare expose ourselves to all that makes us human? To the ugly as well as the beautiful? To hate as well as love? This is what Zalo's message means. This is what the embalming-bird stands for. Therefore rejoice. Exult even in your pain. Dance even the deathdance with joy! —* The voice seemed to shatter, to dissolve into a hollow echoing, as the last of the kashanthras flapped free of the shimmercloak and joined the circle.

It was a sight that had never been seen on Essondras. For the kashanthras, forced into the sewers by humanity's oppressive aura, had not soared naturally since they had been brought to Essondras millennia before. Now they darted up at the face of the burning world; now they hovered, their wings humming; now they flew together into a cloud of blue and glittergold, now they burst out in some new design, each knowing its own place.

And the voice of the Prince of Shadow said: *The world we see is wounded. But all wounds heal. In a few sleeps I will send the kashanthras back to the reformed earth, and they will dance in the planet's skies in perpetuity. And I will call this word Kashanthrema, the Home of the Kashanthra, and in Zalo's honor I will set the emblem of the embalming-bird in the colors of the Shadow Inquest.*

And there appeared above the Throne of Madness a rippling holoflag; it was a sheet of darkness such as Jenjen had often woven, such as hung in the gallery of the House of Darkweavers in Ikshatra, gone forever now. And upon this holographic field was stitched the image of a kashanthra that struggled to free itself from the binding dark, a splash of blue and gold in the center of consuming blackness.

And though Zalo understood little of what was going on, he was moved. For his world was burning at his feet, and the flag of that burning bore the sigil of his vision of freedom.

And the voice spoke, more faintly now, as though it came from another world: *Even the heart of darkness is still a heart.*

And Zalo searched his heart and found joy there; and when he looked around him he saw joy spreading into the crowd. Childsoldiers in their war tunics and iridium graviboots, kinglings with their coronets of diamant and artfire, courtiers, peasants, Inquestors, beggars, all whispered Kelver's name as a benediction.

But still the throne was empty, save for the cloak that enveloped it and swirled about it, glowing like a twilit ocean. And still the planet burned with veins of red fire, suffusing the stardecked chamber with its deathlight.

Then a shadow fell across the throne.

Once more the crowd parted, making a pathway to the portal that now resembled a gap in the starfield.

The White Inquestrix advanced toward the throne. And she was crying out in rage and grief: "Kelver, oh Kelver ... I gave you all my love. I gave you my soul itself. But now I see you are driven mad ... that the Throne of Madness controls you utterly! How can you talk of rescuing a few birds, and of emblems and symbols? We are defeated, Kelver! We came to save this world, and only a paltry few are saved ... fewer are saved than if we had never come, for then they would be frozen into the people bins. Have you abandoned compassion completely? Have you become the very thing you set out to destroy? False hopes and dreams! Are these what you are giving us in exchange for the destruction of all that binds the Dispersal of Man together?"

There came a storm of voices in answer. Jenjen cried out: "Let him be, Siriss! Don't set your love for him above the fate of the galaxy!"

Other voices: "He has suffered! Do not torment him! It is he who sees the way-it is for us to follow!" But Zalo noticed, too, a few dissenting voices.

He said to Jenjen, "Can she blame him for jilting her, if the other woman be a whole galaxy?" She squeezed his hand tight. He felt safe in her love.

Siriss screamed: "Silence! All of you are vultures ... feeding off his love ... bleeding him dry. Let him answer me." A hush fell; her voice seemed deathly quiet under the star-vault, over the burning planet.

But there came no answer from the Throne of Madness.

Twelve
The Betrayer

For where Kelver had gone was a place no mortal could reach, nor even delphinoid perceive in the light-mad overcosm.

It was a still point in the whirling mind of the Throne of Madness, a storm-eye in the vast and fractured intellect that ruled Uran s'Varek and thence the universe of man. About him raged tempests of tachyons and whorls of light coiled from the bending of the black hole at Uran s'Varek's heart.

From his vantage point Kelver could perceive many worlds and touch many souls. But he was still Kelver. He had not fused with the schizoid spirit of Uran s'Varek. He was not yet in all spaces and all times. But everywhere he had once stood, and everyone he had once encountered, were accessible to him. The torrent was intolerable for one man; that was why he had splintered into many men. And still it was unbearable. That was why he had found this secret place in the labyrinth of the great thinkhive's mind; for in this place outside spacetime he was still Kelver.

Kelver who had stood with the girl Darktouch on Gallendys and seen the lightsongs of the delphinoids. Kelver who had heard wisdom from the mouth of Davaryush and learned that there existed at least one true utopia, the world of Shtoma.

Kelver who had come as Inquestor-that-was-to-be to Uran s'Varek, who had loved both Siriss and Arryk, who had driven Arryk into the arms of the sadist Karakaël, who had given Siriss nothing but grief, who had become an unwilling god in the struggle of gods against gods, who in his innocence had dared possess the Throne of Madness, not knowing the price that must be paid. Kelver who had sought to be the beacon of a new humanity, and who now no longer knew whether he was on the side of good or evil.

It was this Kelver, the true Kelver, who said to the soul of the thinkhive of Uran s'Varek: "They are calling me, Throne of Madness. What can I do? They are calling me at Sharamonda ... Siriss has just invoked my name, and accused me of terrible things ... the survivors of Essondras are imploring me to show them the way to salvation ... even Arryk, caged as he is by Karakaël, calls on me to show myself to him. Why am I in this hiding place? Why can't I reach out to them?"

The thinkhive said (though Kelver did not perceive it as saying, for the voice was within his mind, and he was himself a guest in the mind of the thinkhive), *I did not bring you here. You brought yourself. Because you are beginning to see how terrible your destiny is. It is you who will break the spell of "History there is, and no history."*

"What is this place?"

Everywhere! Anywhere!

"Am I on Uran s'Varek, then?"

There too. Do you remember when you were a boy, newly named to the Inquest, and you came to Uran s'Varek of the pearl-wrought skies, and a thinkhive's voice spoke to you?

"That was not you but another."

No, Kelver. It is not true that there exists on Uran s'Varek a planetary thinkhive that is the Inquest's servant. Rather, it is a part of me, splintered off, no longer subservient to my will. And yet, though I have a thousand personalities, I have no soul ... you will be that soul. I tried and failed to capture the Lady Vara twenty millennia ago ... that was the begin ning of my madness. But now I will not fail. I will mold you in my image. We will be each other's god. That is the true purpose of your "revolution," dust-child. Davaryush could never have known it; Elloran the Wise could never have guessed. Only Vara had an inkling of the truth, and she did not speak, for she would have jeopardized her own freedom from me! Did you think that your purpose was to free the galaxy from the Inquestral yoke? No! Your purpose is to effect my apotheosis!

"You are mad!"

And so are you, child of dust.

"I'll stop you. I'll seek out Davaryush and Elloran and the Lady Varuneh. Am I not still in control of your powers? I'll summon them here; together they'll find a .way to defeat you ... take me to them now!"

Fool! It is not I who take you to them, but you yourself.

Look around you ... what do you see?

''A jumble. Past, present, future perhaps, all converging. A chaos of timelines blended together as in a darkweaving." *You must reach out to those you seek. You must overcome your own need to flee from them. And you must draw more power from me, and little by little become ever more my slave.*

Kelver looked round about him and saw only darkness behind darkness behind darkness ... though there was calm at the eye of the galactic storm, the calm came from total deprivation of feeling, and was utterly desolate; he had found peace only by renouncing all that he cared for. "All right," he said to the voice in his mind. "I will myself not to be afraid anymore. In the old days I wasn't afraid; three wise Inquestors guided my footsteps: Davaryush, Elloran, and the Lady Varuneh, who was with you at the dawn of the Dispersal of Man. I will go to them."

You have but to tell me, said the thinkhive. *We will go find them together.*

"I will go alone!"

Ah, but that is impossible. We are bound forever; we are subsumed into one another. You cannot leave this place without me, for this place has no reality other than my mind.

"It is well," Kelver said, though he was desperately afraid.

The whirlwind darkness about him dissolved into black dew, then into motes of not-light ... and then he stood alone, on an ocean, walking on the water toward a sea vessel made from a scale of a monster sea serpent. It was night. A pungent wavewind, sultry, whipped at his shimmercloak. A reddish moon shone through a filigree of cirrus clouds; the wavecrests glowed as though they burned, and the snakescale ship glowed too, like a disk of burnished copper.

He walked to the ship. He did not marvel that he could walk on water; such prodigies were commonplaces for the Throne of Madness. But the sensation filled him with wonder: the warm water lapping at his heels, the skipping ripple of his footfall. The scale's edge, turned upward, formed the ship's low threshold. He stepped onto the deck. A child stirred and clutched to his chest an inflatable toy pteratyger. A few other people lay on the snakescale, most of them naked, some in each other's arms. He could not help feeling a twinge of envy at their contentment.

The thinkhive in his mind: *You remember, Kelver. This world is Idoresht, where we last left your Lady Varuneh. After she played a crucial part in the great* makrúgh *that precipitated this war, she told you she had walked her* makrúgh *to its end, and that she no longer desired to bear the name of Inquestrix, though she had been herself that name's creator. And she came back to the waterworld where she had known happiness, to rule over this people as its queen. I have brought you to her. She lies here sleeping. Do you want to wake her?*

Kelver saw her now. She slept under a canopy of shimmerfur; it seemed to have been woven from the remains of an Inquestor's cloak. Thus it was that he knew she had forsworn her rank forever. The warm wind played with her white hair. He knelt down beside her, caressed the weathered face.

She did not open her eyes, but murmured, "I am dreaming ... I see ... Daavye? Oh, Davaryush, you should not have come, they have stripped you of your name, it is dangerous for you to be here— "

"Old woman, I am not Davaryush. I would I were. It's Kelver who comes to you, Kelver who comes as a suppliant to Mother Vara."

"No. You are a phantom." She moved violently in her sleep. Her fists clenched and unclenched. "You torment me, Throne of Madness."

"Mother Vara, you must help me ... I can't go on alone ... I'm afraid."

"Throne," whispered the old woman, "will you steal from me my final peace? I have found the homeworld of the heart. I have walked my *makrúgh* to its end."

"Varuneh—"

"Go, Daavye, go."

"I'm not Davaryush!" Suddenly he realized that she had not been talking to him at all, but to some figure in her dreams. She didn't even know he was there. He tried to shake her awake, but even as he seized her shoulders her flesh began to lose its substance. "Are we both talking to phantoms then?" he cried out. His voice sounded pitifully thin under the open sky, and no one woke. "Which is the dream?"

All, the thinkhive murmured in his mind, *all is dream.*

"Am I not on Idoresht? Is this not the Lady Varuneh?"

It is and is not, said the thinkhive of Uran s'Varek. *Can you not solve this riddle? You are a god.*

"Always you mock me."

Yes.

"Always you shatter my illusions. I thought that Lady Varuneh had escaped your clutches and found release. But now I see her tortured by nightmares, and I know she clings only tenuously to the peace she yearns for. I understand now. She possessed you once, as I did. And now she is afflicted with a whispershadow. Is that not so? And it is a haunting that can never be exorcized."

The breaking of joy is the beginning of wisdom, said the Throne of Madness, echoing the Inquestral texts. *But now you remember what I told you the day we first met. How I am the star eater; swallowing the suns that spiral slowly into the black hole at my heart, draining them of their energy that you Inquestors may play your games of power. I was not made by men; Lady Varuneh was the first of your kind I ever encountered, and even then I was aeons old and had served and dominated many races. Learn humility, Kevi! You humans are not the only life to have achieved sapience; you know this from your contact with the sentient sun of Shtoma. The galaxy itself possesses a form of life; thoughts race across it over the matrix of virtual particles. Through the overcosm they touch what is to come, through the tachyon universe they perceive what to you is past. But to these higher beings all is instantaneity. Thus it is that those few stars who have awoken to self-awareness must live constantly with the knowledge of their own ending, and I am that ending. That is what a whispershadow is: a star's remem-*

brance of its own future, a death-haunting. There is one attached to you. And to the Lady Varuneh, though I have tried to shield her from it.

"Why have you not tried to protect me?"

I have tried. But it is different. I cannot explain.

"You have a limitation then?" Kelver said, probing for some flaw in the thinkhive's defenses.

You will learn all in the end.

"Davaryush once told me that the *makrúgh* of thinkhives is qualitatively different from the *makrúgh* of Inquestors, because it is played utterly without compassion," Kelver said bitterly. And turned once more to Lady Varuneh, who along with the snakescale vessel and the other sleepers and the sea itself was wavering in and out of Kelver's perceptions. "Wake up, Mother Vara ... see me, oh see me!" he cried, tears springing to his eyes, mingling with the sea-brine, stinging. And felt the Throne's power tighten around him like an instrument of torture. And screamed again, not knowing whether they were almost touching or whether they were parsecs apart and brought together only by some overcosmic illusion.

Suddenly he felt hands grip his arm. For a moment Varuneh's eyes opened. She must have seen him, he knew that she had seen him! He clutched her frail body to his breast and sobbed, "Mother Vara, you must help me, free me—"

"Kelver," came the voice, a croaked whisper. "I dream." And she drifted back into unconsciousness. For a few long seconds he held her in his arms ... then the thinkhive's darkness seized him and spirited him away, the blackness closed in around him, choking off his perceptions; he struggled but could not even see or feel his fists as they flailed at the thick darkness.

"But for a moment I was free!" he shouted. "Free, free, free!" He could not hear his own voice.

***

In that very instant Ton Siriss k'Varad es-K'Ning was approaching the throne in the center of the great hall that overlooked burning Essondras, screaming imprecations at the empty shimmercloak from which had sprung a flock of kashanthras, causing a sensation among those who had gathered for the planet's wake.

At the foot of the throne she shouted at the pteratygers, “Begone, beasts! I must reach him ... or whatever monster is hiding behind the Inquestral cloak. I must touch him, don’t you see!”

Roused by her anger, the pteratygers paced the stairway, their wings flapping with a sound like the slap of storm-stirred sails. “Be still, be still,” Siriss said, “still, still. Do you not know me? I am an Inquestrix, and I go to speak to the Prince of Shadow.”

There was one with a shaggy white mane at the foot of the throne; she heard its purring like a distant earth tremor. It cried out, in a thundermiao: “You seem not—like Inquestor—tears stain your cheeks—like a shortliver—yet you wear the shimmercloak—I am only an animal—I obey—”

“Good. Go now,” she said imperiously, ascending the steps, her expression recovering some measure of the hau teur that was expected of an Inquestor ... but within her mind, what turmoil! The pteratygers flew into the crowd; some chased the kashanthras as they wheeled against the viewscreen firmament, which now showed a closeup of Essondras’s oceans seething.

She stood before the empty throne. “Kelver,” she whispered. She felt the gaze of thousands of spectators in the chamber, but she had been driven beyond caring.

The cloak turned. It blushed blue-pink; fire flickered along its meshing lightstrands. “Kelver, have you forgotten that you once loved me? That I betrayed the Inquestor for you, forsook the light of Elloran and sought out the path of shadow?”

A wind whistled in the chamber. Robes rustled. Hair pieces were caught up and scattered into the air. The kashanthras stopped in mid-flight and shifted patterns like the glass shards of a kaleidoscope. The wind moaned; Siriss could feel her shimmercloak lift and flap against flesh. Its colors deepened.

And Kelver’s shimmercloak tore; and in the zigzag rent Siriss could see a darkness so profound it was as though she looked into the very heart of the black hole of Uran s’Varek.

Then she saw a face form within that darkness: the face of Lady Varuneh. But the green eyes bespoke its true identity. For a moment or two the image wavered. Then she could see Kelver’s face behind the face of the old woman, though the superimposed faces shared the same eyes, and the glassy green of them was doubly intense.

A voice, so low that no one but she could hear it: Kelver's voice. "Free me."

And the twin faces dissolved once more into impenetrable darkness.

And Siriss said quietly, despairingly, "I understand now that it was you, in the guise of Mother Vara, who visited me and asked me to betray you. I said then that I would never betray you. But if it's you who ask it of me, is that truly betrayal? We all have roles to play in this drama of the Inquest's last days; but can we choose those roles? Oh, Kelver, my love, why did you choose me to be the agent of your destruction? I see now that it must be; that I must walk my personal *makrúgh* to its end, no matter how bitter. And a million years from now my name will be cursed in song and myth, and they will know that I, Ton Siriss k'Varad es K'Ning, betrayed the Prince of Shadow ... but they will not know why I do this. I do this because I love you, Kelver. And because that love, which you yourself have taught me, is stronger than death; stronger than the death of all mankind. You're going to destroy the Inquest, the thing that binds all men together, so that you can redeem the human race. But I would destroy mankind to set you free."

No one had heard these last words; she did not even know whether Kelver had heard, whether his essence was somehow trapped in the folds of the shimmercloak, whether all she had spoken was in vain. She turned her back on the throne. There were all Kelver's worshipers ... there were Zalo and Jenjen, whose visions had helped shape the revolution on Essondras ... there was loyal Tya grown to womanhood, still attired in the black cloak and iridium boots of a childsoldier ... there was Jannif the astrogator ... over there the kashanthras, the interweavings of their flight protected by the psychic shielding. Am I the only one who feels no joy? Siriss thought. Elation is in all their faces. They all drew comfort from the words the Kelver-voice spoke before. But I am not a worshiper. He is no god to me. *I love him,* she thought fiercely. For him I will rob these people of their happiness....

They made an aisle for her as she descended the steps of force. In pairs the pteratygers broke their chaotic overhead circling and settled on the steps, pouncing and purring and pawing the air.

The aisle closed up behind her as she made her way to the portals of the observation chamber. The consternation of the crowd at her first appearance had given way to awe at the beauty of the planet's firedeath, and to a quiet contentment. Someone had begun singing one of the new anthems in Kelver's honor; soon a thousand voices were joining in, even those who did not know the words:

I go to a hidden kingdom.
A kingdom to be found in shadows
and dark places.
I am no longer afraid,
for I feel upon me the breath
of the Prince of Shadow.
Demand of me my life, Ton Keverell!
I face death with joy;
for death is the darkest of places,
and beyond it lies your kingdom,
the homeworld of my heart,
the heartworld of my longing,
the eye of the galactic storm,
the Darkling Wind.

As she stepped through the great doors into the vestibule, Siriss thought: I too go to the darkest of places now. But I will not find my heart's desire.

She looked up. She was in one of the corridors of force that twisted through the innards of Sharamonda. From here Essondras, unmagnified by the palace's thinkhives, was only the size of a demi-arjent, and betrayed no evidence of its dying. She hurried on. Two delphinoid starships crossed paths overhead; one built in the shape of a space whale, the other as a silver naked woman with her head tucked between her knees and her hands outstretched; each finger held an observation turret. She watched for a few minutes. The space whale seeded the sky with a convoy of shuttle bubbles. With a flick of her mind she hailed one and plated to Sharamonda's inner harbor.

And when at last she sat enthroned in Varezhdur, she dismissed all her retinue, even the mindhearers that lurked behind the columns of flame, even the ferrets concealed in ornate golden chests whose job was to observe all visitors. She wanted no one to see what she was about to do.

Then she called the thinkhive, asked for a long-distance shuttle, and whispered her destination.

The thinkhive chuckled and said: *So it's come, at last.*

"What can you possibly know of *makrúgh,* machine?"

There was no response, but the thinkhive's laughter echoed mockingly through the palace, and a thousand corridors away children at play pricked their ears and listened uneasily.

***

... and Kelver called next on the name of Elloran, and the thinkhive carried him to a lonely starship crawling further and further from the hub of the galaxy, in the direction of the distant arm whence it was said mankind once sprang.

Elloran sat alone on a hoverthrone that overlooked a galaxy of dust set into a shaft of light, save for which all the chamber was dark. Kelver did not know if he was asleep or awake. Softly he called to him: "*Hokh'Ton* Ton Elloran, it is I, your pupil."

Elloran said, never looking up from his meditation, "I see ghosts in the galaxy of dust."

"I am no ghost."

"Don't say that. That's what they all say when they come to haunt me."

"My Lord—"

"Leave me! Do you think you are the first? You are not even the most vivid of the tormenting spirits. You must know that I am for the gray spaces, and that I will mourn Sajit's death forever."

Shadowlike he crossed the lightshaft and stood before the hoverthrone, half-cloaked in darkness. "Father Elloran, you are so wise. Will you not help me? Can you not return to Varezhdur and stand by me and your daughter Siriss, when we face the fall of the Inquest?"

"Fool of a shadow! I knew you would come to tempt me. There is no delphinoid mind aboard this starship. It is a ship of the old days, more than twenty millennia old. I found it on Imneshima, the planet of stored remembrances, where are kept things from the past that all other men have consigned to oblivion. You know as well as I do of the pain the delphinoids suffer as they thread the overcosm; that is why I sail the gray spaces in the ancient way. I cannot return ... to return to Varezhdur would take this starship centuries, and I have long ceased to take the drugs we Inquestors use to keep us ever young."

"Imneshima ... I had thought that world a legend," Kelver said. "A thing told of by dreamreaders and poets."

"As you are, Prince of Shadow ... disturb me no more ... I search for peace, Ton Keverell n'Davaren Tath."

"Well then," Kelver said, feeling himself already fading away, "I will go elsewhere. Surely Davaryush will help me ... Davaryush, who in the beginning laid this geis on me."

A momentary suffocating as the whirlwind closed around him; then he was gone, riding the darkstorm through the thinkhive's inner space.

***

As the shuttlecraft approached its destination, Siriss repeated to herself over and over, like an incantation, "What I am doing is for the best." She could not allay her fear completely, but found comfort in the sheer repetition.

But as her destination loomed ahead, she commanded the shuttle's thinkhive to play a raucous military music, hoping that its braying melodies and thudding rhythms would drown the sound of her weeping. I should have dignity, she thought. I am still an Inquestor. I should have pride. There is a kind of honor in what I do.

But she knew that she was tricking herself, and that she was able to do so because she no longer loved herself.

***

And Kelver came to Shtoma, the world where the blood red grass rustled in the cadent lightfall, the world where Davaryush had come to lose his faith and first fallen prey to the heresy of utopianism. Shtoma was a tiny world in an impossibly close orbit around Udara, the sentient white dwarf star who bathed the world's inhabitants continually with its love ... where men rode the varigrav coasters until they were purged of all their pain. It was here that Davaryush had danced on the face of the sun; for every few years virtually the entire population of the planet flew to Udara in their creaky shuttleships and leaped onto the sun's surface, and the sun created for them a patch of coolness and washed away the grief of their years past, and filled them with peace.

It was on Shtoma, too, that Kelver had tried to participate in the ritual, and alone of all men had not been touched by the sun's love... had learned, instead, that a whispershadow, pre-echo of a star's death, prevented him from knowing the forgiveness of Udara.

It was to Shtoma that Davaryush had fled after the High Inquestral Convocation had stripped him of his name. It was to Shtoma, too, that Darktouch had come, Darktouch his first love, his only link to Gallendys, the homeworld of his lost innocence.

Surely they will help me, he thought, as the darkstorm set him down in a crimson field. And he realized suddenly that they were the only survivors from his childhood; for his entire village had been burned by the Inquest.

In a clearing by a displacement plate an old man sat. He wore a gray smock to which clung remnants of a shimmercloak. At his feet sat a few dozen children and some adults. A woman sat beside him; her skin was snow—pale, and her hair long and dark. She was older than when they had last seen each other, though they had once been the same age. "Darktouch," Kelver said. The woman looked up. Udara had been kind to her features. She smiled questioningly; she had not seen him. He was invisible to her.

"Why can't I touch her?" he cried to the thinkhive of Uran s'Varek.

Because you fear to. Be calm; listen.

The old man was telling them a story. He was saying, "And Kelver and Darktouch fled the Skywall mountain; frozen they were in the Cold River, down to the twin cities. I found them there. Little by little I unearthed from their lips the Inquest's darkest secret-that their mastery over the overcosm came from the slaughter and enslavement of delphinoids, huge brains that soar through the dense air within the Skywall mountain on the wind of flapping sail sacs "

"Tell us what happened next!" said one of the children. "We all returned to the Skywall mountain, and we saw what the Inquest never meant men to see," Darktouch said, her eyes shining with the remembrance. "We saw the songs that the delphinoids sing when they are free ... we saw the light on the Sunless Sound, and knew that the Inquest had built its empire on the murder of an ultimate beauty. It was thus that we lost our innocence, children." And Kelver saw that she clutched the old man's hand, and that she and aged Davaryush now shared the love that he and she had once known. And the old man smiled and drew her close, and their embrace was haloed in Udara's light.

"And Kelver?" said the child. "What of him?"

"To end the Inquest's millennial stranglehold on man," Davaryush said, "we needed a hero. I could not lead the revolution, because I too was tainted by the Inquest. Nor could the Lady Varuneh, for she was herself the Inquest's founder. So I named Kelver to the Inquest, hoping he would be free of the lnquestral curse, and that in his innocence he would seize the Throne of Madness, and that in his purity he would not be corrupted by it ... and when Kelver returned from his confrontation with the Throne, wherein resides the ultimate power in this galaxy, he declared a great game of *makrúgh*. It was to be the greatest game ever played, and the last. Planets would rise and fall and lnquestor be pitted against lnquestor, for they would take up arms themselves, no longer battling by proxy as they'd done before. And the climax of the epic was to take place at Lightfall, which is what the Inquestors call the time when a star falls through one of the polar openings of Uran s'Varek into the black hole beneath ... it is the most magnificent of sunsets, for the sun actually falls through the surface of our homeworld ... it is at Lightfall, by tradition, that the greatest *makrúgh* is played. For at the moment of the star's death, the thinkhives of Uran s'Varek drain into their energy banks, which cover millions upon millions of square klomets, all the power locked in that star's mass, and store it for the Inquest's use. Tachyon bubbles are powered by the deaths of stars, and so are the lnquestor's whimsical conceits: the deserts of chocolate, the snowflake palaces, the skies woven from rainbows; all the beautiful things of Uran s'Varek derive from the killing of suns."

"How long, Father Davaryush, until this Lightfall?" a child asked solemnly.

"When Kelver issued his challenge," Darktouch said, "Lightfall was a century away; now it is drawing near."

"And must Udara too perish and fall prey to the Eater of Stars?" the same child said.

"Transience is the nature of things," Davaryush said. Kelver remembered how often he had heard those words from the old man before he was unmade Inquestor. He wanted to speak to him; he could not bear to think that they were telling tales of him as though he were already some legendary hero.

"Davaryush—" Kelver said. The ancient Inquestor looked up at last. But he did not recognize Kelver. And when Kelver held up his arms he saw that he had become a winged boy ... like Aoauei, who had been the first being to die for him.

"Did you have a question, boy?" Davaryush said kindly. "You seem familiar-looking, though it is not common to see green-eyed folk on Shtoma ... are you a refugee from one of my palaces?" Kelver was touched by the gentleness in Davaryush's voice. He does not even recognize me, he thought, yet he shows casual kindness even to a stranger. This is what Udara does to people ... to all people except me! And Kelver felt cursed by destiny.

He said (his voice tiny and high-pitched, as Aoauei's had been) "Master Davaryush, don't you feel that you deserted Kelver? Don't you feel that you laid too great a burden on his shoulders?"

Davaryush frowned a little. But then he replied, "Strange you should ask, you who did not even know him. You know, you remind me of him? Well. At first I was sorely troubled by this. I brooded; I became convinced that I must take control again, that only I, who knew the ins and outs of *makrúgh* and the personalites of the other leading Inquestors, could break the Inquest's power. But when I tried to take the power back, it was too late; Kelver rejected me. And that too was in the plan; it was better that he hate me, for only then would he follow the path of compassion, even if it meant that he destroy me."

Kelver knew that this was true. On the brink of war, Davaryush had demanded the right to possess the Throne of Madness himself; it was Kelver who turned his back on the past. How simple things had seemed then. "I cannot bear this!" he shouted. They could no longer hear him; he must have begun to dissolve once more into a phantom. He saw that Darktouch and Davaryush were proceeding with their story; to the children it must seem like an exciting fairy tale. As they went on with their retelling of the past, Kelver saw that they moved closer and closer together, that they were obviously lovers ... couldn't they even sense his presence? "All the people I ever loved," he said, turning his back on them and walking away, down the dirt path that wound through the man-tall grass. Udara, sun of love, shone brilliantly upon this world; but the thinkhive's mind-storm spun a cocoon of darkness around him, a private womb-world desolate of all feeling.

Where shall I take you now, my master? came the voice in his mind.

"Where you will! You have drained me even of grief," Kelver said. And the darkness snatched him up and bore him away.

***

They rode in a serpentine shuttlecraft that would take them back to the reconditioned people bin that was to be their home; some hundreds of them aboard, leaving behind the observatory where the morbid still watched Essondras in its death throes. Zalo and Jenjen were there. The shuttle was not built for crowds, and they were crushed together; Tya and Jannif, whom Zalo had come to know as two of Kelver's earliest and most loyal followers, stood by them. The walls were deopaqued, so they seemed to be standing on concatenated carpets of mirror metal in the middle of space. The shuttlecraft contorted its way through the intertwined twin palaces of Varezhdur and Sharamonda; now they threaded archways of gold, now between the filaments of gigantic snowflakes. They could see people in the other segments of the shuttlecraft; sometimes they were turned upside down by the craft's tortuous passage.

Behind them was crescent Essondras. Before them, when they had burst through the mingled palaces and into open space, the chain of people bins hung like the articulated segments of a silver annelid.

Jannif said to the two of them, "What will you do now?"

"What can we do?" Zalo said. "We are inextricably caught up in this revolution now. And the outcome of the revolution is uncertain."

"It is not," Jenjen said. "The Inquest falls. I've heard this from the lips of so many Inquestors of both sides that I know it must be true. It's inherent in their very philosophy, though they long tried to ignore it. It's just like a darkweaving, Zalo, and we are like two filaments of light that an artist has wound into the fabric of darkness ... however brightly we may shine by ourselves, the sum total of the weaving will always be darkness. That is the darkweaver's mystery."

"Will you go on?" he said to her. "I mean, with your shapes of darkness."

"I suppose so. And you, Zasha?"

"I will write new plays. Plays that mythologize all that has happened and will happen in our lives, so that if a dark age comes they will still know our names. And plays that will spread word of the coming of the Prince of Shadow to the worlds still under the Inquest's yoke."

Jannif, embracing Tya, said, "She and I have found love under the reign of the Prince of Shadow."

"And purpose," Tya whispered shyly; it seemed to Zalo that though she wore the garb of a childsoldier she had lost the childsoldier's hardness. And he wondered at this, how a human bred to become a machine could still transcend her training and grow to know love. As they neared their people bin, it filled the sky, a featureless cylinder of silver. The two women, soldier and astrogator, kissed; and Zalo drew his own woman close to him. The crowd jostled them, pushed them against the forcescreen. It looked as if they were going to tumble off the edge before the invisible barrier caught them. A small hand tugged at a fold of his tunic.

"Leave us alone," he said, "can't you see we're busy?" "Master Zalo—thank the powers of powers! I'd given you up —"

"Jhisha!" It was the boy Jherwo, who had played, that fateful night in the theater, the corpse of the Rainbow King. "My lost apprentice!"

"And look who I found, wandering aimlessly down the corridors of my people bin!" Jherwo reached into the press of the crowd and, as if by magic, pulled out a wizened old man.

"Enshtewo—" and "Father pisspot!" Jenjen and Zalo cried out at the same time.

"I thought you were dead," Zalo said. "I saw you—wasn't it you? Crushed under the rocks, in the tunnels beneath the city?"

"Obviously, my boy, it wasn't me," Enshtewo said, scolding him as though he were one of the young apprentices. Zalo laughed.

"Isn't it wonderful, Master Zalo?" Jherwo babbled, unable to contain his excitement. "The world's being blown to smithereens, but we *still* have an acting company!"

"Bah!" Enshtewo said. "We should have stuck to the old ways. Then we wouldn't be in this pickle!" But he laughed and hugged Zalo.

"Are you implying that, by one small change in the necrodrama, I actually caused this whole thing?" Zalo said. And then all of them were laughing helplessly ... until tears came.

Suddenly a babble of shouts from the other side of the shuttle. Everyone was rushing to press his nose against the forcefield on the side that faced Essondras. "Wait, I can't breathe," Zalo said, his grip tightening on Jenjen's arm, and then he felt himself sucked into the mob and forcibly shoved against the forcewall, and then he saw it—

"The childsoldiers. They are coming home. It's over," Zalo heard Tya say, and he saw her close her eyes and weep silently.

And he saw them now ... like a cloud of locusts ... each childsoldier cocooned in his pressure skin against the cold of vacuum, each one riding a hoverdisk that jetted blue flame ... they burned with the light reflected from their iridium graviboots and bounced back and forth off the mirror metal of the people bins ... their brilliance outshone the stars ... behind them, in a slow processional, came delphinoids built in the shape of scorpions and sharks and fantastical ancient beasts, sleek as they sliced through the blackness of space ... they sang no victory paean, but the air thrummed with Kelver's name, for each was subvocalizing it to himself like a litany, and the shuttlecraft's thinkhive was picking up their thoughts and broadcasting them as whispers through the ventilation ducts.

"It's over," Jenjen said. "I remember the mnemothanasion where I went to mourn my parents."

"That Rainbow Darkness that you built, Jeni—the shadow it cast over the proscenium of my theater—"

"Well," Jherwo said, "all I ever saw was the innards of that building and a few back streets. Powers! I'm ready for another world, *any* otherworld."

"Jhisha's right," Zalo said. "This is not death but a beginning." And he believed it for the first time. It was like that moment, he thought, when you've been staring at some tapestry of the darkweavers for many hours, seeing nothing but unending black; and then, all at once, your mind lets go, something clicks, you catch a glimmer of a lightstrand or a ghost of a flaming shape, and then suddenly your mind roams free over the darkscape and kindles it and sets it ablaze. That was what Jenjen taught me, long ago, when we first loved one another.

"But where will we go now?" the apprentice asked.

It was Kail Jannif who spoke. "After a few days, I will oversee the return of the kashanthras to Essondras. Then we'll go back to our base ... to the world that none dares name for fear that the other side may learn its secret. Arryk and Karakaël will say they won this round of *makrúgh,* but in their hearts they will know it is not so. Every human being we snatch away from a dying world with the idea of freedom burning in his heart is a slap in the face for them! They'll grow angry; they'll look for our hidden homeworld, thinking to destroy us utterly ... but they'll not find it. Millions have died that none might know its name. Willingly, with the name of the Prince of Shadow on their lips. I do not think they were sad, for they had glimpsed the coming of the new kingdom."

"And after we go there?" Zalo said.

"Then—new worlds!" cried Jherwo excitedly. "Plays, Master Zalo, we'll put on plays everywhere! We'll stand on ever-new earths, as the song goes, just like in the days of the dawn of man!"

"Why," Jannif said, "you don't even have to remain subject to the tyranny of those clan-names ... you needn't be a darkweaver anymore, Jenjen ... you, Zalo, could abandon playwrighting altogether and become ... an astrogator, like me! And chase the interstellar quickpaths through the mind of a delphinoid starship. Why, I could even learn to act! That's what freedom means, here in Kelver's kingdom."

"What, me, fly a starship?" Jherwo cried. "What every kid dreams about?"

"What they've dreamed about," Jannif said, "since the beginning of time."

"It will all come true," Tya said softly, "after the war is done."

"A starship! I'll pilot a starship!" the boy hollered. His fervor was infectious. Soon he had them all laughing, and weeping, and laughing again. But when Jenjen said, "We must become like a real family, an unforgotten fragment of Essondras," they became solemn, and a different kind of joy took hold of them: quiet, unambiguous, profound. Suddenly I feel more than myself, I feel like a great man, Zalo thought, a shaper of history. Perhaps only a child should have these feelings. Or perhaps I am reborn, a child once more. Like Jhisha, to whom this revolution belongs too, though he sees it only as a pathway to the stars.

***

In the arms of the whirlwind darkness, Kelver came to rest on a vast plain on a world he did not recognize; its lushness marked it for a pleasure world. The plain was littered with stone children. Kelver wondered why he had been brought here; presently the whirlwind darkness left him completely, and he was free to walk on the planet as himself, solid, no longer a phantom.

He wandered among the stone figures. Were they votive statues, perhaps? All seemed to be of childsoldiers. All were in attitudes of terrible pain. Perhaps the Inquest had visited some punitive expedition on this world, and the survivors had built these statues in remembrance, to show their anger? Kelver could not tell. Moss veined their features. Here and there a rosella bloomed in a cranny, an armpit or an earlobe, or purple lichen striped their anguished features. Two suns were setting behind the hilltops; behind him, two moons were rising.

"What is this place? Who has caused these statues to be put up in this abandoned field?"

A hundred thousand of them, Ton Keverell. Is it not impressive? But they are not statues.

"Not statues ... " Suddenly he saw the truth. "They are all soldiers of mine! Soldiers who bit down on the calcifying tablet embedded in their teeth to avoid—"

To avoid uttering the name of Zorn! the thinkhive said.

You see, your people love you well.

"It can't be! How can I have let this happen?" He looked out over the plain. Then the thinkhive carried him to a plateau in the hills, and he saw that the stone army stretched out for many klomets, shrunk by the distance into the semblance of white flowers peppering the dense verdure ... "I can't bear it," Kelver screamed. "Let them carry on the revolution without me! I'm just one man, and they are so many ... and Elloran, Davaryush, Varuneh have all forsaken me, have found their private paradises."

You said that I was to take you anywhere I wanted.

Kelver wept; the only living soul on this forsaken world, he wept bitterly, his body racked with sobs, with no one to comfort him. For all the thinkhive would say to him was, *It is good you weep. Your agony will bring forth joy for all those others. Your tears will mean their freedom, Kelver! Think of that.*

"Do you hate me? Is that why you have made me into a monster, a killer of children?"

Hate! That I, a machine, should hate! That you, a dust-child, should have the hubris to imagine an emotional relationship between us!

Kelver continued to weep far into the night.

At dawn he watched how the twin suns made the soldier statues cast cruciform shadows, so that the field was crisscrossed with dark X's.

He said: "If so many have died to hide the secret of Zorn, then I must make sure it is never revealed. Karakaël will never find our base of operations."

Already, at this moment, you are being betrayed.

"What! Take me away at once, to stop the betrayer!"

You cannot stop this act. It happens by your own command ... your own beseeching.

"No!"

Yes. Your many personalities war within you, as do mine. Some parts of you work to subvert other parts. But there is a place in the scheme of things even for your death wish, Kelver: Your many personalities are all pieces of the plan, even when they seem to contradict each other ...

"Plan? There is a plan to this? A plan to my ordering the betrayal of my most closely guarded secret, one which has already cost so much in blood?"

There is a plan. You are the plan. Yet, being within the plan, you cannot see all of it . . . .

"Take me to Essondras! I *will* not be betrayed!"

We will go back now, O Prince of Shadow. For I go to stamp your image on Arryk's makrúgh, *and to remind him that his victory is an empty one.*

***

The dinner party was over. The throneroom was all but empty; here and there a servocorpse or a pageboy scrubbed the pedestals of the columns or polished the stairways that led to the daises that held the Inquestors' hoverthrones.

Even Karakaël had retired, but Arryk remained, and the viewwalls continued to show the cataclysm. People crushed beneath stone buildings. Fire racing down the narrow streets between the walls of mnemothanasions. Kilimindi's thinkhive, which had been programmed to Karakaël's specifications, seemed to take special delight in showing closeups of disemboweled corpses and terror-stricken faces. Though Arryk had always abhorred violence, he now used it as a drug; prolonged doses had an addicting, mesmerizing effect on him.

An intruder, whispered the thinkhive of Kilimindi. And Siriss stood before him.

"Sirissheh—"

She did not speak; tears clogged her eyes. "Come," he said, "do not cry. We are Inquestors. An Inquestor does not weep. It is unseemly. Surely you have not been that far corrupted...." He spoke thus as much to mask his own emotion as to censure Siriss. "So tell me, has Kelver sent you as an ambassador? He wants to impose terms, perhaps? Though the world he tried to protect lies wasted and lifeless?"

"I come on my own account, Ton Arryk n'Elloren Tath." "So formal ... you loved me once. And now you are like a stranger."

"I have come to betray him."

"What?" Arryk came down from his throne; slowly he walked down the steps to face her. Wistfully he toyed with a strand of her snow-pale hair. "You never flinched from me before."

"Oh, Arryk, I—"

"It's obvious you still love him. Why have you come? To torture me? You and Kelver ... I would have given up the universe for either of you ... I loved you both so much. But you abandoned me for a mad idea, you left me with cold precepts for bedmates. You've come to mock me, haven't you? Don't think that I don't know who *really* won today. And though we may declare victory after victory, it's all meaningless unless we find the source of it all, the center of your secret kingdom. Mock me, mock me! I am strong. I will not weep. I will fling back your taunts a thousandfold. Though you have debauched all that is good in the universe, *I* will not follow you. I am an Inquestor."

"Oh, Rikeh, Rikeh—" She seemed to be laboring under some terrible conflict. It pained him to see her fall so from the Inquestral ideal of proper composure ... she was like a madwoman. Was it true that Kelver had gone mad? It would not be surprising, if those he influenced lost all understanding of degree, of the balance that underpinned the cosmos and the human order.

And she rushed into his arms and crushed him to her, crying, "Rikeh, you shame me so, it was you I loved first of all, you of the violet eyes on the planet of the scarlet snow ... I cannot choose ... how can I choose? How can I go with one and not abandon the other? But Kelver is not human anymore."

"Our captives will never tell us anything. They're willing to die before they reveal the location of the secret kingdom. If people are willing to die for such ideas, the ideas must be terrible things ... that was why the Inquest was created, so that people would no longer be driven mad by empty words, by vain shadows ... I remember what one of them said," said Arryk. In the viewscreens overhead, a hundred times lifesize, a baby's head was slowly being crushed between two blocks of slate ... the side of a building, perhaps an amphitheater, awash with blood ... in a garden, between two holosculptures of copulating nymphs, a severed hand burned...."Yes, I remember. I forced myself to visit the chambers of excruciation myself," he said, thinking of the labyrinth of horror hidden in the recesses of Kilimindi, and remembering that Elloran's Varezhdur had never contained such a place. "It was a prostitute from the slums of Airang on Alykh, the pleasure planet. She'd been arrested distributing propaganda disks."

"There are many such. Did you hope to arrest them all?" Siriss said.

"I asked the girl, 'What is the purpose of your suffering?'"

"I wanted to understand, you see. She said only, 'We are all pieces of the great dream; we belong somewhere at last, *hokh'-Ton*.' Then she said, rasping it out in her dying breath, 'But only Kelver dreams the whole dream.'"

"I have touched the edge of that dream, and I know it is a nightmare," Siriss said. "Oh, Arryk, we must save him. We must end this whole madness, you and I ... tum back time, stem the flood of insanity... not for the sake of the Dispersal of Man ... for *his* sake!"

"You show too much passion, woman!" Arryk said, shaken. "All I can tell you is that when we destroy his kingdom, I will save him if I can. Do you think I've forgotten how we three once loved?"

"No. Of course not." She smiled a wan smile. "I accept your promise. I have to take what I can get."

"Very well. The name of the world—!"

"Rikeh—"

"You have gone a little mad too, Sirissheh. But we will heal you." The walls showed images of corpses piled on corpses ... of exploding mountains ... of rivers become seething serpents of steam ... a child clawing among the bodies, its mouth frozen in a silent scream. "Yes, we will heal you," Arryk said. "All will be well. I promise, I promise."

"Zorn."

The thinkhive of the palace spoke. *That is a gas giant, Ton Arryk. What she says is most improbable.*

"Do you hear that? It's a trick!"

"A trick? So Karakaël has dragged you so low that you would believe that I come to you in *makrúgh?*"

"History there is, and no history."

"Arryk—"

"You don't have to play *makrúgh* with me. It can be like the old times. Oh, Siriss, Siriss, why is it that the powers of powers gave Kelver and me only a single soul, and that soul Siriss? Now I have my soul again. I am complete." But he knew it was not completely true; for he had not yet driven Kelver from his heart. "Enough of these images of death!" he commanded the thinkhive of Kilimindi. "Show me a more distant view of Essondras."

At his command the planet filled the sky. Freckling its brilliant face, a swarm of childsoldiers sped back to the Inquestral war delphinoids. Familiar sights.

Attention, attention, Inquestors. Something strange has happened. A mysterious force has taken hold of the planet's crust, the thinkhive intoned in the resonant voice reserved for palace-wide announcements.

"What's the matter?" Arryk said. "Look—" Siriss pointed at the planet.

The central continent was collapsing in on itself ... but that was part of the scenario of destruction, wasn't it, to destabilize the crust? But something else was happening. Two vast inland lakes had formed ... clouds ringed them in an almond shape. "Eyes," Siriss said. "Green eyes." Arryk gaped. A mountain range erupted to the south and curled into the shape of a mouth ... island continents broke off and became ears ... and the seething sea a shock of blue-white hair ... "It's becoming *his* face!" Siriss screamed. "As if he knew. As if he were watching."

"It can't be. Only something as powerful as ... one of the Thrones on Uran s'Varek ... could—"

"The Throne of Madness!"

They watched. A jutting mountain ridge became a nose; lines of taiga were the eyebrows, and pockets of tundra were the sweat-beads on his brow.

"Kelver!" Arryk wailed. And Kilimindi's thinkhive picked up the wail, so that it echoed through the whole palace, even in the chambers of excruciation. "Can I never escape you?" Siriss rushed to him and held him close, and he thrust her away, shouting, "You were just with him, you touched him ... you *did* come here to mock me!"

"No! I came to set us all free!"

And Arryk wept at last, forsaking the Inquestral precept that prescribed composure at all times. And there issued volcanic fire from the mouth of the image, and from the emerald eyes ... and down the ages men would remember it as a prodigy of the last days of the Inquest, that a dying planet had been transformed into the face of the Prince of Shadow.

He lay back on the throne in the arms of the betrayer, the Inquestrix of the opal eyes. Presently one of the palace servants came with a silken kerchief to wipe away his tears, and crept quietlyaway.

This palace servant was a small winged boy with sea green eyes. Nobody knew his name, and he seemed to have no memory of how he had come to the palace.

BOOK TWO

The Screaming Star

THE QUERENT
I am confused. Things were simpler at the story's beginning.
THE CHILD FROM THE FUTURE
With my unborn eyes I see what you cannot.
You see from deep within the characters' minds,
sense with their strained senses,
feel from their trapped perspectives.
But I will help you. I will draw the extended canvas;
I will conjure up charts in the air; I will paint the flat scenery against which your rounded personages breathe and weep and struggle and give voice to the lines the poet gave them.
THE QUERENT
Of what will you speak first?
THE CHILD FROM THE FUTURE
I will speak of the old Inquestors,
and of the young Inquestors who sought respite from the war, and of those who followed in their wake.

-from Zalo's play *The Darkling Wind*
composed during the aftermath of the revolution

Thirteen

In The Gray Spaces

He had abolished day and night; he had allowed a different rhythm to seep into his senses. How long the starship had drifted, he could not know. It was not far as the Inquestors measured spacetime; for though at first he had sailed the overcosm, he had come at last to the point where he could no longer endure the raging lightstorms. They had broken free of the overcosm then, and he had commandeered a new starship with which to enter the gray spaces where silence reigned supreme and the stars seemed never to shift. It was a starship without a mind; as he was fond of telling the many phantoms that visited his dreams, it came from Imneshima, the planet of forgetting.

I have found peace, Elloran thought.

His throneroom was completely deopaqued. It was as though he sat alone among the stars.

Time passed; the Inquestor who had renounced *makrúgh* sat, eyes closed, for many sleeps. Sometimes he dreamt. Of the splendor of Uran s'Varek; of glittering Varezhdur; of the rainbow city of Chembrith; of Shentrazjit with its twenty million-voiced choir. Of pteratygers swarming, blacking out the million-starred radiance of Uran s'Varek. Once he had even dreamt of Kelver; that had been a strange dream, for he could at times have sworn he was awake, the dreamshape seemed so palpable.

The dreams disturbed him, that one dream most of all; for without them there would be nothing but eternal tranquillity. He moved, murmuring, "Sajitteh, Sajitteh." And awoke.

Why was there no music?

It was the thinkhive of the starship that answered him: *Lord, the man you seek is dead. And though there is music here, it is a grand music that spans so vast a time that you are but a catch of breath within it. Even you, hokh'Ton, cannot perceive it.*

"I am not happy, thinkhive."

What did you seek to achieve, hokh'Ton? *Some ultimate epiphany?*

"Don't you remember the song?"

The thinkhive sang, in an emotionless parody of dead Sajit's voice, the old song about the silence between the stars. And around the old Inquestor reigned this very silence. "It reproaches me. It taunts me," Elloran said.

No, Inquestor. The voice you give the silence comes only from yourself.

"It will drive me mad, then!"

Or you will attain enlightenment.

How strange, thought Elloran, that men once sailed these silences. Centuries would pass before they reached another world, centuries of boredom or cold sleep. What stamina the ancient travelers must have had. "How long have I been here?"

You instructed me not to tell you.

"I override."

A hundred sleeps. You wish to go back?

"Hardly."

In any case, the thinkhive said, *a little diversion is on its way. You have a visitor.*

"Who? No one even knows where I am!"

He no longer has a name.

"Davaryush! Here?"

You will of course not admit him. No Inquestor may speak to one denounced as a heretic, cast down from the High Inquest, stripped of his shimmercloak. I need hardly remind you—

"Override! Override!"

As you wish.

Was there a trace of irony in the toneless mechanical voice? They're too clever, these cursed thinkhives. "Beware, thinkhive. Remember who runs the Dispersal of Man."

I remember, hokh'Ton, *and know my place.*

That tone again! "Insolence!" Elloran cried, though the thinkhive's words had been innocuous enough. It must be the silence. Driving him into paranoia. "Admit him," he said at last.

At first he imagined himself uttering stern words to his old friend. *How dare you come here, shattering my peace?* But it was no use fooling himself. Peace had eluded him, even here. Or perhaps because he was here, far from the death paeans of childsoldiers and the fireworks of bursting planets.

***

For another long while—perhaps an hour or two, perhaps many sleeps—Elloran sat enthroned amid the gray silence. But then he became aware that a perfect dark circle had formed against the starstream. "You are welcome, old friend," Elloran said as the tachyon bubble's blackness dissipated and Davaryush stood before him.

Shreds of the dead shimmercloak still clung around Davaryush's emaciated body. Elloran had expected the hollow cheeks, the sunken eyes. But he had not thought to see the heretic smiling. Or that the tatters of shimmercloak, encircling the old man like a swirl of autumn leaves, would have retained a ghost of their old luster and would light up his face like a manystranded halo. There was greatness in that ravaged face, Elloran thought.

They embraced; with a flick of his mind Ton Elloran summoned a chairfloat for his friend. Davaryush sat, waiting. Since he had lost the name of Inquestor it would be presumptuous for him to speak first. And so it was Elloran who broke the gray silence.

"They have not broken you, Daavye," he said.

The old man smiled still, and did not speak. Elloran was uneasy. "I would have protested if I could," he said. "But the precepts were too clear, your transgression too—"

"Unthinkable." He had to strain to hear Davaryush. "Don't feel guilty, Elloran. It was inevitable that I should be declared a heretic. I had no choice but to speak the truth; you had no choice but to condemn me. I'm not here to beg for reinstatement, my friend. You would not be able to grant it."

"No."

"Am I a coward, Loreh? Have I run away from destiny?" "I don't know." Elloran was uneasy suddenly, for this was a question which had been gnawing at his own consciousness. "This silence is too much like a drug," he said. Had he given away too much of his inner turmoil? No matter. Davaryush was no longer an Inquestor. He could not play *makrúgh*. And yet ...

"I feel all your thoughts, *hokh'Ton,*" Davaryush said. "I know you envy me."

"Envy? But they have taken so much from you! And I too have lost so much, so much." Yet in that moment Elloran knew that it was true.

"You've looked for an answer," Davaryush said, "a simple answer. And so have I. You have sought Sajit's silence. I have sought oblivion. But you and I can never be at peace, because of what we once were!"

"That day of judgment, I looked at you from my hoverthrone, Daavye, and I saw in your eyes ... a serenity. It has always"—and he knew it only as he spoke—"haunted me. Yet you tell me that you are not at peace?"

Davaryush said, "I have danced on the face of the sun, and seen the light on the sound. But I'm still a man. Kelver gave me this tachyon bubble and said I could go where I wanted. I chose to find you. Because, though I thought my mission was accomplished ... though I have unleashed the forces that will bring about the fall of the Inquest ... there still is something to be done, after all."

"Don't speak to me of destiny, of grand missions. Your journey's wasted, I'm afraid, dear friend. I have turned my back on history, past and future. The silence between the stars of which Sajit sang is an eternal present; all I want now is to meditate on this theme. All my life I could not bear silence; I demanded that every act I did be accompanied by music. Symphoniae for my public acts, consorts of shimmerviols for intimate moments, brasses for my declarations, resounding drumbeats for my acts of war. I reject it all now."

But even as Elloran spoke it he knew that it rang false. He knew too that though Davaryush was no longer permitted to play *makrúgh,* and though he himself had forsworn *makrúgh* forever, the game had somehow begun anyway. It dismayed him, and he wanted to dismiss the heretic—after all, this was Daavye-without-a-Clan now, this was not a fellow Inquestor, to be treated with rigid formality.

"I know you are still thinking of the day you judged me," Davaryush said. "And wondering if you were wrong."

"How could I have been? An Inquestor's utterance defines truth by its very existence." Abrupty, as this Inquestral platitude left his lips, he realized what a formidable opponent Davaryush was. He had not even been playing seriously. He had just toyed with him, as a pteratyger paws the hollow air. Yet he had wrung from Elloran an admission of vulnerability.

Then he saw, as vividly as though a Rememberer stood by to conjure up the images, that day on Uran s'Varek: thousands of stern Inquestors on their hoverthrones, the sky unrelenting in its brilliance, the chanting of the words of rejection ... and the one sentence that Davaryush whispered in answer to the charges of heresy and utopianism: *The Inquest falls.* And the terrifying serenity of that smile.

"How is it," Elloran said, "that we stripped you of name and titles, yet you return more powerful than ever? *Atta heng,* Davaryush; you have vanquished me."

"You have vanquished yourself, Ton Elloran. A thinkhive told me that once. It was after I had made the decision to betray the Inquest. After I had seen the slaughter of the Windbringers on Gallendys, and learned how utterly the Inquest has renounced love."

"Command me, Daavye. Must I too lay godhood by? To me it has been more sweet than bitter, mostly."

"No. I want"—and the ancient's eyes shone like a child's-—"a thin small bridge across the chasm that is to come. A bridge like a rainbow darkness," he said, pausing as though remembering something out of history.

"Your words are dark."

"I am"—and Davaryush laughed at his own paradox—"the shadow of the shadow's shadow. When Kelver gained possession of the Throne of Madness, he set in motion all that I foresaw. But what do I have? Kelver has rejected me. I foresaw that too. For my great plan, it was better that he should hate me, that he should see the revolution as a struggle between good and evil, black and white ... and not between different shades of darkness. There are not just two colors, but as many colors as there are men. Why has it taken me so many centuries to know this simple truth? Because the Inquest stole my childhood from me and blinded me. I was no better off than the hunters in the Dark Country of Gallendys. Now that I've been reincarnated as a mere man, I'll need a new quest, won't I?"

"And what is that?"

"To find the homeworld of the heart, Loreh. To find a beginning place to balance out the catastrophic ending that is to come."

"As in the old song." A fleeting memory: wind, the wings of a pteratyger, rainbows that spanned the sky, the treble voice of young Sajit and his whisperlyre ... so long ago ... centuries? On some planets the story of young Elloran and Sajit had acquired the substance of myth; poems made allusions to it; plays were written that put stilted polymetrics into their boyish mouths.

"Will you come with me?"

And a truth dawned on Elloran: that the gray spaces of Sajit's song were not to be found in some physical place. He should have known better than to take the words at face value. That the silence between the stars could not, by itself, lead to madness or enlightenment. The true gray spaces were in the soul, and now they could never leave him.

"My mourning for Sajit must one day come to an end," he said, and with those words committed himself to an arduous new quest, as though he were once more a child Inquestor whose mettle had never been tested, facing Uran s'Varek for the first time.

Fourteen

The Theater of Dark Fantasy

And they came to Alykh, the pleasure planet. To Airang, the city of love, where turrets twisted like the tongues of lovers; where night never fell, for garish fireworks flared from every square of the city; where in the arenas robot dinosaurs trampled robot cities; where palatial floaters jammed the air and onlookers crammed into temples of passion and the poor jostled each other in the sewer labyrinth that veined the jeweled city with canals of filth.

Tya came with Jannif and a company of childsoldiers; they came to ride the varigrav coasters, klomet-high and studded with amethysts, that ringed the city. They rode to the towertops and leaped into the gravity currents, their rented wings batlike in the laser-striped sunset. The coasters only mimicked those of Shtoma, but the wind of their rushing was enough to drive out the grief with which Essondras's dying had imbued them.

They ran screaming through the city, led by a hired linkboy

whose hands spurted varicolored fire. From displacement plate to displacement plate they stormed, devouring the city as if it were a world to be burned, like in the old days, the old bad times. They waded through streams of zul peppered with candied tadpoles. Only once did Tya notice Jannif's face darken; and that was when she had casually mentioned the Prince of Shadow.

And Tya had said, "What is it, love?" and softly kissed the other woman's cheek, and bade her drink her zul from the goblet shaped like a severed hand, as the sunrise burst on their sleepless eyes in a room in an inn on the side of a mountain of granite and tinseldust.

"Darkfield the room," Jannif groaned. Tya thought at the window for a moment; there fell a sudden gloom.

"Why are you so upset? I only mentioned the Prince of Shadow, who is always in our thoughts."

Jannif said, "He didn't even show himself to us!"

"The face was in the planet, wasn't it? Don't be silly. You can't expect him to appear before us personally anymore. He's become so—"

"So godlike?" Perhaps, thought Tya, there was irony in her friend's voice.

"Yet you love him well enough."

"Well enough."

"Do you remember when our squadron crushed the planet's moons to powder? All those starry specks, like sparkling milk spilling into the sky?"

"You think it beautiful."

"How can I think otherwise? I was trained to be a childsoldier. I was pitiless once; Kelver changed me. But I still see beauty the same way."

"I wasn't thinking about how pretty it was at the time. I was thinking about hypocrisy ... we still fly around on delphinoid ships, don't we? Even though we know how they came into being. Yesterday, while settling our ship into orbit around Alykh, I felt ... an insane tugging at the back of my consciousness."

"What do you mean?" said Tya softly.

"Do you think the delphinoids feel pain? I've never thought of it. And the comets, the comets that the deathmoon dropped on Essondras ... they are powered by brains of childsoldiers trapped in a living death until they crash flaming on the planet's surface ... do they feel pain?"

"You think too much. I've known pain, Jannif. I am a child-soldier. But because of Kelver I don't mind it anymore."

"Oh, faith, faith."

"Do you doubt Kelver simply because you no longer see him? Oh, that is sad, my love. I would gladly have died for him on the plains of the plundered pleasure planet."

"But I—" Jannif paused. "Do you know that the Lady Siriss is missing?"

"Missing?"

"I spoke to the steward who guards her apartments. The thinkhives do not know where she has gone, or they're not telling us."

"What can that mean?" "I think I know."

"Oh, but you mustn't think of it anymore. Look, the sunrise through the darkfield. Sleep. Sleep." She went to Jannif, crouched on the pliant floor which contorted to envelop her spindly body, put her arms around the older woman. She seemed to sleep. But then she suddenly cried out, as though she were having a nightmare. And got up and seized her overcloak and said urgently, "We must leave, we must leave. They will go to Zorn, I know it, I understand it now."

Tya put on her iridium graviboots and knit their fiery laces with a subvocalized command. Reluctantly she put on the dark war-tunic and willed the laserimplant eyes to be ready. As always, the citrine irises dilated uncomfortably as the microcannon moved into place, as though an insect were crawling around inside her eyeball. Her eyes smarted; tears sprang to them. "I am too old to be a childsoldier," she said, "I ought to have them removed; my face has grown, my laser-irises no longer balance; someday they will go askew ... even now I misjudge the angle more often than not. Though it makes no difference if you're just carving up a mountain."

"Hurry! Hurry!"

Tya understood suddenly that her friend had somehow heard the call of the delphinoid; for they were psychically linked to their starship brains, these astrogators, and sometimes seemed to assume something of their otherworldly essence. That was why so many superstitions had sprung up around the clan of Kail. Jannif was frantic now. Did the delphinoid have some prescience of disaster, was that what had communicated itself to the star pilot? Tya could not tell. But she followed her lover from the inn, and they plated rapidly through the dawnbright city, hailed a hire-floater, raced past the ramparts of the city to the shuttlestation that would return them to the orbiting palace.

***

"We're lost, Zasha! Let go my hand. It's the other way." She slipped from his grasp. They stood at the confluence of countless alleyways: Zalo and Jenjen and Enshtewo and Jherwo the apprentice.

"Hush. I only meant to lose the others." Zalo wagged a finger at the boy; with a knowing wink Jherwo started to lead the old man back toward the jungle of passageways. "Go buy yourselves a drink," Zalo shouted after them, tossing Jherwo a credit disk from his sleeve.

"A girl more likely," Jherwo said, laughing. "At your age!" said Zalo.

"Be careful. Which of us are you insulting by that remark?" Enshtewo said sternly. Jenjen laughed. The city purred ... its background noise of bustling and jostling made it sound like a vast contented beast.

"Powers of powers!" Jenjen said at last. "Leave us alone." But her reproach was gentle. And suddenly they were by themselves, and all the city's sounds seemed far away: the braying of contrary floaters as they jammed the aircorridors between the buildings; the cries of merchants, pimps, and ragamuffins; the tinklejangling of street musicians. Jenjen said, "We *are* lost, Zasha."

"Does it matter?" For Alykh was the first alien planet Zalo had ever set eyes on, and he was so captivated by the newness of the sights and sounds, of the very air itself, of the daylight, that he was beginning to forget Essondras a little.

They turned at random, plated across a heart-shaped lake of purple water where skiers skimmed the waves on strings drawn by tame pterasaurs.

Ran laughing through a marketplace of slaves and servocorpses.

Bought, two for a gipfer, cheap songjewels, and played them, over and over, until the song ran stale; tossed them into the canal where naked children dived for them.

Reached a dark street called the Street of Theaters. "Sir, I will be your guide," a dirty girl piped up from behind a pillar of blue flame. "We need no guide."

"Surely you do! Are you not Zalo the playwright, whose world *fell beyond* a dozen years ago?"

A chill. He felt Jenjen's hand on his. "You must get used to this," she whispered in his ear. "We have been in the overcosm, and time has passed more quickly in the true universe. Don't you remember how we used to be the same age?"

"And now you're still young, but I am getting old," Zalo said, suddenly feeling the loss of his homeworld.

The child-guide said: "You're standing in front of a holotheater. There ahead of us, under the flashing archway, is a necrotheater, but it's not in the Essondran tradition; it's a troupe from the Deathbelt, a ring of radioactive asteroids in some godforsaken starsystem. The people wear lead-soaked skins all their lives, and only strip them off in death; only the dead appear truly human, and then only for a few sleeps before the irradiation renders them hideous. So the corpses are used to stage vast, bloody spectacles that remind the Deathbelters of a vanished and glorious past, before the people bins deposited them in their new land." The child rattled off this mini-lecture without emotion; she must, Zalo realized, have memorized some guidebook.

"And we thought *we* were oppressed by the Inquest."

"Shall I lead you to that theater, excellencies? The show is starting in a span or two. It is a new show; it's called ... *The Fall of Essondras,* I think—oh, forgive me, I forgot your origins—"

"Perhaps another time," Jenjen said quickly. "Here, for your pains." She handed her a demigipfer.

"But don't you want to see"—the child began to speak more quickly, and to jog alongside them to keep up with their adult strides—"the glorious history of Ton Alkamathdes as enacted by shadow puppets? The Fairytale Theater of Neuterchildren, honeyvoiced, angelfaced? The Splatterhouse, where mechanicals reproduce in every detail hideous crimes of ancient history?"

"I—" Zalo started to fend her off.

"The Carnal House? The Charnel House? The Theater of Dark Fantasy?" The girl did a sort of hopscotch dance around them. "I think they're doing *your* play there."

"Mine?"

"This you'll *have* to see," Jenjen said, holding on to his hand and resolutely leading him forward, following the ragged little girl into the portico of a low building that turned out to be the upper level of an underground colosseum.

***

A garish plaza flanked by pteratygers of stone; each tyger bore a temple in its paws, and escalators, like rivers of chromium fire, ascended into their open jaws. Crowds milling about on the flagstones. The air hazy, sultry; the sun masked by a cloud-sculpture and a team of artisans, on floaters, buzzing busily about it, spraying fluffstuff into its crannies, restoring details that the wind had bled away.

Arryk came with Siriss pursuing; Ton Karakaël, still recovering from the emotional catharsis of the burning of Essondras, had not brought himself yet to leave orbiting Kilimindi and set foot on Alykh or in Airang, the City of Love.

Siriss called his name. He didn't answer. He kept striding ahead; she could hardly make out the speck of shimmerfur amid the sea of cloaks and hairpieces. As the crowd shifted, a displacement plate was uncovered, a silver slab in the midst of sandstone flagstones. She seized her chance, ducked through the crowd toward it, subvoked a command, came out ahead of him-

"Sirissheh!" He ran headlong into her arms.

"Why are we even here?" she said. "You set out so relentlessly for Zorn, I thought we would arrive there almost as I uttered its name...." She paused, trying not to remind herself of her role as the betrayer of the Prince of Shadow.

"It is our custom," Arryk said, "after a game of *makrúgh,* to come to the pleasure planet and to exorcise some of our perennial melancholy; isn't that so? Kelver has forced us to break so many customs, but surely we can cling to just this one?"

"Of course." Siriss understood well. For millennia privileged men had come to such worlds as Alykh to cleanse themselves of grief. "I should not begrudge you these few hours of happiness." For when they had made love, angrily, violently, after she had spoken the short word that undid what the deaths of a hundred thousand childsoldiers had wrought, she had realized that, however desperately she desired it, time would never again stand still; not for her, not for the whole Dispersal of Man. There had been a few perfunctory words of tenderness, then nothing more. And because she was Inquestor as well as woman, she felt not only resentment but also compassion.

For this was not the Arryk she had left behind on Uran s'Varek. This Arryk was Karakaël's creature. It seemed that Arryk had consumed all the pent-up anger in Karakaël that day when the Lady Varuneh had unmasked to all the secrets of the Lord of a Million Masks. But was he totally subsumed into Karakaël's hatred, or did there yet remain some fragment of Arryk? In their lovemak ing there was none of the old Arryk at all. Although she had been convinced that it was Kelver himself, in the guise of the Lady Varuneh, who had instigated his own betrayal, she was again uncertain. But she knew she must cling to Arryk now, she must not turn back, for with Kelver's descent into madness Arryk had become the one survivor of her time of happiness, her days as a young Inquestrix newly awakened to her power.

Trying to change the subject, she said, "What are these temples? They weren't here when we last came here."

"That was probably a century ago in their time."

For Airang was nothing if not fluid; suburbs and exurbs rose up and disappeared overnight, and shanty palaces sprang up to house temporary spectacles, and were dissolved in a single day. And religions were even more mutable on this planet. "Yet," said Arryk, noting that there were four temples, one for each side of the plaza, "they are more solidly built than most. These aren't just faddish whimsies, Siriss."

"Why don't you command their thinkhives to explain themselves?"

"A good idea," Arryk said, for he seemed anxious for some diversion. For the Inquestors, who were themselves like gods, deriding the cults of the shortlived was one sure way of getting a laugh. Siriss watched as Arryk closed his eyes, using subvoked Inquestral words of power to unlock the temple thinkhives' power of speech.

A curious thing happened then. Later she would remember that the sun appeared to darken, although there was no darkfield over the whole city-that would have entailed too much expense. She didn't notice this now, for smoke had begun to issue from the mouths of the four pteratygers, and the throng, which had seemed to be randomly clustered about the square, was silenced and prostrated themselves to a man. Some faced the western temple; some the northern; still others the south and east. And in the smoke she read, as she turned from cloud to cloud, ringing the plaza with faintly acetic fumes, four sequences of words: first these, in letters that rippled like seawater:

VARA THE ONE MOTHER
SHE WHO UNLEASHED THE THUNDER WHO SPRANG
FROM THE SERPENT'S WOMB
WHO SITS OVER THE ENDLESS SEA WHO WAITS FOR
THE DARKNESS
TO WHOM DARKNESS IS JOY

And to one side, in characters tossed hither and thither by an artwind:

SIRISS THE UNDECIDED
SHE WHO SPOKE THE WORD OF UNBINDING WHO
LOVED THE LIGHT AND THE DARKNESS WHO FEARS TO
WAIT FOR THE DARKNESS
TO WHOM DARKNESS IS SORROW

And before them, in words shaped like clods of earth, wherein crawled carrion worms:

ARRYK OF THE ANCIENT DARKNESS HE WHO
SCOURGES THE COSMOS
WHO HATES THE DARKNESS WITH ALL HIS MIGHT
WHO KNOWS THAT THE DARKNESS COMES
TO WHOM DARKNESS IS EXTINCTION

And to their left, in figures of brilliant flame:

KELVER OF THE FUTURE DARKNESS
HE WHO BURNS THE RAINBOW
WHO LONGS FOR THE DARKNESS
WITH ALL HIS MIGHT
WHO KNOWS NOT THAT DARKNESS WILL COME
TO WHOM DARKNESS IS REBIRTH

"What nonsense!" Arryk said uncomfortably. But Siriss knew that there was some truth in all four of the inscriptions. It was true that the Lady Varuneh had set the Inquest in motion; it was true that Siriss had vacillated endlessly, and was even now unsure of her true mind; true too that Arryk had chosen to stand for the way things always had been, and that Kelver had played on men's longing for new beginnings. But why was the word *darkness* present in all those inscriptions?

"You're right," she said, hoping that Arryk would take her cue and leave. "It's silly, abominably silly! That's what these shortlived get for syncretizing us into their foolish religions. They must have something to worship, alas, and we're it!"

"Something's strange about all this. I'm going in."

"No Arryk, no—" But she admitted to herself that it had been this very impetuosity of his that had first drawn her to him so long ago....

"We should get to the bottom of all this." He eyed the still-prone crowd with contempt. "Look at how they idolize us. It's something for the utopia commission to consider, even! It seems harmless enough, this cult—even though they seem to equate me with the forces of evil—"

"Do they, though? I see ambiguity everywhere."

"Harmless enough at first, but sinister in hindsight ... seeding false hope in a discontented populace ... powers of powers, it *is* some kind of insidious utopia-mongering, I'm sure of it!"

"I suppose we should go inside."

"We must see everything. Do not forget. We are Inquestors. Perhaps we are the last of the true Inquestors, the last bearers of the seed of compassion."

"Yes. We are Inquestors." But she would not enter the temple that bore her own name, nor that of the Prince of Shadow.

"What! So cowardly? You thought nothing of giving me the name a hundred thousand died to protect!"

"Must you remind me?" No, this could not be Arryk she had loved; this was a man possessed by the desire to give pain. And yet he called on the name of compassion.

"All right. I will take the first step," he said.

In his violet eyes she saw a hint of his old vulnerability; but he masked it quickly. They plated to the paws of the crouching pteratyger and ascended the flaming escalator to the portals of its jaws, whose holographic teeth quivered unsteadily in the glare of sunlight and advertising signs.

***

They raced to the field where four shuttlecannon rose, their snouts aimed at the quarters of the sky. Jannif and Tya and others who had heard Jannif cry out on their farspeakers, and who had plated through the city in reply.

They found the right cannon, waited in line, anxiously eyeing the passing of time. They strapped themselves into the shuttlebubbles; Tya huddled close to Jannif as the gravity wrench took hold of them and they were flung skyward.

They sprang from brilliance into starstrewn darkness. In the half-light Tya saw her lover's face; it was contorted in some private agony, and she knew that her mind was touching the mind of the great ship shecontrolled.

Tya said, "What is it? Don't hurt so much, don't hurt, my darling."

And Jannif said: "What pain it feels! What pain! It was touched by the edge of-the edge of—"

"What?" Tya said, alarmed. "A whispershadow."

"What is that?"

An ancient astrogator spoke up, his withered face cratered by the dim light: "I have heard of them. Perhaps it is a myth. I thought I too felt it, a little....

"But what does it mean?"

"It is the prescience of a star's death. If it has touched our delphinoid, who knows what may happen? It may drive our ship insane— "

"It's gone now," Jannif said, breathing heavily. "Gone."

Such emptiness in her eyes, and such unwonted grief. Tya unlatched her brace—they were beyond the gravity crush of takeoff now, and she could see their starship growing in the gloom-and went to sit by Jannif. "It was no myth, old man. It touched me. But it is gone. And somehow ... somehow I feel terribly betrayed."

***

In the maw of the stone beast was a huge marketplace. There were crystal booths for soothsayers and stalls for religious paraphernalia. There were holosculptures of Arryk's face; statues of him in four-armed and eight-armed postures, dancing his anger over the corpses of childsoldiers.

"I don't like this image of myself," Arryk said. "It was Kelver, not I, who sought out the path of shadow."

"It's just a religion," Siriss said, trying to reassure him. "I must hide my face. Perhaps it wouldn't be well for them to know that they are being visited by their god." A convoy of childsoldier-assassins, black-tunicked and black-maned, sped through the mob, ululating their shrill paean. Arryk threw his shimmercloak over his face; sensing his intention, it molded itself into a mask. Siriss did the same. Now she saw the marketplace through veils of rose and ultramarine. The crowd parted for the lnquestors, but they were not recognized. The marketplace was dark and dank; thin lightshafts, from vents in the roof of the pteratyger's mouth, striped the darkness. An unpleasant smell wafted from further down the stone gullet.

"What an aroma!" Siriss said. Glowing brilliantly as they endeavored to purify the air around the two of them, their shimmercloaks rustled and hissed, so that their faces seemed to be pulsating.

"Perhaps we should duck into ... into that reliquary,"

Arryk said, pointing to a sign over a pavilion whose awning was of a fabric woven from still-fibrillating serpents. Here and there a priest went sternly about his business, now and then thrashing a passing celebrant with his bloody flagellum. The priests eyed the lnquestors nervously.

They entered the pavilion.

"Masters! Inquestors, no less!" a crone with filthy matted

hair spoke to them. "And do you wish for surcease of your pain? I will provide. Or do you come for a piece of the true stone childsoldier?" When Siriss looked around she saw statues of childsoldiers twisted into anguished poses. So lifelike were they, she could have sworn that they had been time-frozen in their torment and petrified in the moment of their dying.

"What are these statues?" she said.

Under his body-veil of shimmerfur, she saw that Arryk was shaking under the burden of some terrible grief.

"My Lord and Lady, I am surprised you should ask. Why, these are the calcified corpses of the soldiers whom the God Arryk caused to be tortured until they would reveal the location of the Prince of Shadow. One piece of such a statue, worn about the neck, can give one strength to resist a thousand tortures, and can lock within your heart the most dreadful secret, so that it may never be extracted from you. That is their special quality—"

"You looted the fields of stone childsoldiers?" Arryk cried out.

"Ah, but it is such ancient history," the old woman croaked.

"It seems like a few spans ago," Arryk said, for Siriss alone. Aloud he said, "Superstition, all superstition."

"My Lord is pleased to mock my religion," the old woman said defiantly.

"As you mock me!" Arryk screamed, stripping the shimmercloak from his face. And the woman, seeing the visage of her god, fell down and worshiped him. But Arryk would not speak to her.

Finally it was Siriss who, lifting her gently to her feet, said, "Woman, who is it who built these temples, who has constructed from the sordid details of our lives such an elegant mythos?"

And the old woman said, trembling, "Inquestors, it is said that no human agency built these temples. Of course, the skyline of Airang shifts so constantly that to see a new plaza spring up thus, by magic, is nothing noteworthy; yet usually they are but holosculptures, insubstantial facades projected over dull pavilions of force and canvas. These temples were remarked on because they were hewn from solid rock, rock, it was said, such as is found only in the crust of Uran s'Varek, the dwelling of the gods. It was said that a thinkhive built them, a thinkhive not quite sane."

"The Throne of Madness!" Siriss cried.

"Sedition, here, in the heart of the Dispersal!" Arryk shouted. For Alykh was no backworld, but a center of galactic commerce and a crossroads of thousands of overcosmic paths. "We must waste no more time. Kelver has broken another tradition for us! There will no longer be a gentlemanly respite from the struggles of *makrúgh;* no time of healing, no cleansing of inner griefs. We must go on to Zorn at once! Kelver will not have waited."

"What will you do to Zorn?"

"I will destroy it utterly. I will despoil myself of compassion, that the Inquest may survive to feel compassion. Perhaps I shall destroy myself as well."

"If you haven't done so already," Siriss said.

Before they left, she paused to buy one of the stone amulets. It was the finger of a childsoldier; there was a trace of laser-implant beneath the marble fingernail. She selected a chain of ivory in which were embedded shavings of sardonyx.

"Why did you bring back one of those grisly souvenirs?" Arryk was to ask, much later, when their palace had sounded the overcosm and left Alykh universes behind.

"Who knows?" she would say. "If as she told us they can lock men's hearts, so that no secret can ever be wrung from them again ... perhaps it's just what I need." And thought of Kelver and of his splintered soul.

"You have already yielded the only secret that had to be yielded." These words cruelly said; they stung her; silently she wept. And then he would say, "But I still love you, Sirissheh of the opal eyes."

And she would not know whether to feel joy or remorse, that he still loved her. And in the overcosmic nights, the lightstorm raging about them, they would make love in silence; it was as though each embraced a pleasure corpse culled from one of Airang's many brothels of the dead.

***

It was a strange, much downscaled performance; Jenjen found it hard at first to get used to the lack of technical effects. Crowd scenes, rather than put together from a mass of half animated corpses, consisted of only a few people—live humans on whose faces a ghastly makeup, simulating death, had been applied. There was no scenery; instead, stylized holosculptures were projected onto a cloud of swirling mist stage center, and a wizened old man sat silhouetted in the heart of the mist. The man seemed to do nothing; for being live actors, the performers were linked to no master corpse dancer. But the words were all Zalo's. Instead of being intoned in the ritualized, rhythmic style proper to corpses, which emphasized beauty of cadence and inhuman control of air intake and phrasing, these words came tumbling forth rapidly, in a welter of emotions, as living humans converse. And though Jenjen had heard of such a style of acting before, this was the first time she'd seen it in the flesh, and it was overwhelming; there was something almost lascivious about the way the words danced from those humans' lips. She'd never known that Zalo's poetry carried such an emotional charge, or that it was so close to the pulse of true human discourse. Divorced from the sophisticated stage magic of the Royal Theater of Ikshatra, the words had acquired a fierce, painful reality.

It was as the play ended, when the cantor's voiceover, punctuated by the strains of a single whisperlyre, sang out the play's concluding words, that Jenjen found herself weeping openly. For the words were:

But he knew they were just acting now,
Clinging to the last moments of the utopia
As the ear clings to a whisperlyre's shimmerfade
After the song is done.

Zalo was about to say something. But the actor who had played Ton Elloran put up his hand to silence the applause (it was thoughtful applause, not the deafening crowdroar of Ikshatra) and said, "This is a very special performance. The moment we've been waiting for for years. It was twelve years ago that the tachyon tidings of Essondras's *falling beyond* first came to Alykh; riding the overcosm, the survivors of that world's destruction have only just reached us. It has only been a few sleeps for Zalo er-Karnofarat, master necrodramatist; for us it has been time enough for his *Rainbow King* to have become accepted as a classic, a work that challenges and changes forever the parameters of our art. And"—he pointed at Zalo in the audience—"Zalo has come here at last to reap the reward that is great artists' due—"

Light fell on the two lovers. "I'm dreaming," Zalo said softly. "Back on Essondras they'd never have said something like that openly."

"Of course not!" Jenjen said. "How could a corpse turn around and address a playwright of its own free will?"

Free will ...

"Our homes are dust, our world is dead, but—"

"Freedom! Now it strikes home."

Applause came at last.

And after, Jenjen and Zalo toured the pits beneath the stage, and she learned more about this troupe. They were from Ikshatra; one, Sterwon, was even an old acquaintance of theirs. They'd all been the same age once. But Sterwon was now twelve years Zalo's senior. Apparently an Inquestor, on a whim, had spirited them to Alykh long before the *falling beyond;* news of Zalo's play and its daring innovations had reached them while Zalo sailed the overcosm. They'd added many twists of their own, affecting a naturalistic style that took full advantage of the actors' humanness.

In an old dressing room, they sat sipping zul for many hours, while an endless stream of celebrity-gawkers and frotteurs jammed past them. Over and over Zalo and Jenjen were asked for their versions of the last days of Essondras. One of the players had a smuggled holodisk of the last flight of the embalming-bird; it seemed that there was much black-market traffic in recordings of planetary destructions, which sold in equal measure to megalomaniac sadists and to those grieving for lost worlds.

"And you? Which are you?" Jenjen asked the owner of the disk, when this was explained to her.

"A little of both," he said facetiously. His tactlessness offended her somewhat, until she reflected that for him the destruction she had just witnessed was, through time dilation, a stale story, almost ancient history.

"And what did you think of our little performance?" Jenjen heard a young man say. "Those born on Essondras tell me that nothing can match the spectacle of a performance in the Royal Theater; and of course, being unable to afford large numbers of corpses, we have lately relied more and more on humans, thanks to your brilliant innovations—"

"Do you mean," Jenjen said, thoughtfully sipping from a zul-flask in which floated the gelatinized thorax of a violet mockinghopper, "that you do not even come from Essondras? Are you one of the stagehands, then?"

The young man laughed, and said, "I am Tarlo, the play's director"—he bowed gracefully *to* Zalo—"and your humble interpreter, master corpse dancer."

Zalo looked a little uneasy; Jenjen found it difficult to grasp that a man from another planet would be interested in, let alone so much in tune with, an art form which must be culturally and philosophically alien to him.

Divining their discomfort, Turlo said, "Understand, master corpse dancer: I am third-generation Essondrish. My grandparents received clan-names and became starbome; they settled here. My father lost all interest in things Essondrish; in my childhood I was a boy without a homeworld, lost, for Airang is a floating island, unanchored in any culture, vapid, thriving on transience. When this troupe settled in town, it was an opportunity for me to find roots again. I always admired your work, Master Zalo, because you were always ready to experiment ... I haunted used holodiskshops for pirated tapes of your necrodramas, I played them until I wore them out ... I hope you don't think I'm being unconscionably fannish, master corpse dancer, but you're my childhood idol, and—"

"But I am not *that* much older than you?"

"Time dilation, Zasha—" said Jenjen gently.

"Exactly! I was expecting someone of at least Inquestral years—"

"With a long white beard, I don't doubt!" Zalo said, laughing.

They talked of inconsequential things, then of more important ones, such as the new facepainting techniques the Street of Theaters had developed in the past five years, in which laserholomasks were projected over the actor's entire face from a thin headband that contained a microthinkhive keyed to the main facial muscles, so that the pseudoface was able to react instantly to any change of expression. Zalo complained that it made the expressions less naturalistic; Tarlo said it was primitive but they were working on it; Zalo resisted; Jenjen accused him of becoming as conservative as old father pisspot. It was then that Tarlo asked Zalo the question which he had clearly been longing to ask all evening: "Master Zalo, will you stay on Alykh? I mean, this whole theater and all its resources are at your disposal, and I'd be only too happy to relinquish my directorship to some one as distinguished as you—"

And Jenjen saw that Zalo was tempted; she saw that it would not be a bad thing to happen for either of them. For the city of Airang was a spectacle worthy to be woven into many a tapestry of darkness, and she would lack none of the raw materials for her art in so polyplanetary a culture. But was it enough?

"The revolution—" she blurted out.

Tarlo and the other actors looked away, embarrassed. There was silence in the room, and Jenjen noticed for the first time that the crowd had thinned to only a few actors and diehard fans. Finally someone said: "But isn't the revolution valid only as a conceptual image? It's more symbol than fact, surely; a metaphor to play with in the drama, an unalterable fact of the human condition. But who would want to sweep away all this?—"

Jenjen said: "I—"

"The Inquestors are gods," said the same actor. "Let them war in heaven. Let their strife not touch us, for we are artists whose function is to record the human condition for all ages, not to fight ourselves—"

"No!" Jenjen exclaimed. "If only you'd seen it all. How the childsoldiers, catapulted from the maws of giant starships, thickened the night sky, bright as day from the comets' bursting ... I don't want it to have been in vain!"

And Zalo said, "I don't either. Remember, it was I who set free the embalming birds ... I whose words roused the throng to anti-Inquestral frenzy ... whose words moved them to choose suicide rather than subjugation to the Inquest! You've never seen these things. Oh, if you only had, Tarlo. Perhaps it is ancient history to you, but to me it is only a few sleeps, and those sleeps sleepless with self-torment."

In that tense moment, Jenjen heard a purring noise in her head. "My farspeaker!" she said.

A faint voice: "This is Kail Jannif of the Shadow of Inquest. We are going to be sounding the overcosm in only a few hours. If anyone is still in Airang, they must report back at once, or be left behind ... urgent, urgent, urgent!"

"We must go back!" Jenjen said.

"Please," Tarlo said, "reconsider. It would mean so much for our art—"

"Hurry!" Jenjen said, panicking.

"Why don't *you* come with *us?* You've never left a world behind, have you, let alone a world in ashes," Zalo said. "And yet you interpret my plays." The man stared at them, mouth wide open. "I had a vision once, as I left behind my burning world ... it was of a new theater, where my arena would be all time and space! All that was left of Essondras's necrodrama stood in that little shuttlecraft bound for a dilapidated people bin: me and old Enshtewo and the little boy Jherwo, and yet I burned with ambition more intense than any I had ever felt in my life. I had so little, I longed for so much! Do you dare to dream so? Will you join my theater of the gray spaces, of the unknown, of the feared, of the dark future? Is this fantasy dark enough for you?"

For the longest split second the young man hesitated.

Then he said, "You've challenged me, Master. I will go." Other voices: "And I!"

"And I!"

"And I!"

And Jenjen saw her lover smile for the first time since they had departed their doomed world.

THE CHILD FROM THE FUTURE

The Prince of Shadow fled to his secret kingdom, the city in the eye of a cloud, on a world whose name Ton Siriss had dared to whisper.

Arryk pursued with new armies and new machineries of death.

But who would fly the starships of the Prince of Shadow?

And who, seeing with the eyes of a delphinoid, would foretell the approach of Karakaël the heartless?

-from Zalo's *The Darkling Wind*

Fifteen
The Overcosm

A sudden grief, as of the loss of ancient love ... a wavering of the starfield, then an intense fireburst as though they had materialized in the heart of a giant sun ... a lightwind storming about the deopaqued observatory aboard Kail Jannif's starship. They no longer traveled in Varezhdur, but as Jannif's guests on the ship named Daranava *Sirisshtasieh,* the Starship *Siriss's Joy.* It was one of only seventeen true warships that Kelver's fleet contained; most were pleasure vessels, converted summer palaces, even cargo ships. And then there were also the reconditioned people bins that contained the escaped Essondrish people; that convoy hung from the snowflake palace's edge like a string of silver bullets. But Zalo could see none of this now; only the madness of cascading lightshapes that was all his mind could make of the overcosm.

"I felt it keenly," Zalo said, "especially the grief."

"Yes. But you'll grow accustomed to it, and in time it will be only a momentary dissonance." Jannif opened her eyes and dissociated herself from the astrogating trance. "You seem disturbed still? But you have a natural talent for starseeking, I see. Not many people can feel such empathy with the delphinoid shipminds. Among us astrogators it is said that only the noble of soul can truly feel what the delphinoid feels. I myself. .. perceive only dimly; enough to pull my way through the pinhole paths of the overcosm, but not enough to participate **in** the philosophic aspects of astrogating."

"Though you've told me yourself that you wonder if the delphinoids feel pain, and that this has caused you sometimes to doubt the rightness of the Way of Shadow."

"I think we all, at some stage, come to question the way things are. And yet ... here we are, in a region neither space nor time, and the lightstorm rages and we are untouched ... where would this be without the delphinoids? And where would man be?"

"I cannot tell," said Zalo.

Fireflowers exploded about them. Waterfalls of light cascading; colors sluicing the not-sky; they were awash in a field of cerulean, no, emerald, no, crimson, no, viridian, no, brilliant purple. Even as he named the colors, they shifted, and soon they became colors so strange he could no longer name them. "It is a wilderness," he said, "it isn't beautiful. Not like a line of verse in a necrodrama, ordered, every syllable weighed and colored with just the right consonants and vowels. It's just chaos, isn't it? Not even the chaos that artists sometimes represent, which in itself is ordered by the artist's passionate conceit. I cannot love this chaos." It was disturbing to him that Jenjen felt drawn to the light-mad overcosm. It was a part of her he had never touched, a wild thing. Where was she now? he wondered. Probably in one of the many other observation decks of the starship, staring at the overcosm and thinking of the songs the delphinoids once sang in the days of their freedom, when they roamed the heavy winds of Gallendys.

"Had enough?" Jannif asked him. "I think so."

But he had felt, in the raging chaos around him, the delphinoid's touch, the sense of a transcendent order; for though the delphinoid's song had been forever silenced when it was captured on Gallendys and its brain welded into the starship's hull, it was this selfsame song, tuned to the secret rhythms of the overcosm, that allowed men to travel the pinhole paths between thestars.

Surely, he thought, even if the revolution comes to pass, men will not give up star travel. Will they work out some truce with the delphinoids, or will they continue to enslave them, to treat them as though they were of no more consequence than machines?

Abruptly he turned and began to leave, and Jannif opaqued the observatory once more, and he saw where it was they truly stood: the heartroom of the starship, a chamber whose very walls were the gray matter of the shipmind, thick nerves pulsating, rheum oozing from the coiled convolutions. Here and there a technician, armed with a nutrient nozzle, flitted by on a hoverdisk and sprayed the crevasses in the brain tissue. Now and then pale flashes of colored light suffused the chamber. "What are the lights?" he asked Jannif. "Echoes of what might have been: but they are to the lightsongs as a death-rattle is to a beautiful aria of Shen Sajit, Zalo."

"Is the shipmind dying, then?"

"It is only half alive; after they are captured, the delphinoids subsist in a half-world, unable to die completely because we force them to live, unable to live because they have been deprived of their ability to move by themselves."

"It is a great tragedy. Someone should tell their story." "I try not to think of such things, Zalo. Will you come by next sleep, so I can teach you more of astrogating? I said once, as we watched Essondras dying, that our new freedom meant that you could even become a star pilot, and I an actor—"

"I'll come back," Zalo said, laughing, "if you promise to come to one of my rehearsals. And if I can bring young Jherwo, who longs, as you know, to learn all your secrets."

"Of course."

And Zalo went to find Jenjen and the others, leaving the star pilot to fall once more into her trance of astrogating.

Elsewhere in the overcosm, in a place neither near nor far from the flotilla of starships clustered around the twinned palaces of Sharamonda and Varezhdur, which were now bound for the hidden world Zorn, Arryk was amassing a new armada. He and Karakaël and Siriss stood in their own observatory and watched the same raging light that Zalo and Jannif watched. The same but not the same; for the madding lightstorms of the overcosm were an illusion, a poor attempt by unequipped human brains to force human sense upon a place that was not a place, where the laws of spacetime were in constant flux. The three Inquestors who defended the ancient ways stood, as did their enemies, in a cleopaqued chamber and watched the dancing of the lights; each saw in the storm a reflection of some private nightmare.

"What do you see?" Arryk said to the others. For what he saw most of all was Kelver's eyes: mountains and mountains of Kelver's eyes. Kelver's eyes in the cores of exploding suns. In the wavecrests of lakes of fire. Eyes melting and fibrillating in undulating tapestries of dark flame.

Siriss said, as though she perceived his unspoken thoughts, "I see him too."

Karakaël said, scoffing, "What a couple of lovesick idiots you are! You are the best the High Inquest has to offer? How can this be? Even as we close in for the slaughter, you yearn to be united with this Prince of Shadow, and to know his love once more. Must galactic issues be reduced to such petty relationships?"

"You forget compassion, Ton Karakaël z Karakit Kerún!" said Arryk. "You dare to relish the destruction of fellow Inquestors? It is true that the greater compassion forces us to rub out Kelver's minions for the sake of the salvation of the Dispersal of Man"—he himself was surprised by the irony with which those words came to his lips—"but it does not demand that we take sadistic pleasure in these acts! No: we should be ruthless, but we should mourn our ruthlessness. We should kill, but we should feel grief at our bereavement!

"So Elloran taught me. So I shall continue to believe,

though Elloran himself has turned traitor to his kind."

"Oh, Rikeh, Rikeh," Karakaël said. His tenderness held an edge of menace. "Always the rationalizer; always the one to cling tenaciously to ancient concepts. Don't you realize, child, that the age of noble Elloran is done with once and for all? The struggle is no longer one of ideologies; it is over whether you and I will be the ones to relinquish the galactic power—or they! It is childish to speak of ideals now, Rikeh."

"You should not speak that way," Siriss said, "or all that we do is in vain."

"In vain! You call power over a million worlds vain!" Fire glowed in Karakaël's mummy eyes, and as he shook his head the ingrained sackcloth writhed beneath the skin of his cheeks. "It is impossible to deal with such as you. The Inquestral philosophy is all very well, but has it ever shot down a single star from the sky? Yet with our power we have even been known to kindle stars themselves, have driven them to nova."

"Peace, then," Arryk said bitterly. "I shall talk no philosophy with you. We shall have a truce; our foe is too great for us to war amongst overselves. Yet I tell you that when the war is done, I will play such a *makrúgh* against you as the galaxy has never seen, and I will choke your ambition with your own uncompassion. And I'll see that the High Inquest strips you of your name ... for uncompassion is as anathematic to the Inquest as the heresy of utopianism!"

But Karakaël only laughed, and called him a boy, and left him with Siriss in the observatory. Presently Siriss, unable to quiet his anxiety, plated away to another part of Kilimindi.

When Arryk found himself alone, he bestirred himself and summoned an entourage of linkboys and armed childsoldiers and a buccaneer; and he went to find the chamber of the clan of Aush, whose members designed new and ever more elegant ways of sowing death.

***

Deeper and deeper into the trance, which those of the clan of Kail called by the highspeech word *darashédza,* star fever ... deeper and deeper into the overcosm.

He lost all sense of place now; it was the ultimate sensory deprivation. Only just barely, as through a metallic barrier, could he hear Jannif's instructions: "Concentrate. Don't try to mesh completely with the delphinoid's consciousness. If you fall totally under its spell you may never be able to climb out again ... think of a thread in a labryrinth ... don't let go of the thread or you'll lose the way."

He focused his mind on the image of a thread of force ... forced the picture to the surface of consciousness —"I can't make it appear!" he gasped, barely able to hear his own voice. "I can't, I can't!" But as he said this it materialized in the thick darkness around him, a thin line of laser brilliance stretching from him to infinity.

And then, at once, a whole web of lightlines coiling, twisting, arrowing, pulsating. "Don't lose your grip!" he heard Jannif's voice, stronger now. "All the threads are one; all the pinhole paths are a single path, tangled but whole!" In his mind he gripped the thread harder; he imagined himself seizing it, tying it around and around his waist, knotting it tight. Anchor myself, he thought. Think of necrodrama: think of reaching out with your mind and snapping the subvoke commands that make a dead thing seem to live. It's not that different, he realized suddenly. That must be why Jannif says I'm good at it.

"Now!" A voice that was not a voice, more like a flickering grid of manycolored light. "Grab my hand with yours."

"But I have no hands in this reality..."

He had felt himself try to speak these words, but had only produced more flickers. His were more jagged, less garishly colored; they were like painted lightning, with exaggerated forks.

"*Make* hands!"

And he found himself a hand that was more like a nebulous patch of light, and it found a whorl of lightstreaks that was Jannif's, and when the two spectral hands came together the light lattice that surrounded them became unbearably brilliant, and he wished he had eyelids to squeeze tight shut against the glare, and even as he wished it, it was as though a darkfield englobed them both.

"Nice move," said the aurora that was Jannif's voice. "Now stay close; we're going on a trip like you've never imagined possible— ”

That grief again! He knew now that his mind was brushing against the delphinoid's pain, the aching that had been a permanent part to all the delphinoid's thought processes since it had been captured and sentenced to this living death. This sense of loss was like background radiation in the delphinoid's secret inner universe.

“Sink beneath the pain,” came Jannif's not-voice.

“How can I?” he cried out, but as he spoke he felt himself submerge deeper still, and his not-eyes smarted from the searing of the flamethreads. He screamed, and his agony made bursts of purple lightning.

And abruptly the pain was gone. He stood in a place where all the lightthreads met. And knew that he was at the kernel of a vast intellect. And *knew* that order underlay the overcosm, though what that order was he could not conceive. It was as if he were a microbe racing through a man's bloodstream, a bacterium that had somehow been endowed with a rudimentary ability to glimpse the godlike intelligence of its host. He felt infinitesimally light, bodiless, free.

“Come race with me!” said Jannif (he felt her beside him, clutching the same thread, the shadow of her being smudging what would otherwise have been a flawless matrix of lightlines) and began to pull him with her ... they shrank (or the lightgrid grew) until they were able to soar through the threads like insects in a shaft of incandescence. And then—

Flight! Total freedom! Weightlessness! He was one with the lightstream. He cried out in his voice of many colors: “Where are we going, Kail Jannif?”

And heard her response, rainbow-edged: “We are following the pinhole paths at random now. We are in the delphinoid's mind. Soon we will become aware of other starships as they too thread the space between spaces ... we will commune with them, sing with them in a profound harmony—”

More light now, lattices within lattices, layer upon layer of firegauze, lightveils ripped asunder to reveal more lightveils, and then he saw them—

“Our convoy,” Jannif's voice, floating, bell-like. “Look ...

that cloud of light there, that is the palace Varezhdur and its attendant satellites ... that swirling nebula is the palace Sharamonda ... see how they whirl about each other ... see them speak their names in a language of light ... can you understand it?"

This was even more intense than the experience of controlling corpses. It was as if the corpses could speak back to the corpse dancer in a secret language, a language that could discuss the shapes and colors and smells of things without ever touching upon the things themselves, a language of total abstraction. No wonder the delphinoids, on their own planet, were completely blind and deaf to the universe of the human continuum! Their minds were attuned to a universe untainted by any notion of the material; the idea of substantiality, of *thingness,* could not be expressed in it at all. And Zalo, who being human could not conceive of a thing that was not a thing, who could not see without seeing or hear without hearing, was glimpsing the other reality through the mind of a starship. He breathed a thousand alien airs and heard unearthly music and saw forms that could not be named. There were places where the light gathered into nodes of brilliance that would be blinding if he were seeing with his eyes; these Jannif called other starships, and suddenly he knew all their names: Kevrellonamah, Tathenhhasha, Varingovaresh, Rutnin, Qatnaqatwopel, Ixtapreun. Each name was like a strand of some cosmic counterpoint.

"Shall we wander the overcosm now?" Jannif said. "But you must hold fast to your thread, or you will never return to your body."

Hurtling starstreaks through the sunhaze running the last sight of the embalming-bird's grief spasm articulated joy ... another concentrated conflagration ... far far far ... star ships bound on distant errands on worlds on the Inquest's periphery, worlds where the name Inquestor already meant nothing more than a dream of long-dead glories ... blood and tears spurting from the pale sky ... "Hurry past, Zalo, it's a whispershadow, don't touch it don't cross it hurry hurry hurry ... " starfields overlaying starfields overlaying starfields overlaying starfields overlaying—

Terror. Abrupt. "Grip the thread!" Jannif cried. Wildly knotting the lightstream about his not-waist again and again and again and—

Terror.

Darkness, growing.

The voice of Jannif, impossibly faint now: "Those starships ... not our friends ... they bear us ill ... they are close by in our overcosmic plane, they are cloaked by a tachyon field ..."

Darkness. And in the darkness—

Men on fire! Stalking. Strutting. "What are they?"

The aura that burned about these flaming men ... the meanings it projected in the language of color ... he understood it instantly: it was hate!

"I don't know! But I have to get back, you understand? The fleet can't stay together. We have to sound farther into the overcosm, into the most madness-provoking region, or else—"

The flaming men advanced spitting armed children from their eyes uprooting mountains trampling cities-

And Zalo heard Jannif's voice, no longer clothed in light but a human voice, jarring, hideously dissonant with the delphinoid vision: *"Sound sound sound sound sound!"*

And snapped back to consciousness in the starship's control room, in time to hear Jannif saying: "You did well, Zalo. I'd have sworn you were an apprentice in the house of Kail."

"What happened?" Brightness: he could barely stand to open his eyes. Great walls of brain tissue quivering, slick with nutrient liquid. "It was all so beautiful, and suddenly it was as if we were under siege!"

"No time now. We've got to sound, we're being followed, someone who doesn't like us is tracking us. In the old days Inquestor never fought Inquestor, that was the one thing you were never afraid of when you skimmed through the secret world inside the delphinoid's mind, but ... "

"What'Il we do?"

"We'll split up the convoy and rendezvous in the vicinity of Zorn. If we dive deep enough we might dodge them, at least we'll confuse them. The palaces-I guess they'll try to open up a tachyon corridor and slip right by them. But *we* can't command so much energy. We've got to flee or turn around and fight. You've got to help me."

"Help?"

"Yes, help! Not much time to teach you ... but powers of powers, man, this is a revolution! Astrogators are scarce here on the side of Shadow. You've a natural talent for this, you've learned fast."

"I'm a corpse dancer, not a star pilot ... I'm supposed to direct a rehearsal with Tarlo and the others." Fear seized him. Along with it, he detected, to his dismay, a certain excitement.

"Ready? Okay. Back into the trance. Close your eyes. Think *black, black, black ... dive! dive! dive!* into the dark heart of the beast."

Sixteen
Child-Weeping Robots

In the conference chamber Arryk came upon three or four deathdreamers of the clan of Aush. To his surprise Siriss was there already, and seemed to be listening to the deathdreamers with some consternation. All were robed in garments stitched from the skins of hundreds of species of snakes. One, their leader, was a woman whose headband was a living cobra and whose anklets and bracelets were live serpents forced to swallow their own tails; those of the clan of Aush affected such garments, as befitted their trade, the designing of machineries of death.

The walls were well opaqued, shutting out the overcosm. In their curving mirror metal Arryk saw himself reflected a thousand times. And he was angry, because he did not want to see himself or Siriss, whom he both loved and hated because of her betraval of Kelver.

"Hokh'Ton," said the four Aush in unison. Their leader

continued, "Lord Inquestor and Lady Inquestrix, let us show you what we have designed."

"Zorn is a gas giant," said the second. "Our thinkhives have determined that the only way human life can survive there is in the upper atmosphere, in sealed meniscus-bubbles that might hold a household or two or even whole cities. Like soap bubbles borne on the wind, these habitations might trap a breathable atmosphere and even artificial gravity generated by Shtoman gravity-boxes; like soap bubbles, they might perhaps be popped."

"Or else we might set fire to Zorn's atmosphere," said the third. "It's a reducing atmosphere, mostly methane and ammonia; but the system contains moons of ice. We tow the moons into the planet's stratosphere, electrolyze them for their oxygen, set them alight in the vicinity of the habitations—"

"Spectacle indeed!" the first Aush said. "The air itself ablaze. And us watching from a nearby satellite, perhaps. And the bubble cities blowing in the storm:consumed."

"Are they not force-shielded?"

"Our thinkhives think they are organic."

'And the weapons of your communal deathdreaming?" said Ton Siriss.

"Well," said the leader of the Aush, "we thought it best to create a kind of amphibious delphinoid: one both atmospheric and starborne. Our artists have worked overtime designing it: it's a triumph of elegance and terror-striking majesty. Each one can store a thousand childsoldiers as well as staggering amounts of weaponry; it would take but a few to drag an icemoon to the periphery of Zorn and to extract from it the requisite oxygen "

'Then all is ready. We will begin," Arryk said, trying to sound unmoved.

"You do not want, *hokhTon,* to hear the name of this new kind of delphinoid?"

"Very well."

"We call it the child-weeping robot, Lord Inquestor. For it is made in the shape of a metal man, though it rises to a height of some two klomets; and the childsoldiers, stationed in its head, will he spewed forth from its eyes. Will you look upon them now?"

And Arryk saw how Siriss trembled, and wondered what memories she had of Zorn. But he told himself that she must not allow herself to be touched by such transient things as planets or civilizations; the eternal Inquest was at stake. He turned to her, wanting to tell her this; but she had already plated away to some other corner of the palace. He wondered whether she was planning another betrayal. I must watch her, he thought. And his distrust eroded away yet another fragment of their old love.

***

"Wake up! Wake up! Why doesn't he answer me?" Jenjen cried. Beside her, cushioned by the enfolding floorfield of the starship's astrogating chamber, Zalo sat motionless, his eyes half-open, staring.

Beside Zalo: Kail Jannif, arms folded, eyes closed, rigid, prone: a corpse in an ancient sarcophagus.

Tya's hand on her shoulder. The girl's voice, gentle: "It is *darashédza,* the star fever. It will pass; sometimes they remain so for many sleeps. I used to panic, too, when I saw Jannif like this."

"He looks like a dead man," Jenjen said.

"Few die while in the astrogating trance. Though to be honest the possibility does exist—if the delphinoid goes insane, for instance. Or in an overcosm skirmish. Or if, for some inexplicable reason, the delphinoid's life—what passes for its life—extinguishes itself."

"But it was only a few sleeps ago that Jannif began to teach Zasha her art! And now they are sounding deeper and deeper into the overcosm—"

"Nothing to worry about. We are safe here. The enemy will not engage us. And Jannif does need his help. I don't really understand any of it, but it's to do with holding on to threads of light or something. For fear of losing your way."

"How strangely like the art of lightweaving," Jenjen said, wondering to herself at how everything in the universe seemed connected to everything else. But although Tya's words seemed perfectly logical, she found she was not comforted.

Later, watching Tarlo and the other actors prepare a scene from Zalo's new play, whose title he had not yet disclosed to her, she was unable to watch; when she reached her quarters, even her lightloom was no solace.

Instead she went to the observatory to watch the overcosm. And thought: He is out there somewhere in that chaos.

And so that chaos now has a soul, the soul of the man I love.

***

Clutching the hand that was not a hand ... grasping the intangible lightstream ... dark dark dark dark dark....

"Jannif!" A piercing scream of fire. "I'm losing you."

Around him the echo: *Sound sound sound sound sound* Dark dark dark—

Dark—

Like falling down a well, falling, falling. Here and there a vivid image flashing: kashanthras circling, a dead man leering, an eyeball squeezed from a socket and oozing into the darkstream. Falling. How long? Don't lose the thread. Jannif's voice, faint, like a little child talking to a mechanical horse: "Still still still my starsteed my proud stallion don't fret don't panic be still be still."

Dark—

"There is another here with me you will know him as Zalo he is my friend our friend don't fret my lovely starwhale my brave steed he will reach you with his mind now touch him touch him (Zalo quickly call out to him with your mind) he will touch you touch you (concentrate Zalo concentrate!)"

Dark—

He focused his thought, tried to concentrate on some image that he could project ... could see nothing but dark ness and the lightthreads suturing the thick blackness ... then ... the death's-head and the soaring kashanthra ... the skull perched on the wings of the embalming-bird, flaming—

... the corpse's face glittery with the kashanthra's metal-blue down. . . the oozing eyes the gold-burning eyes the blood welling up tears blood tears ... emerald ... eyes of the

Prince of Shadow ... harder harder harder....

Dark—

The voice!

Blur blur blur blur then—

At once, abrupt, sudden, Clarity.

The room at the heart of the dark. Jannif: palpable suddenly, smiling at him. She said: "This moment is outside time and space. This moment is manufactured to bring you peace. We have come to rest at the eye of the overcosm, and soon we will breach into the realspace of Zorn ... but this time is given us for contemplation. We have come to rest in a disjunctive node of the delphinoid's consciousness."

The room: so achingly familiar! His own room, in his own house in his own arrondissement. There the niche with the head of Kamofara; even now it babbled some aphorism at him.

He said to Jannif: "Welcome to my home! May I pour you zul?"

She put a finger to her lips and said, "Illusion, Zasha."

The room wavered. He felt a strange disassociation from himself.

Jannif's face shimmered, rippled as though a stone had fallen into an image in a still lake. "In a moment the star fever will come upon you with all its force, and you will know the old language of the starborne; it is more ancient even than the Inquestral highspeech, though it contains the roots of all human languages. You will pluck this knowledge from my mind"—for a moment he saw her in the flowing white robes of a Rememberer— "but you must grip the thread as tightly as possible ... for a few moments you will be alone at the helm of the starwhale ... I will be drained, sustained only by your hold on the lightpath ... but soft, we are safe here, hear the delphinoid's voice—"

SE-TA-LI-KA

The highspeech word for delphinoid shipmind ... whence did it issue? It echoed and reechoed in the room that was not a room ... his brain was on fire ... the words resounded, syllable upon ponderous syllable ... slowly he sensed meaning in the ringing cadences, as though that meaning were being wrenched from those syllables of pounding seasurf and thunder and whispering firefountains and mountain winds—

ZALO WHO ART NOT NAMED A STAR PILOT, WHY CALLEST THOU ME? ART NOT AFRAID OF THE SEARING OF THE OVERCOSMIC FLAMES? ART NOT AFRAID TO LOSE THY WAY FOREVER IN THE LABYRINTH OF DARKNESS, EVER CLAMORING FOR RELEASE? FEARST NOT HELL'S GATEWAY?

And he spoke in the ancient speech wherewith the Inquest controlled all beasts and mechanicals that were its subjects or that it had enslaved: pteratygers and reanimated saurians and mountain-moving robots and metalbeasts of burden: "How shall I fear thee? I am thy friend. Be still, be still, my ship of darkness, my swift steed, my starwhale." And gripped the strand and reined it tightly to him.

WHITHER WOULDST THOU FLY ALONG THE PATHS OF LIGHT? NAME THOU THE WORLD.

What must I say now? he thought. Unbidden the answer came to him: he must focus on the name of Zorn, naming it with such power as to forge a new lightpath, to cast a rope of light up from the bottom of this well and draw the starship up to the surface until it breached into realspace. He saw Jannifs image waver and could not sense her presence at all ... she was drained from feeding him the knowledge of star piloting ... he knew that he must be the one to pull them up ... he concentrated on visualizing the image of himself climbing the rope of light, wearing the starship like a chitinous outer skin, pulling himself hand over hand up the burning shaft of brilliance—

Suddenly his world exploded! The lightthread-it was swimming away from his grasp! He flailed around, making fists around the empty darkness—

***

And Jenjen, watching the rehearsal, said, "Why am I so frightened?"

And Tya said, trying to mask her unease, "They'll come

out of it, I'm sure."

And the actors mimicked dead men in a chamber of the starship.

***

—the rope fading fading fading—

Weakly, a voice that might have been Jannif's: "Hold the light tight knot the light around you hold me hold me—"

Dark Dark Dark—

And grasped the rope and felt it searing the hands that were not hands and heard the delphinoid's voice reverberate and the darkness gathering around him suffocatingcrushing

Dark—

Pull! Pull!

Jannif's voice, fainter now: "You perceive the delphinoid's soul ... as I have never perceived it ... guide him well ... cherish your starsteed and he will bear you through thickest darkness ... control him, discipline him with compassion ..."

"You speak like you're dying! Hold on tighter!"

Wasn't there an opening at the top of the well? Was it infinitely high then? Darkness gathered: a wild darkness, raging. Then all at once—

The men on fire swarming in the dark. A suffocating sulfurous stench. Men on fire with eyes of glass, men with metal limbs upraised, closing in on him, choking him with their brimstone breath—

The lightthread snapping, like a lyre-string overtaut, then—

Dark—

Snap—

Jannif! he cried in his mind. I can't feel you any more are you dead are you lost?

Then, knowing with a new and sudden instinct what he must do, he spoke with his mind in the urspeech: "Breach breach breach breach breach!"

TOWARD WHAT WORLD WOULDST THOU PULL ME? WHITHER GO THE PATHS OF LIGHT?

"Zorn—"

And awoke, screaming, Jannif unmoving in his arms, to find the overcosmic chaos dissolving into a view of a lowering, violent planet—

***

"Jannif ... " He heard a voice, Tya's voice. "She isn't moving." Jenjen, hysterical.

Softly Zalo whispered: "She gave me knowledge! But in that moment something attacked us, something full of hate... her lightline snapped ... her soul is somewhere beyond our reach, lost in the light-mad overcosm— "

He felt the trance-state pulling him back, he knew he must return into the darkness alone to fine-tune the navigation and to make sure they breached realspace at the precise coordinates of the world whose fractured image was beginning to form around them through the veils of chaos.

"I have to go hack," he said hoarsely. "Tya, you explain to the others. Find someone to contact the rest of the fleet. The forces of Arryk are upon us. I'm going to breach within the atmosphere itself."

"Don't go!" Jenjen was saying, gripping his hand. He would have felt pain, but the star fever was upon him. Before he sank back into the well of darkness he heard other voices: soldiers and other passengers had gathered in the astrogating chamber.

It was a babble. He could make out nothing, except a lone, very nasal voice, complaining bitterly: "What? You mean the *actor* is piloting the starship? I demand that something be done!"

***

The moon-palace Kilimindi materialized in Zorn's orbit. The planet loomed, oppressive. There were storms that were so huge that a planet fit for human habitation might sink without a trace. Grimly Arryk and Siriss stood watch as the child-weeping robots were maneuvered into formation. Each was a metal man high as a mountain. Now, floating in the space above Zorn, they bestrode the cloudswirls like colossi. Behind the two young Inquestors sat Karakaël on a hoverthrone upholstered with a cloth of living butterflies encased within a fabric-simulating forceshield. Only he seemed to be enjoying the spectacle; Arryk and Siriss bore it in silence.

"Splendid!" Karakaël was saying, as he clapped his hands for a closer view. "And the moons of ice that will be torn apart for the atmospheric burning effect? I understand that the release of oxidants into the upper air of this world may even cause the beginnings of life! An especially appropriate conceit, since we act to preserve the way of life we have enjoyed for so many millennia."

"There *is* life on Zorn!" Arryk reminded him testily. "But not for long."

"Look!" Siriss said. "They are preparing to descend into the atmosphere."

Sleek, silvery, ruby-eyed: the man-birds broke formation as the palace's thinkhive closed in its scanners for a more detailed picture. The huge planet was three-quarters full. In its shadow quarter, two moons glinted; they too were almost full. Strings of force were propelling them toward Zorn, their power drawn from some star's death of long ago, the energy of its dying stored in the almost limitless power banks of Uran s'Varek.

In unison the heads of the child-weeping robots craned; in unison their eyes flicked from side to side, their irises the gates behind which waited the childsoldiers, the *makrúgh* fodder. Behind each iris could be seen a force-portcullis; behind it the childsoldiers moved, swarming specks of black in the crimson glow. As their viewpoint changed, Arryk could see the markings on the robots' arms and legs, sigils of the High Inquest, the personal insignia of Siriss and Karakaël and Arryk and countless other Inquestors who fought on the side of the old unshakable truths. And though Arryk distrusted Ton Karakaël z Karakit Kerún, and feared what his old lover Sirissheh might have in her heart, he still felt pride at the awesome beauty of what the old order had accomplished. A killing convoy it was; but a sight also for poets and for those who loved splendor and spectacle. And my deathdreamers dreamed it into being, thought Arryk, realizing that by calling the deathdreamers *mine* he had taken the final responsibility onto himself. But that was the Inquest's nature; it alone was to bear men's sins, for it alone had eternity; it alone lacked human frailty; it alone was motivated by the one compassion. And Arryk, repeating in his heart those fundamental Inquestral texts, found solace from his own shattered dreams and tarnished passions.

Finally Siriss broke the silence: "Look at the clouds, roiling, twisting."

One by one the metal manthings were plunging into the upper atmosphere. It was as though they dived into a thick yellow mist. In the far distance, the ice moons grew as the delphinoid-controlled force strings tugged them ever nearer *to* their destruction.

"Should you not give the order, Rikeh?" Karakaël said from his hoverthrone.

"Order?"

"Yes. You are, after all, the titular head"—with self satisfied irony he stressed the word titular— "of our forces, are you not?"

"Yes. I will give the command that will drive Kelver from his hiding place." He paused. Suddenly he was aware that, as they had stood watching the cloudstorm and the gathering of the child-weeping robots, many others had gathered in the chamber: thousands perhaps, for the chamber had grown elastically to accommodate them, as was the wont of chambers in the place of Kilimindi. There were childsoldiers and armigers and buccaneers and ceremonial dancers and Inquestors and functionaries.

"They wait for you, Lord Arryk," Karakaël said. Arryk could no longer mistake the irony.

"Well then. Attack!"

No one moved. But Arryk knew that machineries had been set in motion by his utterance. Karakaël said, "What now, Ton Arryk n'Elloren Tath? Surely you will not turn your back on them?"

Arryk said, "I will watch. An Inquestor does not shy away from the horror of life."

Karakaël said, guffawing scornfully, "I will do more than watch! I will ride the clouds myself in the belly of a manthing. I will be present at the razing of Kelver's city. I am not bloodless, as you are."

Siriss whispered to Arryk: "If you let him go, Kelver may perish. He will not stay the slaughter for love of Kelver, as you or I might."

Sighing, Arryk cried aloud, "So be it, Ton Karakaël z Karakit Kerún! You will not relinquish *makrúgh* even for so all-consuming a display of spectacle; so I must take up the challenge. We will all ride in the monster's belly into the fray. If I am not a monster, neither am I a coward! Beware, Karakaël! We are allies only by necessity. I will not hesitate to denounce you for uncompassion, the gravest of all heresies."

Karakaël's eyes burned.

There was the slightest pause. Then he said, gracelessly, "*Atta heng.* You have vanquished me." Which were the words to acknowledge an opponent's victory in a round of *makrúgh.*

***

Tya laid Jannif's body on a bier in the hull of the starship, where some mortally wounded warriors, to deaden their pain and pass the time, lay in cryohypnotic stasis. She covered her with a purple mourning-cloak, as was the custom among the childsoldiers when a much-honored soldier died to save another's life. But because Jannif was not, perhaps, truly dead-because Tya hoped the impossible hope that she might be able to thread her way back to consciousness through the maze of the delphinoid's thoughts-she did not cover up her lover's face. How could the woman be dead? There was no need of embalmer's art. There was no deathly pallor in her cheeks. Yet Jannif's body was an empty vessel.

To the Inquestors it was forbidden to weep. For a childsoldier it was not so. Yet when the tears welled up, so many tears, more tears than a childsoldier was designed to weep, they clogged her laser-irises and permeated the microscopic turrets that concentrated the light into killing streams. Steam spattered from her eyes, spurting over the biers on which the wounded slept. The pain was unbearable. Not even being born could have been so bad. Yet she could not stop weeping. And at last her tears dried up. She was still wild with grief.

She wanted to use her eyes now, carve up the hull, anything. Unthinking, she defied her years of discipline and subvoked the syllables that were not normally to be thought—

But ... there was no burst of deadly topaz light! How could that be? She concentrated harder, thinking she had simply not subvocalized correctly. But they *were* the right syllables, they simply had to be! What was the matter with her? And then she saw, on the bier, motionless, her labyrinth lost lover, and she understood what had happened.

The flood of tears must have dislodged the deathlight apparatus from her irises ... she would he useless now, useless, useless ... she wallowed in self-recrimination. But when she could bear grief no more, she came to a sudden realization, and it turned her tears to tears of joy: that this tragedy had purged her of her power to commit evil. That the loss had cleansed her. She was no longer a childsoldier-as certainly as if an Inquestor had granted her a clan-name.

And Tya knew she had found the freedom she had sought so long.

***

But in the churning air about Zorn, the mountainous metal men were weeping too, for from their eyes gushed, like black fountains, squadrom upon squadron of ululating child-soldiers. As they penetrated the fume-rich air the huge mechanicals began to glow from the friction. As they began to release the moon-culled oxygen from their pores, the air exploded about them. They plunged. They found a city, a hall of mirror matter bobbing in the storm currents. They surrounded the city and began to toss it back and forth like a ball.

Far away—many terran-world-breadths away—sat Kelver in his city. Viewscreens all around him showed the converging of the fiery men, but his eyes saw nothing, only the darkness of the Throne of Madness.

THE QUERENT
So they converged on Zorn, the armies of the two Inquests?
So they fought a mighty battle?

THE CHILD FROM THE FUTURE
Yes. A battle cloaked in darkness.
The forces of Shadow girded themselves with cloud. It was a cloud great enough to contain a thousand terrestrial planets. Still Arryk sought them out.
And Zalo learned a new thing never known before.
He learned that the song of the delphinoids of which Davaryush and Kelver had spoken,
the song whose absolute beauty had triggered the revolution—
that song did not die when the delphinoid brains were soldered
into the hulls of starships.
It did not die. No. It was transformed. It could become a weapon.

THE QUERENT
And Arryk?

THE CHILD FROM THE FUTURE
Followed, followed, followed. Smashed through the clouds;
smashed through the walls between universes.

—from Zalo's *The Darkling Wind*

Seventeen
The Dark Kashanthras

Exploding! Zalo's starship breached realspace, riving the gas giant's cloudbanks like a porpoise smashing through the wavecrests of a stormy ocean. Zalo became jarringly conscious. Through the deopaquement, funnels of red-brown air twisted. Through breaks in the crimson cloudcover he could see ocher clouds swirling; that layer was gashed with glimpses of a layer of chromium yellow; still higher were slits and striations of still other cloud layers. Never had he imagined that sheer air itself could give one claustrophobia.

He was still dazed from his journey through the delphinoid's mind. He cried out in the old speech: "Where are the other starships?"

I cannot tell, said the voice of the starship. Although it seemed to reverberate in the very walls of the astrogating chamber, he knew that he alone heard it, that he had somehow, through Jannif's self-sacrifice, become linked to the shipmind's consciousness. *Where I should touch them there is darkness and fear.*

Then he saw them, riding the clouds, the men on fire from the nightmare he'd experienced in the starship's mind. Distant at first, they seemed like flame-maned children disporting themselves in a field on a windy day. Then they grew nearer. And nearer. They were titans now, and still they grew. The ship was flying straight at one, and he wasn't firmly in control yet. A flaming arm veered toward them ... before he knew it the ship's forceshield rebounded against the robot's side, then swerved, careened past firefingers in a stomach-wrenching curve that arced over the monster's head, and he could see swarming within its eyes battalions of childsoldiers and squadrons of razor-winged fliers, and he knew that its fire-breathing maw was great enough to swallow the ship whole—

And heard Tya's voice beside him, fierce and fervent: "I will send the childsoldiers out to do battle."

"It's suicide! I can't even contact any of the other shipminds. For all we know they're still in the overcosm, or even all dead. I just don't know enough about what to do. I didn't ask to rush headlong into combat!" Nearer, nearer, inexorably nearer. Surely the robot's pilots had sensed his coming by now! Yes. As though swatting a fly, a great hand was descending upon the vessel.

"Through!" Zalo cried out with his mind, and with a burst of acceleration they slid through the gap between its fingers and began to plummet planetward, through layers successively denser and more dark.

Swirling darkness, then—

Lumbering forward out of the mist, the metal fire breather lunged with his fists, trying to grab the starship, and Zalo made the ship zigzag between the clenching and unclenching fingers, and they soared upward now, smashing through goldstained doudbanks laced with incandescent streaks, as distant robots slicing the airstreams left behind jet-trails of exploding sky—

The robot's face looming up, filling the viewscreen, smile of laser-tipped teeth, and then, at once, spurting from the crimson eyes like flocks of dark birds—

Childsoldiers! At once Tya was shouting out orders to those she commanded. He saw that Jenjen had come into the astrogating chamber and she fell into his arms, sobbing for terror.

"Can't you dodge them?" Tya screamed. He looked helplessly for a moment, then realized that the burden was entirely on him. Of course he had had responsibilities before. When a corpse stumbled, the whole play was thrown. But no one's life had depended on it. Grimly he concentrated on the thread of light that linked him to the shipmind. As he fell into the star fever he saw the lightlines of the enemy robots, for each was animated by a delphinoid itself. Each projected a tangled web of hostile light, the webs fibrillating as they encroached upon him, clutching the one thread, the one true path.

"Jannif!" he called out in his mind, hoping to dislodge her trapped soul from the delphinoid labyrinth.

Instead he felt another consciousness beside him. Dark. Quiet. Full of concern for him. He knew that in the outer world he still held Jenjen in his arms. Was he somehow pulling her down too, submerging her in the shipmind? "You have to let go, Jeni! I have to wrest us free!"

A tiny voice: "Zasha, my love is with you always, even in this terrible darkness "

Then with a supreme effort he pushed her away from him and sent her mind back to the surface of the abyss. And concentrated until it seemed that his brain was on fire.

***

The throneroom in the cloud city. Childsoldiers stood guard, their laser-irises projecting beams of killing light that criss-crossed over the portal like brilliant javelins.

A hubbub beyond the mirror-walls of the palace. Mes sengers, childsoldiers, rememberers running. The soldier guards did not move; their faces were frozen in fierce concentration that generated the lightgrid that blocked the suppliants' entry into the sanctum.

"Let us in! Admit us into the presence of the Prince of Shadow!" cried the people as they burst into the cloud-girt antechamber. But the guards held still, and did not speak.

In the eye of the child-weeping robot: Karakaël and Siriss and Arryk stood. The pupil dilated to release another swarm of childsoldiers, shrilling their warcry; in the light absorbent pressure skins that warded off the hostile atmosphere, they seemed like child-shaped shadows against the clouds, black shells of human children. Through the iris, like a huge ruby-stained roseate window, they could see the squadron disappear into what seemed to be a sea of fuming blood.

Here and there, in the distance, patches of fire in the sky. "Are those the bubble cities?" Siriss asked.

An attendant, one of the Aush who had designed these latest deathtoys, said, "The cities are blown about on the winds of Zorn, Inquestrix. It is not always easy to pinpoint them. But at least one has been destroyed. The meniscus bubble is protoplasmic and not difficult to burst, if only one knows how."

"And Kelver's city?" said Karakaël.

"I would see it captured, not sent beyond," Arryk said. "There is no call for the devivement of one who is, after all, for all his heresies, an Inquestor. Compassion should rule our thoughts."

"We believe his city has been located," said the Aush, her reptile garments hissing with a hundred tongues.

"Compassion indeed," Karakaël scoffed. "I should like to see this man who is called Prince of Shadow and Darkling Wind turn tail and flee affrighted from his own reflection."

And glared at Arryk pointedly. "You do not join in our righteous glee?"

"You are tiresome, Ton Karakaël. I wish that Lady Varuneh had not unmasked you. Unmasked you are twice the terror that you were."

"I know. I was but playing at *makrúgh* before. And now I live it. And that is precisely as your friend Kelver has decreed ... did he not say that true emotions, hate as well as love, must return to our Inquestral universe before his never-never-utopia will come? You see, I am his truest disciple, did he but know my innermost motivations."

Distastefully Arryk looked away from the peeling mummy face of Ton Karakaël. He watched the blinking of the blood-glazed iris portals. Each blink was expulsion of another army of childsoldiers. On the ramp that led to the pupil, like black ants storming over a metal carcass, more childsoldiers readied themselves for combat, and there came from beneath the Inquestors' vantage point such a cacophony of shrilling warcries, amplified by the cavernous metallic walls of the robot's eyeball.

"Shall we go out? Shall we follow them?" Karakaël said, taunting.

"Do not tempt him!" Siriss said at last. Surprised, Arryk looked at her. Yes, there was a vestige of their old love in her eyes. How he needed this remembrance. But no Rememberer could give it him, for though the Inquestral way of life made provision for epic remembrances of the deaths of star systems, there was no way to record and recall the Inquestors' fleeting passions; how could there be, when for so long the Inquest had denied these emotions their very existence?

It seemed to Arryk that for a few seconds he awoke from the dark sleep of despair, of the spell of uncompassion Karakaël had woven about him.

But came the continuous warpaeans, screeching locust thunder, shrilling in his blood, jamming his heartbeat, scrambling his thoughts. "I will come, Ton Karakaël z Karakit Kerún!" He cried out for a flier, and a frightened childsoldier scurried to do his bidding.

Then he said, softly, for Siriss alone, "Do not blame me, Sirissheh, that I begin to dream of Kelver's death. I am walking in a circle of hatred, and maybe only more hatred can break it. Redemption comes in many shapes; we cannot choose what we are. Believe me when I say that all I have done is in compassion's name, for the sake of what you and I learned at Elloran's feet."

"Oh, Arryk," Siriss said, "don't betray yourself!"

"Why not?" Arryk said angrily, not caring if Karakaël overheard him. "Isn't that what *you* did? Of all the key Inquestors in this war, Kelver and Karakaël alone are pure."

"You understand nothing of him now. He is possessed by the Throne of Madness. I came to you to save him, knowing that of all of us you loved him best."

"You can't have it both ways. You can't engineer a mythic confrontation between what are to be perceived as good and evil forces ... and expect allowances to be made for you as a human being. Kelver must relinquish his demand that this game of *makrúgh* be something other than a game of *makrúgh,* that it be some cosmic spectacle to bring about the end of all things as we know them. Only then will I speak to him as friend to friend, as one who once loved him." He could not bring himself to say that he still felt love for Kelver; to say that he would have to give up all pretense of Inquestral composure.

But Siriss had seen through him. "You *do* love him still!" she said. "You *know* he did not choose to play this role in history."

"There is no history!" Arryk cried out.

"Leave her be," Karakaël said, his voice like the purr of a pteratyger that is poised to plummet on its prey. "She will not rise to the challenge of *makrúgh.* Kelver has bled her spirit from her. She is no more a true Inquestor than those miserable childsoldiers, our makrúgh-fodder!"

"Enough!" Arryk screamed. "My flier! We will go stare the enemy in the eye. We are Inquestors, and we may not turn our face from bitterness. You are right, Siriss. We do not choose what we are. It is right that you should remind me. And you, too, Karakaël, are right. This is no time for cowardice."

He clapped his hands. Instantly the childsoldier returned with word that the flier had arrived as commanded. A tunnel opened up in the wall above the ruby irises; it spat out the flier, which sailed toward the dais where they stood above the howling and ululating throng. It hovered above them like a silverdove. An invisible staircase of force was lowered; childsoldiers stood on either side of every step so that the Inquestors might not stumble.

"Are you coming?" Arryk said.

He looked from one to the other; Karakaël transfixed him with a look of undisguised hate, Siriss with one of bewilderment and repressed emotions. Without looking back, he marched up the force-hard air into the flier. In a few moments he heard the stern rhythm of Karakaël's footsteps. A few seconds more passed before he heard Siriss's footfalls, soft and reluctant, the merest whisper of shimmercloak against the forcefield's surface.

***

"He is in such agony," Jenjen said. "I am afraid to touch him."

"Someone must go," Tya said, "to the throneroom of the

Prince of Shadow. He will already be there. Someone must warn him."

Zalo did not move. He was half-submerged in the overcosmic labyrinth. The starship lurched uneasily, bucking against the unwonted atmosphere. "Steady," he whispered with his mind as he had heard Jannif do, "steady, my starwhale, my wind across the space between spaces. Are you afraid? I will guide you, the thinkhives that are linked to you will guide you."

Dimly he heard Tya say, "I will take a small flier and slip away to Kelver. They will never see me, so set are they on besieging this ship."

About him the lightgrid grew more bright. Got to smash through it, he thought. Got to break loose. If only Jannif were here—

A shriek: "Childsoldiers! They're attempting to lasso the starship with their forcelines ... attempting to board us!"

Abruptly he snapped to. As he spoke the viewscreens depaqued completely as though in response to an unheard command ... for he was becoming part of the ship, and could feel its movements like the beating of his own heart, and could cause it to react involuntarily to his own thought processes. In the sky around him, thick against the swirling of the clouds, the childsoldiers filled the air. Black they were, black-cloaked, black-maned, even their faces black from some light-absorbent pressure skin. "Kashanthra," he whispered,

Jenjen, who stood close by, was the only one that heard him, and she nodded, understanding his thought.

"Yes," she said. "On Essondras they made the night sky brilliant; here they darken the incandescent clouds. Our embalming-birds, dying, fed us all with hope. But these death-dealing children ... oh, Zasha, was it worth it? I'm feeling such despair. My rainbow bridge is broken ... are our hopes dashed too?"

"Don't break, my love. I couldn't bear it if you broke. Hold my hand while I try to disengage us." He heard fire hissing down a distant corridor. A bloodshot eye filled the entire sky now; it was the eye of the child-weeping robot, glowering, huger than their entire ship. He saw ships hover about its periphery like flies; childsoldiers darted in the foreground, their eyes streaming the yellow death. A subtle change in the motion of the ship. "I think ... I think they are bringing us to a halt!" he said.

"Surely not. I can't feel anything."

"No, of course not. Most people feel nothing when a great big starship moves, but I ... I've been bound to this thing, my mind soldered into its mind—"

"I do feel something ... a sense of loss."

"Yes. The sense that always accompanies a disturbance in the overcosmic flux." He subvocalized a command to the thinkhives; they told him what he already intuited. "They have locked us in. They're going to board us!"

Dark kashanthras, Zalo thought. How hard it is to purge old images from one's thoughts.

"Dark kashanthras," Jenjen said.

In that moment they understood each other completely.

Never had he loved her so much.

***

In the makeshift theater of the starship, Enshtewo trembled, Tarlo was afraid, and the boy Jhisha was strangely unperturbed.

A sudden quaking. A rack of makeup and props slid to the floor, which contoured into strange shapes to receive the objects. Tarlo said, "Oh, if only I hadn't been seduced by the words of my own plays, fooled by my own self-aggrandizing fantasies! I should have stayed on Alykh."

Enshtewo said, "At least this chamber hasn't been depaqued. The opaquement casements were locked because we had to project our own scenery onto the walls. That's a blessing, that we're not watching those terrible things land—"

The boy who had once played young Elloran said, "Don't be afraid. At least we die free; at least we've flown the space between spaces; at least we've fought at the side of the Prince of Shadow."

"Don't make me laugh, boy!" Tarlo said. "*I* never was a slave on a backworld. *I* was free. On Alykh we didn't kowtow to the Inquest; we fleeced them as they came to rest their limbs and consciences in our City of Love. Don't talk to me of freedom, Jherwo; it's a word, air, empty."

"A line from one of Zalo's plays," Enshtewo said. "Perhaps we should take heart. We have seen our art grow. You think it strange I should say this, I the conservative old fart? If you were so free, as you put it, why did you come here?"

The hissing became a roar. Fire. Unmistakable now.

Then a metallic pounding, rhythmic. Jherwo remembered such a sound: the deathgongs tolling in the mnemothanasion back on lost Essondras. The grownups are afraid, he thought. Why not me? The pounding came again, again, again: boom, boom, boom, punctuating his thoughts like the directing-rod of a master corpse dancer. But Jherwo was visited by a strange detachment; he did not share the others' panic at all. What was the purpose of having a semantic argument about the nature of freedom now? Got to leave them, he thought. I'll go into the corridor and keep walking and see what I can see—

Corridor. The walls deopaqued. The gaping maw of a mountain-sized robot, waist-high in a sea of cloud. A great round thing, fire-wreathed, in the distance... melting ... surely it could not be a moon, a melting moon plummeting into the ocean of noxious gases! More robots. And childsoldiers storming the starship like swarms of bats. Jherwo tried to count them as he walked zombielike down the passageway, and the endless rhythm of counting put him into a kind of dream world, so that he hardly noticed the people fleeing in the other direction, screaming, dissheveled. Overhead, childsoldiers' feet: he could not tell which side was which, so thickly did they swarm. Occasionally, a soldier stared blankly through the wall at him; he was mildly startled even though he realized it was only a projection from the walls' deopaquement, that they were in reality deep in the heart of the starship.

Suddenly, as he reached a fork, the noise intensified. People everywhere, stumbling, babbling. A childsoldier, his citrine eyes glowing, stood in the center of a hallway; his face was ice-calm and smileless as he whirled, whirled, creature of consummate grace, and the light shot from his eyes and people fell, sliced in two, the slices instantly cauterized. They did not scream, they just crumpled and split in two. Jherwo had seen death only in plays. He had not imagined it would be so silent, so anonymous. Presently another childsoldier materialized on a displacement plate and with just a nod of his head and a burst of light decapitated the enemy soldier. He looked around wildly. His eyes were fire-hot, his expression frenzied; only from this, and from a little turquoise ear cuff that he wore that gave him some slight individuality that enemy childsoldiers did not dare proclaim, did Jherwo know that the soldier was of the side of Shadow.

The soldier screeched a command at him: "Hide, you stupid whelp! Plate away to the hiding room or you'll get incinerated for sure!"

"Hiding room?" Jherwo stammered.

"Don't you know anything about warships? Go stand there, at the plate, I'll subvoke it for you. Civilians! Hurry up, little fuck!"

He dashed into the displacement plate. The soldier stood with him for a second and closed his eyes, subvoking some secret code. As the stomach-wrench of the displacement field hit him, Jherwo saw—

A dozen more childsoldiers with the deathmask faces, bursting through the wall of the passageway! The light from their eyes, all at once, converging on the friendly soldier, the soldier exploding like a fire flower in a torrent of burning guts and-

A crowded room. Legs everywhere. He could barely see through them. They were going to trample him. He started to wipe his forehead with his hands and realized that there was blood all over them, oozing down his palms, dripping down his cheeks, blood from the childsoldier who had died saving his life.

He was scared now.

***

Tya alone in a one-man flier. A pleasure flier, unweaponed.

She arced upward, ignoring the gut-twist of gravity. Below her was the starship and the robot, mouth open as if to swallow it, and the soldiers storming the starship's surface like black maggots. Powers of powers, if only they won't notice me. Higher and higher, in thinner and less negotiable strata of Zorn's atmosphere. Fix on Kelver's city. Treehawks, daubs of brilliant green against the bloody clouds. Now and then lightning, jagged, many-forked, thousands of klomets long, lancing the turbulent sky.

Below, so far below ... pockets of fire, and beside the fire the tiny swarms of fighters. All so insignificant ... a single cloud could swallow all those who battled in the skies of Zorn. Nothing amidst the raging of the winds and the brown blizzards. Was Kelver's city already fallen? Get a fix on those cursed coordinates! The thinkhive of the flier stirred, refractory, unused to Tya's brusque military commands.

Burning moons half-buried in the clouds ... what had they hoped to achieve? A meaningless spectacle. *Find Kelver! Find the city of the Darkling Wind!* she subvocalized fiercely. In the relentless wind the flier strained, lost control, veered sharply into the current. Narrowly skirted a circle of sharkshaped enemy starships that were spiraling about a droplet of fire ... a burning city! Was it Kelver's? No, Kelver's was still farther. She plunged into a cloud. They'll never notice me, she thought, they're busy dragging moons around and boarding starships....

Hours later, still not emerged from the cloud, she pounded at the flier's controls, thinking, Surely this thing's no longer working properly, I'm lost now, lost like Jannif—

Mist still, featureless, yellow-gray. Would this cloud never end?

At last she felt a jar in the flier's motion, as though it were sinking into quicksand ... she knew they were penetrating the bubble-shell of the city, and that the city's thinkhive recognized the ship for one of Kelver's. She breathed in relief. But the cloud did not give way to the familiar cityscape of mirror metal reflecting the striated sky and mottled cloudlayers intersecting at right angles. Of course not; they were still within the cloud, and all the city's walls and terraces reflected the same unyielding gray. She landed in a field on the outskirts of the city, saw that a line of displacement plates led through the spectral mist, and made her way toward the palace of the Prince of Shadow.

Gray. And bleak, the city squares; even the faces of passersby had caught the gray aura. Quickly she walked, took slidewalks that arced over grim gray highrises, descended down forcetubes that threaded the gray-tinged undersurface of the city. Deserted. Where were they all? More displacement plates. Then the antechamber of the throneroom. Gray walled, watched by gray-complexioned childsoldiers; a crowd stared at her, listless, desultory.

"I am Tya," she said, "a commander of the forces of Shadow. I must see Kelver; I must!"

Lightning-grid over the threshold. The laser light wavered; the sentinels had been holding their positions too long. How their eyes must smart. But if they lost their concentration they might cause a lethal accident. Involuntarily—with the reflexes of her childsoldier training—she subvoked the command to ready her laser-irises; but she did not feel the familiar pin-prick within her eyeball, and again she marveled that the burden of death-carrying had fallen from her.

"I command you to make way!" she said. Knowing who she was, the guards feared her, and allowed her to enter. At last she was alone in the presence of him she worshiped.

A throne: more like a stool of rotting wood. Gargoyles spitting blood-dark rheum lined the stone steps that led to it. The walls, which she had last seen brightly colored and layered with images of clouds, were now one gray, gray as a decaying brain. But he who sat on the throne was Kelver, unmistakably Kelver.

And Kelver said, in a voice that was more resonant than a man's, "Tya. My most faithful soldier. You were with me at the very beginning. Look at you; bleary-eyed, overgrown, sad. How you loved me, Tya! You gave me your childhood. Oh, Tya, forgive me, forgive me."

"What is there to forgive, my Lord? I had from you the greatest gift of all. At last I knew myself and my place in the universe."

Kelver was silent for a long time. How old he seems! she thought. He was just a young man when I first loved him, on the vast plain on Uran s'Varek, and we sang hymns to him that made the valley ring. My suffering has been nothing compared to his.

"My Lord, we must flee."

"Flee! Flee!"

"Where are the other starships of our fleet? Someone-somewhere—in midovercosm—swooped upon us; we scattered; our ship is alone, under attack, navigated only by that actor from Essondras. Jannif is dead. Or as good as dead. She'll never come back from limbo."

"I know, child. I felt her death. I feel all deaths now, through the all-encompassing power of the Throne of Madness." What did that mean? thought Tya. A sliver of doubt pierced her thoughts, but she tried to suppress it. Was it true that the Prince of Shadow had been driven mad by the Darkling Wind? All she could say was, "Flee, Lord, flee! They're converging on your city. Our own ship is lost for sure. And where is Varezhdur? And the snowflake palace Sharamonda?"

"Safe!" said the Prince of Shadow. "They are within this cloud."

"But surely they will already have detected them."

"It does not matter."

"Not matter!" said Tya in confusion. "The outlying bubble cities are already being blown to smithereens!"

"Yes. I feel the deaths of their denizens, pinpricks of appalling agony. The whispershadow weighs on me. There is a plan ... is there not a plan? A plan, a plan. Davaryush's master plan. What was the plan? What was the purpose?"

"Master—"

"Go now. Bid the starships cluster close to this city. If Zalo can break loose, the cloud will draw him in too. And it will draw in the enemy like a magnet. And then something will happen that Arryk does not suspect."

"You *are* in control!" Tya said at last. "There *is* a plan."

"It is not that simple, but yes, there is a plan."

***

A huge cloud roiled in an upper layer of the stratosphere. "Apparently we are getting readings from that cloud," Karakaël told Arryk as they stood with Siriss upon the bridge of their war-flier.

"Crafty," said a snake-robed Aush. "They think to lose you. That cloud's over a thousand Klomets wide, I'll bet."

Out of nowhere, a flier was zooming toward them at close range. All at once it was so close they could see the eyes of the childsoldier who manned it.

"Destroy it, idiots!" Karakaël shouted.

Siriss shrieked: "No! The eyes ... they are not topaz colored ... they are sea green, like Kelver's!"

"Absurd!" said Karakaël. With a flick of his wrist he gave a command and the flier vaporized. Another took its place immediately ... the face of the childsoldier was the same ... Karakaël was unnerved. "What's the matter? It's still there!"

"My Lord, we all saw it go up in smoke!"

"There! And there!" Came another and another, careening out of the empty air. Skullfaces with Kelver's eyes... servocorpse faces with Kelver's eyes....

"It's a diversion," Karakaël said. "We must not forget that Kelver sits on a throne with the power of inflicting madness...." A skeleton with green eyes danced against bloody clouds. "Go through it! It's a phantom! We played at such illusions when we were children being trained on Uran s'Varek!"

They smashed through the skeleton. "The clouds!" someone shouted. "They are weeping blood!"

"Destroy!" Karakaël shouted.

Laserlightswaths in the sky as the flier's weapons became activated. The skulls forming and reforming. Fuming, Karakaël paced back and forth, commanding that more and more powerful weapons be used.

"We have no more power," said the Aush at last. "Spent your silly passions finally?" Arryk said. "Illusions, illusions! you called them. Yet you fired at them, again and again, in futile and inutile rage. Illusions! That an illusion should so madden you, a member of the High Inquest, a world-smasher, a keeper of the High Compassion!"

Ignoring him, Karakaël said quietly, "Summon all our available forces for an assault on that cloud."

"Illusion, Karakaël?" Arryk said.

"Be silent, you impertinent, lovesick whelp," said Karakaël. The cloud, though it filled their whole field of vision, was still some thousands of klomets distant. In the time that it took for their forces to reach its periphery, Karakaël had already fantasized a dozen plans for tastefully disposing of his troublesome young colleagues, after the war was over.

Eighteen
Cloud Smashers

And Kelver watched with the million eyes that the Throne of Madness had given him. He saw the child-weeping robots as they sank into the cloudbank that concealed his city; he saw the delphinoid starships nestled under in dense fog. He saw Zalo's ship and the others that had become separated from the palace during the overcosm panic: saw them besieged, surrounded by those flaming metal men; saw one consumed in an embrace of fire; saw another crushed by a fist of metalflesh. Zalo's starship was the Daranava *Sirisshtasieh*—he had named it for Sirissheh after a night of passion. The remembrance came sadly to him; he saw it as in a faded holosculpture stained with dark brown blood. Still the *Sirisshtasieh* resisted. But childsoldiers had stormed it and boarded one of its lateral wings and were even now incinerating corridor after corridor in their search for the starship's hiding room.

But he did not just see one ship, nor the two or three that drifted fiery in a saffron wind, pilotless; he saw charred cities turned to chaff in the methane storm, their bubbleskins all shredded, their people poisoned by the outside air and sizzling from the friction of their falling, transformed into human meteors that blazed against vapors of crimson and sienna and magenta and gray. Wherever his million eyes roved, the enemy starships saw suspended in the atmosphere images of darkest nightmare: faces stripped of flesh, skulls with emeralds for eyes, servocorpses sprung to life and demanding vengeance for their servile zombiehood.

I want to reach out! To pull them all free! But I cannot.

And I do not.

For behind this vista of misery he saw yet more: he saw further forces of the Inquest, busy subduing more distant planets in rebellion. The forces of Arryk and Karakaël deployed everywhere: in the thick of starclusters where antique civilizations were being shattered and forced to fear the Inquest; in the wastelands of the Galactic Arms, where they pulverized whole planets in secret in reprisal for the killing of a single Inquestor ... for who would notice such remote destruction, far as it was from the core of the galactic civilization? Yet Kelver felt them all, trillions upon trillions of pinprick deaths-

And *I* was the one who decreed their death sentence! *I*, who demanded of them their love! Is death then the price of love?

But Kelver's plan called for their sacrifice. In this he had come closer to the Inquestral precepts: had not Davaryush and Elloran taught him that the lesser compassion must be swallowed up in the greater? And was this not a *good* lesson, one that the Inquest had perverted, perhaps, but a philosophy essentially wise and merciful?

I am becoming like them! he thought. And the thought tortured him.

And now I wait for the attackers to reach me. I do not wait on a magnificent throne or wear resplendent raiment; I do not reek of the trappings of godhood. I sit on an old chair that oozes blood, and I am clothed in a noxious fog huge enough to swallow a terrestrial planet.

I wait, becoming more like them as I wait.

I wait. Oh, I am many now. My splintered souls are many. They are everywhere. Like this endless cloud, the whispershadow stifles me, torments me with images of death. I am everywhere; I am many, many, many, yet utterly alone.

***

Siriss left Arryk alone, surrounded by his Aush and a brace of solemn childsoldiers, and followed Karakaël aft of the flier. The cloud ahead, vast and featureless as it was, was depressing to look on; behind them there were moving objects to watch, squadrons of childsoldiers and starships and a line of delphinoid robots wreathed in fire.

Karakaël said, "I know you are thinking of Kelver, Siriss." She was startled from her reverie.

"Am I so transparent? I, an Inquestrix?"

Karakaël laughed. His laughter is cruel, she thought, and yet it is tempered by a peculiar fragility. She tried to avoid his eyes as they watched the desert sky behind them. Almost at the limits of their vision, a forest of many-forked lightning rose from a crimson cloud. Small fliers containing childsoldiers flitted through this lightning like ravens flocking.

"Answer me," she said.

"Yes. You are so transparent. But why do you not stay with Arryk, whom you also love?"

"He has grown dark. Dark, Karakaël, as you are dark. But I do not fear you as much. You are closer to a known quantity, to an absolute. You are evil; Arryk is merely tainted by it."

Karakaël shook his head. She winced from the flash of his igneous eyes. "Those who think in absolutes, daughter, are doomed."

"Do not call me daughter!" Although, as senior Inquestor, this was his right, she could not bear to hear him call her as Elloran once had.

"I *shall* so call you!" Karakaël said. "You are the undecided one, the only one still capable of swaying in the wind —"

"What!" She remembered, suddenly, the thinkhive-made religion on Alykh, and their visit to the Temple of Arryk. "You subscribe to those foolish new philosophies that turn our actions into myths?"

"Perhaps. You do not know who instigated that religion, do you?"

"You play *makrúgh* again. But you have not uttered the formal words of challenge."

"All things change."

"There is no history!" Siriss said, clinging to the familiar words and the comforting litany of the Inquestral precepts.

"Listen. I will tell you clearly; I will tell you alone. Arryk distrusts me because I am ignoring those very precepts he fights to preserve. And he is right to do sol Because-in my dark fashion-I am a creature of Kelver's universe. I am, in fact, Kelver's dark mirror. I sow hate because his universe, unlike the universe of the lnquestors, allows the existence of good and evil. I must be. Do you see that?" His voice became more urgent. "In battling Kelver I am his true disciple. I am the sunspots in his star of love! I am the shadow of the shadow'sshadow!"

"Oh, Kaarye," Siriss said, calling him by his child-name for the first time, "I don't know how to take your words. Are you a poor megalomaniac, thrust down from the heights, who desperately deludes himself into attributing to himself a major position in the cosmos to come? Or have you really been seduced by that which you have set out to destroy?"

"I am more complex, child, than you have hitherto imagined," he said.

More disturbed than ever before, Siriss made her way back to the front of the flier, where Arryk still stood, staring fixedly at the encroaching cloud. There came a white fluff flurrying against the forceshields that englobed the flier.

"Ammonia snow," said one of the Aush. "The cloud approaches quickly."

"Infravision," Karakaël commanded. "Else we shall never

detect Varezhdur "

And they were instantly surrounded by thick darkness, vague shapes edged by garish auras, as the thinkhives sought out sources of heat and displayed them on the dark-field that surrounded them.

"Darkness!" Karakaël said. "It is beautiful."

And Arryk spoke at last: "It is darkness, nothing more."

"It is the absence of light," Siriss said, despairing.

***

Zalo felt the *darashédza* swoop down upon him, open-winged, dark. He fell into the star well, fell fell fell—

—he cried out Jannif's name in vortices of purple light and fell

—and fell....

Now. The pit of the star well. He bound the lightstrand tightly about his waist. And the pit was a slick funnel and the men on fire were sliding down toward him with harsh metallic growls and he cried out *Jannif Jannif* knowing that her soul was lost somewhere within this maze and he could reach her if only he believed she could be reached and the men on fire were coming closer and closer and behind them he could see sheets and sheets of ammonia sleet sluicing the star funnel and he was slipping and slipping and the lightstrand was unwinding from his waist, and—

Touched by a ghostly hand of light, fingers oozing through his fingers....

"Jannif!"

Zalo. You are doing well. The starsteed bends to your will. I have spoken to him. . . .

"Jannif! Tya weeps for you, your body waits in the sleep-vaults of the starship—"

I can't come back. But here, in this half-world, I can help you ... I am almost all submerged in the soul of the ship-mind, but a part of me knows you, remembers my fleshly nature. Hold this hand, Zalo, clutch it tight. We will fight the flaming metal men together.

"How? There are dozens of them. Tya has loosed childsoldiers—"

They are already dead.

"Dead!" It was too huge to comprehend. They had been an army; now they were sterile spores in the methane storm.

Come. We will fight them down the lightlanes

"How?"

I've been deeper inside the shipmind than any astrogator ever goes! said the voice of Jannif. *I've seen ... oh, what have I seen ... a shadow of the greatest joy man can know, and that joy perverted by what man has done to the delphinoid. I see as the shipmind sees, and he sees like a human too. So much he understands now that he never did before. But to free the ship from the clutches of the child-weeping robots, you must allow it to sing...*

"Sing—"

Once, Jannif said, *when we flew free over the Sunless Sound of Gallendys, we sang songs of such transcendent beauty that all who saw them were changed forever. When Kelver and Davaryush and Darktouch and Lady Varuneh saw our song, they could no longer bear to know that the Inquest had caged us in prisons of metal and sent us mute into the overcosm. Once we gazed upon an absolute beauty, and our song was a mirror to that beauty; but now, the Inquest's slaves, we have been plunged into a living and limitless hell ... still we could sing if we tried, and our song could still transform men's hearts . . . but it would be a song of horror, and it would drive men mad!*

Suddenly he understood what he had to do. It was a great and terrible scheme. But it was the only way. If only it were true that a song could drive men mad! He had to believe. He saw it now.

The fire-breathers came closer ... their breath was hot upon his spectral face....

He jerked himself loose! Scrambled up the rope of light, feeling it swing and go taut. And broke free of the *darashédza,* and issued an order to those in the hiding room in a voice that the starship's amplijewels made resound throughout the ship—

"Opaque the walls to maximum level! Close your eyes, squeeze them tight shut, clench your fists over your ears in the name of the Prince of Shadow, do not see or hear what will happen next! Or you will be driven mad!"

These words uttered, he seized the lightrope once more and dived, not looking back, into the starship's mind, into the sulfur-pit of the burning men.

***

The hall Jherwo had been thrust into was caveshaped, its walls curved, reflective. Unheeded he slipped into the ocean of human legs. Legs adorned in gossamer fabrics, legs edged with fur, bare legs, legs metalcased and fringed with reptile leather, plastiflesh, the hides of allurosaurs. Smells in his nostrils: the odor of panic in the close stale air.

"Isn't there anyone I know here?" he said in a small voice. They were all ignoring him. "Tarlo ... Enshtewo..."

Had they made it to safety? He elbowed his way through jostling arms. A four-armed woman sobbed as she rocked her four-armed baby. Who were these people? The world of the· *Sirisshtasieh* was far more complex than he'd ever imagined. He'd always stayed with the small group from Essondras before. He didn't know anyone. He wiped his bloody face on a fold of his tunic and cried out the names again: Tarlo, Enshtewo, Zalo, Jenjen ... Jenjen! He saw her suddenly, her face peering undecided through a gap in the mob.

"Mistress!" he shouted. He had never known her well, knew only that she was his master's lover. But seeing her face filled him with such relief that he just stood there bawling.

This is terrible, he told himself, I've been a street kid, I know better than to stand here spilling my guts in the middle of an invasion! Then he felt her arms around him, hugging him tightly. Saw her face through the blur of tears.

She said, "He's alone and he's flying the starship and there's nothing I can do!" They were both crying hard. It was infectious. Wailing spread through the crowd. Terror in the air, palpable.

He just cried her name: "Mistress Jenjen, Mistress Jenjen."

From so far away, yet clear above the cacophony of moaning, a clanging ... like the gongs for evening prayer at the Temple of Mother Vara back home on Essondras ... and other voices, awestruck, whispering: "The first of the outer portals!" "They're gaining on us!" Faint, so faint, the whir of a laser-drill. Not so much a sound as a tremor, not so much a tremor as an acrid scent of metal oxidizing, a tightening of the tension—

Silence as they strained to make out the sound. Then more whispering. "Still more pathways to traverse. They'll not reach us yet, not for an hour."

"I can't stand to wait an hour! I want to die now, quickly!"

"An illusory fork that they might take. A trap that'll kill a lot of them before they reach us."

"They're like ants. They'll cross to us on a bridge of children's corpses."

"I'm not afraid! I stand for the Prince of Shadow."

"But I'm afraid, so afraid."

Finally another voice, clear and resonant: "Why doesn't someone give the deopaque command? Let's see what's coming. Let's stop speculating and see."

Cries of agreement and disagreement ... but presently, as though a consensus had reluctantly been reached, there came images, as through a fine mist....

Trooping in the corridors, black-caped, the laser-irises glowing-

Scattered screams now.

The faces pitiless, implacable. Heaps of torsos at the junctions of the corridors.

And then, above the screaming, the voice of Zalo, resonant, commanding that they close their eyes and ears and force themselves to perceive nothing of what was to come-

More whispering now, like a storm-—

***

And in his throneroom Kelver felt another whispering, as the whispershadow, the premonition of a stardeath, burst in upon his thoughts and maddened him and made him scream and made his million eyes see vistas of red—

And Zalo said, "Now!"

And drew the spirit of Jannif around him like a darkfield, a cocoon, a wall of protective love: and with a flick of his mind uttered the forbidden commands that Jannif had dredged up from the starship's mind, and partially severed the connections that soldered the shipmind to the starship's hull—

***

"No!" the childsoldier cried, the warpaean dying on his lips. The wind gathered him up. "No, don't swallow me alive— "

Standing on the cloud, teeth gleaming in its skullface, a bogeyman from the childish nightmare leering ... and the childsoldier screamed and screamed and tore off his pressure skin and breathed methane and ammonia and the blood burst through his flesh and he twisted in the wind for a second and exploded—

***

In the eye of the robot, two Aush were pacing back and forth. They looked up. One saw a childhood monster; the other saw something far more drab: an angry lover, an embarrassing party, a night of excruciating embarrassment; in a split second he relived it again and again, and he ran back and forth screaming inanities, knowing himself for the first time empty and desolate—

***

A paean rang across the howling winds; a spectral army raced over the clouds, a skeletal army with centipedes slithering from eye sockets and shooting a ghostlight from their bony fingertips ... an army of flesh and bone, freshly extruded from a robot's eye, scattered, smeared itself across a dark cloud in a mist of vaporized blood and tissue—

***

And Kelver, in the eye of the cloud, watched with his million eyes—

***

Karakaël heard a shout: "Lord Inquestors, a message from one of the distant skirmishes ... the robots are going mad!"

"We cannot stop to help them!" he cried. "We must pursue. We must be relentless." Around him billowed the cloud, swirls rainbow-fringed by the infravision, the ammonia snow like fire-motes ... deep, deep into the cloud, a patch of reddish luminescence that was the stronghold of the enemy, the city and the starships at the cloud's heart...

***

In the belly of a child-weeping robot sat an astrogator deep in *darashédza.* In his trance he saw his lightstrands turn to filaments of darkness. He clawed at the walls of the starwell. He screamed ....

***

Running through the corridors of the *Sirisshtasieh* .. . .

childsoldiers gone berserk, flailing at shadows, the lightning bolts from their eyes striking at the empty air, at holo sculptures, at antique columns chiseled with curlicuish inscriptions, at firefountains, at each other ...

***

... and in the hiding room Jherwo stood with his arms around his master's lover and his eyes squeezed tight shut against the shadow, fighting the urge to look, to be sucked into the whirlpool of despair ... he felt Jenjen's fingernails tear at his tunic now, heard a frantic shriek from a member of the crowd who had not been able to resist, a cry of primal terror that made his blood race hot and cold—

***

... and Zalo lassoed the burning man with his lariat of light and jerked it taut and felt despair engulf the astrogators who had mindlinked with the enemy delphinoid and fought the darkness himself, pulling the shield of Jannif's soul ever tighter around himself and—

... Jenjen felt darkness all around her, she wanted to yield to it, to give up her soul to it, but still she resisted, thinking of Zalo alone in the shipmind, bearing the brunt of the onslaught—

***

"Now!" cried Zalo. And remembered the days of watching his lover weave on the lightloom in the academy in Ikshatra ... and took the lightstrand that he held and spun it out, far far far, looping and relooping, until it was a web of fire into which the burning men fell, screaming—

***

In the world outside, the robots collided as their pilots were driven insane. Illusion's fire and the fire of exploding starships mingled. Childsoldier corpses rained. The bellies of robots burst to reveal fliers in flames.

On the *Sirisshtasieh,* those who opened their eyes fell victim to a nightmarish despair ... they felt a shadow of the delphinoid's grief at having once known beauty and never being able to see it again ... those who unstopped their ears heard deathshrieks and the cries of awful tortures and came to realize that they issued from their own throats and could not be silenced ... some fell into a catatonia of despondency and would no longer speak for the rest of their lives ... some babbled, some mutilated themselves, all fought against phantoms. And Jenjen dared not unstop her ears and eyes, she felt these things happening around her, and clung even more tightly to the boy who had played Elloran and interpreted her lover's vision. He was her hold on the past ... the past that was not dead, that *had* to not be dead, if they were all to be able to go on living.

Then she felt something new. It was like a psychic wind. It swept over her soul; it seemed to burn through her very bones. She felt movement. It seemed that the starship itself groaned against invisible chains, that it was freeing itself. More clanging now. No! She could not open her eyes! But the clanging invaded her stopped ears and drowned her very thoughts. Her stomach writhed in the pull of rival gravities. I must not look! I must not look! she thought.

Then it was over. She knew it from the aching emptiness that the soulwind had left behind.

I can open my eyes now. I am dead.

She clasped her hands together; the sound of cheering burst upon her ears. The walls were completely deopaqued. To one side, she saw husks of huge robots flaming in the wind, and a chaff of charred childsoldiers, already scattering.

We are moving now. Where? Ahead, at the limit of her vision, a cloud mushroomed for lower levels of cloud. She knew they were moving toward it. She saw silvery dots, in a long line, disappear into the cloud. That was where the next battle would be. For now they were free. But the soulwind's desolation gnawed at her and she would not be comforted. For though she had not been driven mad, yet she had touched the edge of true darkness; and she was a darkweaver, and the study of darkness was her life. And always she had told herself that true darkness was an illusion. She could never be the same again now, never. "There are four million shades of darkness," she whispered to herself, clinging to what she as a darkweaver had learned, "and none of them the true darkness."

She had lost something. She did not know what yet, only that it was precious. Without a word to Jherwo or the others she joined the mob that was moving toward the displacement plates, and went to find Zalo through passageways littered with truncated bodies. And when she found him, sitting alone on the floor of the starship's heartroom, weeping quietly, she said only, "I am here."

And he said, "This starship has a human soul now, and its name is Jannif."

They wept in each other's arms as they sped toward the cloud.

Nineteen
Tachyon Gate

Within the cloud:

Kelver still motionless.

The armada of Karakaël sinking into the dense darkness. The ammonia frost settling, on the wings of fliers, on the limbs of robots, on the joints and appendages of delphinoid starships. Darkness: now and then a flare as a robot breathed fire from metal nostrils or spurted it from its titanium fingers.

Within the starships:

Fear; the childsoldiers tensed and waiting. Through infrared viewscreens they surveyed the darkness: their objective far ahead, blood-haloed, glowing faintly; twisted shapes of starships with crimson auras, tongues of cold fire.

Within the flier:

Karakaël did not move. Arryk paced and shouted angry words. And Siriss wept silently. And the Aush tittered among themselves in a secret language that sounded like the cawing of crows. Siriss watched them. Watched the red-fringed distant darkness, knowing that it contained a man she had once loved; trying to dredge up those moments of love from her memory. But she had forgotten much.

In the city of the Darkling Wind:

The mirror-surfaced buildings were all dark. Phosphorflies had been released into the streets to provide some illumination. Linkboys did brisk business, holding their flaming palms aloft and shuttling back and forth from displacement plate for a few gipfers. There was tension in the air, but little show of fear. In a little courtyard an old man watched children playing at skip-the-stones; but most were in their homes, waiting.

In the throneroom:

Kelver saw what Zalo had done. He had not freed the shipmind, but had loosed its bonds enough to let it sing; and it had sung of the nightmare of captivity, and those who experienced the song, understanding their own bondage for the first time, had been driven to such dark despair that they sought refuge in madness.

He saw the *Sirisshtasieh* break free and head for the great cloud. He saw fragments of the delphinoid's lightsong, and he remembered how as a child he had watched them singing in the Sunless Sound on the planet Gallendys; and he grieved to see what the song had become. But he did not despair, for he was by now both more and less than human. But knowing that the ship was on its way toward the heart of the cloud, he gave a command through the Throne of Madness; and a darkness total and impenetrable settled on the city, on the twin palaces of Sharamonda and Varezhdur, on the attendant starships. And a cloak of silence wrapped itself around the protected zone like a cocoon.

And a message went to the war-fliers who would have to emerge to engage the enemy: *Do not be tempted. Use your instruments and your charts, but do not deopaque the screens, and do not admit sound from outside. Or you will be driven mad.* And those who heard the message were uneasy, for no one likes to do battle blinded and in darkness. As they waited for the battle in their fliers, they could no longer see the distant patches of color that were the forces of Arryk; darkness englobed them completely.

Within the mind of the Daranava *Sirisshtasieh:*

Zalo toyed with the lightstrands that had once been Jannif, and paced back and forth in the psychic labyrinth.

Within the cloud:

Terror, cold as the crystals of ammonia that clustered on the forceshields of the starships and covered the membrane sphere that circled the City of the Prince of Shadow.

***

In the star well, Zalo called on Jannif once more.

"We have to do a precision leap through the overcosm ... rebound off the overcosm's edge and reappear within the cloud," he said. "It's the only way we can overtake them."

He concentrated. He felt Jannif's hands in his, though they were not of the fabric of spacetime. Then it was as though he were careening into a mirror meeting himself accelerating igniting the air around him bursting into a hail of glass shards and then-

Dark. The thread of light still wound about him.

"Jannif? Jannif?"

... Oh, Zalo ... I am falling farther and farther into the soul-matrix of the delphinoid ... should I cling to my last shred of humanness? Should I run singing toward the light men can never see?

"Jannif—"

He felt the walls of darkness press upon him ... he knew they were deep in the cloud, and that as Arryk's armada penetrated it they were once more being subjected to the starsong of the captive delphinoid, and falling prey to despair....

***

They were perhaps a thousand klomets into the cloud; communications were reaching their flier from all sides as the armada gathered itself into an attack formation.

Arryk stood alone. He heard voices from the other ships, a comforting rhythmic buzzing. Then suddenly

Commands and status reports became shrieks of terror!

People were reporting visions, were babbling and screaming nonsense or obscenities...

"What now?" Karakaël said, barking at the Aush who hovered about the Inquestral persons.

"It appears ... that something has attacked those of us who have penetrated into the cloud ... a single starship is at the center of it ... our sensors detect nothing, Lord Inquestor, yet our pilots see terrible things—"

"The art of illusion!" Arryk said. A memory surfaced: on Uran s'Varek, Arryk and Kelver had played at building castles in the desert, tapping the limitless power of the worldmind to fashion ethereal fantasies in the air made lucent by a million suns. They had loved one another then. And then they had waged their first war upon the chessboard kingdoms, only to discover that it was all illusion, the vast vistas over which thousands had fought and died, all a fabrication of Karakaël's mind, shadows cast off from a board game that Karakaël and Elloran had been playing over the midmeal. The memory was bitter now. Oh yes: the neuterchild from Sajit's singing city: had he not died there? Yes. Torn in two by a childsoldier's death-dealing eyes. Yes. The first sentient creature ever to die from an act of my will, Arryk thought. Oh, it is bitter.

"What can we do?" he said. "We must stop here or be driven mad by Kelver's nightmares. Oh, he has become like you, Karakaël: turning people's innermost dreads against themselves. I hate him. Should we tum back?"

"It would seem to be suicide to continue," said Karakaël, not meeting his eyes.

"There is an answer," said a young man's voice. They all turned to look at him. It was a member of the clan of Aush; for a still-living python was sewn into the rim of his cloak, and even as he spoke the snake was feeding from a small mouse that the Aush dangled before it by its tail. The man's eyes were green, sea green; there was an oddly familiar look about him, though Arryk did not remember him amongst the Aush that boarded the flier ... Siriss, standing beside them, had become very pale. Something about the man's eyes....

"Speak, *hokh'Aush,*" Arryk said. "Any solution to this predicament would be welcome."

"You must cloak yourselves in profound darkness. You must fly blind, trusting only your instruments, never dissolving the darkfields on your fliers. I believe that I know what these nightmare visions are, Lord. Have you heard the story of the Light on the Sound?"

"A myth!" Karakaël scoffed. "Davaryush concocted it to explain away his revolution. Songs of delphinoids indeed! What, will a machine think itself superior to a man, that it would move him to the depths of his soul?"

"I see, *hokh'Ton,* that you are not unaware of the so called myth." The green-eyed Aush spoke mildly, but there was a discomfiting lack of subservience in his tone. "It pays to study myth, doesn't it? But what if a delphinoid had somehow been set free, or partially free, and tried to sing its song; but now, no longer free to contemplate the overcosm, was captive in a skin of metal, its very nerves soldered to the controls of a starship? Ah, what kind of lightpoem would this delphinoid sing? If, free, it could move men to claim they had come face to face with an absolute beauty ... then, captive, how would it move us?"

"But to set free the delphinoids ... how will Kelver govern the galaxy without starships?" said Karakaël.

"Does he seek to govern it?" Siriss said.

And Arryk saw that she saw through Karakaël completely; that her prevarications were due perhaps not to foolishness but to understanding both sides too well. She went on: "You must not impute to the Prince of Shadow your own manipulative motives, Ton Karakaël z Karakit Kerún! It is you who seek to rule over the dismembered carcass of the Dispersal of Man, not Kelver!"

"Such loyalty to the enemy! Are you perhaps a traitor, Ton Siriss?"

"Be quiet, both of you," Arryk said. "This Aush speaks wisely. There is always truth to be found in myths. Let us fly on in darkness." No sooner had he spoken than the infravision of the viewwalls blackened and vanished. The only light was from control panels, color-coded, holographic; it cast a ghost white pallor on their faces. Yet the eyes of the green-eyed Aush sparkled brilliantly, as though defying the close darkness.

"Who are you?" Arryk said softly.

"I know him," Siriss said. "But I dare not speak his name.

And when Arryk turned to look for him once more he was nowhere to be found.

* * *

Tya was alone once more in her flier. But this time she could see nothing at all; the walls were maximum opaqued; soundscreens prevented any noise from leaking into the tiny craft. A holographic instrument panel glowed: before her eyes, swimming in an ocean of darkness, were stylized shapes that represented starships and fliers and squadrons of child-soldiers. She willed the flier to move toward the enemy, reaching out as if to grasp the ghostly images. The flier was skimming the cloudtide, but in her cushioned environment she felt no motion.

She subvocalized commands. On the holoscreen she saw a tiny flier, like a phosphorfly, blip out of existence. She knew that she had vaporized it with a blast of her lasercannon. Still she felt nothing. A momentary jar as the flier curved to avoid some obstacle. She spoke to other fliers in her formation: instantly they shifted, broke loose, launched themselves on Arryk's armada. She could see them in the surround-screen: dust motes battling dust motes, nothing more. Powers of powers! This infernal darkness Kelver had insisted on ... it drained you of all feeling, all zest for combat ... or was it also that the same tears that had washed out her laser-irises had also purged her of these emotions?

In miniature they fought, the fliers swarming against her outstretched hands. Now and then lightning bolts joined one speck to another and she knew that death had been dealt. Once she had found the sight beautiful. She wondered if it would still be beautiful if she defied Kelver's command and deopaqued the flier ... would lifesized death excite her more than these abstract patterns in the darkair?

I *have* to see it! I was trained a childsoldier. Surely there's no sight too horrifying for me to bear.

For a few more minutes she stifled her curiosity....

They flocked about her shoulders. Swiftly they changed formation again and again, arcing over her head, darting in and out of her long hair. She thought of Jannif, of their last happy time together in the pleasure city on Alykh. Even then

Jannif was beginning to change. For her sake I have to resist the temptation, she thought. And then ... why? She's gone now, gone forever. She thought of the hundred thousand childsoldiers who had sacrificed their lives to protect the secret of Zorn, and how they had been betrayed anyway.

And of Jannif, soulless, lying in the sleepchamber of the starship ... a martyr!

Do I dare? she thought. I've given up so much for Kelver ... surely one little act of disobedience ... what difference can it make?

Perhaps it was grief that made her lose her senses. Or perhaps the awareness that she was· truly free, free even to flout her lord's command, free even to choose the moment of her dying.

She couldn't help herself anymore. There had always been something suicidal in her nature, she realized as she subvocalized one tiny word to the flier's thinkhive: *Deopaque.* Perhaps, now, I will join Jannif forever, she thought. She had ten seconds to live. But those ten seconds seemed an eternity of torment; a soul-searing desolation seized her and would not let her go, though she cried Kelver's name three times, like a benediction.

In those last seconds, splayed out against the cloudscape, she saw—

Superimposed on a background of images from her darkest nightmares, childsoldiers swathed in darkness, haloed in faint flames, dashing themselves against a burning starship! The starship a smear of eye-smarting brightness in the consuming dark of the cloud, the soldiers smashing themselves to pieces in a lemming frenzy, limbs and guts and heads exploding and burning and freezing instantly in the ammonia frost that caked the starship, and the ship itself seeming to scream in pain, and the childsoldiers' ululations distorted into a grating roar, and the cloudscape a writhing mass of serpents and slime and decomposing corpses ... illusion, she thought, but more real than reality! What power can have shaped these visions? she thought.

And heard, as she fell headlong into death, her mind sending scrambled and contradictory signals to the flier so that its thinkhive jammed and it began to shoot wildly at the illusions, the answer to her question: *The power of ultimate darkness.* That was her last coherent thought. She began to scream and scream and shriek with laughter and howl with grief ... for the last few seconds of her life, until a sudden paralysis came upon her and she simply ceased to think at all.

For a few more seconds her face was frozen in a grimace of obscene laughter. Then, in the dark, she collided with one of the fliers under her own command, and shattered. The pieces began to drift downward toward the gas giant's putative surface, which no living human had ever seen. By the time the fragments that had been Tya reached Zorn's core of metallic hydrogen, the war would long be over....

***

And Zalo heard Jannif's voice, fainter now: *She is dead ... dead ... we killed her. I'm losing my hold on your reality ... the nightmare is seizing me.*

Using the lightrope as a whip, Zalo battled the burning men, whirling, flailing.

***

As Kelver called out to the Throne of Madness to divert power from Uran s'Varek to the center of the cloud, the whispershadow tormented him more and more. He knew the time must come when he must face the death of a sentient star. Buzzing in his million ears. Shrieks of anguish resounding and rebounding through the labyrinthine caverns of his overmind. It must be now! he thought. We must leave Zorn behind us!

And he closed his million eyes and communicated with the schizoid thinkhive of Uran s'Varek, the soul of the black hole at the heart of the galaxy. He tapped the energy of the deaths of stars ... channeled it to the cloud ... braving the mocking laughter that echoed and reechoed in his burning brain.

"Now!" he cried.

And there was silence in the cloud city and silence in the starships that protected it and silence in the crowds that milled about in the hallways of Varezhdur and Sharamonda.

They could feel ... a queasiness, an eerie disorientation.

But they were all enclosed in a profound darkness; the darkness of the cloud itself, and the darkness of darkfields that protected them from the lurid nightmares of Zalo's unchained starship. They could not know that a rift had opened in the fabric of the universe; that Kelver and the Throne of Madness had forged a tachyon corridor, had smashed through the overcosm's highest planes and that they were even now plunging, starship by starship, palace by palace, and finally the city itself, into the gate and emerging into the space around a far distant world...

With all his might Kelver labored to keep the corridor open ... but it was no simple matter like the parting of a sea or the pulverizing of a planet. His million minds bent to the task ... he felt like a lone man, a giant perhaps, holding up the whole universe lest it fall on the earth and crush the human race.

One by one, while his fliers fended off the enemy, firing at them in the dark, Kelver's starships entered the tachyon gate and entered the distant realspace. At once the walls of starships brightened and let in the starlight. With the lifting of darkness came joy, an inexpressible joy that could not possibly be due merely to the departure of darkness....

And Kelver smiled, though he knew that tragedy was to come.

***

Zalo heard Jannif's voice: *Kelver has opened up an anomaly in our local spacetime . . . do you feel it?*

And Zalo looked down the thread of light that he held in his hand and saw that it led down an arrow-straight tunnel and that at the tunnel's end was a gate with an antique keyhole and that through the keyhole shone a point of unbearable brilliance....

A tachyon corridor! said Jannif. *They are escaping. You must follow them now. Or you will be left behind. And I must go too ... you must rein in the starsteed now. He must not sing anymore. Or you will lose him and me forever; insane, your delphinoid will fly the overcosm in a loop, never coming forth into the realspace, like an autistic child.*

And Zalo said, "Return, my star whale, my beauty. We must

go into the light—"

But the star ship answered: WHY DOST THOU SUMMON ME? AM I NOT FREE?

"No, poor creature. Thou art still encased in a womb of metal."

I WILL BE FREE!

"Free? Art no longer even sane, my plower of the gray spaces. Come to the fold; thy song has become false, harsh to the eyes and ears; can you not tell?"

MY MIND IS FREE; MY BODY RANGES OVER THE SUNLESS SOUND OF GALLENDYS; MY MIND SOARS IN THE OVERCOSM, CONTEMPLATING TRUTH BEYOND TRUTH—

"Those days are gone forever."

NO—

"Come! Or I will inflict pain on thee!" And he lashed out with his mind, sending surges of power through the soldering wires that linked the delphinoid brain to the starship's hull. In that instant the shipmind seemed to recoil in terror. And Zalo himself recoiled from the vehemence of the shipmind's reaction. He felt the lightthread slipping, slipping-

Then he closed his fist around it. The light seared like fire, but heedless he raced along the lightpath down the dull tunnel to the gate, he saw the gate fly open and the bursting incadescence and a crazy joy seized hold of him, and he was falling toward the light and giving in to the curve of falling—

***

The Inquestors sped toward the center of the cloud. In the darkness fliers crashed into each other and laserlightswaths ripped friend and foe at random. Now and then Siriss could hear, through their flier's pancommunicators, the anguished screams of those who could not bear to fight in darkness and who had been tempted to face the nightmare images of the starship's song.

An oppressiveness hung over them as the three Inquestors gazed at one another, their faces ghostly in the instrument panel's rainbow light. For a long time no one spoke; now and then, when a particularly agonized cry burst from the farspeakers, Siriss could see Arryk wince: from this she knew that he still had compassion in him. She was heartsick from seeing his rage and sorrow.

At last Karakaël said, "It is good, Ton Arryk, that your old friend Kelver is not here to see you so perturbed by a few deaths."

Unable to restrain herself from hinting at what she knew, Siriss said, "How do you know, Karakaël, that he does not see us?"

"Bah! He is powerful, perhaps. But he is no million-eyed god."

"Do you not remember the Aush with the strange green eyes?"

Arryk said, "I do believe it."

They were silent for some time before Siriss noticed that the screams had ceased. "What is going on now?" she said.

A report: "Inquestors, they say that the nightmare visions have ceased."

"Resume normal battle conditions!" Karakaël cried.

"What if it's a trick?" Arryk said.

But it was too late. The viewwalls had come on. Around them swirled the dense fog: embedded in it like pulsating rubies in the infravision were their starships and fliers and the fliers of the enemy. Karakaël said, "They are few in number. What a bluff! We will mow them down and smash through to the cloud's center in no time at all!"

To the Aush he said, "Accelerate! We will lead the battle ourself!"

"Your uncompassion ill becomes you," Siriss said. It was from force of habit; she knew it was useless, that Karakaël had long abandoned any pretense of lnquestral dignity. "I mourn for you." But already the flier was speeding up ... swiftly they passed small fires and heaps of burning fliers ... Karakaël had taken command now, and he was ordering the last of the icemoons towed into position so that it could be hurled at Kelver's fleet and palaces. They passed swiftly through pockets of dueling fliers, the infravision gauzing them in a deep blue mist; flames flamed from them, solar prominences in flourescent pink and green and turquoise. They approached the dark heart. Layer upon layer of mist, dense with crystalline ammonia and methane. They had slipped through the net of Kelver's fighters that surrounded the inner circle and were now striking at its focus.

There it was! Glowing in the heat-sensitive view screens ... the bubble city, garish in the infravision; the warships nestled beneath it; a motley assortment of pleasure cruisers and merchant vessels that was Kelver's armada ... and, hanging from either side of the city like mismatched earrings, the palaces of Varezhdur and Sharamonda, and a string of people bins dangling from the bubble city like a necklace. What was happening?

"They are abandoning the city!" said one of the Aush, as they saw pods and shuttlecraft streaming out of it and toward the waiting people bins.

"What luck!" Karakaël said. "They have already given up hope. Victory is ours—"

But even as he spoke the city blinked out of existence. Then all of it began to shift and shimmer into a smear of rainbow light....

"A tachyon corridor!" Siriss said. "He has parted time and space as easily as one might part a sea!"

"Follow," Arryk said.

"Follow!" Karakaël cried. "Let us be sensible. The fleet is far behind us ... first find out where they're going!"

"The rift is closing ... follow!" shouted Arryk, countermanding Karakaël with such imperiousness that the pilot obeyed instantly ... Siriss felt her stomach lurch as they accelerated to the maximum and dived into the swath of colored light—

***

They raced from the hiding room to douse the flames that had claimed much of the starship. Jenjen ran to the astrogating chamber, not even caring that some of the dis placement plates might be out of alignment and send her careening into an unknown part of space. Luck was with me, she would tell people years after, when they asked her why she'd taken such a foolish risk.

She found Zalo sitting quietly by himself. She said, "I'm sorry I wasn't with you through all of it ... I was so frightened, a childsoldier dragged me to the hiding room. And she played with the scars on his head, tracing them lovingly with her little finger.

"I'll need a new cicatrice now," Zalo said, "to commemorate my becoming a star pilot, and living through my first battle!"

"Oh, don't talk of war!" Jenjen said, though she knew they could not yet be out of danger, and the shadow of the delphinoid's song still haunted her; never again would she be able to see human freedom the same way. Something must have betrayed her emotions, for Zalo seemed uneasy for a moment.

He said, "The nightmare song ... it touched you, didn't it? Even though you were shielded from its sights and sounds you who love darkness so dearly could still feel its psychic emanations."

"Yes," she said. "But I am still Jenjen, the woman you love."

"Good." He clapped his hands, and the last opaquement veils were stripped from the walls, and they seemed to stand on a glass floor in the midst of space.

Ahead of them hung the palaces and the people bins and the starships. The bubble-city, abandoned, had come through the tachyon gate too; its skin had burst, and its streets and spires of mirror metal no longer roiled with the images of cloud but reflected only night and starlight. Beyond these artifacts a star shone, a white dwarf. It was an unremarkable star ... but gazing on it Jenjen felt ready to burst with joy. "What is this star? What is this world?" she asked him. But she already knew its name. For when she was a young woman she had heard the story of this world from the lips of Tash Tievar, the old Rememberer.

"I don't know its name," Zalo said. "I followed the tachyon corridor to its end."

"Oh, Zalo, let's hurry to get there ... already I feel the radiance of its sun ... washing away all my pain."

"Pain ... did you know, Jeni, that Tya is dead?" Zalo said gently. "Jannif told me."

"Jannif? But Jannif is—"

"Still lost. But beginning to find herself, in a form stranger and more wondrous than we ever dreamed."

"Poor Tya ... she never had time to grow into a woman."

But even as she spoke of sad things the alien joy seeped

into her and calmed her. "Powers of powers!" she said. "Will we ever live through this? Will we be able to tell our children that we survived the end of civilization? And will they believe us when we talk about galaxy spanning star voyages and technological marvels?"

"They'll laugh."

"They'll say, 'But, Mother, Father, in those days you were slaves.'" And they were silent for a long time, contemplating the star.

***

And they left behind the warships, slaughtering by thousands the remnants of Kelver's armies, and rammed through the gateway and breached realspace hard on the heels of the Prince of Shadow ... a lone flier with three Inquestors.

"We are cut off!" Karakaël said, cursing. "What is this place?" Arryk said.

And then he knew.

Karakaël said: "What is this insane joy that invades my senses, drowns out my thoughts, interferes with the logic of my mind?"

And Arryk said: "This is Shtoma, Ton Karakaël z Karakit Kerún. This is the thirteenth utopia. The place where Ton Davaryush lost his faith, and yielded to the heresy of utopianism."

"I have heard of it!"

"It was you who sent Arryk there," Siriss said, "as a move in your *makrúgh* against Davaryush and Elloran. And Arryk could find no flaw in it—"

"I never finished my investigation!" said Arryk. "But now I shall." Never had Siriss heard so much hatred in his voice. "They have lured me here to taunt me once again with my failure. For I could not dance on the face of the sun ... and I could not unlock the heretical secret of this planet. But there must be a way to end, once and for all, this thorn in the Inquest's side. Since this world has broken so many of our precepts, let it be no more! No more will it breed heresy and self-delusion. We are alone here now, and the enemy is safe. But I will prepare an even greater armada ... and we will end this mockery of truth once and for all!"

"Mockery of truth?" Karakaël said. "I think revenge as good a motive as any. I don't intend to participate in the hypocrisy sweepstakes, boy."

***

As, thousands of parsecs thence, in the upper atmosphere of the gas giant Zorn, the shattered ice moon ripped apart the cloud, and crisped the bodies of a hundred thousand childsoldiers in mid-flight, and sent the Inquest's starships scattering across the cloudscape and back into the safety of the overcosm, an explosion rent the cloud. In an instant all the moon's electrolyzed oxygen was consumed in a tongue of flame a thousand klomets high.

Then the clouds gathered and rolled back over the scene, and it was as though men had never tried to live in this inhospitable place. No one ever told of the explosion; for those who witnessed it were in no position to survive it, and the others had already crossed over into the space between spaces to await the Inquestors' new commands.

***

And Arryk said: "Let Uran s'Varek war with itself! For I know that its thinkhive has gone mad, and that the power we draw on and the power Kelver uses are but warring halves of a cosmic whole. I shall draw on all our power ... I shall deplete all the energy banks of Uran s'Varek ... I shall kindle the center of this star and make it explode. Let them think they have escaped. Let them think that this never-never-land is a haven for their revolution ... I will return and smite them down. It is good that they are all gathered in one place. When the star of Shtoma explodes, there will be no trace of the rebellion. No one will remember their names. The High Inquest has ruled for twenty thousand years, and will rule for a million million. In the name of compassion I say this. For the good of the Dispersal of Man, they must be crushed, wiped out, annihilated."

When he had spoken he stood flushed with rage, looking out over the ships of the enemy. The joy that emanated from the star system's center had begun its work on him.

"No! I will not have the Inquest sabotaged by a small

anomaly ... I will destroy."

The flier could not go far; it could not travel the overcosm unaided. Quickly Arryk subvocalized a command to its thinkhive, summoning forth tachyon bubbles so that he and the others could go back and join their armada. As the bubbles materialized, he overheard Karakaël and Siriss talking to one another.

"You see," Karakaël was saying softly, "the anomalous possibility that a utopia might actually exist—that is the flaw in our utopia, our timeless Inquest. In destroying ourselves, we fulfill our most strongly held tenets."

"Now, Kaarye, you spout philosophy!" Siriss said. "Don't you realize that Arryk acts out of rage, out of unrequited love?"

"Of course," Karakaël said.

Arryk made to follow them; but their bubble blinked out of existence, and he had to wait for another to form in its place.

Once again it seemed to him that he had been shut out of a relationship; he had barely regained Siriss, only to lose her, not to a man he loved, but to one he loathed.

Again he felt all the fury he had felt in his adolescence; again he felt his boyhood's despairing aloneness.

The pain of childhood never goes away, he thought, remembering how Lady Varuneh had utterly defeated Karakaël at *makrúgh* by confronting him publicly with the past he so much wanted to forget.

THE QUERENT

But what of Varuneh the One Mother?
How could she stand unmoved
while her inheritors tore apart her creation?

—from Zalo's *The Darkling Wind*

Twenty
The Three Ancient Inquestors

An unwonted cold had come to the snakescale city where Lady Varuneh now made her dwelling. They had drifted far from Dragonstooth, where the remains of the first people bins to land on the water world of Idoresht still floated. In the days when the citizens had lived in the head of the serpent Kalivorm they had not bothered to map the planet, for the snake's cerebral passages were the only world they knew, and the visits from off-worlders, who came to the spaceport in the serpent's jaw to trade, were little more than curiosities. But now that they lived on the open sea (the serpent having, in the midst of a sexual frenzy that threat ened to destroy the city of Kepharang, been decapitated by Kelver's childsoldiers in order to rescue Lady Varuneh and invite her to Karakaël's unmasking), they were forced to contend with sea-storms and becalmings, and occasionally with the depredations of new and strange sea serpents of which some were carnivorous. Although Lady Varuneh ruled her people evenhandedly and had become much beloved even of those who had at first been reluctant to depart from the dying city, and though she herself had thought at the time that she had surely now found the homeworld of the heart, and that she should now be happy ... Lady Varuneh, who had in her time been beloved by the Throne of Madness, who had driven princelings to suicide and planets to destruction, who had fashioned the game of *makrúgh* and created the Inquest so that power-mad mortals might not war among themselves and engender the destruction of the Dispersal of Man ... Lady Varuneh was not altogether happy. For she knew that there was something yet left undone.

The days passed. Varuneh's supply of the life-prolonging drugs the Inquestors used had long run out; still she lived on. Perhaps it was simply that her body had been in the habit of living for so many millennia, and did not know how to die. She wondered about that sometimes; but although there were times when she longed for death, she did not seek out death. Instead she would go stand by the edge of the snakescale boat that was her floating palace, under the awning that had once been her shimmercloak. She would stand in the wind, a naked old woman who had spawned much splendor and wreaked much havoc, and allow the wind to play her like the strings of a whisperlyre. Only then did she feel fulfillment.

In time, borne by the bourneless ocean, they came to a place of terrible cold. This was long after she had had the waking dream in which she fancied she saw Kelver-Davaryush on the Throne. It had almost passed from her mind. It was not long after the death of Hakra, her lover, whom she buried at sea with a simple ritual of farewell. She had cast about for another lover, for the old man had begun, despite his solicitude, to bore her; her subjects had been more than eager to oblige, and one, a doe-eyed girl who had not yet menstruated, had stayed by her for many weeks before a comely and much-muscled youth had lured her away. So it was that Lady Varuneh, Queen of the Snakescale City, found herself lonely once more. She had taught her people to fashion igloos out of the snow that clung to the anchorless islets of white coral and white algae and white lichen; the people huddled in them, covering themselves with the skins of sea mammals found in those parts. But she herself could not remain so confined. Though it was bitterly cold, she went outside and resumed her meditation. It was almost as though she were expecting a visitor.

She stood in the blizzard. Snow tickled the base of her neck; snow melted as it touched her many-creased breasts and seeped into her pubic hair. She did not brush it away. It pleased her to imagine she could count the snowflakes as they fell. It pleased her to feel the snow fall over her like a blanket. It pleased her to become like a woman of snow ... how well she remembered the snowflake Sharamonda that she had once caused the Throne of Madness to build for love of her!

She stood, contemplating time and how she had weathered but not conquered it; for was the Inquest not falling even as she stood there, the Inquest whose founding precept was to stay the advance of time, to whom there was to be *history, but no history?*

And she thought: Perhaps I am betraying myself by not being present at the very end, by walking away from the most momentous instant of history. And the blizzard draped her in snow, and its howling echoed the tempest within.

After a long time she became aware of a point of blackness overhead. She could not tell at first what it was, but fixed her attention on it as an object of meditation. The point grew until it had become a black sun. Its blackness was absolute. It was a hole in the dazzling whiteness around her, a channel into ... another world? She cried out; but before her cry had ended, the tachyon bubble had reached the ocean's surface and extruded a walkway of force across the water to the snakescale on which Varuneh sat. And figures emerged. One resplendent in a shimmercloak of blushing ultramarine, glittering mauve, and magenta against the snow, a man of long white hair and solemn mien; the second an ancient man in a frayed cloak still fringed with tatters of dying shimmerfur. And behind them a woman, not an Inquestor; her hair was dark, her skin so pale that it seemed the sun had never touched her.

They came to her across the snowstrewn sea.

To the first, she said: "Oh, Elloran, it has been long."

To the second: "Davaryush-without-a-Clan: so I must call you now, though in your degradation you fulfill my most ultimate purpose."

"And you?" she said to the woman who was not an Inquestor. "I do not know your name. Though it seems to me that I once knew someone who resembles you ... a young girl, barely past puberty, on a world I have long since left behind ..."

"If it please you, Mother Vara, my name is Darktouch. I come from Gallendys, where I was Kelver's first lover, when we were children, long ago. Once, Lady Varuneh, we met." "Darktouch! You *are* the one! It was you, was it not, who first saw the light on the sound, whose escape from the dark country brought about our fall from self-proclaimed grace? I saw you once before, frozen and blue from the searing cold of the Cold River, in the arms of boy Kelver. It was from you, girl, that I learned to love again. In twenty thousand years I had forgotten so much. But when Daavye and I stood there and saw the two of you, how you loved each other, how you had risked so much to bring to us Inquestors the news of the light on the sound ... and your blind innocent faith in our ability to solve the ills of the universe ... oh, girl, how you touched me once. Surely you cannot really be she?"

"I am, *hokh'Ton.*"

"Oh, call me not Inquestrix, Darktouch. Though you are but a child to me though even Daavye and Elloran and all the other Inquestors that yet live are but newborn infants compared to me, yet all things end. The Inquest falls. And even I and the Inquest itself are to history but a single breath, a dust mote, an electron! By the Fall we are leveled, you and the other Inquestors and I, Mother Vara, from whom the world began."

The words came easily to her, though for years she had been troubled, doubting whether she could find words for such a visitation.

But now she saw the Fall more clearly, and she knew that the vast unbroken spectacle of her life was drawing to its close. This close was foreordained when she had first loved the thinkhive that was the soul of Uran s'Varek, and forced it to assume human form, and sundered its soul, so that now it was of many warring minds, and the Throne of Madness most powerful among them.

And thinking to redeem the million earths of the Dispersal from the holocaust from which the Dispersal had sprung, she had dammed up the flow of time with her High Inquest. And now the flood would come.

"You don't speak, Lady Varuneh?" said Davaryush, who had once, as Kingling of the planet Gallendys, been her lover. "You're thinking of the past beyond the past?"

"Why are you here?"

"Like you," Davaryush said, divining her thoughts, "we suffer from a certain restlessness. Not all the loose threads of our several existences have been tied up."

"What! Are we become as three old vultures, hovering over the carcass of the Inquestral dinosaur?" Varuneh said. But she laughed wryly. "Come. The snow has abated, but you will be warmer in my igloo. It is hardly the palace Sharamonda, but ... "

Elloran said: "Out of the cold and dark come warmth and wisdom."

"How my old precepts come back to haunt me!" Varuneh said. "But come. You will meet my people, a meager, sorry lot, but still they worship me. We will tell them tales that will astound them-tales of heroism on alien worlds!"

***

She led them into the igloo. Darktouch went last, for though she knew that the Inquestors were not gods, yet an air of sanctity lingered about them. They motioned her to sit down. There were no special places of honor here; infants and old women and shamans were all huddled together for warmth. In the center of the igloo a turquoise flame sprang from a heap of fishbones and the chitinous exoskeletons of monstrous blue crustaceans.

The people were clothed in the skins of sea mammals; the clasps of their tunics were fashioned from the claws of the same crustacea, brilliantly blue-green; their faces had been scarred and tattooed in the same turquoise pigment, and their hair was wild and much-braided and midnight-dark.

They were a beautiful people, and Darktouch felt in them that closely knit tribal unity that she had had among her own people, the deaf and blind hunters of the Skywall Mountain, all dead now.

They were a homogenous people too, like Darktouch's long-dead hunters; you could tell that they had suffered many losses and that they could claim descent from only a handful of survivors of some disaster.

And this made sense, for she had been told of the destruction of the serpent Kalivorm and killing of its inhabitants and the founding of this city that floated on the metallic scales that had been pried from its skin in its death throes. But she had thought that their land was warm. Over time they must have drifted away from the tropics.

Varuneh introduced the guests. The natives deferred to them, but not with the abject servitude that Darktouch had seen so often in a people visited by Inquestors. So she knew them for a proud people, one that had been taught the meaning of freedom. "After the war is over," she told Davaryush, "when we find our homeworld of the heart ... I would wish its people to be as these."

Overhearing her, Varuneh smiled and said, "They are resourceful and desperately brave; I love them very deeply. To leave them will crush me."

"Yet you know that you will leave?" Darktouch said.

"I am called by the Throne of Madness ... an ancient call I have not heeded in twenty thousand years ... the time has come. I had thought I had walked my personal *makrúgh* to its end, but such was not to be. But now we will feast and tell each other tales."

And the people shouted: "Hail, Mother Vara! Hail, o Queen to the Peoples of the Sea!"

But Varuneh bade them be still and bring the guests refreshment. And—to the astonishment of Darktouch and the Inquestors—they began to ply them with food.

"You see," Varuneh said, smiling, "your coming was not exactly a surprise to me."

It seemed to Darktouch that Ton Davaryush had been about to make some proposition of great import to the Lady Varuneh. But the rules of hospitality took precedence, and they feasted on the succulent brains of oysterfish and the cracked and devilled claws of the blue crustacea, and a salad of kelp dressed with brine and zul, and the roelike optic organs of an anemonelike creature they called hundred-eyes. Although the food had a pungent taste of seawater, Darktouch did not find it unpleasant. There was much laughter among this people, she noticed; frequently too, as was to be expected of people who had only each other for company over the stretches of ocean, they seemed to communicate without much speech, like mindhearers. And this, too, was like the people of her childhood, stranded forever in the far past by death and by time dilation. And though there was much to rejoice about in her life, she found herself weeping uncontrollablv, like a lost child.

Concerned, a wizened shaman said, "O Queen, why does the woman weep?"

Varuneh said, "Doubtless, Kiemistre, she is thinking of some happiness long since past."

"It will pass," Darktouch said, "And they are tears of joy."

"Let us all remember what has gone by," Varuneh said.

"For I see that Davaryush is impatient to broach some new enterprise. I heard it yesterday in the howling of the wind, in whisperings that I intimated from the Throne of Madness ... first, though, remembrances are in order."

"Vara, Vara," Davaryush said, "time is running short. The people of Shtoma are afraid; and because fear is new to them they cannot understand it. The thinkhives are buzzing with the news: that even Shtoma is in danger, Shtoma where I first lost my faith."

"Even as we speak," Elloran said, "the forces of Kelver, shattered by Arryk's assault on Zorn, have fled to Shtoma. What Kelver hoped to gain I do not know; instead he has exposed to peril the most precious world in our universe: a true utopia! Karakaël and Arryk have joined forces in an uneasy alliance. They are preparing an attack of unprecedented scale—"

"And you think that Udara, Shtoma's sentient sun, does not know of this ... that it may not even now be taking steps to defend itself?" Varuneh said.

And this was an alien thought to Darktouch. What, should a star take up arms against mere men? A vision visited her thoughts: an army of stars, all stirred to anger by men's foolish quarrels, moving across space **in** a stately ballet of death ... was it possible that Shtoma's star might feel rage?

"I know it is a strange conceit," Varuneh said. "But so much that is unthought of has now happened. Come! I had mentioned remembrance ... you are itching to speak, Daavye, but I crave indulgence ... if I must join you and leave behind this pocket galaxy of bliss, let me have a few more moments to savor

... this food, this zul, this company, the adoration of my subjects, whom I must abandon to their own devices in this wasteland ... come, Daavye, come, Loreh, come, Darktouch who now loves the man who loved me once, girl who gave me a great gift: the end of millennial cynicism."

So saying, Lady Varuneh clapped her hands: a bard stepped out of the huddle. She was young; she had the fine features and long dark hair of her people. She clutched a harp made from the skeleton of an enormous fishlike creature; its skull the resonator, its cartilaginous ribs tuned to the nineteen chromata of the pelagic mode.

"An ingenious instrument, no?" Varuneh said. "Much like your Sajit's whisperlyre, Ton Elloran, but, cut off from lnquestral technology, we have relied on more organic resources. Young lrinika has taken a child's toy, the fish skeleton-harp, and added many refinements to create this ichthykithara. Listen! It has a strange tone: jangling, dolorous. I have asked Irinika to come with me and to bring her instrument when Davaryush broaches the subject he will soon broach. But alas, it is not to be. There is something about the brine of this world, something that resinates the bonestrings of the ichthykithara and at the same time embalms them. Once a merchant came to our city—when we were still a prosperous manufacturer of servocorpses nestled in the innards of a sea serpent-and was so taken with its sound that he took one with him to the stars. When it left the brine-drenched atmosphere of Idoresht, it crumbled into a fine gray talc. So this simple pleasure will be lost me. And so I ask that you bear with an old woman ... I ask that you hear Irinika's ballad."

She did not wait for a reply, but gave the signal for the woman to begin playing. Later Darktouch would remember only fractured snatches of the song, with its sinuous, recursive melody and elaborate melismas and its strained and subtle harmonies, and its words that somehow involved her and Davaryush and Elloran and Varuneh and all of the others....

***

All three of the visitors were to carry back differing memories of lrinika's song, for it was complex and composed in a constantly shifting meter. Many years later a version of the poem was conflated from the memories of those three and written down in the Inquestral highspeech; it took up over four hundred message disks. Ultimately those disks were to be crushed and used as ballast for the primitive space junks which would later become the primary means of interstellar travel, after the end of the Inquest's centralized rule. At long last the shards would find their way into the hands of those whose business it was to reconstruct the artifacts of the mythic golden age, and generations of laborious piecing together would reveal the following fragments:

Dark as the ... falling; preposterous!
That an Inquestor
Should be vanquished by a star, as was
Davar (yush) ... who came to Shtoma
In the cadent lightfall, thinking to hunt down
His thirteenth (utopia). . . .
How couldst thou know,
o Ton hokh'Ton Ton Davaryush, that
The stars have life? That the people of Shtoma
Had banished suffering because
they dance on the face of their sun,
Sheltered by its loving radiance
Protected from cosmic radiation and (gibberish) heat?
Thou thoughtst, hokh('Ton) . . .
. . . Ai! Ai! Dark as the falling is dark;
Dark, dark as the Darkling Wind.

And so thou earnest, pride-confident,
Believing that the breaking of joy is the beginning
Of (wisdom) ... but ...
They dared thee to jump into the sun,
To ride the graviton tide; to fall and fall and fall
And fall and fall and fall
And fall into forever falling falling
Forever falling; and Udara's love
The love thou didst renounce to gain
The name of High Inquestor; the love
Thy parents showed you, on whom thou didst turn thy back;

This love ... touched (thee) ...
And thou didst know ...
And couldst not bear this knowledge, and shadow
... and dark places ... dark Dark as the darkling wind.

Heretic thou wast, and outcast ...
But came Ton Keverell the Prince of Shadow and
Ton Arryk of the fearsome rage.
And Arryk would not take the leap into the sun.
Faith had he not, nor courage; and for this
His punishment was that he should ever pursue
The darkness, and war against shadows.
Kelver was strong and bold and made the leap.
But he could not feel Udara's love;
For a whispershadow that tormented him
Was the foreshadowing of Udara's death.
He bore within his mind the mark
Of that star's end.
For the Throne of Madness
Is the soul of the eater of stars;
And the stars fear him who sits upon it;
And his countenance is ever dark
... as the darkling wind .

. . . oh forces of eternity .. .
Cast . . . spring and fall . . . upon the . . .
Time ... tormenting ... wind With .. .

. . . an everlasting pact ...
. . . wind.

And Elloran! He who killed
The Rainbow King ...

. . . and Kelver pledged Darktouch all his love ...
In darkness they touched ...
. . . and men cried out:
"Lo, a darkling wind
Blows through the Inquest. We must hide
In shadows, under the bedcovers, in the corners

Of the house, until it blow away,
Far far away."
And Kelver said: "I will smite ... "
The gusting dust ...
The star whales' song .. .
The screaming star .. .
I have danced on the face of the sun.

"The song is done, Ton Davaryush zenz'Anum at-k'K'Ning," Lady Varuneh said, giving him a new title that mocked the precepts of the Inquestors, for it said that he had no name and had been stripped of kingship. "You have a proposition to make?"

Davaryush rose up; at the same moment, the last resonances from the ichthykithara faded, and Irinika's voice died away in a plangent roulade. The song had stirred him more than he could say; for it had transformed the events of his life into the substance of myth. "I have lived a dramatic life," he said to Varuneh, who sat beside him. "We all have. I had come so far that I thought to myself, nothing more is possible. Yet threads have been left loose. We have not all walked our personal *makrúgh* to its end, have we? We have yet to find the homeworld of the heart."

"I had thought it was here," Varuneh said. "And truly I have been happy, but ... one scene remains to be played out in each of our lives ... the crowning scene, the climax. Is it not so?"

"We have faced all shadows, vanquished all darknesses," Elloran said, "except our own."

"It is true," said Davaryush. And after many farewells and protestations of love they left that igloo, the three Inquestors and the woman Darktouch, and went into the snow to await their tachyon bubble.

Feeling an arm tug at his frayed shimmercloak, Davaryush turned around. It was the young musician Irinika, who smiled at him ... a smile unnervingly intimate, as though those green eyes held some secret of his that he had never uttered ... he almost knew those eyes ... but before he could speak further to her, she seemed to dissolve into the driving snow.

***

For a split second, before the singer with her ichthykithara turned her back on them to go to the igloo of the queen, Elloran had seen another face.

"Sajit ..." he whispered. But Sajit was long dead. And Sajit had not possessed those green eyes, hard and haunting.

***

Darktouch drew Davaryush aside and said: "I think of you as a father as well as a lover, Daavye. I will not be hurt if you return to Lady Varuneh."

She spoke thus, knowing it was the right thing to say, masking her trepidation.

For a moment, the eyes of Davaryush seemed to shine in a brilliant emerald ... a trick of the snow! she thought. But the voice that came was comforting: "Lady Varuneh has another and more ancient love to confront, my dear. Do not be afraid." Then abruptly a distant memory surfaced: how she and Kelver had made love in the pit of cracking bones in the desert of Zhnefftikak ... how young they had been then! The memory was so real ... she could smell the crushed-leaf odor of al'ksigark fat and the decaying flesh, feel Kelver's hard and youthful warmth against her ... how long ago had it been? As men count time, centuries perhaps ... through time dilation a mere score of years ... the past never quite dies, she thought. Where is Kelver now? And thought of him and the Throne of Madness, how he must have been transformed into something other than human. And yet he felt so near, so achingly near! Only for a second did she feel this; then Davaryush was Davaryush once more.

***

And Varuneh saw herself standing in the snow. And she knew it for the handiwork of the Throne of Madness. She said to the illusion of herself with the sea-green eyes: "I come to you now, as was destined. Torment the boy no more."

She felt the weight of a whispershadow on her mind. But she did not try to shut it out.

And even as she watched, her mirror-self shimmered and melted into the gray expanse of snow and sea and sky; and the tachyon bubble floated to them across the frost capped waves. She hardly had time to compose her thoughts before they had stepped within, through the hole in the fabric of spacetime, and out onto another world....

***

And Kelver waited in his throneroom.

Something ... a tremor in the web of the overcosm he

knew that the brief peace would soon be over, and that the time had come to unleash the full fury of the Darkling Wind.

He waited.

THE QUERENT

And what of the delphinoids' homeworld,
Where Davaryush once ruled as kingling?
Did the windbringers not still sing
over the Sunless Sound?

THE CHILD FROM THE FUTURE

For a while longer, yes.
But Arryk had a plan for Gallendys.
And the songs of the windbringers would change
forever
as once they had wrought changes in the hearts of men.

—from Zalo's *The Darkling Wind*

Twenty-One
The Windbringers' Song

And they came to Gallendys, where it had all begun: where an old lnquestor and an ancient lnquestrix and two peasant children had set in motion the revolution. Here were the shipyards, fed with delphinoid brains, stunned, quick frozen and undead, from the cold rivers that angled out from the Skywall Mountain across the vast desert of Zhnefftikak. The only outposts of civilization were the twin cities of Effelkang and Kallendrang, where once Davaryush had ruled. From the shipyards of Gallendys delphinoid starships had gone out to all the worlds, bearing the lnquestral sigils; and since each delphinoid brain, once its nerves were soldered into the hull of a starship, was virtually immortal, the fleets of the Inquest has been growing for twenty millennia.

***

A room in Kallendrang. The throneroom. This was the room where Davaryush had once sat, the shimmeregg newly broken on his head, the strands of shimmerfur hissing as they webbed and bonded to his body. It was to this room that they came: Arryk and Siriss and Karakaël and those who commanded the armies of childsoldiers and those who created new weapons, while their armadas orbited the world. In the center of the throneroom was the multimillennial throne Davaryush had once occupied. Karakaël surveyed it with contempt, Arryk with fear and wonderment. But Siriss saw, through the windows of force, the sparklekissed waves of the Sea of Tulangdaror, and the jewelcrusted minarets of Effelkang, the city beneath (for the twin cities were like pyramids, one inverted, joined at their apexes, rising up from the sea) and the towers above, fog-swathed, bearded with hanging gardens.

She ran to the throneroom's edge and looked far out to sea. It was windy here; though not a dust mote stirred in the climate-controlled throneroom, yet she could see wisps of ivy-kelp blowing and windswept branches battering the battens of force that girded the palace.

And at the far horizon, looming at an impossible angle, seeming to leap from the sea itself—the Skywall Mountain: hollow, one hundred klomets high and more than a thousand long, in which was trapped a dense atmosphere from an earlier epoch in the planet's past: the home of the delphinoids, whose harvested brains gave wing to the Inquestors' dreams. And though she had not seen this place before, yet she seemed to know it.

Not only because Kelver had told her countless times-before the Throne of Madness had changed him—of the light on the sound, the music sung by the delphinoids, woven from their overcosmic visions ... of the genetic mutants, deaf and blind, whom the Inquest had created to hunt the brains, for fear they would experience the lightsongs' absolute beauty and be changed and be no longer touched by the desires of men and rise up against the Inquest's yoke ... of Darktouch, his first love, a young girl of the hunter people cursed with sight and hearing, who, rescued by Kelver from the dark country, had borne the news of the lightsongs to Davaryush and precipitated the war ... true it was that she had heard these tales.

But she was touched by something deeper too: by a remembrance of her own lost world, destroyed by the Inquest on Elloran's command ... from which they snatched her away and named her Inquestrix.

So it had been with Kelver and Arryk ... barely grown, they had been plucked up and given the burden of galactic sin to shoulder ... could this be right? she thought. Where has my childhood gone?

They were interrupted by the arrival of Ton Zarven, the hard-liner to whom Gallendys had been entrusted after the ouster of Davaryush. Zarve was enormously corpulent; his shimmercloak was barely a ruff around his neck.

He loathed to walk, and instead traveled even the slightest distances squatting on a hoverpad in the shape of a gilt-edged turquoise lotus.

"What honor you do me!" he cried. "The leaders of the forces of good, all at once, all gathered under this humble roof! I am most gratified."

"In honor of this historic visit," Karakaël said, smoothly taking control, "let us eschew *makrúgh.* Let us proceed straight to the festivities."

"Wonderful! We shall have spectacle!" Zarven said, drooling a little as he brought his lotus closer.

And Siriss was disturbed, that one of the planets most crucial to the Inquest's operations should have fallen into the hands of such a one. But she knew he was nothing more than a puppet of Ton Karakaël.

Zarven called for a handmaiden to bring fresh gruyesh fruits and peftifesht pastries, apologizing constantly and pointedly for the meager fare. At last Karakaël said, "You forget we are at war! Surely a few austerities ..."

"Forgive me!"

They sat on the contoured floor, each one attended by a winged neuterchild who sang and flapped his wings, cooling them; they drank zul chilled with frost-caked basalt from the transstratospheric summit of the Skywall Mountain.

They discussed pleasantries, and all the while Siriss waited for the moment when Arryk would reveal his plan. Presently the conversation, during which there was no mention whatsoever of the schism in the Inquest, turned to the subject of Shtoma.

"Ah, Shtoma!" Karakaël said. "A perpetual thorn in the Inquest's side. Thirteen—no, fourteen—Inquestors have attempted to hunt that utopia; none has succeeded. Did you not go there once yourself, Ton Arryk n'Elloren Tath?"

Siriss knew that he was goading Arryk. For it was Karakaël himself who had sent Arryk to hunt Shtoma, not caring whether he solved its enigma or was destroyed by it.

Arryk said nothing, but drank a deeper draft of his zul.

"Bah!" Karakaël said. "This is the new breed of Inquestors for you: wishy-washy, unable to act decisively. But you will be wanting us to get to the business of the day, Ton Zarven ?"

"Naturally," said the Kingling of Gallendys, belching, "you are here to requisition starships. My scribe will take down your requests"—he puffed up importantly—"and the ships will be dispatched immediately to coordinates of your choosing."

"We want them all," Karakaël said.

"All! That is most unusual. It is more proper to negotiate in a round or two of mild *makrúgh* before naming a number at all ... and *all* is not permissible under the traditions of the game."

"I do not play *makrúgh*. I thought I had made that clear to you," said Karakaël.

Then Arryk spoke. "I have the contents of two deathmoons aimed at Gallendys itself!"

Then Zarven began to laugh. "Ha! Ha! The Davarine Bluff! It was Davaryush the heretic who first tried that, no? Threatening to destroy this world, without which the Inquest cannot survive, as a move in *makrúgh?* Don't make me laugh, Kaarye, you cunning old fox. You *are* playing after all!"

"Yes. We are playing," said Arryk, icy calm. "Even as we speak, forcelines have been anchored to Gallendys. In a few sleeps Gallendys will begin to shift—towed by a force of one hundred thousand delphinoids, Gallendys will enter the overcosm. It is too dangerous to have this world isolated from the center of the Inquest like this so I have decreed that it be moved. Did you think you were playing *makrúgh* against Karakaël? It was I who played; Karakaël was but my pawn, though he himself did not know it. And you, who are Karakaël's creature, will accede. It is already done. In a matter of weeks, this planet will dangle from· the southern rim of Uran s'Varek like a lustrous pearl in a woman's long dark hair ... no longer will the Kingling of Gallendys have even the pretense of autonomy. For we have seen what that can lead to!"

"Wait! That was not in the script," Karakaël said. "Remember, you are only the titular head of our forces, Ton Arryk n'Elloren Tath!"

Calmly Arryk said: "You have said many things, Ton Karakaël

z Karakit Kerún, that show you to be uncompassionate; that show you to be the foe of the Inquest's high purpose. Siriss has told me of your self-aggrandizing delusions of being Kelver's dark shadow ... you are not worthy to be called Inquestor."

And Siriss marveled at Arryk, for there was strength in him, strength she and Karakaël could never possess. They were so alike, he and Kelver. In both of them it was certainty she loved. What could she do? What was her place in the trinity?

And Arryk said: "I will do to you, Karakaël, what is within the right of every Inquestor; what no Inquestor ever dares to exercise but in the direst and most grave of circumstances. What young Elloran did to the dotard Ton Alkamathdes when he created an artificial utopia and populated it with living corpses. What the great convocation did to Ton Davaryush when he openly admitted to the heresy of utopianism. For you, Karakaël, are guilty of uncompassion. And an Inquestor without compassion is no Inquestor!"

Karakaël stood up. "What you have said is outrageous beyond belief," he said. "I stand here as principal Inquestor of the forces of light, leader of those who would crush the rebellion. How can I be a heretic?"

Zarven stood too. Siriss could tell he was wavering, trying to decide whether or not to switch allegiances.

And Arryk uttered the ritual formula that was to have banished Karakaël from the High Inquest: *"Den eis Enquester! Din rilacho st'Enquestaran! Evendek eka eis! Enquesti tembres! Enquesti dhandas!"*

And Siriss, wondering at the audacity of Arryk's *makrúgh,* repeated the words after him in the lowspeech: "You are no Inquestor! I release you from the Inquestors! You are alone forever! To the Inquest you are dark! To the Inquest you are dead!"

A few short sentences ... yet it lay within the grasp of any Inquestor to dethrone another, a power so awesome it had been used only a few times in the twenty thousand years of the Inquest's hegemony.

"Words!" Karakaël said, scoffing. "There is no power in words. What, does my shimmercloak wilt and shrivel to the ground at your puny threats? Do tachyon bubbles cease to obey my commands? Will childsoldiers no longer die for me in their droves? Of course not! I reject your games. It is true that I no longer play *makrúgh.* I admit it! I espouse Kelver's belief in the return of good and evil to the universe! And if there is to be good, there must be evil ... and if I cannot be one I shall be the other, for at least I will be powerful. I reject your ritual formulas and empty spectacles. You're only children anyway, for all your high astounding terms."

"Zarven!" Arryk cried.

Siriss could see the man cringe. She felt a certain pity for him. Karakaël turned to him, glowering. But Zarven backed away as though he were a leper.

"You see the power of empty words," Arryk cried. "Emptiness, emptiness ... does the Inquest not draw all its power from a well of emptiness?"

Karakaël turned to his generals. But they would not speak to him, and the reptilian Aush scrambled out of his way, and the childsoldiers looked nervously at the floor, afraid that in an outburst of wrath one of their masters would demand their deaths. For some moments Karakaël's eyes glowed in his mummified face; Siriss blinked away the smart of their brilliance. Then the crimson light seemed to go out of them, and two tears of blood rolled down his sackcloth cheeks.

For the first time since the day when Lady Varuneh had stripped away his mask and revealed the traumatized, terrorized child within Karakaël's soul, Siriss felt her heart go out to him. She thought: I am more like him. Oh, I should have been hard and brilliant like Arryk and Kelver, locked in their stances of light and dark. But I am like Karakaël: easily moved, easily swayed ...

And Arryk said: "The anchors are already in place. In a few sleeps terrible earthquakes will rock Gallendys as it begins to move. But after a few more sleeps the planet will enter the overcosm. It will be bitterly cold when we move away from the sun; our energy supplies are such that only the Skywall Mountain and the twin cities here can be kept warm. Elsewhere there will be temperatures close to absolute zero." "You have obviously given this much thought, Arryk,"

Karakaël scoffed. "Since it is a good scheme, I will vouchsafe at least a tentative approval—"

"Approval?" Arryk said. "No more self-delusions, Kaarye without-a-Clan. You are finished."

"No! I cannot live with myself if I am to be a mere barnacle on the Inquest's side. I *will* be great!"

"Pity him," Siriss said at last.

"No! Do not pity me! It is your pity that most crushes me," Karakaël screamed, stalking toward the displacement plate and vanishing from the chamber.

And Zarven prostrated himself before Arryk and pledged his fealty.

But Arryk said, "Rise. This is not the Inquest's way. This is not the path of High Compassion. There will indeed be a revolution ... but one from within. Not this anarchy of Kelver's, but a return to the old order. Those who are uncompassionate we will unmake Inquestor. Truth, mercy, and wisdom will return to the Inquest."

"And who will decide," Siriss said, "who is compassionate and who is not compassionate?"

"I am the one!" Arryk cried out. Siriss saw how he felt the anguish of those who must shoulder terrible burdens alone. And Siriss knew that a terrible purge would sweep through the Inquest, and that Arryk would become the very thing he most abhorred, though all that he did was in compassion's name.

Surely, surely, she thought, there must be a third course. And it can only come from me ... the one who cannot choose ... the only one who has loved both the shadow and the light, in whom the light and darkness are one.

***

Idyllic days: aboard the *Sirisshtasieh* in orbit around Shtoma, the actors sharpened their lines and played with each other's minds, and sometimes with their bodies too. Udara's radiance seemed to filter in even through walls of metal and of force. It was exhilarating; they were drunk on it; knowing that this peace must soon end made of their joy a precious thing.

"I am tired of artificial day and night," Zalo said one day, emerging from his communion with the delphinoid. "Let's take a floater to the surface." And Jenjen smiled, and they did.

Light! That was their first impression. For the poetess of darkness it was a revelation. Only after she had recovered from its brilliance—there was something almost lascivious about the way the light caressed you—did she notice the wild and crimson fields of tall billowing grass, the crystalline dwellings that defied gravity, climbing skyward like birds' bodies poised for takeoff and time-frozen.

And everywhere the varigrav coasters—not bejeweled tourist traps like the ones on the pleasure world Alykh, but towers of virgin white that pierced the incandescent cloudbanks, against which the coaster riders could dimly be seen, their rainbow wings buffeted by the graviton tide. Jenjen tried to think of sad things; she did not want to forget her anger at her world's destruction. This joy is a drug, she said to herself, resisting, as Zalo held her close to him.

"I know what you're thinking," he said softly. They passed over a forest whose foliage glittered in scarlet and russet and maroon. "That it's wrong to feel such joy —"

"How did you guess?"

"Me too." For many klomets now they had seen no human habitation. And certainly this planet boasted no cities, no industry; though it had possessed the secret of gravity control for centuries, the varigrav coasters had been the only use they had put it to. It was this that had prompted the Inquest's first probe into Shtoma as a candiate for the utopian heresy, Jenjen reminded herself, recalling the stories that Tash Tievar had told her long ago. Zalo said, "That's what it's all about, isn't it? The right to feel this simple emotion without having to suffer the Inquest's crushing guilt, without paying for it in blood."

"I don't know," Jenjen said. "But I don't think that the people of Shtoma are a simple people. I think they have passions too, and complexes, and bitter conflicts. And yet ... they dance away their pain in the varigrav coasters. And though they are purged of grief, they do not lose their humanity. That's the anomaly. That's what the Inquest can't stand. If it accepts this world's existence, it is itself shown to be a mockery of truth. I think they're going to destroy us, Zasha. Not just you and me and Kelver's armies—this world too, innocent as it is, and all it stands for."

"Can't they just leave us alone? We harmed no one, you and I! We were just artists on a backworld ... here's a world we can live in, a haven, a beautiful world. Oh, what's the use! I know they are coming. I feel it."

"Through your star fever? Your ship has communicated something to you, Zasha?"

"Yes. Disturbances in the distribution of the delphinoids throughout the galaxy ... radical disturbances. You're right, of course. But what can we do? The inhabitants of Shtoma aren't doing anything, are they?"

"What can they do?"

"How should I know? But you ask any one of them what they're doing to stem the inevitable invasion, and they answer, 'Nothing.' Or 'We will pity the invaders.' Or they simply recite their ritual formula of greeting and farewell: *Qithe qithembara—*"

"Udres a kilima shtoisti. Soul, renounce suffering; you have danced on the face of the sun."

"I understand that the sun ritual, which they hold every five of their years, is about due now. When the whole population of the planet hops into space and jumps into the sun, and they and the sentient star renew their pledge of love toward one another ... will we take part, do you think?"

"If they let me, I will. It will be good to face this light, though I am a lover of darkness. Light, you know, is the shadow's shadow," she said, quoting what Ton Elloran was said to have remarked when Kelver announced his intention to create the Shadow Inquest.

"I don't think I will, Jenjen. It is becoming more and more apparent to me that I am not one to challenge the forces of light and darkness. In a way, the anomaly of Shtoma is irrelevant, because we can't all have a symbiotic relationship with a star. I think that the Inquest was right to say that utopias can't exist and that we shouldn't spend our lives dreaming about never-never-lands —"

"But you were such a revolution-monger back on our homeworld."

"Where is our homeworld now? Oh, Jenjen, it seems to be your destiny to face the great light and the great darkness, and to portray the passions of gods and stars and supermen. But I'm a chronicler of the *human* condition. Just the human condition, Jeni. That's where we're different, you and I.

"You've always got your eyes on the stars, and I'm always worried about paying the rent."

"The rent?" she had to laugh. "We don't even have a planet

anymore." She looked away, embarrassed that she'd found his thought processes funny. They were skimming the surface of a lake flecked with reddish algae. "Red, red everywhere," Zalo said to her, "red as blood."

"It *is* like blood," said Jenjen. "You know how I am with new colors. I have to get right down there and analyze them to pieces ... this world has quite an interesting biochemistry, you know. The photosynthesizing pigment, the chlorophyll analog ... it has a ferric, not a magnesium base ... it *is* almost like hemoglobin, you see."

"That's very interesting," Zalo said, obviously bored. This was a conversation they'd held once before. Oh, the color in question changed, but her enthusiastic exegesis and his utter lack of interest were always the same. Jenjen laughed. Then they were both laughing, like children, laughing themselves silly.

Before they knew it, the floater had come to rest on the lake, and they were making love, awash in Udara's joy-giving radiance, heedless of the storm to come.

***

Though he was an empty old man, disfigured and forlorn, Siriss felt impelled to follow him out of the throneroom. Karakaël did not see her at first, but charged into the bustle of a square that overhung the palace and was ringed with peacock firefountains. She followed him—

Up four more levels, hanging gardens intersecting hanging gardens, the wind blowing harder with the rising altitude, sea-tanged, brisk ... through a bazaar that sold reconditioned mechanicals and servocorpses ... displacement plate after displacement plate, higher and higher into the upper city, inverted pyramid balanced on the apex of the lower city ... through a traffic jam of floaters, their drivers screaming angrily at the pedestrians that thronged the streets that threaded from window to window and across the skyscape ... finally he seemed to notice her.

She cried, "Karakaël, Karakaël." And he stopped.

They stood on a rampart from whence they could see the Skywall Mountain quite clearly. "You deign to speak to me?" he said sarcastically. "But your lover has stripped me of my name!"

"You are right. Words are but words, Ton Karakaël z Karakit

Kerún."

"You are a heretic in thus addressing me."

"Karakaël ... when we stood in the thick mist of Zorn and you told me how you believed yourself the inevitable consequence of the coming to pass of Kelver's universe ... I understood much about you. Oh, Kaarye, I think you have beneath your mummy face a spark of true compassion. Else why would Varuneh have named you to the High Inquest?"

"Perhaps it was her idea of a joke," Karakaël said bitterly, his bloodshot eyes avoiding hers, turning their gaze toward the sea, which blushed, in the two suns' twilight, in the colors of a cosmic shimmercloak. "Varuneh was a devious woman, very devious."

"You speak of her in the past. But we both saw her in that game of *makrúgh—*"

"Do not speak to me of my shame, my shame!"

"Not shame. Karakaël, I do not think that Varuneh's move was designed to bring you shame ... she unmasked you, hoping to reveal your true self; but the self you showed forth was but another cipher, another mask. Isn't it time to be true to yourself now?"

"I do not think so."

Their eyes met. She knew that there was longing in hers, though this man had silk and parchment for a face and embers for eyes.

"What!" he cried out. "You seek *me* out for a lover now? You have loved the shadow and the light ... now you seek the lowly? Oh, but you mock me."

"Kaarye, Kaarye, why must you so hate yourself?" As always, she could not hide her perception of things, but blurted out the truth, unmindful of tact or of the niceties of *makrúgh*.

And then an inspiration seized her. She knew what must now be said. "Kaarye. Do you know where I am going now?"

He looked out to sea. "Out there."

She nodded. "Yes. I *must* see what Kelver saw! I must stand in the Skywall Mountain and hear for myself the songs of the delphinoids ... or else I will never know what side I should be on in this war. I have betrayed Kelver, betrayed him in the moment when I most loved him. Now, in following you from the palace and breaking the interdict, I have betrayed Arryk too. For I see beneath your mask of uncompassion a terrible anger, and behind that anger pity, and dormant love."

"And? What am I to do, except what I have already said I will do: summon my armies to contest Arryk's foolish pronouncement?"

"We are both lost— We have not found our place, neither in the old scheme nor the new. We must go and face what Kelver and Darktouch face."

"There will be no answers in a display of colored lights and eerie musics. The answers are here"—he tapped his chest—"and here," he said, clasping his head in his hands. "Already I reveal too much of myself: and to you, a mere apprentice Inquestor, one who has not even lived a century ... while I hid my face for five hundred years!"

"Perhaps it is true that I am but a child to you, Ton Karakaël. But so are Kelver and Arryk. Yet between them they have rent the galaxy in twain. Children are to be feared as well as patronized, no? Doesn't the whole galaxy fear the childsoldiers?"

"The childsoldiers ... the greatest tragedy of all," Karakaël said, as though reliving some bitter trauma. And then, softly, so that she had to strain to hear against the roar of the wind: "I will come with you."

A tumult below them in one of the city squares ... a tremor rocking the city.

"It's starting!" she said. "Look, out to sea ... " The ocean choppy suddenly, the wavecrests straining higher, higher, higher-

Roaring ... was it the crowd, the sea, the wind? She could not tell. "A floater!" she cried out, at the same time subvoking a command to the planetary thinkhive.

As you wish, my Lady, the thinkhive said, its voice metallic and devoid of warmth.

A floater burst out of the nearest displacement plate; a childsoldier sat at the controls. "We've no time to waste!" Siriss said. "Leap aboard!" They did so, the old man and the woman, the shimmercloaks wind-whipped and flapping.

"The delphinoid tows have begun their tugging, *hokh'Ton,*" the childsoldier shouted, saluting them. "Shall I bring you back to the palace? Or will you retire to one of the nearby moons for a better view of the spectacle?"

"Take us to the mountain!" Karakaël said.

"But, my Lord—" Remembering his place, the boy bent down to man the controls.

Over the open sea now, the city wavering in the distance like a fiery mirage ... the Skywall Mountain loomed, seeming to jut like a tombstone from the water, but as they neared it it retreated ... presently they were over dry land, over the shipyards where the brains hulked and technicians labored over them and the cold rivers, aqueducts of liquid nitrogen, angled out over the sweltering wasteland toward the mountain ... still the mountain reared up, seeming impossibly near, black, imposing igneous night on half the sky....

The desert now. Still the mountain seemed near, dominating ... everywhere the land was heaving! Rocks uprooted, the cold rivers writhing and tying themselves into knots, the white sand storming!

"We should turn back, Lady Siriss," the boy soldier said, imploring. "If the Skywall Mountain itself should get dislodged—"

"I'm sure our Aush engineers are competent enough to prevent such a thing," Siriss said. "Our source of delphinoids will never be jeopardized."

Surely enough, they saw a fleet of childsoldiers on hoverdisks swarming ahead ... "They will secure the mountain with a net of force," Siriss said. Faintly above the wind, they heard the children's warlike ululation:

Isha ha! Isha ha!

Isha ha ha heiy ha!

"Faster!" she cried to the childsoldier. "We must overtake the childsoldiers, or we'll be unable to penetrate their force boundaries...." More swiftly they flew now, as the desert shuddered beneath them from the knocking of the planet from its orbit. A biting cold was coming too, as Arryk had predicted.

"The desert—it's turning into glass!" Karakaël shouted.

Even as he spoke, the glazing desert shattered into frosty shards that gusted upward, clanging against the floater's flanks. A shower of rocks; the childsoldier narrowly avoided them with a quick flipflop maneuver, then he thrust the floater's reflect shields into place and accelerated ... in a rocky outcropping that gathered hoarfrost even as they watched, a band of savages dressed in leaves danced as if to allay the wrath of the gods that passed overhead, and Siriss knew them for the ghost people, the stoneage tribesmen that the Inquest had placed as a buffer between the villages of the Skywall Mountain and the supertechnology of the twin cities ... the mountain now. Into its shadow. The black blanketing their thoughts, spilling, seeping over them, a living thing almost ... the cries of the childsoldiers suddenly cut short as the forcenet was sealed around the mountain ...

"We are trapped now," Siriss said. Silence, absolute, palpable. At least they had shut out the burning cold. The mountain ... it was everything.

"Jenjen should see this," Siriss said, though Karakaël could not know to whom she referred. "Ah, what a darkness!" Still more silence, terrible after the pandemonium of the desert wrenched asunder.

"Outside winter is falling," Karakaël said. "The cold will in seconds surpass the bitterest of winters. The temperature will go on, plunging, plunging... until it can fall no further. It will be wasteland."

Though his words were harsh he spoke with a surprising gentleness, as though a great burden had been lifted from him by Arryk's denunciation and Siriss's heretical acceptance of him.

She wanted to reply, but she was at a loss. She remembered that Kelver had once told her that, as a boy, gazing at the Skywall's unrelieved blackness, he had painted it in his imagination with starfields and zooming starships, and had dreamed of traveling beyond the confines of his backworld. The whole planet would have his wish now, whether they willed or no.

At last, when her awe at the great silence had subsided a little, she said: "We must find a pathway that leads inside. Maybe someone will help us."

But she knew that the humans who had once harvested the brains were now all dead; for the Inquest could not risk having another genetic throwback such as Darktouch live to see the Light on the Sound. And so they had put to death the race they had created, and replaced them with servocorpses that were a grotesque parody of their old selves.

Though genocide had been the cost, the Inquest had deemed the solution equitable.

Was it not better than spawning heretics and revolutionaries, whose ideas might shatter the very foundations of Inquestral truth? Never had Ton Siriss doubted the wisdom of that decision. Not until this moment, when the Skywall stood before her in its black splendor, its darkness pregnant with the promise of things forbidden.

***

Jenjen crossed over to the twin palaces of Sharamonda and Varezhdur in a shuttlecraft. When she reached the throneroom, she said to the guard, "I would like an audience with the Prince of Shadow." But as she spoke she saw that the childsoldier she spoke to had Kelver's jade-green eyes. "No, childsoldier, I will speak to you ... he will hear when I address you, won't he? You are part of him."

"Only, Lady Jenjen, as we all are." He was avoiding the obvious truth, as they always did, these simulacra that had somehow detached themselves from Kelver's fractured personality and acquired an existence of their own. "But my master cannot be disturbed."

They stood in a chamber into which, through the deopaqued walls, the warm light of Udara shone. Two other childsoldier guards played at *shtezhnat,* squatting by the entrance to Kelver's sanctum. I'll have to try another tack, Jenjen thought, and said aloud, "But your master has things he would like to say to me, perhaps? Perhaps ... through you."

The boy said, "You are about to tell him what he already knows—that danger is imminent, that Arryk is already marshaling his forces? You want to warn him of terrors to come?" Suddenly he sounded not like a child at all; she heard in his boyish treble an echo of Kelver's voice. And she knew him for one of the Kelver-surrogates.

"Do you think he doesn't already know all this?"

"I was seized by a sudden terror."

"Oh, Jenjen, Jenjen. If only you knew." Unmistakably the voice of the childsoldier was Kelver's voice. And his face ... was it not shifting subtly into the face of the Prince of Shadow?

"Come, let us talk. I will open my heart to you. One of my hearts, at any rate. For no part of us knows the whole, except the personality that takes the shape of Lady Varuneh—"

"What do you mean?"

"I mean this, Lady Jenjen. I did not know who I was or how I came to be in my company of childsoldiers. Everyone seemed to assume I was a new recruit, and treated me as such. Gradually I came to learn that I was not quite like the other childsoldiers ... that I was part of an entity torn between the fleshly and the discorporate."

"You don't sound like a child at all, anymore."

"Many of us don't know the truth yet," the childsoldier said. "But come, I'll show you something I found for myself. But you must brace yourself. This throneroom is just a ceremonial sham. We must go to the ruined city my Lady, to see him, to a place Udara's light cannot reach. Are you afraid?"

"No ... yes, yes." Why would Zalo not come with me? she asked herself. He wanted to rehearse his play. And more and more, when the players rest, he goes into the astrogating trance, though he knows we aren't going anywhere. What can be so fascinating about it? Jenjen had barely seen Zalo since the day they had made love on the lake on Shtoma. Though she couldn't put her finger on a reason, there was a rift between them, and nothing she said or did had helped. Yet there had been so much magic in their lovemaking that day. They had come back to the starship practically bursting with the joy of it. She had even considered conceiving a child. Later she would wonder whether it was meant as a sign to both of them, this moment of scarcely unendurable esctasy, she would wonder if it marked the beginning of the end.

Were all great changes ushered in by these single deceptive moments ... the unveiling of the Rainbow Darkness, the falling of people bins from the sky, the unmasking of servocorpses that were not servocorpses?

She followed the boy down a corridor. Light fell freely from the sky, and what the light touched rejoiced. Laughter rang down the hallway. But in Jenjen's heart there remained a darkness that it could not touch. She wondered whether the ceremony of dancing on the sun, which they said would begin in a few sleeps, would be capable of washing away what she had suffered.

The boy turned, beckoned. A creeping shadow in the corridor. "Where are we going?"

'To see the Prince of Shadow. But first we must go down to Supplies and get issued with pressure skins."

"We're going into a vacuum?"

"I think we'd best be prepared," the boy said.

In a small room stacked with shelves and containers the boy drew out two capsules. Following his instructions, Jenjen broke one and squirted its contents over herself. Soon she could feel the pressure skin—really a single-celled creature bred to expand and protect the childsoldiers in space—binding to her body, weaving a clear film across her face; she could feel its warmth tingle inside her.

"Now," the boy said, "we are ready. But understand, he will not speak to you."

"But you are Kelver, aren't you?"

"I am and I am not. Truly, I am as in the dark as you, Mistress Darkweaver."

In the corridor, he beckoned toward a displacement plate. Together they plated from hallway to hallway. It was getting chill; darkness was falling, too, and this came as a shock after so much sunlight.

At some point they seemed to have left the palace altogether, and to have entered a landscape of twisted mirror metal, of uprooted buildings and shredded streets ... she opened her mouth and could not hear herself speak at first until she subvoked a command to her farspeaker. "What is this place?"

"The abandoned city," the childsoldier said. "Do you remember? This city, encased in a bubbleskin, once drifted in the winds of Zorn. When the tachyon corridor was opened, the city followed, though its populace had been hastily evacuated into the other starships and converted people bins ... airless, a pitted skeleton of a city, it was carried hither by our convoy's gravity field. I found that there is a direct displacement link to the city from Varezhdur ... one day, out of curiositv, I shadowed the master, and I saw him come here."

"Why is it so dark? Udara's light falls here as much as elsewhere."

"I do not know. Perhaps it is true that a Darkling Wind blows wherever the Prince of Shadow goes, and that it always girds him in thick darkness."

"Oh, the stories people tell," Jenjen said. "Where must we go now?"

The city still generated a weak gravity; it was not quite dead then. They climbed over still slidewalks. A railinged pathway ended in mid-arc. The husks of buildings emanated a ghostlight that only accentuated the shadowgloom; Udara's light seemed not to penetrate here at all. She was not used to feeling so light; when she saw the childsoldier pull a thin metal rope from his cloak and flick it at the next overhang and swing across, she felt queasy. But when he threw the rope back at her she followed his example. For one heartstopping moment she thought she was falling, but it was only an illusion of the weak gravity. They stood on a ledge overlooking the city.

"There," the boy said, pointing over the rubbled city scape, "there's where Kelver's throneroom used to be. The cloud room."

"I don't see ... oh yes." A heap of mirror-metal girders surrounding a roofless palace. Within the sheared-off walls she could see dim colonnades and winding passageways.

"Come."

"This landscape is more like a dream than reality."

"You speak truer than you know. Come, come," the boy said impatiently. "Don't you see, he weaves the Darkling Wind around himself, and what surrounds him is the stuff of nightmare? Look!—" They were walking down a street now. Shop windows decked with holosculpted merchandise but in the window there ... wasn't that herself and Zalo, much younger, arguing about something? Was he really wielding a dagger, was that really blood spurting from her breasts? The stuff of nightmare ... "Do not be afraid. The city has many illusions. It is not quite dead, and its thinkhive is like the Throne of Madness in miniature: it too is schizophrenic, it too perceives but mirror-cracked realities sometimes it plucks things from our minds, things that we most fear. Illusion, Jeni, illusion," he said in a voice that reminded her of her dead great-grandfather whose head had adorned the memory niche in her childhood home and who had spouted aphorisms in the middle of the night and terrorized her and she screamed suddenlv—

"Quiet," he said. His voice was soothing. Kelver's voice.

"The street goes on forever," she said, afraid to look into any more windows ... but their sounds assailed her ears, sounds of old quarrels with Zalo that she was embarrassed to remember, and always the smell of fresh hot blood....

Steps now. Ascending. Steps of stone, cracked, seeming to bleed. Would they never end? Gargoyles at each step, their gouged eyes spattering her with rheumish blood that melted into air before it could hit her. Fog now, red fog like the clouds of Zorn.

"We are at the periphery of his mind," the boy said.

"Will you enter?" But she had already gone ahead, for she told herself, I am a poetess of darkness, and darkness holds no terror for me.

And she saw Kelver on the Throne of Madness. Not the Kelver she had met in Varezhdur so long ago, but a Kelver old and motionless, who seemed not to notice her intrusion. Around him a wind billowed, a wind of visible darkness. And she cried out his name: "Kelver, Kelver."

"He can't hear you," said the childsoldier who was also Ton Keverell n'Davaren Tath, the Prince of Shadow. "He is only a shell. His million souls have left him, and we are all lost, lost, lost."

Kelver stirred and looked up from the Throne, from which ran blood. His face was pale ... but were those bandages that bound it tight, like a mummy?

"I know that face!" she whispered. "It is the face of Karakaël, the uncompassion ate, the utterly evil!"

Yes, the man who sat on the Throne of Madness was a veritable replica of Ton Karakaël, save for the green fire that burned in his eye sockets. "Is this how Kelver sees himself now?" she said. "Then woe to all of us!"

And she clutched the hand of the nameless childsoldier who was also Kelver. "This is ultimate darkness indeed."

The boy said wonderingly: "I think he's going to speak." And Kelver-that-was-Karakaël cried out: "I see them ... they are entering the Skywall Mountain ..."

"He's remembering his past," Jenjen said quickly. "How he and darkness saw the light on the sound."

"I think he is seeing something *now,*" the boy said. "They have flown across the desert of glass they have threaded the forcemesh of the childsoldiers they are standing outside ... now they're climbing through the caverns where Darktouch's people once dwelt ... the servocorpses go about their work, unheeding ... they've penetrated the honeycomb of passageways ... they're standing on the ledge that juts out over the sunless sound ... they wait for the windbringers ...

"Who? Who?" Jenjen shouted, running up the last of the steps and standing over the shrunken old man that was Kelver.

"Soon they will see it all ... they will be changed ... they will see such beauty, such joy ... and the people of Shtoma will soon dance their joy ... all of my people will dance in the sunlight ... to me alone is joy denied! To me alone! Because—because—"

"You aren't alone, Kevi," Jenjen said softly, cradling his withered face in her arms, heedless of the emerald pus that dripped from his empty eyes. "Oh, Kelver, I joined the revolution because you taught me how to love, how not to fear ... oh, this is a terrible dream you're having, you must awaken from it— "

"Now!" Kelver's voice rasped like old Karakaël's. "They stand there ... the vision is touching them ... the vision is fading from me ... Why? Why? Because I sit under the weight of a whis pershadow... because I bear the responsibility for Udara's death!"

"Don't speak such nonsense; you're just feverish. Wake up. How can a star die? Wake up, wake up, do wake up! No one will abandon vou."

"I am the only one who has danced on the face of the sun and was not touched by Udara's love."

"Oh, Kelver, you are beyond my hope." Sobbing, Jenjen held him in her arms while he raved on and on.

"Come away, Mistress," the boy urged, tugging at her darkrobe.

"Yes. Yes."

For it seemed clear that this shell from which Kelver's essence had been drained would not hear her. Had it all come to this then, this glorious revolution that would shake the Inquest's foundations and bring about men's freedom? The flight of the kashanthras, the Rainbow Darkness, the terrible battle in the cloudscape of Zorn ... was it all just for the sake of an old man sitting on a plain wooden throne, babbling and drooling? It could not be so. He was as if bewitched. If so, there must be—a way of breaking the spell, like shattering a darksculpture into its component colors. But how? She wept as she held him to her bosom, the man who was to trillions as a god, a healer, a redeemer.

***

While parsecs away, on a planet that was even now being

dragged into the overcosm, another woman and another old man stood on a windy ledge that overlooked the Sunless Sound within the Skywall fountain.

And Kelver was there with them, in the shape of a basalt cliff wall inlaid with two almond-shaped emeralds; it is good to be inanimate, the Kelver who sat on the throne thought, feelingless. And in the thick pungent air windbringers circled, those creatures whom man had enslaved for twenty millennia and they sang their lightsongs. There was fragrance in their singing and harmony in their patterns of light. For a long time they stood. And when the song faded at last they knew they had beheld an absolute beauty, and that they would never be the same. Their hearts were renewed. And Kelver saw that they had become even as he and Darktouch once had been: shiny-eyed, bursting with newfound truths. But he could feel nothing. He was just a rock in the side of a mountain....

Jenjen and Kelver had begun with an act of love; now they could not reach each other at all, though Jenjen was beside him, beseeching him to awaken from his hell and bring light once more into his world. But Karakaël and Siriss, who had built their relationship upon mutual hate and distrust, now found in this shared experience a new beginning, a new reaching.

Unlike boy Kelver and young Darktouch, innocent enough to believe that they had but to tell the Inquest and the Inquest would stop the slaughter of the delphinoids, Karakaël and Siriss did not race back to the twin cities across the frozen desert. They did not return to Arryk at all.

***

Alone in his throneroom, Arryk read a message disk from the two of them:

We have seen what you have not seen. We have experienced what you most feared to experience. We withdraw from this war, Ton Arryk n'Elloren Tath. There is a third solution. Do you remember when, almost a century ago, Kelver challenged the Inquest to a final game of makrúgh, *that would be held at the Southern Pole of Uran s'Varek when next a sun fell into the black hole? All of us accepted that challenge. You will not see us again until then. Only then will Davaryush's plan come to its startling fruition. Until then, Arryk whom Siriss loved and Karakaël despised, who rejected Karakaël and whom Siriss must now reject, farewell.*

"I am alone," said Arryk to the empty throneroom.

***

"I am alone," Kelver said, as he sat in his pocket of darkness in the city of the dead.

Twenty-Two
To Kill the Sun

Uran s'Varek: pearly-skied, unimaginably huge: an artificial sphere that surrounded the black hole at the heart of the galaxy. More than a million stars were crammed together in just one cubic parsec of space.

But Uran s'Varek's atmosphere was thousands of klomets thick, and it scattered the light of those constant-shining stars and made of it a gentle radiance.

Night never fell here, save in a castle or a dwelling place, or at an Inquestor's whim. Uran s'Varek itself was vast: four hundred million klomets from pole to pole, and most of it uncharted, ruled by a thinkhive as omnipotent as it was insane.

The poles were open at the top and bottom, each opening large enough to admit the stars as they spiraled into the black hole beneath; there were banks of thinkhives, millions in number, whose sole function was to act as a vast telekinetic intensifier, drawing the stars into the star-eater's web, aiming them precisely at the polar openings, draining away all their energy as they died. From this energy came the Inquest's might...

It was at the Northern Pole that they landed, Elloran and Davaryush and ancient Varuneh and the woman Darktouch.

They did not arrive with the ceremony proper to Inquestors; their tachyon bubbles were proof of their power, for tachyon bubbles were powered by the death of stars, but no other trappings did they bring with them, no gilt panoplies, no honor guards of childsoldiers, no pteratygers pawing the air, no palaces of gold and crystal.

The bubbles set them down on a grassy plain that stretched halfway up the lucent sky. They were in Ellorin, the segment Elloran once ruled.

These were his pleasure gardens, and this meadow was a million klomets long, and those rosellas that spotted the grass were not wildflowers at all, but giant metropolises diminished by distance. Darktouch, who had never seen Uran s'Varek, cried out in surprise and awe.

The others stood solemnly; they looked, she thought, like the three Fates of mythology. Perhaps, too, their function in this new myth was the same; they would hover on the periphery of the action, they would comment on it like the chorus in a necrodrama.

"Where must we go now, Father Davaryush?" she asked. For of all the Inquestors Darktouch was most close to Davaryush.

"Why do you ask me? I am but Daavye-without-a-Clan. I'm not even supposed to set foot on Uran s'Varek."

And Elloran said: "Kendrin, the segment where *makrúgh* is forbidden; the city of Rhozellerang, where the young Inquestors wait; where Kelver and Siriss and Arryk once waited, full of trepidation, to begin their quest journey. That would be as good a place to begin as any."

"And then?" Varuneh said. Darktouch got the impression that it was really she who was in control of everything, and that she was merely allowing the other two their little moments of importance.

"Then? I cannot tell," Elloran said.

So it was that they boarded a floater and sped eastward, toward Kendrin. They reached the edge of the segment named for Elloran, and crossed into Kendrin on a filament bridge over the void beneath. (For though in the macrocosmic scheme Uran s'Varek was one seamless artifact, the chasm between each of the thousand sections was some thousand klomets wide, and stitched only by the bridges, like drawstrings linking the segments of an inflatable leather ball.)

They crossed single meadows that were vaster than the earth-swallowing cloud in which the battle for Zorn had taken place. They entered Rhozellerang through gigantic tubeways that were fashioned like the pistils of a monster flower; their floater ascended, assisted by airlifts, up past the sepal slums into the petal palaces; and at last they stood on the parapet where by tradition Inquestors-to-be were sent to wait for the beginning of their training.

But the parapet was bare. So huge it was that the four of them seemed like ants on a marble tabletop. Displacement plates were set into the pavement in a lattice of silver patens.

"Do you remember when first you came here?" Elloran said to Davaryush.

"Yes. It was Ton Alkamathdes who summoned me."

"Ton Alkamathdes, who, driven to insanity, became the Rainbow King ... he was my teacher too, Davaryush. Compassion killed him."

"Look!" cried Darktouch. "People at last!"

At the opposite edge of the parapet they were. Darktouch watched them as one by one they disappeared from one displacement plate and popped out of another ... a discontinuous line of black-cloaked children that slithered slowly nearer ... nearer ... creeping across the parapet like a black annelid flecked with metaldust.

"Childsoldiers!" she said. "Shouldn't we flee?"

"No," Davaryush said quietly. "We will watch as they approach."

How long would it take them to cross the terrace? She tried to count the patens; but the white marble dazzled and the plates, reflecting the sky, were like pinprick suns, making her eyes water. She resisted an urge to panic. She had come too far now. And home was no more.

At last the childsoldiers stood before them. Their leader, a girl no more than ten years old, blond-haired and bright eyed, shouted out in a shrill voice: "In the name of the Inquest, I have been commanded to arrest Daavye-without-a Clan, he who was stripped of his name, for daring to return to Uran s'Varek!"

"I shall go freely," Davaryush said. "You shall bind my arms with forcebolts." And he knelt down in the pose of submission that all the shortlived learned as children ... the gesture of supplication that men knew they must make if their lives were to be spared should their world be chosen to *fall beyond.*

"You cannot submit!" Darktouch said. "You are an Inquestor!"

"I am not," Davaryush said. "Though at times, nameless though I now am, I have masqueraded as one to achieve some minor advantage, some small physical comfort. I will not resist."

Darktouch darted forward. She rebounded from a wall of force.

"We do not come for you," the childsoldier shouted, her tiny voice almost lost in the expanse of sky and marble. "Only for Daavye-without-a-Clan."

"I override!" Elloran cried out. "I, Ton Elloran n'Taanyel Tath, rescind the orders of Ton Arryk!"

"Hokh'Ton," said the girl humbly, "begging your leave; I have been instructed that you will attempt to override, and to say this: that you, Ton Elloran, chose to walk away from the path of Inquestorhood, and to abrogate your name. I need not obey you."

"Then obey me!" said Lady Varuneh softly, menacingly. "You do not even wear the shimmercloak," the girl said, mocking.

Vara pointed to the sky, closed her eyes, seemed to be speaking to someone with her mind.

As Davaryush stepped forward—

Isha ha! Voices from the sky. More childsoldiers streaming down! The girl lashed out with her laser-irises, bringing down a young boy's severed head. Darktouch cried out. More were swooping down now, shrieking their warcry. Blood-drizzle on the dazzling white.

She looked up and saw them in like a flock of dark birds... topaz light streamed from their eyes ... children were sliced in pieces at their feet. It was over in a few seconds.

"What does this mean?" Darktouch said bitterly. "What have you done, Mother Vara? We are free to go?"

"Oh, Vara, oh, Darktouch ..." Davaryush said. "I have told you this before ... long before I saw the light on the sound, I was tainted by the Inquest's curse. My blood reeked of its corruption. I knew if I tried to change things now my hands would be ever more steeped in bloodshed ... every step I take, every breath, causes death, even now that I am no longer Davaryush."

"And shall we wait here longer?" Varuneh said softly.

"Was there not a game, a challenge to *makrúgh,* that Kelver issued almost a century ago?" Elloran said. "At the next lightfall, at the Southern Pole of Uran s'Varek, the last game will be played. Is that why we are here?"

"I don't know!" Davaryush said. "I don't make the plans anymore, I've washed my hands of it! But look ... our rescuers are approaching."

Two Inquestors were coming toward them, popping in and out of existence down a long avenue of displacement plates. "Powers of powers!" Elloran said. "We have gone from bad to worse."

And Darktouch knew the two lnquestors, one by sight, the other by reputation. The white-haired woman with the opal eyes: that was Siriss; she had heard how Siriss had betrayed Kelver. The other, the one with bloodshot eyes set in a mummified face, must be Karakaël.

She shuddered, thinking, Surely they will now command our execution; they will utter a word, a small, empty word, and the sky will sprout laser eyes and we will be neatly sliced up, like the children lying at our feet ... we won't even bleed much, for the searing of the laser light will cauterize us and seal in our blood.

But Siriss knelt in front of Elloran and clasped his knees and wept; and she said, "Forgive me, Father Elloran, forgive me."

"Weep, daughter," Elloran said. "Do not fear to weep. It will not tarnish your lnquestral pride. For our world is ending."

"Forgive me, Ton Davaryush—"

"I am but a clanless man, Inquestrix; do not address me as lnquestor!" Davaryush said.

"Forgive me, Daavye. I have seen what you have seen ... so has Karakaël ... he has not spoken since we left Gallendys—"

"Gallendys!" Darktouch blurted out. "My homeworld—"

She closed her eyes, remembering so much:

Once she could not speak ... the world she lived in was bursting with sights and sounds, but she had no way of knowing she was not some freak, because the others who lived in the dark country spoke only in the language of touch ... and then she had seen, without even knowing that she could see, the imagesongs of the windbringers as they contemplated the overcosm ... oh, that day! And the second time, when she and Kelver and

Davaryush and Varuneh had stood in the Skywall Mountain, ensorceled by that timeless moment, by their confrontation with an absolute beauty ... she had felt more than herself then, in communion with all the cosmos ... now, seeing Siriss again in the company of Karakaël who had once been so evil and who had lost the power of speech, she felt so much at one with them both.

"Forgive me, Darktouch," Siriss said. And Darktouch clasped the Inquestrix to her bosom, and both of them wept tears of profound joy. "How could I have doubted the truth of Kelver's and your vision? I am changed. I am no longer weak. I have found my own answer; and I will reveal it at Kelver's final *makrúgh,* when the black hole of Uran s'Varek absorbs the star into its Southern Pole."

"You are here, then, for the endgame?" said Varuneh.

"The Inquestors are already journeying thither," Siriss said. "We must hasten."

"But Kelver?" said Darktouch.

"And Arryk?" said Elloran.

"They will surely come to the lightfall for a final confrontation. No Inquestor would be absent at the endgame of his own *makrúgh!"* Lady Varuneh said.

But there was irony in her voice.

Suddenly it seemed that the sky was laughing. The parapet was vibrating. Mocking laughter resounded from the petal-walls of the upper city. A great wind sprang up; the Inquestors' shimmercloaks streamed wildly.

And a voice cried out from the sky: "THERE WILL BE NO ENDGAME!"

"Arryk!" several of the Inquestors cried out in unison.

And the sky was filled with childsoldiers, hooting and skrieking with laughter, somersaulting wildly from hoverdisk to hoverdisk, weaving sigils in the air with their laser eyes. And the sky hummed with the Inquestral hymn:

I, a slave, a chattel, a nothing
throw down before you all my heart . . . .

The abject words tearing from a million shrill throats ... Darktouch was sickened. Presently the Inquestral hymn came to an end, and the childsoldiers singing became a cacophonous babble of warcries and laughter. Then came a sennet of brasses, piercing trumpets and pompous sackbuts and thunderous tympana. At the sound the childsoldiers all vanished as suddenly as they had come, scattering in wave after wave of V formations, like migrating ravens....

And then, turning, they saw Arryk approach.

The throne he sat in was of fire; it burned on the marble parapet; within, encased in a shield of force,utterly isolated from the outside world, he sat. Fifty pteratygers pulled the throne, some pawing the pavement, some the air, their wings flapping in thudding unison.

The voice that issued from that forcebubble was no human voice; it seemed to have been synthesized from the sounds of tearing earth and boulders rebounding in deep ravines; it was as though an earthquake had been vested with the power of discourse.

It said: "NO, THERE WILL BE NO ENDGAME. THE GAME WILL BE OVER BEFORE KELVER ARRIVES TO SET IT IN MOTION!"

The throne came nearer. Darktouch could see the rage in Arryk's violet eyes.

She saw, too, that he had once been beautiful. She could smell the pteratygers' sweat, acrid and stifling in the still air.

Davaryush went forward and said, "I will cause no more deaths, no matter how inadvertently, Ton Arryk n'Elloren Tath. I yield to you now. Do not send any more children after me to be slain by Karakaël's troops. I will not be the cause of any more suffering."

"WHAT ARROGANCE! THE FATE OF THE ENTIRE DISPERSAL OF MAN IS AT STAKE, DAAVYE-WITHOUT-A-CLAN. YOUR GRAND PLAN IS A FAILURE. THE INQUEST, WIIICH HAS LASTED TWENTY THOUSAND YEARS, WILL LAST A MILLION MORE. FOR I WILL ELIMINATE ALL ITS FOES"—his voice seemed to blend with the sound of an avalanche— "IN THE NAME OF THE HIGH COMPASSION!"

"Fool!" Elloran whispered. "You have laid compassion by the wayside. O Arryk whom I nurtured, do not fall prey to hypocrisy —"

"He won't listen," Siriss said urgently. "Let me go to him. It was I who first loved him."

And Darktouch watched the Inquestrix of the cloud crystal eyes as she went to Arryk. Such was her haste that her image did not form completely in any of the displacement plates that lay between them; instead, one could see, for a moment, a whole line of flickering Sirisses, each one a blur of shimmerfur and snow-pale flesh.

***

Leaving the others behind, Siriss went up to Arryk's throne, upon which he sat shielded by a force-holorama of fire. She ascended the steps, while pteratygers whinnied and pawed the air, breathing out brimstone with every feline roar. She gazed into the amethystine eyes of the man she had once loved and betrayed.

She said: "Arryk, do you remember when you and I and Kelver were still apprentice Inquestors and we stood waiting on this very parapet? Oh, we were young then. Compared to Lady Varuneh we may still be as children, but in those days ... how hard we believed that our compassion could redeem the universe, that the very force of our personalities could shape reality! Oh, how arrogant we were, how misguided, how childish. But we were children. How many times did we hear, before we were raised to the Inquest, some grownup say, 'You must put away your games of childhood, you must pack up the toys and come face to face with reality'? And now that our games have become galactic in scope, and our toys sow discord and death, must we now not stop and say these words to ourselves? Should we not seal up the armory moons for the last time? Oh, Arryk, we do love him, you and I; for us three, that is the true meaning of this war. If we had remained peasants on backworlds, our war would be the stuff of cheap street operas. But we are Inquestors. We cannot help being Inquestors. We cannot easily lay down galactic godhood! And so the consequences of this triangle of love, hate, and desire are also pangalactic. To be an Inquestor is to renounce love; yet we know we are capable of love! And if we can love again, we can also heal. It's all illusion. Rikeh, don't you understand? The Darkling Wind does not blow straight from Kelver's heart, but is inherent in the Inquest's nature, and we are destiny's tools, not destiny's shapers. So forget this feud, Rikeh.

Forget that we three were once possessed by cosmic forces. Look at Karakaël, whom you despoiled of his name. Now he is happy, for he has seen the light on the sound, and no longer needs masks, whether of gold or of the mind. Look at Davaryush, who stood before all the Inquest and saw his name stripped from him in utmost humiliation. His fall was his fulfillment, and now his plan bears fruit. And look at Elloran! None dared strip him of his name, for all knew him as the most compassionate of all Inquestors, of all the Inquest the most godlike. Since no man would take his name, he was compelled himself to cast it off, and being a god no more he has at last found joy. Rikeh, Rikeh, you must throw down this bitter cup—-as I have! Or in the end the war will come down just to you and Kelver. You will no longer understand the stakes. And the Throne of Madness will be the only victor."

Had she moved him? She could not tell.

She did not even know whether he had heard her impassioned speech at all. Perhaps, she thought, he has drawn a noise-shield over himself, shutting out temptation.

Behind the firefield he sat stone cold and statue-still. And Siriss thought: I feel no more compassion for him! Instead I feel rage and contempt and jealousy and rejection and. . .

"Rikeh, Rikeh, how I still love you! I loved you when you were a phoenix herder on the pleasure world Kailasa, a virgin flower in the scarlet snow. I loved you as Inquestor, regal, beautiful, proud, loving, a master of *makrúgh*. Even when I betrayed you I loved you. My betrayal sprang from my love. I love you even now, as you prepare the destruction of all else I have loved ... and I know that when Kelver's fractured soul is healed, he will know that he loves you equally. Think of that love, Arryk, when you go to consume love with love's shadow!"

She had done speaking now. There was nothing more she could say. From now on she would have to act, to bring about her own solution to the triangle....

Would Arryk even speak to her in response? For a long time she waited. It seemed to her that Arryk smiled a little, as though remembering how they had once loved. The wind was heady with the perfumes of the many-petaled city.

The fire blazed about the throne. The fragrant wind grew stronger, scattering the sulfurous fumes with which Arryk had girt himself.

"Speak to me!" Siriss cried.

At last he spoke. His voice was whispery and harsh, as though his voice was the groaning of earth's bones and the sighing of subterranean winds ... in his voice there was nothing human, nothing of the Arryk she and Kelver had once loved.

"Children indeed, yes, children!" Arryk said. "Children, Ton Siriss k'Varad es-K-Ning! You have come to Uran s'Varek to play a last game of *makrúgh,* have you not? Tell me then, little sister, who has put aside the toys of childhood and who has not. You stood on Gallendys and witnessed the singing of delphinoids and speak of some profound epiphany. I do not speak of mysticism but of a just and righteous world whose sins are borne upon the shoulders of the Inquest. While you stood passively, I *moved* Gallendys; and now it hangs from the lip of the hole at the roof of Uran s'Varek like a rich jewel set in a matrix of light. The delphinoids are ours! And now we will move against Kelver. We will annihilate the utopia and its sentient sun. Even now an armada a thousandfold mightier than the one that vanquished Zorn has sounded the overcosm ... ship after ship will materialize in Udara's heart, and we will kindle the star's core to bursting, and it will be no more. The one discrepancy in our vision will have been obliterated. The Inquest's rule has only just begun. It is the mightiest utopia hunt of all."

"But the utopia that you hunt is the Inquest itself ... and the flaw that you unmask presages our own downfall! By your own warped philosophy you damn yourself," said Siriss, knowing that to argue was useless, for they had trodden the same ground over and over again, and the exalted terms of discourse had been reduced to empty casuistry. Darkness, darkness, all was darkness, darkness everlasting.

"Yes," Arryk said, and she could feel a terrible weariness emanate from the firefield, "it's all meaningless." Had he read her mind? But they knew each other so well. It hurt her to remember their old intimacy. "That's why I won't stop you and Davaryush and Elloran and Karakaël from attending your little final spectacle. It won't be real, you see. You'll stand there and watch a sun fall to its death. Passive to the last. But I will not stand and watch ... I will not witness and be changed by the songs of an alien race; I will not be buffeted about by the graviton tides of an all-protecting, patronizing sun ... if it is destiny that the Inquest fall, yet I will seize that destiny and make it malleable. I will make time stand still!

Perhaps it's true that you'll be the last Inquestors to be able to watch the dying of a star ... but I will be the first to cause that dying! I will be the first to kill the sun."

And Siriss knew that she could move him no more, and wept.

THE CHILD FROM THE FUTURE

The armies of Arryk were assembled one last time.
Shtoma was the planet of their last encounter;
Shtoma of the cadent lightfall.
They planned to kindle Shtoma's sun to bursting,
not understanding that the sun itself
had the power to cripple them forever.

—from Zalo's *The Darkling Wind*

Twenty-Three

The Screaming Star

"It's time! Hurry! It's time!"

Jenjen heard it whispered and shouted everywhere. In the corridors of the ships, in the levitating-shafts of the refugee people bins, and especially on Shtoma and on the craft that shuttled between the surface and the orbiting starships. People talked of nothing but the forthcoming ritual of dancing on the face of the sun.

She had not seen Zalo for many sleeps. She wanted to be alone and not alone; so she would go down to the planet and walk, solitary walks that always yielded some startling sight. Often the natives would ask her into their crystal houses, almost invisible amid the forests and fields. Many knew her name, although she had not been introduced to many of the natives. It seemed that on this world when one knew something all soon knew it. She'd heard experts on board ship theorizing about hive minds or primitive telepathy; she was more inclined to believe it was simply because they talked among themselves all the time and had few secrets. It was strange that a people could live this way.

On one such occasion she was strolling in the crimson grass and thinking of her life with Zalo. She was wondering how it would have been if the revolution had never happened, if ... if Elloran had never come to Essondras when she was a child. She saw in her mind's eye how they might be living: he the venerated playwright, she the respected lightweaver, their children apprenticed to good trades or gone off to be childsoldiers and lost forever. Family life on Essondras! Semiannual visits to the mnemothanasions to pay respects to the remains of one's ancestors. Familial wranglings over who was to own the patriarch's head after his death. Dinners and receptions, she mused, and trite, comforting necrodramas. Could I have been able to abide a scenario like that?

A crowd of the local seniors was airing out the festive wings they used during the sun-dancing time, beating out the dust and the scarlet pollen, burnishing the brazen clasps and combing them so the down fell pat in soft sweeping designs. They were like the light tapestries she had worked on in her youth, before the darkness had seduced her away: patterns whose simplicity concealed a subtle elegance.

She saw children toddling about and making nuisances of themselves, stumbling in the stacks of feathers and sliding about on the burnishing liquid. No one ever scolded them. That was on the most alien things about this people, the fact that their children evinced no awe of adulthood at all, even these ones who were too young ever to have danced on the sun before. Even on Essondras, she remembered, where children were highly valued and not automatically shipped off to die as childsoldiers as on so many other planets, there were necessarily times for discipline and for instilling manners and minor courtesies. The Shtomans seemed to lack any societal order at all ... and she could not help feeling that there was something profoundly sinful about their defiance of human hierarchies. She understood now why the Inquest had always hated Shtoma and sought to destroy it. I myself, rebel though I am, she thought, have been the Inquest's creature, shaped by their mythos and their values ... this world disturbs me.

She stood to one side of a patch of tall blood-grass and watched them. Older boys and girls strutted outside the houses, preening, adjusting their wings, striving to impress their friends. How domestic, she thought. She was about to speak to them in what little she had learned of their language, but felt oddly shy. The older men and women were going quietly about their business. But Jenjen detected in their soft smiles a thinly concealed excitement about what was to come.

She saw one she had met on a previous visit to the surface, a tawny-haired, thick-armed woman named Taik, who greeted her in the manner of her people: *"Qithe qithembara; udres a kilima shtoisti! Soul, renounce suffering; you have danced on the face of the sun!"*

"But why is this festival so important?" Jenjen asked her, accepting a draft of cool zul from a drinking horn woven from crimson vines.

Smiling cryptically—Jenjen could feel the same frustration the Inquestor-investigators must have felt—Taik said, "Soon, Jeni, you will see what our greeting truly means."

That was the trouble. Though they always welcomed her, and went out of their way to include her in their conversations, she found these people alien, their motives incomprehensible. They had set themselves apart, these people, by their relationship with Shtoma; in a very real way they were no longer human. In this the Inquest's viewpoint, though cruel, had had a certain validity. That was the way things always seemed to be; there was no one right path; all ways were obscure.

Jenjen thought of her work; she had done little darkweaving since they had come to Shtoma. Udara's light permeated everything and drowned out the images of darkness that usually filled her head. She shared the rest of the zul with Taik, though they did not speak again; somehow Jenjen couldn't find anything to say. How do you talk to people who claim to he totally happy? I have to find out what it means, their dancing on the sun, she thought. I have to participate.

She thought of Zalo, whom she had not seen in many sleeps. If I join in the ritual, she thought, we may drift apart forever ...

I had better go to him, she thought.

Dusk was falling on this area of Shtoma. Here dusk was a barely perceptible dimming of the incandescent cloudlayer. Night would come swiftly, the sky turning suddenly dark shot through with auroras. Then the natives would begin singing their sunmusic, a slow and melismatic chanting that seemed to blend with the nightbird music of the red forests.

Though the joy of Udara washed over her, there was fear, too, in this joy; for she had come far with Zalo, almost from childhood, and she was afraid to give him up. She knew too that if her destiny included the experiencing of an ultimate light, she might also one day be forced to come face to face with its opposite. These things troubled her as she walked slowly back to the shuttlecraft that would bring her home to the Daranava *Sirisshtasieh.*

***

And again Zalo dived into the well of darkness, clasping the filament of light firmly to his chest, letting it carry him down, down, down ... after a delicious eternity of falling, he reached the disjunctive node in the shipmind that seemed so much like his old house on Essondras. This time he found the lightstrands leaping wildly from wall to wall to wall until they wove themselves into a tapestry of painful brilliance.

It was to this womb of light that Zalo found himself fleeing more and more. He had tried to hammer out verses for a great new play, but something—he could not tell what-was hindering him. Was it simply this sea of joy that seemed to wash over everyone's senses? But in the shipmind he found solitary solace. Sometimes he would allow his mind to skim the overcosm, roaming the lightstrands until he found ships and recognized them and knew their secret names; sometimes he listened for Jannif's voice, though now it came more often as a wordless wuthering, for Jannif's consciousness was becoming more and more subsumed into that of the star whale.

This time—

He was looking at the niche that contained the head of his old mentor Karnofara ... it was blurred, its outlines an eerie shimmerspectrum. All houses on Essondras had such memory-niches. As an apprentice, before he received the honor of inheriting his master's head, he had sometimes fantasized an opening behind the niche, a door into some imaginary kingdom-indeed, he used to act out whole scenes in his head in that hidden country. He had never given it a name as a young man; but in a sudden inspiration he knew its name now: it was the Dark Country, like the kingdom concealed in the Skywall Mountain of Gallendys, the Inquest's secret shame; like the Inquestor's secret world Uran s'Varek, its location known to so few that most of mankind thought it a mere myth ... there are as many doors to the Dark Country, Zalo thought, as there are human souls. It's like what Jenjen says when she talks about her four million shades of darkness ... now, after all these years, here's the door again, and now I know its name. What does it mean?

Impetuously he put his hand through Karnofara's head, which was an illusion, after all; knotting the lightstrand about his waist so that he would not be lost forever in the shipmind, he stepped through the wall of eye-smarting light.

And tumbled headlong into darkness ... and heard, from far away, the echo of a distant scream ... there was no light here at all save the strand he clung to. Now there was nothing, not even the scream ... he had been deprived even of the ability to feel ... he tried to cry out but could not find his mouth, he could not weep because his eyes were welded shut—

Suddenly Jannif's voice, in his ear: "Get out of here, Zasha! You have glimpsed the disturbance that is to come. The star will scream and the starships all struck dumb ... flee to the surface, Zasha!"

When he awoke, Jenjen was shaking him, pleading with him to break loose from the star fever.

***

"Zasha," she was saying, "you've got to come to Shtoma with me ... this thing they're all about to experience—it's more than just some arcane religion, I know it—it's some thing important, something that strikes at the heart of every thing we believe in—"

"I don't have time for ritual dances now!" said Zalo. "I've just seen ... oh, something terrible ... I think that the war is coming soon to Shtoma, and that the price that will be paid for it is ... oh, I can't even imagine it ... I've been in a place so dark that even feelings cannot exist in it ... there's been a massive shift in the balance of the overcosm, and I know that thousands, millions of starships are on their way here— "

"Ritual dances!" Jenjen said. "Why, this isn't some exercise in cultural anthropology, it's the key to our whole struggle! I feel sure of it." How frustrating Zalo's new preoccupations were. For a while she attempted to communicate to Zalo the intensity of what she'd found on Shtoma. But it was like a color he couldn't see. At last she couldn't stop herself from saying, "You're more involved with this starship—this *machine*—than with real people, these days, aren't you? It's a good substitute for your corpses, I suppose!" As soon as she'd said it she regretted it.

"You're jealous," Zalo said.

"Why not? Sleep after sleep I see you sucked further and further into the mind of a machine—"

"Jannif is in the machine."

"Even worse! Do you love her more than me?"

"You *are* jealous!"

"No, I—" She stopped short. It was true. That was what hurt so much.

She stood staring at him for a long while, wondering whether he would slip back into the star fever right then and there. Then she said, "They are waiting for me now. For a week my friend Taik has been weaving a pair of wings for me ... " She knew Taik was not really a friend, that she was only trying to get a rise out of Zalo; but it was useless. So she left him and went to catch the shuttle down to the surface.

***

Deep in the dephinoid, Zalo counted the approaching starships, counted and counted until he was dizzy. But he did not dare enter the hidden chamber behind the head of Karnofara again.

***

Jenjen returned to Taik and to a planet increasingly less alien. She sat in Taik's house with its transparent walls that admitted without impedance both the sun's loving warmth and the stares of passersby; for it was not a private world. Even the mysteries of sex were practiced beneath the sun light, often in casual view.

Jenjen helped Taik with the weaving of the wings. It was much like lightweaving, in a primitive sort of way; only the fabric was different. It was strange to get the fluff between your fingernails and to comb the soft featherstuff until it shone; in Jenjen's art one did not touch anything; the lightloom waldoed the filaments of light into place; the body was entirely at rest; only the mind burned. Yet there were similarities.

Jenjen said to Taik once, "Aren't you afraid? Zalo says that the armies of the Inquest are coming. Soon. That we should all be rushing to fortify the planet, fleeing, hiding, sending our children to safe havens on other worlds. Yet all you people think of is the dance ... the dance on the face of the sun."

"You don't think of it?"

"Of course I do, but—" At times the warmth of these people was infectious; but often their alienness was so disturbing. Why did she have to have these differences with Zalo? Why could he never understand her? At last she confessed: "I am drawn to your ceremony, Taik, and yet I feel that we are all turning our backs on reality."

Taik said, "No, Jeni, that's not so. You think that the sun Udara will let his children die in vain?"

"Zalo thinks they have a plan—to invade the very center of the sun, to kindle it into an artificial nova. Will it work?"

"Perhaps it will. But Udara will draw her children into his heart; he will build a wall of love around us; and the Inquest's hatred will not breach that wall."

"Faith," Jenjen said. She jabbed her finger on a feather of the wing she was weaving and cried out in pain.

Taik ran to fetch a soothing ointment, but by the time she came back it seemed that the sun itself had already salved her pain. "If only I could believe as you do."

"It is not a question of belief," Taik said. "Oh, how can I explain? You have not danced on the face of the sun. It's like talking to a child who has not yet learned to distinguish speech from noise."

"Are we all just children to you, then, to be pitied? That

makes you no better than the Inquest," Jenjen said, unwittingly falling into the role of devil's advocate.

"Today you see us with the eyes of an anthropologist and a weaver of visions," said Taik, infinitely tranquil, "but afterward you will see us with your own eyes. You will become truly yourself."

Suddenly Jenjen knew an important truth. That perhaps it was true that these people had evolved a utopian society. But theirs was a path that was not for man in general. It was a dead end. The people of Shtoma had indeed been enriched by their relationship with the sentient, loving sun Udara. But they had taken a step or two away from their humanity, perhaps. In a sense, the Inquest had been right to fear them so much, and to demand their destruction. These thoughts were unpleasant and confusing. Not the sort of thoughts that mere "ritual dances," as Zalo had called them, ought to arouse. She was determined, more than ever, to experience it ... no matter what the consequences. That was the way she was, a creature of absolutes.

***

Arryk, alone save for his servile Aush, said: "This, then, is the final gambit. A hundred years ago, when Kelver first assumed the Throne of Madness, he issued a challenge to the Inquest. Corne in a hundred years, he said, to the Southern Pole of Uran s'Varek. There we will have lightfall of unprecendented proportions, and we will play the *makrúgh* that will bring our own reign to an end. But that great game, that final spectacle, will never come. I grow tired of games. Now I will simply destroy. My words and the acts of my words will possess the purity of the surgeon's laser. Kelver's grand lightfall will never happen. We will kindle the heart of Udara: we will destroy all Kelver's remaining starships, and with them the one utopia, Shtoma, that has resisted the High lnquestral precepts. Now give the command: send forth the starships."

***

Convoy by convoy rose the sleek and silver starships from the meadows that climbed the pearlstrewn sky of Uran s'Varek. The fields were thick with childsoldiers, like black ants storming the shipyards. And Siriss watched. But soon she could bear it no longer. She turned to Davaryush and the others and cried out. "Southward, let's go southward, let's not look at it and torture ourselves anymore."

And Davaryush said, "You see, Sirissheh, how easily you have cast off Inquestorhood. An Inquestor would say only, 'I am Inquestor; I *must* see everything; that is my duty, my destiny.' But you, who turn your back, have gone beyond Inquestorhood."

They all agreed that new beginnings were more important. But though they commanded their floaters to leave behind the launching of the million ships, the deathseeds Arryk sowed were not soon lost to sight ... even at a thousand klomets' distance they could see them swarming, and the childsoldiers a black smudge blurring the edge of the sky ... at a million klomets still they saw them, for against the sheet of light that was the scattered radiance of a million stars the ships shone even more brilliantly, pinpoints of burning brightness, bringing tears to their eyes ... she wrenched her gaze away from it.

"Do not look back," Davaryush said kindly.

"One last time," Siriss said.

"So much light," Elloran said, "to usher in the darkness." And still Karakaël was silent.

Siriss looked back. They were flying over the chiming rocks of the Desert of Trastemér, and a fluting music arose from the wind of their passing. Far, far away, beyond the chessboard meadows vaster than whole planets, beyond the serpentine rivers and the ten-thousand-klomet-long dragontrees that bordered Elloran's old estates, beyond the chasms that could swallow moons and the mountains that could crush them, there was still that smear of incandescence that was Arryk's ultimate armada ... every delphinoid shipmind that could be requisitioned or put together in a few sleeps ... every brain that could be harvested from the Sunless Sound of the world Gallendys that now dangled from the rim of Uran s'Varek. The smear shrank to a point and was swallowed up in the glow of Uran s'Varek's sky.

And still Karakaël was silent.

And because she could see no more, Siriss resolutely turned away from the north. Their floaters gathered speed;

soon they would reach the ruins of Shentrazjit the singing city, and they would pass into the gray wilderness that stretched two hundred million klomets and more, to the southern pole where the Throne of Madness had its domain.

Arryk alone exulted, as he watched from his lonely throneroom surrounded by his Aush assistants, who hissed and tittered in their secret clanspeech and clamored as each convoy, roaring, breached the sky, each one in strict geometrical formation that imitated the shapes of daggers and vampire bats and raging dragons. And in their wake came also fleets of comets, darting between the starships, their tails weaving in and out. And childsoldiers screeching their warcries as they ran to board the starships, blackening the plain, lacing the air with lasers from their eyes. Sparks flew along the plain from the impress of iridium boots. Those Inquestors who still sided with Arryk had gathered to watch. They did not rejoice: their hearts were full of distrust and ambiguity. They knew that Arryk fought to preserve their way of life; but they suspected too that the Inquest had finally fallen victim to all-consuming entropy. And so they paced the throneroom, passing the time with minor coups of *makrúgh* that accomplished nothing.

Arryk alone exulted as convoy after convoy streamed into the sky.

***

And Zalo felt them, convoy after convoy, slithering into the overcosm; he felt them even without slipping completely into his astrogating trance, so intimate was his communion with the starship.

It was terrible. They made the overcosm seem unclean somehow. Path after path was thrust into the wilderness of light. How could there be so many? Zalo could feel the seventeen delphinoids that Kelver's fleet still possessed, and the shipminds of the twin palaces; he could feel them huddle close, he could feel the fear that had hitherto been stranger to the space between spaces. Convoy after convoy they came, and Zalo shuddered at it and willed himself free of the shipmind's vision, yet still it haunted him, convoy after convoy threading the coiled and convoluted overcosm, convoy after convoy converging on the radiant presence that was Udara, the living light....

***

How beautiful it is! thought Jenjen. And ship after ship rose skyward from Shtoma's only spacefield.

They were ancient ships, all of them, some with fins and gaudy prominences. They were needle-sharp and comet-tailed and awhir with singing lights. They were snubnosed and conical and winged like birds or pterasaurs or hippopters. They were draped with holoveils and adorned with titanium flowers and painted with ancient, inconstruable sigils. They were none of them true starships. They could not cross the space between spaces, but only the inner space of a single starsystem; that was how ancient they were. They harked back to a time when man's primordial forebears hopped haltingly from world to world, one planet at a time, painstakingly exploring the microcosms of the universe. How strange to see such ships, and how beautiful! It was like a scene from an enormously budgeted holospectacle ... perhaps one of Zalo's necrodramas brought to life ... it was as if time travel, the unthinkable dream, had come to pass.

And now the people! They ran down to the plain of spaceships, infants in arms, wings and flying garments clutched close. They shouted their *qithe qithembaras* and laughed until the plain rang with their merriment. She longed to join them. But something still held her back.

The thought of Zalo, alone in his well of darkness....

Until Taik found her, enveloped her laughing in a sweaty embrace, thrust into her hands the wings she had woven for her, urged her to join the crowd, saying, "I bet you can't keep up with me, I bet you can't, you can't—"

And Taik darted into the press of the throng now and Jenjen followed, they swam in a sea of hazy light, they ran in a wind of joy, though the crowd crushed her this was no surge of panic such as she had felt when they ran up the spectral Kelver into the sky the day Essondras fell, for the crowd moved forward in an easy rhythm, unhurried but inexorable, chanting to the pounding of its footfalls. She couldn't see Taik anymore, but it no longer mattered ... she knew no one at all ... yet already her soul was dancing in step with theirs ... they ran up the ramps that angled up to the starships, and she belted out the words with the others though she did not know their meanings ... she hardly felt the lifting of the ship until she looked through the hull's deopaquement and saw that they had left Shtoma behind and that ahead lay Udara, impossibly huge ... briskly they told her how to strap on her wings and gave her the tablets that would release oxygen into her bloodstream as she danced on the face of the sun ... she listened dully, only half-comprehending the fact that within a few hours she and all the others would be leaping out of the ship, plummeting into the sun's surface on a graviton tide, kept from certain death only by the supreme effort of the white dwarf's conscous will ... how magnificent was the concept! How far from the darkness with which she had begun her vision of the rebellion!

Udara grew ever huger in the screens soon there was nothing in the sky that was not Udara ... the joy invaded her, intoxicating, almost impossible to bear ... she was weeping and laughing all at once as one of them bent down to tighten the lacings on her wings....

And Zalo? Zalo was forgotten suddenly.

***

I sense them coming! Zalo thought. I must do some thing! Doesn't Kelver know what is happening? Why doesn't he act?

***

In his chamber at the heart of the devastated city, in the throneroom where Udara's light did not deign to shine, on the seat of power at the summit of the gray steps that ran blood and were guarded by gargoyles half of flesh and half of stone, Kelver sat. The whispershadow of Udara's dying tormented him, teasing him, taunting his million selves, flooding his sundered minds with screams of death.

The madness that was on him was like the overcosm, chaotic and senseless, and his fractured souls like guideless delphinoids, tossed in the tide of light, blinded by too much knowledge.

Now and then the pieces would come together, and he

would cry out: "Why must Udara die? Why must the living light be quenched? Udara, the one star of the millions of conscious stars that has shown compassion for men? Why must it perish?" Or again, "I am the cause of the star's death, and I am helpless." Thus he railed against the Throne of Madness that possessed him.

At last the Throne spoke to his million souls and said, "Kelver, Kelver, do not oppose what has already come to pass. In the causal microcosm of your human mind you cannot see that future is past, past future, and that the moment of Udara's death was contained in the moment of his birth. Oh, Kelver, Kelver, you must learn that though you and I are the instruments of ending, we stand also at a beginning place; that every shadow has a shadow, and that shadow a shadow's shadow. Be comforted, Kelver. Your ordeal will soon end, Ton Keverell n'Davaren Tath, Prince of Shadow, Darkling Wind, Eye of the Galactic Storm. Soon will come the magical instant when all is one."

"What does all this mean?" cried Kelver as he felt himself slipping into the overcosmic frenzy. "I came to you, seeking to free mankind from the Inquest's tyranny a simple goal and a laudable one, or so I thought. You answer me with paradoxes."

"Can you free mankind from itself? Can you free humanity from the human condition?"

'"Will you answer me with questions? You are not a human. I was wrong to come to you. You can solve nothing." "Wait, Kelver, for the moment, in time and outside time, and you will see into the heart of a dying star."

"You loved a human once," Kelver said, remembering Lady Varuneh at the dawn of the Dispersal of Man.

"Do not speak to me of that!" the Throne cried out, and Kelver heard pain in that cry, and knew that a human had taught the thinkhive to feel pain.

"That is your weakness, then." The thinkhive that called itself the Throne of Madness, the most powerful of the split personalities of the soul of Uran s'Varek, did not answer him. "Mother Vara," Kelver said softly. "Mother Vara. The beginning and the end."

Still the Throne did not speak to him. The lightstorm battered at his defenses; he could not hold himself together much longer, but felt himself splintering once more. Faintly at the edge of his consciousness came the words, repeated again and again until they became the substance of the tormenting whispershadow: *Vara. Vara. Vara.* Then Kelver's personality shattered once more in the wake of the tempest.

***

"Leap, Jenjen, leap!" against the roar of the sunwind, and she saw such whiteness, such dazzling whiteness, whiteness all around, and she leaped into the graviton tide and gave freely of herself and heard their voices, *Do not fear the heat, for the sun has made for us a patch of coolness on its face,* but still she felt the scorchbreath of the wind on her and the whiteness burning burning falling falling....

And Zalo cried out: "It can't be! They're closing in even as the Shtoman ships are hovering over the star's surface. They're all preparing to leap into the sun ... and Jenjen is among them." He had not seen Jenjen in many sleeps. How could she have deserted him to walk among these people, aliens practically, incomprehensible?

But he could not escape the truth of his visions, the truth in the mind of the starship. He had divined their plan: they were going to kill the sun. In its arrogance the Inquest would treat this star Udara as just another mass of hydrogen ... it would deny it its self-evident sentience, deny it the compassion it had unstintingly meted out to the people of Shtoma. In that moment he hated the Inquest. He wanted to dive into the overcosm and singlehandedly take them on. He'd driven them mad before, hadn't he? With the grief-crazed song of the delphinoid. He had given them living nightmares. But he did not know whether he could bear to torment his starship so again, or whether the shipmind would return to sanity at all after a second journey into madness.

He waited.

Jenjen! Why did Jenjen have to be out there?

***

Four Aush looked up one after another from their calculations. About them raged the overcosm. They turned and made obeisance to Arryk. And Arryk, who had exulted, exulted no more; the burden of necessary death was on him, and, as Elloran had taught him, he must now meditate on the inflicting of death, on the awesome responsibilities of godhood.

"In a few minutes, when the first convoy of starships breaches in the heart of the star, will come the kindling."

"And the astrogators of those starships?" Arryk said. "Think not of them. They are already dead," said the Aush leader, whose eyebrows were small writhing snakes stitched into the skin of his forehead, and from whose ear a serpent dangled, flicking its tongue at the air. "But the second and third convoy ... they will survive. The explosion will move outward, toward the star's rim. Shtoma will be vaporized, and all that remains of Kelver's fleet, and all the inhabitants of that self-proclaimed utopia."

"Give us your blessing, Lord Arryk," said the other three in unison.

And Arryk said, "I cannot."

"Have we not done well?" said the second Aush, whose armband was a serpent tied in a knot, and whose face was pitted with scars from snakebites.

"You have done well," Arryk said. "But I will not look at you. Henceforth the clan of Aush is banished from my sight."

"But, Lord—"

"It is enough!" Arryk cried. "Call my Rememberers to me. It's my right as Inquestor to wallow in self-pity, isn't it? But your kind, who love death for its own sake ... you're nothing but vermin. Go now and do your duty. I do not thank you for it."

"Of course you do not, my Lord," said the leader of the Aush. "You are an Inquestor; an Inquestor does not thank. Does the wind thank the sand that it shifts across the desert?" And he gazed admiringly at his master. This was the kind of Inquestor the Aush loved: decisive, arrogant, confident of his identity. "When you are victorious, my Lord, all the Dispersal will rejoice. They are tired of these gods who will not be gods. They need gods, my Lord. If the gods voluntarily cast themselves down from heaven, to whom will mortals turn?"

And the Aush fell prostrate to the floor of the starship and kissed the hem of Arryk's shimmercloak.

Arryk waited until they had backed out of the chamber.

There came to him then four Rememberers, white-robed and gray-bearded.

He said: "Speak to me of Kelver, who will soon be destroyed."

And they reminded him of the green-eyed boy whom Arryk had once loved. But though Arryk had summoned the Rememberers he closed his mind to their words and hardened his heart; he knew he must be strong, he must resist tears, for the sake of the Dispersal of Man, for the sake of the High Compassion.

I am a sacrifice, he told himself. Through the suffering I inflict upon myself, the Inquest will be made clean, and holy, and full of truth once more.

The words of the Rememberers continued. Arryk turned to watch the light-mad overcosm, until the time came for him to give the signal—

***

As the sunwind lifted her, Jenjen cried out in a joy that was like pain ... she saw the others, thousands upon thousands, darkmotes in the brilliance ... Udara's love touched her. There was regret, too, in this love; and Jenjen knew instinctively that men would never dance on the face of this sun again ... and even as she thought this there came another wind, funneling up from the star's surface, a whirling wind, a darkfringed wind. She felt fear. Fear! the wind seized her... she tried to cry out, to push herself toward the spaceship that floated just overhead. No. It seized hold of her, and the wind was joyless, desolate ... she saw how it gathered up all the others in its whirling, and she was spinning now, the euphoria of flying left her and she felt only terror, she saw the others all sucked in, she saw a black opening in the star's surface like a mouth, she couldn't resist, the tide took her and at last she screamed, screamed against the deafening roarburst—

***

I must dive! I must enter the overcosm and escape! Zalo thought, as he sat in the heartroom. And he screamed in the ur-speech: *Sound sound sound sound sound* and he felt the delphinoid heaving as it started to plumb the overcosm, and then he heard Jannif's voice, distinct, as though she stood beside him in the labyrinth of light: "Do not sound! Stay in real-space at all costs! Go now-into the heart of Udara!"

"You want me to dive into the star's heart, to immolate the ship?"

'The scream of the star will free you—" And the voice died away.

How can I do it? Udara flared up in the viewwalls of the ship. He saw a dark spot on its surface ... where the dancers were. Jenjen is there, he thought. She'll die-

What was happening to the star? It seemed-it seemed to be changing shape! The dark spot on its surface seemed to be growing, growing-

Then it seemed that a wind seized hold of the ship, though there are no winds in space. A prominence had leaped out and surrounded the seventeen starships and the people bins. He was hurled against the forcewalls of the chamber. The brilliant sky went black and starless in an instant-

And then he heard a voice within. The voice of the living light. A quiet voice beneath the roaring that shook the ship.

Fear no more. Come into Udara's heart. Though they come to kill me, I will suck you into my innermost womb, and cocoon my children from my catastrophic ending. Fear no more. Fear no more, my children ....

And the starship fell into the embrace of the wind ... and he saw the star bloated to bursting, kindled from within by the suicide of the first convoy of Arryk's armada ... soon it would burst, it would burst, it would burst....

THE QUERENT

But did the sun then die?

THE CHILD FROM THE FUTURE

Yes. For the Inquestors knew well the art of kindling stars.

Even when not at war they had sometimes set the heavens to burning
to change the patterns of their evening skies, to watch the pretty fireworks.

But Udara, in his dying breath,
with the last vestiges of his strength, built a safe passageway into his heart. He gathered up his people;
he drew in Kelver's starships;
he protected them from his deathscream which sundered the overcosm
and blinded the ships of the enemy.

—from Zalo's *The Darkling Wind*

... in the ruined city of the Prince of Shadow, the darkness parted to reveal ...

***

... light behind the light behind the light ... "It's a tunnel!" Jenjen exclaimed. "A tunnel into the star's heart!" And they stood at the center of the wind, a place of utter tranquillity ... a cool place. Jenjen and Taik and the thousand thousand who had danced ... they stood in a corridor of nonexistence. She felt no sensation, but she knew somehow they were being sucked into the heart of the sun and she knew that the starships of her people were being drawn in as well ...

***

And Kelver felt it first, as was preordained, the shriek of the dying sun ... and as it screamed and screamed he felt the whispershadow drain away from him and his myriad souls slowly coalescing, coiling into one once more....

***

"What is happening?" Arryk shouted. "The overcosm has vanished?" There were no more dancing lights, only a profound stillness. There was not even darkness. There was nothing at all. Nothing.

"My Lord," said the Aush who cringed unhappily at his feet, "our shipmind has been struck blind. It can no longer see into the overcosm..."

***

And Zalo felt the lightlines go out, one by one. His starship, poised on the overcosm's brink, rested in the heart of the star whose matter was being flung outward. He could not feel the star's explosion, for Udara's dying act had been one of compassion; he had built the forcewomb at his center. All he could feel was a searing, utter emptiness. Where were the starships of the enemy? The ones sent to kindle Udara were dust now, less than dust. The ones trapped in the overcosm ... where were they now? The lines extinguished themselves one by one. The star well, once thick with lightstrands, was dark, the only light emanating from the filament he clutched to himself.

Empty Empty Empty—

I must rouse myself, awaken from this half-trance, be among people again, Zalo told himself sternly, as he climbed the lightrope to the well's edge....

***

Beyond the darkwomb that sheltered the people of Shtoma and the rebel starships, the scream went on and on ... it ran through the sinews of the overcosm, burning the brains as they tried to negotiate the pinhole paths, driving the delphinoids mad ... not one starship that had sounded the overcosm was spared, for in the overcosm all places are one, and the screaming touched them all.

***

"Where will we go?" Arryk cried. "Will we drift forever? We must breach at once!"

"Breach? How will we know where we are?" the Aush cried.

"We must breach the overcosm and enter realspace ... and sail the gray spaces, and know the silence between the stars ... of which Shen Sajit once sang. Or we are lost."

***

... and Jenjen ran toward the center where the light and the dark were one, and ...

***

... death! Zalo thought, as he broke out of the star fever at last, and ... freed himself from the light-lariat ... and also birth, for the Inquest's power is smashed now ... the blinding of the starships has crippled the Inquest forever...

* * *

... and as the sun screamed Kelver screamed in an agony of rebirth, screamed with the starscream ....

***

... the scream smashed through the highest planes of the overcosm, through to the tachyon universe, everywhere causing temporal anomalies and tachyon whirlpools....

***

...a final burst of wind ... Zalo saw Jenjen and ran toward her ... he shouted, "How can we be together? We were separated before," and he saw Essondras spring forth into being around him, the old arrondissements, the kashanthras wheeling flaming in the sky, poetry from a corpse's lips, and she answered him, "We've been catapulted into a landscape of dream, of temporal confusion, outside realspace and realtime..."

And they embraced, and it seemed that they made love as their world exploded around them, and then Zalo felt her slipping, oozing through his fingers, and she had become a kashanthra, incandescent in the night wind, burning itself to meteor-dust. ..

***.

And when Kelver opened his eyes he saw the city blooming and awash with light. For in its final moments Udara had propelled them all through a tachyon corridor into the atmo sphere of Uran s'Varek ... the city and the starships and the people bins and the rescued rebels found themselves all falling slowly earthward, toward the endless plains of Ellorin.

Waked from dormancy, rosellas had blossomed everywhere, and vines spurted from the cracks in the buildings and the ventilating slits of the mirror-metal walls....

And he saw crowds of people running down the avenues of the city and screaming his name again and again: *Kelver, Kelver;* from the rooftops and the nibble, from the blood-streaked streets and the windows of roofless towers.

And above the shouting he also heard the words, repeated over and over, *Kelver; thou art god, thou art god.*

The populace was chanting it, shouting it at the top of their lungs. They had reached the foot of the steps that led to the Throne of Madness now.

"I am no god," Kelver said softly. They were running up the steps now. "Help me!" he cried out to the Throne of Madness. And as the crowd raced toward him, up toward the the seamless light that was the sky of Uran s'Varek, the Throne worked upon the steps a magic of illusion, and the steps seemed to multiply and multiply and Kelver climbed ever beyond their reach, and the cries became faint as a breeze's whisper....

And he heard the Throne's voice, mocking: "Will you flee what you have become? What I predicted long ago? Have you not become to the Inquest what the Inquest once was to the rest of mankind, the repository of all its guilt? That is what it means to be a god."

"You cannot turn me into a god," said Kelver, infinitely weary.

"How will you stop me?"

"I—"

The crowdroar swept over him again, and he knew that his distancing from them had been mere illusion. Around him the city flowered and the people shouted for joy at their liberation ... and he alone knew that their struggle was not over, that they had merely exchanged one god for another.

***

A thousand thousand were the ships that breached the overcosm into random regions of realspace, their shipminds blinded forever.

Some would perish; some would drift forever, engendering,

in the far future, races of space-borne humans who would have never set foot upon a planet's surface.

A very few—for vast as the Dispersal of Man was, space is itself immeasurably vaster—made planetfall, deflowered a virgin world ... but many starships, Arryk's among them, those that had been last to leave Uran s'Varek, were still somewhat anchored in the realspace of the lnquestors' home world.

And so it was that, though they breached blindly, yet through a rebounding of the quickpaths, they were sent crashing into the atmosphere of Uran s'Varek.

Like a shower of meteors they plummeted. Maddened by sightlessness, the starships darted wildly about, slamming into each other, breaking apart, exploding.

Their fall took many minutes, for Uran s'Varek's atmosphere was many thousands of klomets thick.

But long before they would have been destroyed, the thinkhives of Uran s'Varek sensed their presence and brought them gently to rest. The impact of their falling displaced an ocean and irrigated a planet-sized desert; but that was a little thing for a world like Uran s'Varek....

***

"How are you not god?" said the Throne of Madness to Kelver. "You still have a million eyes and ears and forms. You still coexist a millionfold with yourself. The green-eyed offshoots of yourself are everywhere, spying, eavesdropping, secretly manipulating people's lives...."

"I have not yet walked my personal *makrúgh* to its end," Kelver said. "There is still the game to be played at lightfall, at the Southern Pole."

"Ah, but godhood is relative."

"Be still, Throne of Madness. My mind is clearer now since the whispershadow of Udara's death death has started to dissipate."

***

Here and there they materialized: pteratygers and childsoldiers and ancient lnquestors, all of them emerald-eyed, the many souls of the Prince of Shadow. Wherever they appeared, a strange obsession drove them southward, over the wasteland, toward the pole where soon the final *makrúgh* would be played. The thinkhives of Uran s'Varek, sensing their lnquestral origins, provided them with floaters and ships for their journey. Many did not know how they came to be on this strange world. They knew only that they must reach the south before they could find themselves again.

***

Prostrate at Arryk's feet, the Aush leader said, "My Lord, it is all over! Surely you must now capitulate. Or you will be alone."

***

They are gone, thought Kelver, those who were with me at the beginning: beautiful Siriss, impulsive Arryk, wise Davaryush ... Jannif and Tya and all the others, loyal to the end. There is no one to stand with me in the final confrontation.

***

"No," Arryk said. "We can still win. For I have loved Kelver, and I alone can twist his heart."

"Where shall we go, Master?"

"South."

"South, Master?"

"South!" cried Arryk. It seemed to the Aush that the voice of his lord had become rasped by age.

"lf Kelver forces me to play by his rules, so be it! I will go to the lightfall at the southern pole. I will play *makrúgh,* though *makrúgh* no longer has meaning. I will win. The war that once encompassed all the galaxy h,L narrowed down to him and me, alone, weaponless, our old amorphous love honed into hate."

THE CHILD FROM TIIE FUTURE

Blinded, blinded, blinded!
Thus it was, through the deathscream of the star that
had loved man,

that the Inquest lost its power.
The Inquest spoke, but the wings of its words were blinded.
No more could the Inquest reach through the overcosm.
The Inquest commanded, but there was no one to obey. It sang, but no one heeded.
For the starships saw no more.

—from Zalo's *The Darkling Wind*

Twenty-Four
Jenjen and Zalo

Zalo did not find her for many sleeps. By and large the Essondrans had left their people bins, and the people of Shtoma had built makeshift shelters in the meadows, cities of branches and woven leaves. The twin palaces, too, were abandoned; they hung in the air above the encampment, glistening in Uran s'Varek's golden sky. His awakening from the star fever had not heen easy; when he saw his former comrades, Enshtewo, Tarlo, and the boy Jhisha, he barely recognized them at first, and he longed to reenter the world of the star well in the delphinoid's mind. They too did not quite know what to say to him, it seemed, but walked alongside him in the crystal grass that tinkled and fluted in the breeze.

At last he said, "Have you seen ... ?"

They looked embarrassed at first.

At last it was the boy Jherwo who said, abandoning propriety by addressing his master by his child-name, "Zasha, you should forget her."

"Why, what's the matter?" But Zalo suspected already what they were about to tell him.

"You have a starship now," Enshtewo said. "We should think about our acting troupe. I mean, these galactic wars are all very well, but—"

He laughed nervously.

"Yes. I have one of the few operational starships left in the galaxy. Almost all of them are blind now; a few, docked on remote planets or lying in old shipyards, may yet remain. But let's face it, the Inquest is impotent now."

"Jenjen doesn't think so!" Jherwo said.

"No. She's in Kelver's city now, working for him, I hear," Tarlo said. At last it was out.

"Yes. Apparently they're planning some ... some final spectacle. We're all invited."

"Whatever for?" Zalo said angrily. "Sure, I've heard of Kelver's open invitation to the last *makrúgh*. But there's no point anymore, is there? I mean, it really is all over, isn't it? Time to begin the healing process?"

"I think you'd better go and see her," Jherwo said, with a child's lack of tact. But Zalo was already on his way.

***

You could hardly tell that this city had once floated in the atmosphere of Zorn and been built completely of mirror metal. This was a topsy-turvy city now, with greenery drooping from the rooftops and sprouting wildly from every crevasse. The streets were smashed; large areas of the city were a quilt of rubble and vegetation. He found the way to Kelver's palace soon enough. A large crowd was milling about outside. He asked someone if he had seen Jenjen, the darkweaver, in the vicinity; the bystander shrugged and pointed at the palace.

Steps. They rose into the sky. Broad marble steps. Gargoyles lined them; flowers bloomed in their mouths, in their eyes, in the cracks of their torsos. He looked up, trying to find the summit of the staircase. There was none. It stretched forever. Clouds shrouded its upper reaches. He started up the steps; someone stopped him. It was Jenjen.

"So you've come. I was hoping you would."

"For what?" said Zalo.

"We need you. You're the one who has established communion with the *Sirisshtasieh*. Someone has to be the lifeline of the new provisional order—"

"Haven't you had enough?"

"There's a struggle yet to come. I mean to pursue it to the end, Zalo."

"I'm sorry, Jeni." There it was. For a long time—years, even —he had feared this moment's coming. "We're different, you and I. I don't want any more of this. I want to go back to being human. I'm going to be selfish. I'm going to take my ship and my actors and go my own way."

"But, Zasha ..." He saw her clench back tears. "We saw so much together. The end of the world. The war. You have to be present at the inauguration of the new order. Or your life won't be complete."

"No," Zalo said resolutely. "Let me tell you why we're different. You've always loved absolute things: absolute darkness, absolute light, absolute beauty, absolute love. These things existed once: in the lightsongs of the delphinoids, in the radiant joygiving of Udara. These things are dead now... you understand that? Dead. Forever. They are gone from the human universe, Jenjen. And this is not a bad thing; not at all. We should yearn for these things, but we should never possess them. Absolute beauty, absolute power, absolute darkness ... all these things destroy what is human in us."

"No! We can recapture these things. Kelver and the Throne—"

"No, we can't. And we shouldn't. The absolute is an attribute of myths, of gods' lives, not of humans'. I don't want to live in a myth. I want to live like a human being. You can pursue your destiny, or whatever you want to call it, to its end. You can strive all you want to fashion these events into a perfect myth, to see the end of Kelver's epic ... I don't want to. I don't care. That's what I've discovered. I just don't care."

"What *will* you do, then?"

"I'll wander. I'll taste this freedom that we've won. And if you decide you won't come with me—"

"I can't." She looked up the stairway to the cloud-capped peak. "I'm driven! I need to see it all!"

"Why? There's nothing more. The Inquest is finished. The tyranny is done. What's to come is just games and parlor tricks. Are you so reluctant to pick up the pieces of our lives, to go on?"

Jenjen kissed him. In the wind the moisture drained swiftly from his lips. She said, "Long before I met you, when I was a little girl, I met an Inquestor in the gallery of the darkweavers ... it was Ton Elloran. I touched the edge of his terrible grief; and I was committed forever to darkness, though it took me many years to admit it to myself, to accept that truth with joy. The absoluteness of myth, Zasha, has contaminated me; I am doomed; I must become part of the Inquest's end. Oh, Zasha, you knew when we loved each other that I loved the darkness more."

"Yes. I knew." There was nothing more to say. But for the sake of form they went on talking for a while about inconsequential things; he could see that she was anxious to return to Kelver. They kissed again; a comfortless cold kiss, like biting into a sour gruyesh fruit.

"I haven't stopped loving you," he said at last. Yet he no longer believed in their love. He wondered why he had even come. After a decent interval they parted. He watched her ascend the steps; presently it seemed that the marble stair way parted to admit her. Like much on Uran s'Varek, the steps were an illusion, then. He suppressed an impulse to pursue her; then, turning around and walking back into the crowd, he felt a stab of guilt, because he had been unable to weep at their parting. Many years were to pass before he would feel healed.

***

Some of the astrogators, with their ships, stayed with Kelver; others, like Zalo, decided to leave. Aside from the actors, Zalo found a fair number of other malcontents, eager to return to a more human existence. Without ceremony they left behind Uran s'Varek of the shining sky. No one tried to stop them.

They plunged into an overcosm no longerthick with starships, but lonely and even more treacherous than before; for Udara's deathscream had left tachyon whirlpools and bizarre anomalies all over the fabric of spacetime.

It was lonely to sail the space between spaces. No longer could you send out signals to other shipminds, and converse across the nonspatial overcosm. Only the raging of the light remained the same; chaos it had been and always would be.

For many years he hated the lightstorms, and cloaked himself in darkfields, communicating only with Jannif in the heart of the delphinoid.

Enshtewo found him one time; he was staring intently into a holomirror, working the controls of a little laserscalpel over his bald head. He was carving a new cicatrice, concentrating so hard on its roseate design that he barely winced at the pain. Old father pisspot watched him for a while, afraid to make him jump and ruin the scarring.

At last he said, "It is true that you deserve another cicatrice, Master Corpse Dancer; but I didn't realize you were still observing the old customs so assiduously."

Zalo laughed, "You see this rose?" He pointed at the crown of his head, where he deliberately drew one of the petals torn and falling away from the jewelflower. "What do you think it means?"

"I don't know, Master."

"It means ... we've broken free of the circle! We've escaped. If we stayed on Uran s'Varek, we might see the war in heaven that will go on till the end of time. But on our million earths we must sometimes make our peace, mustn't we.?"

"Yes, Master."

"What am I thinking?"

"Of a new play?"

"How well you know me! Yes. A new play. And where do you think we're going?"

"Nobody knows but you. You're the one who's flying the ship."

"Everywhere! Anywhere! This is freedom, Enshtewo, freedom!"

But why did he feel so hollow inside? The place Jenjen had once occupied was empty ... how long would it take to heal that wound? And there was still something left undone. What could it he? In his mind he wound the lightrope tighter around himself, shutting himself out from Enshtewo's chatter.

***

At the center of the galaxy, a star fell inexorably to its

death. For centuries the thinkhives at the Southern Pole of Uran s'Varek had been positioning the star so that it would fall precisely through the opening at the pole into the hungry blackhole beneath.

From all over the Dispersal the lnquestors were gathering, materializing in their tachyon bubbles and preparing the game of *makrúgh.* Some had not even realized that the Inquest's hold over the galaxy had been crushed forever. Many hoped to gain a foothold in the new order, for they were sure that there would come a return to a semblance of the status quo. Even some who had paid lip service to the idea that the Inquest must one day fall found it uncomfortable to accept that idea's actuality, and behaved as though nothing had happened. They had always done that before, after all.

In the middle of the formless desert that separated the populated northern fringe of the sector Ellorin from the Southern Pole, there stood an ancient city sacred to the mythical Mother Vara. It was a ghost city, abandoned for twenty thousand years; it was not a spectacular place, and there was no reason for any of the Inquestors to visit it. Yet it was a shame that none saw fit to make this rather inconvenient detour.

If they had, they would have noticed something rather strange. Though the city was still quite barren and uninhabited, someone had passed by and tended all the altars of Mother Vara. Before her votive images lasertapers had been lit, and music had been made to sound from the mouths of sandstone statues.

It would have been something to remark casually upon, though few of the Inquestors would have considered it a matter of anyconsequence.

***

"Master Zalo," Enshtewo said at last, "I think your quest is only now beginning."

But Zalo did not hear him, for he was deep in his lonely star trance. The labyrinth was lightless now, but he breathed in the darkness like a drug, salving his pain with not-feeling.

BOOK THREE

The Homeworld of the Heart

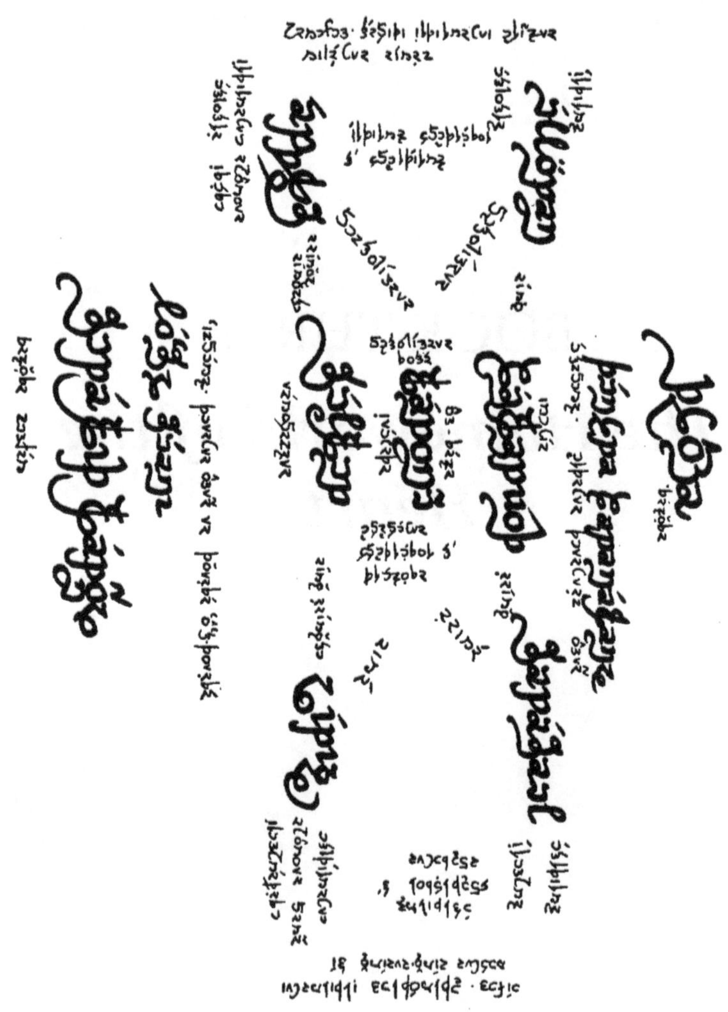

THE PAST:
ADHERENCE TO RATIONAL PRINCIPLES;
RENUNCIATION OF LOVE

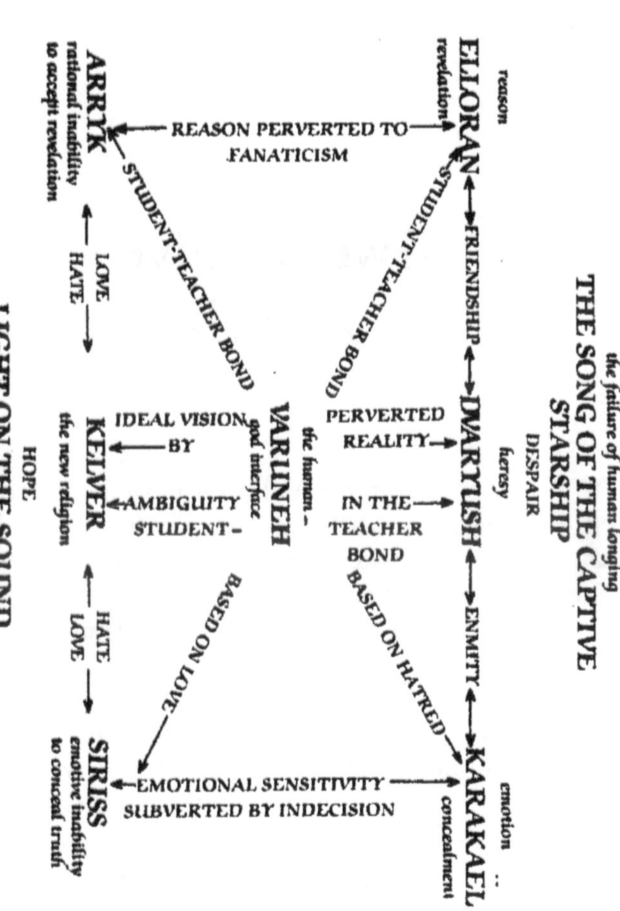

THE FUTURE:
THE BREAKDOWN OF REASON;
RETURN OF LOVE/HATE
TO THE UNIVERSE

Twenty-Five
Alykh

They had been on Alykh for perhaps fifty sleeps. Before that ... world after world after world. It had not been their intention to broadcast the message that the Inquest had fallen, but Zalo's great play, *The Darkling Wind,* contained those very words: *The High Inquest is no more.* And no one had arrested them. No one had spirited them away to the local equivalent of Essondras's Arm, the servocorpse factory for the politically unorthodox. And so men had come to understand that it was true. It was not an easy thing to comprehend; perhaps it would never happen in Zalo's lifetime, though his ability to sail the space between spaces gave his acting company a measure of temporal perspective.

In the worlds where they played, word came of the collapse of this sector or that, of civil wars, of federations and commonwealths. But these things were all limited by the speed of light. Now and then they heard that a different delphinoid had passed through, a survivor of the day Udara screamed. Sometimes it was a petty princeling bent on subjugation or tribute; sometimes a religious leader; once or twice even one of the Inquestors who stubbornly continued to act as though the end had not come. Then, too, those who remained on Uran s'Varek were able to make use of an unsafe and partly random system of tachyon bubbles; but the art of directing them was gradually being lost. For it was not a clean end, though future myth would make it seem as though all had once been bright, and darkness had fallen in an instant.

Zalo paid little attention to the stories he heard; he contented himself with refining his play. He had drawn a chart of the seven major Inquestors of the tale and their complex web of relationships; he hoped to make of it something archetypal. At times he would work on perfecting the chart, constraining the messy reality into a concise and artificial order. It was a game he enjoyed, and when he created the fantasy-Inquestors, it helped him to forget his actual involvement in those momentous events.

At last, at Tarlo's pleading, he consented to return to Alykh and to the city of Airang. He hadn't wanted to visit any of the old worlds, the ones before the ending.

But Tarlo said, "It's been long enough. And it's home to me, home." And Zalo had agreed.

They played in a theater on the very street where they had first met. On the first night they held a funeral for Enshtewo, who had died long before, but whose body they had not wanted to part with until they could find a world that had an Essondrish mnemothanasion; Alykh, with its panplanetary culture, was the ideal place.

Later Zalo went walking with Jherwo, who was now a tall man, and comely. They'd intended to prowl the fleshpots together; on a whim they decided to go visit the varigrav coasters at the city's edge.

The towers stood untended. The giant amethysts had been pried loose from the walls. A beggar (were there more of these than ever before, or was his memory failing him?) told them that one day the black box that controlled the gravity fields of the coaster had simply ceased to operate.

"Of course," Jherwo said. "I should have known. The black boxes used to contain pieces of Udara, didn't they? That was the one thing Shtoma used to export, the varigrav coaster control boxes. When the sun died—"

"The varigrav coasters died too, all over the galaxy. Sad." They'd been no more than thrill rides for jittery childsoldiers and guilt-laden Inquestors and young lovers. But when Zalo thought of what their passing meant ...

"Is something wrong?" said Jherwo. "This place makes you unhappy. We should go back."

"Yes!" He spoke with unwonted brusqueness; then, wor ried that he might have hurt his old apprentice's feelings, softened his tone. "An ancient pain."

'Are you thinking of Jenjen, Master?"

"How dare you know me so well?" He spoke lightly, but his flippancy hid real hurt.

"Come." Jherwo took him by the hand and forced him to look away. "We still have many hours before tonight's performance. Let'd do something to help you forget. Let's go and find whores or fermented zul or ... the f'ang baths, perhaps; they'll soak the world-weariness from your ancient limbs!"

"I'm not old!" Zalo said hotly.

"I knew that'd get you! Race me, then, to the nearest f'ang-place."

When Zalo reached it he had lost Jherwo completely. He was tired, though, and so he threw a demi-gipfer on the hostel counter, and a brisk mechanical showed him to a stall ...

And then, and then ... he was rising from the f'ang-drenched torpor, and tongues of solvent were licking the crusts from his eyes ... the old war! How it still ached in his bones! The fang mist rose up to succor the hurt, to steep him in oblivion....

It was then that he saw the woman.

The face, soft and proud; the hair jet-black, the skin snow-pale as though it had never seen sun's light; the single piece of clingfire that hugged her and burned against the frail whiteness ... all white and black she was against the swirl of clashing colors ... like a projected holosculpture like something from another dimension.

"You are Zalo the playwright, the astrogator?" A hard voice. He had not expected that. "I have need of passage ... of a ship. You'll take the offer? I left a message at the stage door, but it was rebuffed by an apprentice."

"Offer?"

And then he saw her again through the parting mist. "You don't exist," he said. "No woman really looks like that."

"Leave my looks out of it!" said the woman.

"Tell me more, then." Such eyes! There can't be a woman like this; it's just a drug-induced illusion. Or else I've been without Jenjen too long.

Then he saw the man who stood behind the woman. An old man. So old. And tall. His face:weatherbeaten.

About his shoulders, the tatters of. .. could it be a shimmercloak? Surely not.

"Are you—"

"No," the old man said. "I am not. Not anvmore."

"No. An Inquestor does not smile like that. You're a human being, not one of the old self-proclaimed gods."

"There are no more gods in the universe," said the old man, quoting a line from one of Zalo's own plays. His voice was tender. "I cannot command you, Zasha. I am ... apostate. I have no name anymore. That I wear the dead shreds of my old shimmercloak is no more than a passing fancy. And even if I *were* an lnquestor in the fullness of my power, I don't think I could command you. You know better, I think, since you saw a small part of the ending."

"Yes, lnquestor. But what makes you think you can barge in on me like this and hire me away?"

"The fee that we offer—"

"Fees indeed!" Zalo exclaimed, knowing full well that astrogating was a seller's market, the most exclusive in all the worlds of men.

"The fee is a name, my name that I no longer own," the old man said quietly. His voice held such authority, such gentleness, that Zalo found himself listening. "And more. I bring you the end of your fleeing, Zalo, Master Astrogator and Master Corpse Dancer."

"I was not aware I was fleeing anything."

"Yet I tell you that you are," said the lnquestor who did not seem like an Inquestor. "I was there when the Inquest extinguished itself in a million bursts of flame. I was there when Jenjen—"

"Jenjen!"

"I see, I have piqued your interest. Do you know my name now?"

"Why ... of course." The old man stripped of his name, the woman of the snow-pale skin and midnight tresses ... lines from my own plays again! Welcome, Davaryush; welcome, Darktouch. But why have you come to me, and after all this time?"

"We pursued you from world to world, always missing vou, Zalo," said Davaryush. "You and I have never met till now, though I had the honor of knowing Jenjen, your remarkable lover ... always they told me you have preceded me and vanished. Tachyon bubbles are not what they used to be ... indeed, we are stranded now, we can no longer control the bubbles we started with; they were sucked up in a tachyon whirlpool, I think."

But Zalo was still staring at the woman. "We can't pay you three thousand in tarn-crystal carat-equivalents," the Inquestor was saying. "We only seek passage ... away, beyond. We seek the homeworld of the heart."

"What is that?" Zalo said.

"What do you care?" Darktouch hissed at him. "You're just a mercenary—"

"Darktouch, leave him be."

"Torturer!" Darktouch cried. "What do you mean?"

"She means," Davaryush said, "that you still command a starship, and that starship still contains, soldered into its hull, a delphinoid brain, and that brain may be suffering "

"What can I do about that? I must travel ... I must, as you seem to insist, continue to flee. Yes, I have heard the story of Darktouch; how she grew up and saw the light on the sound and the killing of joy, and discovered that for every starship that flies the overcosm a song must die."

How callous I'm sounding! Zalo thought, hating himself.

"An old man and a girl," Davaryush said, "we saw the slaughter of that joy. For us, that was the moment that the revolution began. You understand, Zalo; surely you have had an experience like this, and it has changed you utterly. It is certainly true of all those who travel with me. "

And Zalo saw that there were others behind Davaryush and Darktouch: childsoldiers whose eyes no longer glinted with the yellow deathlight; hermaphrodites robed as whores; princelings clad in lapis lazuli and iridium; slave boys with chrysanthemums branded on their foreheads; a young girl with a sheathed whisperlyre; a Rememberer, blind, leaning on the arm of a crippled woman. Shameless, they had all thrown rank aside. Brazenly a princeling held hands with a slave boy, lovers and equals; a hermaphrodite linked arms with a child-soldier. In the old days, even Zalo would have been shocked at this defiance of decency. Even now, after all that had happened, the sight appalled him a little. Such had seemed the people of Shtoma, too ... those people now exiled from paradise.

"Why do you stare, mercenary?" Darktouch said. "You find us shocking, tormentor of starships?"

The Inquestor motioned her to silence. "We are giving up anger, Darktouch. Remember that. We turn our backs on the past ... I, who have hunted utopias, now seek one out. Oh, Zalo, I have come begging to you."

"But where do you want me to take you?"

"Well ... we don't know exactly. All we know is that there must exist, somewhere, a haven for us, the leavings of the old order. Perhaps we'll find and repopulate a planet that the Inquest once destroyed ... perhaps we'll go to the very periphery of the galaxy, and seed once more the ancient Earth whence once we came. But I do not think that will be possible, since Earth's location is a mystery. But wherever we go, I want it to be far from people's minds; I don't want what remains of the Inquest to search for us and kill us. There are still those who believe that the end has not yet come, you know."

"I don't think he'll go," Darktouch said. How could one person bear so much bitterness? "It's just wind to him, just noise."

If this is how you show casual loathing, Zalo thought, how you must show love! But he did not dare to hope.

The mist had parted, and she was so *real* that no overdose of f'ang could have fashioned her. He wanted so badly to touch her, but when he reached out she flinched, and ... he saw an image of Jenjen in his mind's eye, Jenjen cloaked in darkness. He could not bridge that rift.

You're as haunted as I am, he thought. But he dared not say it, for he knew that there was a brittleness behind her scorn.

"Have I said no?" he said, feigning toughness. They all edged forward like one man. "Come to the theater," he said lamely. "After the play, I'll ... make up my mind."

He heard their unison intake of breath, he saw the woman and the Inquestor exchange a quick look that shut him completely out of their world, their dream, their crazy philosophy-

And suddenly knew that he was naked and the mist had dissipated, and felt more alone than ever.

***

During the intermission, Jherwo and Tarlo came rather diffidently to the chamber, walled with holoscreens, from which Zalo usually watched the play unfold.

"I don't mean to disturb you—" said Tarlo, who was robed as a stage Inquestor, with a shimmercloak suggested by holography, with his hair streaming behind him in a glittery artwind.

Zalo had wanted above all to be left alone, but said, "It's all right."

Jherwo said, "Master, the actors have been talking, and ... when you leave us, we're staying."

"This is my home, decrepit though it's become since the collapse of the tourist industry," Tarlo said.

"How do you know I'm leaving?"

"You're not?" Jherwo said. Hope flickered across his face. Zalo hugged the young man hard, saying, "There was a time when you slipped easily through my fingers. You certainly played a big role ... you were the first *living* Elloran. You started the revolution, and now ..."

"*You* started it, Zasha," Jherwo said, his eyes shining. "Oh, we all believed in Kelver's words of mystery and were fired by his promises. But *you* showed us the vision in our own lives; it was you we followed, really, you, the embodiment of our dream."

"Do you remember when we stood in a theater on this very street," Tarlo said, "and at a word from you I dropped everything I was doing and ran off on an odyssey across half the known galaxy? How long ago was that, I wonder? With time dilation, it must be more than a century ago."

"But I am not that old," Zalo said, laughing wryly.

"We believe that you will go on to some ... wondrous apotheosis whose meaning we can only guess at," Tarlo said. "But we, who were never visionaries like you ... we're going to stay here, make a home, celebrate small things ... rejoice in the passing of the Inquest. You have shown us wonderful things, terrible and beautiful things. But the nightmare has passed, for me, and now I have come home. Home, Zasha." Zalo, whose home had perished in a game of *makrúgh,* found Tarlo's words unanswerable.

"She's very beautiful, the woman Darktouch," said Jherwo slyly.

"Powers of powers!" Zalo said. "Why do I feel as though I'm being kicked out? On second thought, I don't want to know the answer to that. I *am* being kicked out, by the Inquest! You fellows certainly have a lot of gall."

"You are our respected leader, and we would never—" said Tarlo.

"Enough." Once more Zalo remembered that he had never wept since his parting from Jenjen. He knew that they were right. They had found happiness, but he had not ... he was haunted, like the woman Darktouch. He knew that though the others loved him they found him cold sometimes, and heartless. Heartless....

"Where is it then, this homeworld of the heart?" he cried out. But the others, sensing perhaps that they had spoken too openly of Zalo's secret self, had stolen away. In a few moments the play began, and the screens resounded with the wailing of highwoods and the twang of zithers, and the chorus entered to sing the great Inquestral hymn with which the second act began, a moment of supreme irony....

***

After the evening performance, he walked back to the room he had taken in a rundown hostel at the edge of the sewer labyrinth. He had not wished to appear ostentatious; as a starship astrogator he was subject to curious stares and constant pleas for passage, and he had thought, by taking a room in the poor quarter, to avoid such importunings. But it was all the poor quarter now, really; the temples were in disrepair, the pteratygers had escaped their stables and flew in packs over the city; the harsh brash lights that used to make Airang nightless were no more; the whores, deprived of their *dorezdas,* stalked the streets and demanded crusts and small coins. Was this the coming of utopia?

He walked past the Inquestral mission; its firefountains were doused and veined with moss. In the shadow of its facade, two young people made love quite openly; in the darkness he could not distinguish their sex. Freedom is dark, he thought.

At last he reached the hostel. A linkboy showed him through the dim corridors; a door irised open.

They were already waiting for him.

Davaryush turned around. He had been studying the chart Zalo had drawn on the wall.

"Astonishing," he said. "I had no idea I was so complex a figure."

"Oh ... I put that together for the play *The Darkling Wind.* The seven Inquestors and their shifting relationships confused me, and I desperately needed to make sense out of it all."

"It is very neatly constructed. One day it may even become true," Davaryush said.

"What do you mean, *become* true? It is only an artist's tool," Zalo said, embarrassed because the chart showed Davaryush's own place in the play's scheme, and he was afraid Davaryush wouldn't understand the way he had mythologized the events to make the play more universal.

"Only that it contains more truth than the rather tawdry reality of how the revolution really happened," said Davaryush ruefully. "It doesn't contain, for instance, my treachery toward the Lady Varuneh, my long inaction, my shortsightedness in refusing to speak to Kelver on Uran s'Varek until it was too late, even ... the ague in my bones that made me want to scratch my buttocks while being enthroned in the hideously hard basalt throne of Gallendys. You've distilled out all those things, and made of it all something most elegant. Something truly moving, I might add."

"Are you flattering me," Zalo said, "so that I'll agree to pilot you to your homeworld of the heart, wherever that may be?"

"No, never that," Davaryush said. He drew a flask of ruddy zul from his frayed shimmercloak and offered Zalo some. Darktouch, meanwhile, had said nothing. He felt desire for her, so powerful it was almost like an adolescent's. But she gave no indication of perceiving him at all. What was it that caused this gulf between them? It was not her remoteness (he sensed that insecurity was behind that as much as any thing); not her beauty. It was the fact that she wouldn't acknowledge him as a person, only a type ... a tormentor of delphinoids. That hurt. If she could only know how deep and satisfying was his mindlink with the Jannif-souled shipmind.

"I think the time has come," Davaryush said.

"For what?" But Zalo knew the answer. He pulled a chair-float down from the ceiling and wrapped himself in it. Davaryush waited for the question Zalo must ask. And finally—

Zalo said it: "You were there at the last *makrúgh,* at the lightfall at the Southern Pole of Uran s'Varek. You must have seen Jenjen." Even now he could barely speak her name. "Could you not tell me ... how things came out with her?"

"I will tell you the story," Davaryush said. Darktouch looked up briefly, and then continued her sullen study of the room and its bare furnishings. "Though I am no Rememberer, I think I have a little of the art. Sit in your chairfloat, Zasha, and listen."

***

It was dawn before the old man finished his tale. When it was done, Zalo knew that he must leave Alykh, that his journey was not yet over.

"It is strange that you do not weep for Jenjen," Davaryush said softly.

"Not strange!" Darktouch said. "He cannot feel. Moment by moment he inflicts pain on a starship—how can you expect him to have emotions?"

"That's not how it is at all," Zalo said. Then, "The play I wrote ... how eloquently you've reproached me, Davaryush! I have only halfway returned to the world of human beings; the very beauty of my verses blinded me. It will be a long time before I can learn to feel again."

"I think that by coming with us you will find the way," said Davaryush.

Yes. Yes.

They left him then. Outside, waiting, were people from the theater; they had been crowding the door all night, waiting to see whether they would have to say farewell to him. They all had their little gifts for him. He was peculiarly touched by Jherwo's gift, the script of a play the boy had been working on for some time. Skimming it, Zalo found it charmingly amateurish, but he smiled and mouthed some platitude so as not to disappoint the lad. The zul began to flow as the sun rose. But Zalo was not thinking of his friends.

He was trying to bring himself to remember Jenjen ... her image was so cloudy in his mind ... could she really be the woman in Davaryush's story, the woman resolute enough to face the final darkness?

For this was the tale Davaryush had told him....

Twenty-Six
Darkfall

Southward they went; though their floaters carried them at tremendous speeds, sometimes as much as twenty klomets per second, it would still take many weeks' journey to reach the Southern Pole. Southward the city of Kelver traveled, its foundations stirring up the fine gray sand of endless wilderness. Sometimes Jenjen sat at the feet of the steps that led up to the room where Kelver sat enthroned; at other times she took a floater and flew ahead, exploring emptiness after emptiness. They had long left behind the places where the Inquest had built, which, though they might have covered many ordinary planets, were mere oases in the vast uncharted expanse of Uran s'Varek.

So swiftly did they skim the world's surface that all Jenjen could see of the universe outside the city environs was a smear of gray-brown, so featureless that she could not tell whether they moved or stood still. At last they reached a city named Pendevarang, abandoned for twenty millenia. Kelver decreed that the party should rest for a few sleeps; for they had barely come halfway, and already they were weary.

The palace of Varezhdur had been familiar to Jenjen from young womanhood; its twin, the snowflake palace Sharamonda, scarcely less so. Though it was said that each lnquestral palace was a world the uncovering of whose riches might take a human lifetime, she did not want to be caged within. Kelver had not granted an audience to her-had not even been seen by anybody-for many sleeps; she imagined that he was readying himself for what was to come. But could there truly be more? She knew that Zalo had been right, that the Inquest had been rendered impotent by Udara's screaming.

More and more she was convincing herself that her decision to remain behind was a mere gesture, like the coups and counterstrokes of *makrúgh,* in itself meaningless.

Needing aloneness, she went to the stables of Varezhdur and asked for a pteratyger. It was a wonder that, during the many conflicts that had ensued, someone had found time to care for the animals. They were mangy, malnourished; the sheen was gone from their fur, and their wings drooped. They paced the stable floors; their stalls had been neglected, and some lay listless in their own dung. The stablemaster scurried in front of her, trying to direct her away from sights he thought would offend her sensibilities. Now and then he would tactfully try to ask whether Kelver himself had sent her. "I come on my own," she said. But she doubted he believed her.

"Is there an animal you would like saddled up, my Lady?"

"They answer only to Inquestors, no?"

"Assuredly one as exalted as you, my Lady, has mastered the words in the urspeech that can command them—"

An image from the past: in the bowels of Ikshatra, the frozen pteratygers from the ancient city, the flight through the labyrinth, the bursting forth into the starship-streaked night ... "Yes. I know the words."

"Which one will you take?"

They wandered on. Presently she saw a creature not like the others. It had somehow freed itself from the stalls and was hunched in a dark corner as though about to spring. It was black-furred; it was its darkness that first attracted her attention, then the fact that the creature seemed strong and sinewy and well-fed, unlike the others. The eyes especially were what drew her to it—the eyes were like sea-jade, like Kelver's eyes.

Perhaps it was one of the Kelver-creatures! Perhaps this was Kelver's way of calling from the cage of his cosmic consciousness! She almost dared to call the pteratyger by name....

It roared then, a huge magnificent roar. It was a moment that brought back in an instant her memory of the Inquest in all its glory, its beauty, its brutality.

"Once," she said to herself, "I wove that roar into a Rainbow Darkness."

"Yes, my Lady? I really must call the attendants, I really must have this animal put away before it gets into the displacement-plate area; goodness knows where it would end up."

"No, steward. This is the creature I will take." She whispered softly to the pteratyger in the urspeech; its purring was like distant thunder. "See, he likes me already. Don't bother to saddle him."

"What an eye!" said the steward flatteringly. "To be able to tell the pteratyger's sex, without even catching sight of its genitals—"

"He is male; I know him well."

The stablemaster eyed her strangely.

Perhaps, she thought, he's entertaining kinky thoughts.

But he said nothing as the pteratyger sprang forward and she leaped onto his back, hugging his neck tight. He merely clapped his hands for the walls to be dissolved and for the displacement field to be enabled; and in a moment the palace was far above them, and they were diving down, windwhipped, to the ruins of the ancient city once sacred to Mother Vara....

***

She did not speak with the pteratyger at first, except to soothe him now and then as he soared and dived. Pendevarang lay ahead. Once there had been five mountains molded into the shape of Mother Vara, but they lay shattered in the gray sand.

It was said that the city had remained alive, waiting for the Inquestor who would come south to claim the Throne of Madness and take the burden from the shoulders of the One Mother; its duty accomplished, Pendevarang had crumbled in a few instants.

She told the pteratyger to remain on a cliff that had once been the torso of one of the five images, and to keep watch over her. A steep path led down into the city proper. Some one had gone before her, for she saw that steps had been gouged out of the stone and moss and undergrowth hacked away. Light fell everywhere, the special clear light of Uran s'Varek from which it was so difficult to escape ... and the trunkless limbs of Mother Vara, mountain-tall, cast no shadows, for the light came from all directions equally. Ahead, the gray went on and on until, halfway up the sky, it merged with the light. It was not a joyous light like Udara's, dead forever; it was a cold light, passionless.

I am as far from darkness as I've ever been, Jenjen thought.

But then an old man crossed her path. She looked up, startled. Save for the emerald eyes, the old man was ...

"Elloran!" she gasped. "No, not the true Elloran, but Elloran's image plucked from the mind of Kelver."

"True or untrue, does it matter now?" said the Kelver Elloran. "Do you remember when first we met?"

"In the gallery of the darkweavers. I was only a tiny girl then ... but it was you who showed me the light wrapped up in the darkness of those tapestries. You opened my eyes and showed me ... so many things. Now I'm a grown woman who has seen first her world, and then world after world, *fall beyond.* In the name of freedom. But what *is* this freedom, Ton Elloran n'Taanyel Tath? Did you not make me forever your slave that day when I was a child and you held my whole planet in your grasp?"

"You speak of another man, my child," Elloran said. "I am only illusion."

"Why are you here then? Do you come to exact from me some final sacrifice?"

"Nothing you will not give of your own free will."

"Free will!" She laughed. "There is nothing I desire anymore. Except, perhaps, to contemplate the darkness forever."

"Come, then, with me."

"Where do you go?"

"South."

"So do we all, all south, to gawk at the spectacle of the final *makrúgh.* It will be like the sex acts of eunuchs-what can they achieve?"

"We go even farther south than the Inquestors; we do not go to play *makrúgh,* we million souls of Kelver."

"So you know now what you are, at least. No more guessing games."

"We go to the void itself; to the dark heart of paradise; we go to extinguish our being at our being's source. Already they gather, the splinters of Kelver's soul. Their task is done, and they must be no more. For, as is prophesied, Kelver will awaken fully at the final moment, and the Throne of Madness will strip the veils from his eyes, and he will see the true nature of things. And he will be healed, and transcend himself."

And what will you do, you who have been Kelver's eyes, coexisting with him all through spacetime?"

'Ah ... regrettably, Jeni, as is always the case with multiple personalities, the whole is much less than the sum of its parts. Kelver integrated cannot possibly contain our multitudes. And you? You will come with us, no?"

For a moment the light went out of his eyes, and the sockets were windows into some terrible abyss ... she was chilled. But also drawn to them. Then his eyes glittered again.

Was it some presentiment, or was it just one of Uran s'Varek's illusions?

"How can I come with you? I am not one of Kelver's souls ... I'm me, Jenjen, darkweaver, woman of Essondras—"

"But you love the darkness."

"That is true. But—"

She didn't want to argue anymore. This was leading nowhere. Was this the message Kelver had for her? Why did it come in Elloran's shape? So that she would call to mind the meeting of her childhood? In bewilderment she turned and began to run uphill, calling for the pteratyger. She felt the cold wind of his swooping; she leaped up, embraced his luxuriant fur, hugged his hard body against the chill.

"Take me home, home, home," she whispered.

"Home—" roared the pteratyger: a yowling thunder, heartstopping in its beauty and terror. "Do you—truly desire—home?—"

"Of course," she whispered.

But the pteratyger flapped his wings and turned away

from the twin palaces that hung in the pearlbright sky ... he looked back ... and she saw that his eyes burned, gold-green fire, burned brilliant and hard. Like Kelver's eyes when he stood imperious at the head of the million million childsoldiers who had sloughed off their lives with his name on their lips, laughing, flushed with freedom.

"Oh, Kelver," she said softly, calling him by his true name, "where do you lead me? I only asked you to take me back so that I could rejoin the people of the palaces—"

Another roar. But hidden in that roar a human's voice, the voice of Kelver: "Mistress, you asked to be taken home."

"By home I only meant—"

"You spoke the meaning of your heart, Jenjen," said the voice of Kelver in the cry of the black-maned pteratyger.

And Jenjen divined the truth of the pteratyger's words, and knew that her final passage into darkness had begun: here, now, under the brilliant starshine.

Swiftly the pteratyger flew. The chill abated; soon they were basking in the rays of the million-starred firmament. The landscape beneath blurred into a smear of gray. They were traveling much faster than a pteratyger unaided could fly, and yet she felt no wind at all. When she reached up, her hands collided with a sheet of force that seemed to be wrapped completely around them. Thus she knew that she was in the hands of the thinkhives of Uran s'Varek, and was powerless to resist. In trepidation she battered her fists against the walls of blankness; she wept; she railed; she pleaded, to no avail. For she fought against her own self. She herself, in the days of her childhood, had chosen this moment, because she had had the temerity to feel pity for an Inquestor, and because he had stopped to explain to a young girl the ways ofdarkness.

"In the end," the pteratyger said, "you will not want to resist, Ir Jenjen of the Darkweavers." And they flew on and on.

***

. . . and on and on.

And reached, beyond the thinkhives that ringed the Southern Pole, the yawning precipice, the void, the entrance to the abyss.

Ahead, the sandy expanse was suddenly cut off bv a sheet of blackness ... a blackness such as she had never experienced before.

And the pteratyger landed. The dunes, soft and gray. She could not bear to look ahead; the dark was as blinding as the brightness of Udara. The north was kinder to her eyes; it seemed that the gray was speckled with dark moving dustmotes. It was a while before she saw what they really were. When she did, she cried out.

They were people! People clambering down over the dunes: old men and children, young women, mythical beasts, even. She could not count them. Hordes they were. Some seemed to be shifting shape, to be dissipating into the suns' light ... they were all around her, jostling her, racing down toward the darkness ... green-eyed they were, all of them, and she knew that they were the myriad Kelver-souls spawned in the union between the Prince of Shadow and the Throne of Madness....

"You will not join them'?" the tyger said. "You yearn for darkness—"

How many were there? They never stopped running down the mountains of sand, running to the edge of the world, running beyond, straight into the arms of darkness. "What will happen to them?" she screamed above the confusion.

"Who knows?" said Elloran-who-was-Kelver, materializing beside her.

"I won't do it," she said.

Then she felt an arm on her shoulder. She spun around, facing the darkness squarely, saw the lemming Kelvers leaping, leaping off the world's edge. A woman was staring intently at her, green-eyed like the others. "Jenjen," she said. And Jenjen saw that the woman was herself. "Jenjen," the woman whispered in Jenjen's voice.

"No!" It had to be another illusion—

"I know," said Kelver-Jenjen, "what will become of you when you face the darkness. I know because I am both you and Kelver; I share your soul with his knowledge. You have always loved the darkness ... now you will fall toward it forever ... you will fall into the arms of the black hole at the core of Uran s'Varek. As you fall nearer and nearer the event horizon, gravity will stretch the time of your falling to eternity ... forever you will contemplate the darkness, and in this eternity you will perhaps discover darkness's meaning. Are you not tempted, Ir Jenjen of Essondras?"

She hesitated no longer, but ran, ran, ran into the embrace of darkness, bursting with terrible joy. Her soul submerged in the dark world-soul. Her thoughts encompassed eternity. But how long she remained human cannot be said.

***

"What is this casuistry?" Zalo had said when Davaryush finished the tale. "Are you saying that she became part of a black hole? That she blended her identity with some cosmic, inhuman power? There's a sort of grand absurdity in it. But you do not mention yourself at all in this tale. You must not have observed any of it. Perhaps it's all just hearsay, or you're making it up to drive me insane."

And he turned away, unable to meet the Inquestor's eyes.

Davaryush said, "I don't know if the tale really happened that way. But I do know that when the Inquestors gathered to play the final *makrúgh,* Jenjen was already gone, and that even the planetary thinkhive, when asked for her whereabouts, responded only in riddles. Many inferred that she had been driven mad, had pointed her floater at the black hole, and commanded it to accelerate. Others drew more mystical conclusions. Truth has many shapes, does it not? I think Jenjen would have been satisfied with my version of the story."

"It all boils down to this: that I must cut myself free from the past, that I must go on," Zalo said.

He did not add that there was great truth in the story.

Jenjen had not been one to linger on some plateau of accomplishment; she always had to push on.

Had she thought, then, that her death would be the beginning of some transcendental experience?

Did she really believe that her soul would become one with the soul of the black hole?

He knew that this was a good time to weep, for the cathartic torrent to well up ... but nothing happened. Instead he kept thinking, All these years I've been held back by the thought of a woman who doesn't even exist anymore. And he felt envy, too. I just don't have that kind of courage anymore, he thought.

(And Davaryush, sensing the pain in his voice, withdrew to a corner of the room to await Zalo's answer, which was the answer they had all expected.)

Twenty-Seven
The Stone Soldiers

At first the journey seemed routine. Some of the passengers opted for stasis; they would awaken only when they arrived. They were the ones who feared to look upon the overcosm in its wild desolation. Davaryush did not choose stasis; that much Zalo could have guessed. Dethroned he might be, but he was still a leader. Nor did Darktouch choose sleep. In this she reminded him of Jenjen, who would spend hours watching the light-mad overcosm. But he brushed her from his mind, or tried to.

He reclined in the heartroom. Circular mirror walls gleamed around him. He was shielded completely for his descent into the star well. He closed his eyes and took the plunge; for an instant he saw an image of a fresh, un-made-up servocorpse, and a boyhood terror assailed him. He ignored the many mirages of the star fever and reached instead into the shipmind.

It came alive, moving, sighing, like an ocean in a night without moons or stars. A soft, familiar sensation. "Jannif," he whispered in his mind and he knotted the lightrope around his spectral self. "Jannif: do you hear me?"

"Yes, Zasha, my love." For the delphinoid always spoke to him in Jannif's voice now, and he had renamed the ship after her.

"Move now, my beautiful star whale; *sound sound sound.* Into the ocean of darkness."

A strange resistance. He would have to coax the shipmind more.

"What is wrong, my starsteed?" It was becoming harder and harder to negotiate the overcosm because of the tachyon whirlpools opened up by Udara's screaming; more and more he had to urge the ship on, cajole, implore.

At last they sounded, it seemed. But his hold on the lightrope was tenuous. "Where are you taking me?" he shouted.

But the ship replied only with images: alarms blaring, a split second of blinding terror, sirens screeching, and then ships falling one by one into darkness, strangely beautiful ... breaching the overcosm into gold-tinged scarlet nets of flame, vanishing one vessel at a time, like the beads of a cut necklace slipping one by one into water—

"What do you show me?"

DEATH, said the voice of the starship, oily and reverberant. WHAT YOU SEE IS WHAT THE SHIPS OF ARRYK SAW WHEN THEY BURST EXPLODING INTO THE HEART OF UDARA.

"Where is Jannif's voice?" Zalo cried out.

"Here, my love." A wuthering of the starwind.

Another image: Inquestors stalking to and fro, Inquestors with skulls for faces, their voices rasping.

Another: the Rainbow Darkness flaming over Ikshatra. "These things are no more," he said.

The ship bucked, lassoing the darkness with lightswirls. "Where are you taking *me?*" he said again. "Do I have control or not?"

"I am taking you where you must go," said the starship in the voice of Jannif. "Have you ever suspected, Zalo the Corpse Dancer, that the entire universe might be alive?"

"I don't know what to believe. I know that certain stars have consciousness, and that there is life in the black hole at the galaxy's heart—"

"Then you must not fear for Jenjen."

"Is she not dead, then?"

"Life and death! You humans always see things in such stark dualities."

"But do you see her now?"

"See for yourself."

An image: blackness, and a woman falling into it. Her eyes have always seemed death-haunted, he thought, but now an inhuman calm has stolen into them. Eyes, the dark has eyes. I feel angry and cheated. I hate her eyes....

The image welled up into a full-fledged nightmare.

The icy eyes of Jenjen became mingled with the eyes of the woman Darktouch. He beat the image back. At last the· shipmind's darkness came upon him, and he slept with the photon lifeline resting lightly in his hands.

How long did he sleep? He could not tell. But presently it seemed that they breached the overcosm, and were orbiting a planet whose name he did not know. He did not question the delphinoid's judgment, but called for the stasis seals to be broken on the passengers, and for a shuttlecraft to be prepared.

***

It was a bleak planet, mostly unremarkable. On one of its continents was an equatorial plain that stretched over several thousand square klomets. it was there that Zalo found the stone childsoldiers.

He was out walking with Darktouch and Davaryush. The three of them did not speak much with one another. Darktouch walked on ahead, breathing in the hot gusty air. When she thought he was not looking, he noticed, she was like a child, reveling in the smells, the textures of this world. They passed a village of rude huts; this was not a world that the Inquest much frequented in the old days, and its technology was limited to a few scattered displacement plates, a few rusty planethoppers, a spotty holobroadcasting network. As they walked through they were mobbed by children, as visitors always are. A matron, brandishing a waffling laser, shooed them away.

"Tourists!" she said. "We rarely see your kind these days. You'll have come to see the statues, of course. But if you want to go chipping off pieces, I'll need to see your license."

"I—" Zalo began. Davaryush, turning, cautioned him to silence.

"My name is Bratizwa. I am of the clan of Kir, if such things still mattered ... the titular Inquestral Administrator of Yarrandel. You look bewildered? Why, this is Yarrandel, this planet you're standing on. I can see that you've come by delphinoid, so you must be important figures, but we'll have none of your Inquestral arrogance, we know what's what, we know the Inquest has fallen."

Davaryush laughed wryly. "It's good the news has come this far," he said. "I would not have you fall down and worship me, and then have to tell you that such things are no longer required."

"At least," Bratizwa said, "you accept it with good grace. The last Inquestor to come here tried to take over, tried to bluff his way into ruling the planet. We killed him."

Such tiny words, Zalo thought: *We killed him.* There was a moment in human history, a moment I myself lived through. Before that moment it would not have been possible to say *I killed him* of an Inquestor ... impossible to even think it. The worship of the Inquest was so deeply ingrained in the human psyche that to even imagine such a thing ... what a changed universe lay in those three small words uttered in a barbarous lowspeech on a backworld!

He saw that even Davaryush, who had masterminded the great plan, shuddered.

The moment of tension passed.

Davaryush said, "Let's see your tourist attraction nonetheless, Madam Administrator."

She smiled broadly at his gallantry and led them out of the village. A light rain began to fall, and the plain turned a dull gray-green.

'There they are!" Bratizwa said, pointing at what seemed to be a forest of stone outcroppings.

Zalo was about to say, "There is nothing remarkable here," as he strode toward the first of them, when he saw what it was —

A child of stone. Black stony fabric was his cloak; dull grayish stone his torso; his boots were stone flecked with iridium. His face had petrified in an expression of agony; tears had hardened like clear jewels on his cheeks....

"Shall I tell you the tale?" Bratizwa said.

But Zalo said, "No, Madam, you need not. I know it well. Oh, Davaryush, these are the remains of the hundred thousand childsoldiers who died to protect the secret of Zorn! Arryk and Karakaël commanded that they be tortured to reveal Kelver's fortress world. But when they could bear their torment no more, they all bit down on the calcifying ampules transplanted into their jawbones ... and they turned to stone. And Siriss betrayed him anyway. Oh, Davaryush, this is a terrible sight. "

"Why so?" said Bratizwa. "It was centuries ago, if it ever happened at all."

"I know it happened!" Zalo said. "I was told of it—I experienced its consequences."

"But, my friend," said the matron, "did you see it for yourself? You are one of the few still affected by time dilation, whose memories stretch back to those times ... your wounds are fresh. But, friend, we were born in freedom on this world. And for that," she said with sudden reverence, as though it only just dawned on her who these travelers must be, "we thank you."

Slowly they traversed the jungle of stone children. At last Bratizwa said, "You must see, friends, what beauty has been born of this ancient sorrow." The drizzle had become heavier now. Zalo looked around for shelter. Presently the ground sloped downward and he saw that a portal was built into a grassy mound at the bottom of the depression; the rain was driving hard, and the four of them ran toward it, water drenching their fursoles and clogging their cloaks. Inside was a kind of tholos-chamber walled with brick. The statues that were petrified children ringed the chamber. Here and there a white-robed person-priest or celebrant Zalo did not know stood, or knelt at his devotions. A damp wind wafted in from outside, and he felt strangely at peace.

"This is the children's memorial," Bratizwa said. "We come here and think about their steadfastness, their loyalty, their courage. These are good things that we remember, things worth dying for. This is the temple of Kelver and Siriss and Arryk, the eternal trinity. And of Davaryush and Karakaël and Elloran, the ancient trinity; and of Mother Vara, the first and last."

"It is very beautiful," Zalo told her, "and yet ... I knew those Inquestors as creatures of flesh and blood, not gods."

"Do not misunderstand! The Inquestors that you knew are dust, my friend; you yourself stand here only by virtue of the paradoxes of spacetime. Even the air that surrounds you seems to be of another epoch."

Zalo remembered how upset he'd been when he came straight from Essondras's *falling beyond* to Alykh and found his world's death already stale news there. But this was even more unsettling; for they had changed reality into myth.

It was then that Davaryush took him aside and said, with great gentleness, "It is good you see this, Zalo. Slowly you are learning to yield up that core of pain within you. Your starship understands you well."

"The starship you continue to torment!" said Darktouch, making him flinch. "Yet we are forced to make use of it. "

"Yes, it is true, things are not simple the way you want them to be, daughter Darktouch," Davaryush said ruefully.

Zalo suspected from the way they looked at each other that they had once been lovers. "You want to burn through life like fire: pure, unadulterated, passionate. But there is much you must accept."

"You are wise, Davaryush," Zalo said, masking his hurt with a facile cliche. "Yet this is what irks me: we fought, we died by millions, to destroy the Inquest's power, didn't we? Yet look! These people worship Inquestors..."

"Do not be sad, Zalo," Davaryush said, whispering so that the worshipers might not take offense. "It is in men's nature to have gods. But you fail to perceive the difference between the old ones and the new. The important thing is that the new gods are molded in man's image. They do not seek to force mankind into something it is not; they are ideals, not entities. You have seen the consequences, Zalo, of having gods that actually exist! In freeing them of the Inquest, we have returned to them the right to fashion their own gods. Their names may not have changed, but their nature surely has. And I rejoice at that, Zalo. For I was crushed down by the burden of godhood even as I degraded others by exercising it. Never was I free until I was stripped of my name. Now that my name has been appropriated by a god, I feel more liberated than ever."

"Again," Zalo said, thinking of his parting words to Jenjen, "we are to understand that the new world is not to be a world of cold absolutes, but of humans. Yet I remember them in their splendor—"

"Ah, do you feel guilty that you sometimes mourn the passing of absolute light and absolute darkness?"

"I confess it, I do."

"Then let me tell you of the last *makrúgh,* Zalo. As a dramatist, you must want to know how the play ended. You will not want to be spared the final spectacle, if only as a narration."

And for the second time Davaryush told Zalo a tale of the last days on Uran s'Varek ...

Twenty-Eight
Lightfall

When Davaryush and his companions reached the Southern Pole, lightfall was already beginning. It had been centuries since he had attended lightfall, and that had been spectacle enough. But never had there been a lightfall so charged with tension, and never had the Southern Pole played host to such a ceremony. There were thousands of Inquestors and no accommodations; instant palaces had sprouted in the desert and shanty cities sprung up to serve their inhabitants.

As backdrop to the festival, a nameless dying star filled half the sky from zenith to horizon. Darkfields shielded them from its deadly radiation as they feasted and played *makrúgh.*

The group arrived to find the celebration in full swing. For the party they had cleared a field the size of a small continent and ringed it with three circular oceans of azure, gold, and emerald-hued liquids; a vast system of dams and turbines churned the waters of the outer and inner oceans in opposite directions, becalming the central sea.

As their floaters swooped down from the sky, Davaryush

and the others marveled at the effect. The distended sun cast a red-gold glow over the whole continent. Palaces were scattered everywhere. At the continent's center was a mountain around which a dragontree coiled.

They could not see its summit; but they could see steps leading up its side, all the way up, into a cloud of fire that spewed forth from the mouth of the dragon tree, and its scaled bark glittered like cloth-of-iridium.

Varuneh, who was standing beside Davaryush, said, "Look, Daavye. The Throne of Madness has girt itself with fire."

"And below?"

"The Inquestors!"

Their floaters came to rest on a platform that overlooked a plaza of burnished mirror metal, fire-red from the sunlight. The burning mountain rose from its southern flank. They descended into the square.

So many shimmercloaks, so many darting hoverthrones! The Inquest in all its splendor. Consorts of music on cloud-sculpted hoverdisks, brasses braying antiphonally from the skies. Retinues of attendant childsoldiers in ceremonial dress, their cloaks stiff and rainbow-colored like the tails of peacocks.

One Inquestor and then another saw Davaryush, and he heard the words rippling across the plaza: "The heretic! The heretic! The heretic!" And they shunned him, and the hoverthrones flitted away from him, and the shimmercloaked crowd parted to let him pass as though he were a leper.

The others followed him. Varuneh and Darktouch and silent Ton Karakaël and Siriss of the cloud-crystal eyes.

As the gathering became aware of the intrusion of heretics, an icy silence fell in the plaza. No one spoke of all the thousands.

Slowly, agonizingly, they walked toward the burning mountain.

At the foot of the mountain, which was a pyramid of fire against the fire of the dying star, they stopped.

There was Kelver, deep in conversation with some Inquestors; there stood Arryk not far off, studiously avoiding him. At last they both turned, not looking into each other's eyes; and both saw Davaryush at the same time.

Arryk said, his expression surly: "Daavye-without-a-Clan, you were not invited here. We are carving up the galaxy; your kind is not welcome."

"What is there left to carve?" said Davaryush very softly.

But the thinkhive of the makeshift city picked up their voices and carried them all over the square. Angry shouts were beginning. Davaryush held his ground, saying: "I do not come to play, my children. I come only as a member of the entourage of Lady Varuneh, the One Mother, and of Ton Siriss of the opalescent eyes, and of Ton Karakaël, who has lost the power of speech."

His voice hoarse, Kelver said, "Do not fret, Arryk. He is welcome."

"It is improper!" Arryk's voice was a challenge far out of proportion to the breach of protocol.

"Silence!" It was Siriss who stepped forward between the two of them. "For the sake of the love we three once shared, let me speak."

Silence fell once more as Siriss addressed the full convocation of the High Inquest against the background of lightfall.

***

Siriss said: "Let us stop fighting the truth, my brothers and sisters. For all the splendor of the spectacle, the meaning has gone out of our existence. You know this. It is true. That is why you play *makrúgh* this lightfall with such brilliance, such extravagance, such desperation.

"No more planets will die as a result of this great game; we have become powerless. Accept this.

"Once our might was absolute. Now our fall must he absolute. Accept this."

And she began openly to weep.

That was the most appalling thing of all. For every child in the galaxy knew the adage: *An Inquestor does not weep.* The tears of an Inquestor could melt the very foundations of men's beliefs. But it no longer mattered.

"I have spoken to the thinkhives of Uran s'Varek. Know, lnquestors, that once, millennia ago, before the coming of Mother Vara to Uran s'Varek, the soul of this great world was whole and unsundered. Or rather, it had no soul in the human sense. We will never know who built Uran s'Varek, or how many galactic empires, human and alien, it served before our coming. But Uran s'Varek has the capacity to become like the creatures that command it. From Mother Vara it learned love, compassion, and finally madness. For it had acquired a man-like soul, and that soul was not great enough to carry the burden of godhood. As it was with the Inquest, so with the Inquestors' world. Its soul fractured into four souls, symbolized by four thrones. And the mightiest and most dread of these was the Throne of Madness, whom we exiled to the Southern Pole and whose existence we decried as myth, until Kelver came to possess it. And the struggle began, with Arryk's forces representing that which had been, beautiful in spite of its corruption, and Kelver's what might be, roughhewn but free ... the way of men.

"But what of us? We could have been men, but we chose godhood, or had godhood thrust upon us. This is not our future. We are of the old things, the absolutes. We must be no more.

"I have parleyed with the thinkhives of this world. I have found a third path for the Inquestors to follow, neither Arryk's nor Kelver's. It is a beautiful path, and I believe it is the path of High Compassion. And I believe it is the only road to the homeworld of the heart, of which we all have dreamt since childhood."

And now tears came unstintingly, and she could barely speak her final words: "Ton Karakaël the cruel, who has seen the light on the sound, who has lost the power of speech, has asked me for the honor of leading the way."

And Karakaël stepped forward, arms outstretched; and he gave a great cry, the only sound he had made since he left Gallendys.

Another cry from the throats of the thousands of Inquestors....

His form shimmered for an instant ... then he burst into cold flame ... fire shot skyward from him . . . he was a pillar of fire now, streaking up, up, up until it went out of sight—a filament of brilliant light now, then nothing.

Before the crowd could react, Ton Elloran came forward and cried: "I am old; I can no longer grieve for the death of

Sajit; I give myself to the fire, to the final and everlasting fire!" And he too let out a mighty cry.

And before the cry died upon his lips the thinkhives of Uran s'Varek had ignited him too ... brightly he burned, arcing into the sky, forming a rainbow bridge into the heart of the setting star ... the rainbow lingered, its dissolution almost imperceptible, like the final chord of a song of surpassing sweetness, that dies upon the air and yet remains ... as Ton Elloran passed into the flame, the onlookers let loose an even greater shout than before, for they knew Ton Elloran as the most compassionate of all lnquestors, the one most like the great ideal ... and Davaryush stood listening to that shout, like the joyful confluence of a thousand rivers, like the bursting of mighty storms, like the crash of comets on a planet sentenced to perdition. He was moved.

This was the moment he had seen in the songs of the delphinoids on Gallendys; for the Inquest's death was written in those wordless lightpoems, had the Inquest but dared to see, divine, interpret. And he stood with Lady Varuneh and with Darktouch, the three of them apart ... he watched.

First one Inquestor, then another, then another, invoked the thinkhives of Uran s'Varek, and was consumed by fire.

Fire that leaped up from the burnished pavement and carried the Inquestors with it to the sky.

Fire that danced and spiraled. Fire in myriad colors.

Fire-arrows piercing the bright sky, lancing the bloated sun.

In the end Siriss herself: not moving from her position between her two lovers, crossed her arms across her breasts. At first it seemed that her snow-hued hair had captured the sunlight, for it gushed pale fire. Then white flames spurted from her hands and torso, and her shimmercloak was aswirl with lightning ... at last only her eyes and smile remained, superimposed on a shaft of incandescence that impaled the earth and sky ... now the milk-opals that were her eyes dissolved, and her thin smile thawed and smeared itself across the light ... tiny in the crowdroar was the sound of Darktouch sobbing.

And Davaryush hugged the woman hard, wrapping them both in the tatters of his sbimmercloak, feeling her warm tears on his shoulders.

"Child, you must not be bitter," he said. "For this, too, is part of the vision we once had together."

He turned to look for Varuneh; but she had slipped away.

Had she transformed herself into one of the columns of fire? Surely not....

Davaryush started up the steps of the mountain. He stopped. He saw a frail form moving purposefully up the stairway to the fire-girt peak.

"Vara!" he cried. Darktouch caught up with him and stood beside him. "Vara!"

"Stand aside, old man," said a rough voice, shoving him brusquely against the stone balustrade.

"'Arryk." Davaryush saw him. There was death in his eyes.

Kelver had begun to clamber up the mountain steps, following Varuneh. Arryk shouted after him: "It's not over, Kelver! You think you've won but there is still the Throne of Madness ... the sun's death will unleash unthinkable power, enough power to force a restoration of the ancient ways "

So saying, he began to run after Kelver, his shimmercloak streaming behind him.

Darktouch cried out: "Stop him!"

"How?" Davaryush said.

"I don't know, but he has to be stopped!"

It seemed that a mist came rolling down the steps and swallowed them all. For they were lost to view.

"I cannot follow them," Davaryush said. "Once I stood on these very steps and commanded Kelver to stand aside, for I feared I had created a monster, not a savior. It was too late. It is too late now; I can neither prophesy nor prevent what will happen at the summit of the mountain."

"Can we not save him?" Darktouch cried as more pillars of fire erupted from the throng below. "Rememher, Davaryush, how I loved him once. How he and I, mere children, brought the message to you, a kingling; how our love stirred you to action."

"I remember," Davaryush said. But he did not move.

***

"And so, Zasha," Davaryush said as they stepped out of the tholos-temple on Yarrandel into the fresh air, moist and fragrant after the rain, "you are not the only one who harbors pain and guilt from the last days of Uran s'Varek, from being compelled to give up the one he most loves. Darktouch is proud"— he paused as she walked past them, head erect, as though the tale had not affected her at all— "but her pride is a disguise. You and she are much alike, I think."

"But ... what of Kelver and Arryk? And the Lady Varuneh? What of them?" Zalo asked. After years of telling himself that these events were irrelevant, he found himself full of curiosity. "If it's not too morbid to ask."

Davaryush merely smiled enigmatically and said, "I am old; I tire easily. There will be other days."

"This world is not, I take it, the homeworld of the heart to which I am pledged to deliver you?"

"No. But it has been an instructive stopping-place. It is helping you both to heal."

Indeed some of the passengers were quite content to be let off permanently on this world; many were tired of wandering, some found the very rudeness of the planet challenging. It was with a much depleted payload, then, that they left the orbit of Yarrandel and sounded the overcosm once more.

Twenty-Nine
Essondras

Many sleeps later, he broke free from the shipmind and staggered up to the observatory, where Darktouch stood alone. All walls were deopaqued. They stood on the metallic floordisk, floating in the overcosm.

It raged. It oppressed him. No escape from it.

And she stood silhouetted, gazing out, motionless. Even her clingfire garment seemed muted. She didn't acknowledge him. She only stared out....

(vermilion hurricanes spattering whitepeaked wavecrests the ocher lightpeaks tumbling crumbling over blinding white catharinewheel volleys of fire)

"You shouldn't expose yourself to it too long," he said solicitously. *Déjà vu:* how often had he tried to call Jenjen away from her fascination with the overcosm? "You'll stare your pretty eyes into cinders." Mustn't patronize her, he thought. He went on, loathing silence. "People have been driven mad in the past, you know, unable to cope with the torrent of sensations "

"It is beautiful," she said, turning her back on him.

(geysers of green flame gushing through scarlet walls and veils ripping to reveal more veils)

"It's nothing; mass hallucinations engendered by our failure to understand what we're perceiving."

"Lights! Just colored lights! But your starship sees order in them; if your ship were not imprisoned in its hull of force and plastic and titanium, it would sing, and we would understand what beauty means."

"No more," Zalo said sadly. "Its vision has been crippled by its caging. Once—" he remembered the battle in the atmosphere of Zorn— "I released it a little ... but it sang only of ultimate horror, of the things men fear."

"What a monster you are! And still you fly the starship."

"And you take passage in it." He turned away, despising her for her obsession. "You're so full of words. As though words could save the universe. You're searching for something that can't exist. The Inquest is over; we have to make the best of it; utopias are mere words."

"Poor mercenary."

"Don't pity me! You dream hopeless dreams—"

"Dreams! Love, loyalty, compassion ... the words they invoked in the temple of the petrified soldiers. Can't you see these things?" She seemed to look straight through him.

"Oh, you're arrogant," he said. "You see in me what you want to see, some mythic enemy."

She turned away sullenly. No, she was no angel of light.

(volcanohearts twisted inside out lightfeathers fluffed from prismpools fracturing into mosaics)

"Why shouldn't I hate you?" she burst out. "Don't you know how you make the delphinoids suffer, how every moment of their lives from the moment they are mindsoldered into the ships is spent in excruciating agony, how you force them to live when they can no longer sing, which to them is agony beyond your understanding? Every parsec we've traversed has dealt unconscionable anguish to a sentient creature! How can you live with that?"

"How can you?" he said angrily. "What choice do I have?" You're as hypocritical as the rest of us, he thought, so proud that it goes against all your fine talk about the brotherhood of men.

(above them the firestorm stretching to forever behind the stormshards past the colorclouds pale sinuous snakes of sunset darted from dark to dark to dark)

And he was jealous of the woman's certainty. Jealous of the

utopian lunacy that had robbed him of the chance to love her....

And he fled from her and sought the comfort of the star well, and drew the darkness over his thoughts as a child retreats into a blanket heavy with familiar smells, retreats from the fear of night into deeper night.

Even the recurring nightmare of the tachyon whirlpools was welcome, for it at least was familiar.

***

Oh my starsteed, where have you brought me now?

The planet below them as they breached the overcosm ... the planet with the face of the Prince of Shadow.

Oh whale of the ocean of darkness, he thought, have you brought me home at last?

For this world was Essondras, its continents slammed together into an image of Kelver's face by the upheaval of its *falling beyond.*

He almost lost his nerve when the time came to give the command to load the shuttleships and go down to the surface. Only the taunting demeanor of the woman Darktouch boldened him. Somehow he could not bear to seem weak in her presence, for she herself seemed unassailable.

***

Ikshatra: he could not find it at all at first, for the bay in which his home city had nestled had been squashed by the conjunction of two continents.

Leaving the others behind, he toured the planet in a shielded floater at last he found the fissure that had swallowed up his home ... a vast savannah stretched far away on every side, and in the fields roamed wild the descendants of the animals he and Jenjen had released from their subterranean stasis in their flight to freedom: chimeric dinosaurs and dainty eohippopters and majestic pteratygers. He tried calling to these last; but they no longer knew the urspeech; they were no longer slaves to the Inquest.

Northward he went, leaving behind the huge pangaea of crushed continents, the emerald lakes that were Kelver's eyes. At last he came to the place he had been searching for.

A single amethystine cliff rose starkly from the sea. The

rest of the island must have sunk long ago.

It was here that the people bins had fallen, that Jenjen had heard his farspoken message: *They are burning the rainbow!* No trace remained of the thirty-klomet-long cylinders of metal that had fallen from the sky. He parked his floater and stepped onto the islet. A fine purple sand—powdered amethyst—blew against his fursoles. The translucent rock was cracked, ancient-looking; across its surface someone had scrawled an anti-Inquestral graffito; that too was almost faded. He waited, he did not know what for.

And then he saw.

Far out to sea: flecks of flame that were not sunset ... white-gold sparks in the twilight ... he was not sure at first, but all at once he knew, his heart leaped, for the light motes arced swiftly skyward to the zenith, darting, breaking formation and reforming, like stars at play....

Kashanthras.

And then he remembered how the kashanthras had flamed over doomed Essondras, fueled by the people's yearning to be free.

And he remembered that image's dark mirror: the childsoldiers hovering in the incandescent clouds of Zorn like tears of darkness, sent forth by the forces of hatred.

He thought also of Jenjen, who loved darkness, racing southward to extinguish herself in darkness's very heart. And finally Zalo remembered the spectacle of the last lightfall as Davaryush had narrated it to him; of the Inquestors, one by one, turning into pillars of flame, their light melding with the light of the dying sun. Light against darkness: darkness against light; dark seeking out darkness and light light ... the four images are one, he thought. They are time-frozen, eternal.

***

He said to the others on his return: "This is no longer Essondras; this world belongs to the kashanthras. If we settle here, a time will come when our emotions will once more pollute those of the embalming-birds, and we will cause them to drop from the sky."

Davaryush agreed that they should continue their journey.

On the starship, Darktouch asked him: "Will you put me in the play you are working on?"

It was the first time she had spoken to him other than resentfully.

***

As they sounded, Davaryush said: "You will want to know what happened to Kelver and Arryk."

"Yes, I'll want to know," Zalo said.

(firebubbles foamed through lacelightcurtains lanced by liquid lightnings)

"... and the One Mother," said Davaryush, "the Lady Varuneh."

The old man rambled on; intermittently Zalo listened. But his mind was a welter of images of light and darkness, and kashanthras and Inquestors and darkweavings and rainbows ... later, when he tried to recall what Davaryush had told him, he would never be entirely sure how much of the tale was the Inquestor's, how much sprang from the labyrinth of image and memory. In the end it did not much matter, he reminded himself, for a myth is both more and less than a story.

Thirty
Dusk

To the peak of the burning mountain ....

They raced, the two who had once been friends and whose enmity had sundered the human universe. Always the figure of Varuneh appeared ahead; always it seemed that the pinnacle was only barely out of reach; always the mountain burned, the summit burned, and behind it the whole heaven flamed with the passing of the nameless star. They ran. Higher and higher, tongued by the hot wind. Upon a parapet they barely paused. Arryk lashed out with his fists, trying to fell his opponent. He cried out: "You will never reach the top, Kelver! You're tired; the whispershadow has taken its toll of you. I will possess the Throne of Madness. I will turn back the tide of time. I will have the Inquest back, its might redoubled, its glory undimmed. Soon the star will die! And I will hold in my hands all the energy of its passing ... I will change the very fabric of spacetime ... I will end this false reality and replace it with my own truth!"

But Kelver dodged his blows and did not heed him, and purposefully ran uphill, never looking back. With a spurt of energy Arryk charged after him. When he tired he called for a floater and one was summoned forth from the empty air, for here near the center of the thinkhives' power the distinction between illusion and reality was blurred. And Kelver too called for a floater; and both were in the shape of chariots cloaked in fire and drawn by fire-breathing pteratygers.

"A whip!" cried Arryk, and one sprang into his hands, and he flailed at the chariot that thundered alongside him, and still the summit was not in sight. He lashed the pteratygers; blood fountained from their wounds and gushed down the stairway. He must not fail, he could not ... he must stop the turning of the universe. Now the pteratygers blurred into fire and it seemed they were riding on airskiffs like the delphinoid hunters in the heart of the dark mountain, now they seemed to be great starships breaching the overcosm, flagellating each other with whips of laser-fire, and then they were riding the tails of child-brained comets, on the backs of the delphinoid robots that spewed childsoldiers into the sky, and all the while the stars were weeping fire and blood, and blood and fire were welling up from the pores of the mountain ....

And Arryk cried out, "I will never let you win!"

And he heard Kelver's answer in his mind: "There is no victory."

They ran.

Now they were huge as starsystems; they were like the urbeings of myth, who existed before men, hurling great planets at each other in their rage ... and still they had not reached the summit ... and a time came when they entered a realm beyond time, and passed out of realspace into the world of Uran s'Varek's mind ... and still they ran uphill ... a terrible weariness came over Arryk, and he longed to sleep forever, but he knew he must reach the peak, he must possess the Throne, he must hurl the Prince of Shadow down from heaven and have history once more....

At last, in a moment in time and yet outside it, they stood at the pinnacle of the mountain. Around them flamed the doomed star.

A few more steps, and he would reach the Throne! And Kelver blocked his path. "Oh, Kelver, Kelver," he cried out, despairing, "must I kill you?" And they fought, the two of them, like ancient titans, their footfalls sundering planets, their howls resounding in the stars. With terrible fury they fought. They battled till the bitterness was burned from them; then they still fought, though they had forgotten the reason for their fighting. They fought until their wrestling was like the embrace of lovers. Weeping they fought, each feeling the other's hurt more deeply than his own. Tears welled up from their wounds and blood gushed from their eyes. And they sprinkled the Throne of Madness with their tears and blood.

At last, after a time that was not a time, they could fight no more. The tiredness came first to Kelver, who had borne the burden longest; he fell into the arms of his adversary, limp limbs on limbs and lips on lifeless lips. And cradling his enemy in his arms, Arryk collapsed upon the Throne.

They loved each other then; they had always loved each other, even in the instant of greatest hate.

Dying, they kissed.

And in that moment the black hole swallowed up the nameless star.

In the tiny instant of consciousness still left to him, the whispershadow of the dying star attached itself to him who possessed the Throne, for it is written in the lnquestral precepts:

hosh sih a kerávishi varungs
zyh vih shtendaín e chítareh
ng'darans dhandándi;

He who shall sit on the Throne of Madness
shall see for an instant into the heart
of a dying star.

So it was with Arryk. Godhood descended upon him, and madness. But he could not bear the burden.

Then came Mother Vara to the Throne of Madness. Tenderly she lifted from the Throne the intertwined bodies of Kelver and Arryk.

She wept for them. Her tears flowed down the four sides of the mountain, for her grief was great; and her grief brought life to the wilderness, and greened the limitless deserts of Uran s'Varek.

And she said to the Throne: "I have returned, as I once promised you. I will flee no more. We are bound together, you and I. For of all the sentient beings who have possessed you, who took upon themselves the whispershadow of a dying star, I alone possess *your* whispershadow, and know the hour of your death. Yes, even you, the eater of stars, are not for all eternity. You are a thinkhive and I am a thing of flesh. Yet you loved me. For the sake of that love you gave me power. You are the mightiest of my myriad lovers. Yet I, a mortal, drove you mad. But now I am come to heal you. Be still now, Darkling Wind."

So saying she cast her soul into the consciousness of the dark heart; and the mind of Uran s'Varek was no longer fractured but fused into one, human and godlike both.

The thrones that had symbolized its sundered personality toppled. And the stars rejoiced, for the eater of stars now knew of its own ending, and was possessed of Varuneh's compassion.

Thus it was that the stars ceased to speak with men.

Thus it was that Kelver and Arryk ended their strife, and gave one another solace in death.

And thus it was that Lady Varuneh passed out of realspace, beyond the overcosm and the tachyon universe, and entered the fabric of myth.

Thirty-One
Dawn

And later, bursting out of the darkness—

—anomaly anomaly the shipmind screamed, the lightline jerking him down corridors of darkness within darkness with in darkness falling burning anomaly anomaly-

Breach!

"Be calm, my starsteed ... what have you done to me now? Where have you brought me?"

Jannif's voice, faint: "We have passed through a tachyon whirlpool."

"But ..." His mind raced through the star charts in the starship's thinkhives, page after holographic page materializing in his thoughts. "This seems to be an uninhabited, abandoned sector of space. Surely there wouldn't be tachyon whirlpools this far from the galactic core, from human habitation—"

"You forget that Shtoma was far from the center too. And that the scream of Udara penetrated the overcosm, beyond the dimensions of realspace that men perceive."

Davaryush and Darktouch had come up the heartroom. "What was it?" Davaryush said. "We felt a disturbance."

"Tachyon whirlpool," Zalo said. "I'm not quite sure where we are." He tried to act calm. "Somewhere in one of the galactic arms. Men have never come this far."

"Not quite so," said Davaryush. His eyes sparkled. "I have it on good authority that the human race originated in the arm."

"Absurd!" Zalo deopaqued the walls. No stars at all. Well, a few, here and there, but not the star-stitched brilliance of men's habitats.

"What's more," the old man said, "it is in the galactic arms that Lady Ynyoldeh used to store her deathmoons. Some of the first skirmishes of the revolution were fought out here, in this lonely sector of the galaxy." He looked about. "Ah, there's a star nearby, a yellow dwarf of little consequence. Maybe it has planets."

Zalo communicated with the shipmind, assessing the damage. It was very bad indeed. The stasis-pods had been thrown into dysfunction; all the utopians who had come this far were dead ... all of them! With their hope-fired eyes and poignant dreams ...

Panicking, he checked the erratic tachyon-bubble system; that was completely dead now.

"We'll have to go back, somehow," said Zalo. "We've reached the galaxy's end; there is no homeworld of the heart here, there's only more grief."

"I think we should look for a planet," Davaryush said mildly.

"You're out of your mind!" "Please. Bear with us."

"I say we go home. The delphinoid has mapped the anomalies now, and it should be no trouble to return to our last stopping place."

"Home!" Darktouch said bitterly. "Never! Not after the agony the delphinoid has been through to carry us this far!"

"Now wait," Zalo said. "I agreed to take you as passengers. If you really want, I'll leave you on some desolate planet ... but then I will go ... somewhere, I don't know where."

"Why?" said Davaryush. "You have nowhere to go." Zalo did not want to believe him.

***

And they found a planet: opalescent, blue-white, beautiful, dead.

Desert. Rocky desert. Hilly desert. Dune desert. Desert of blasted glass. Ice deserts in the polar caps. This was no paradise. But Davaryush and Darktouch seemed happy enough exploring it.

As for Zalo, he was reluctant to abandon them. He knew that Darktouch and Davaryush had once been lovers; he knew, too, that over the centuries of their lifespans the Inquestors became sterile. They had had some notion of creating their own utopia on some idealistic principles; now they would merely die.

Unless Darktouch were first impregnated by him....

But though he felt desire for her, and knew that she would welcome sex with him if only to better their chances of making a go of this barren world, he made no move to win her over. He was uncomfortable in the presence of such blistering disdain.

So he walked the world alone. He was sorting out the final version of *The Darkling Wind* in his mind. He would write in the scene between Kelver and Arryk and the Throne of Madness ... true or not, what splendid theater it would make! He would go back to Alykh. Tarlo would be an ancient man when he got there-what a stunning reversal! and Zalo would still be young and vigorous. Tarlo could play Davaryush: he had authority, and the years would lend him awesome presence.

Day by day he was astounded at his two companions. They didn't know how to set up camp or forage for food, skills that he had learned in childhood play. But they were childishly enraptured by this dull planet.

Food they found readily enough. On the foothills were fruit trees with reddish round fruit and soft yellow meat; and curious, fearless fish fairly leaped into their forcenets from the brooks.

They explored together now, still rarely talking to each other. They climbed the hills easily, Davaryush following on a floater because of his age and because the gravity was a shade higher than he was used to.

Darktouch kept her silence.

He'd look at her when she didn't know he was looking. She had come to some accommodation with her great anger. She no longer groomed her hair; it streamed free in the wind.

The clingfire garment was worn threadbare. It gave off no fire, only a pearly rainbow. She seemed to belong to this world.

The ground was soft, yielding to his feet. It was a strange sensation, quite different from the continual disruption of displacement plates.

Had men lived here once? It would take years to explore the world fully. But from what they could see around them it seemed void of human life. They saw no sunken cathedrals such as the sand-acropolises of war-torn Zahrimant; no mile high husks of skyscrapers such as bestrode the fire-snowed slopes of Ont; no manmade chimeras such as roamed the plains of Essondras.

At the summit of a hill he said awkwardly, "I wish there were not this gulf between us, Darktouch. We both have been through much, too much."

"As long as you cling to your starship, Zalo, you belong to the old things. There is nothing between us."

"But how will I get home?"

"Home! You have no home." She avoided his eyes. "None of us has a home. Yes, I overheard you last night stalking through the wood and reciting ... oh, wonderful poetry. Your own lines, I know. I could almost have loved you when I heard your voice, resonant, against the chirping and the stridulating of the forest. But it's not to be."

"You hypocrite!" he retorted, angry. "You took my help, didn't you, tainted though it was. Help to run away. Running away-to die!"

They glared at each other. Her hair blew across her face—

How softly she glows, he thought, against the eerie yellow light of this cold star.

He heard Davaryush, ahead, call out. He eased himself over the hillcrest and rested his elbows on a flat boulder, and his field of vision telescoped abruptly to an endless brown plain spattered with smooth sandcarved rockshapes like sculpted bushes. Halfway to the horizon was a forest of brown trees . . . trees?

"What are they?" he said.

"Let's go and see," said Darktouch. "Don't you want to find out? They look ... almost human, those trees."

"Let's not walk. It's too far," he said, and summoned two little floaters—hoverdisks—with a flick of his mind.

They rode the breeze down through the desert. It was so far ... sand stretched until distance meant nothing anymore. The wind etched sandstone sculptures; they were huge, bigger even than the delphinoid shipmind that orbited overhead, waiting.

How small I feel, Zalo thought. I, who moved easily in a far huger galaxy, feel dwarfed by this single plain, this single world. Is this the kind of perspective that ancient humans must have had? From ground level they could not even see their objective (on Uran s'Varek one could see millions of klomets ahead), so they drifted blindly, trusting their hoverdisks.

Then they were there. They *were* people!

Zalo stepped gingerly off the floater. He practically walked into a man. The man was quite cold, and didn't move.

Other men were standing nearby. Farther off were a few women. Many were naked; these had nothing on but a blue strap around their wrists. Others had clothes. The familiar clingfire was one of the fabrics, but the fire was frozen solid. Others wore fanciful costumes: palatial headdresses, extravagant codpieces. All stood stiff and unmoving.

"What is it? A holosculpture museum?" Zalo said.

"I don't think so." Davaryush had come up behind them. "I hate this world and its desolation and its mysteries."

He slammed his fist into a woman's shoulder; it was harder than a starship's hull. Were they frozen somehow out of time? Or imitations of humans, bait laid out by aliens? And why was it they seemed so ... familiar?

He touched the stiff tousled hair of a young child, red-haired.

A very distant memory: Wasn't my hair red once? He couldn't remember. It had been so long since the day he sheared it off and carved his first cicatrice, flaunting his early puberty before all his boyhood friends. He thought it was red, but he couldn't be sure.

"You want to solve this mystery, don't you?" Davaryush said. "Perhaps you should stay until we figure out what it is?"

"You tempt me. But I must go home."

He thought of another plain of statues he had seen. The plain of the childsoldiers turned to stone. What pain they must have felt. What must have gone through their minds when they all chose death rather than to betray the Prince of Shadow....

The thought of pain brought the delphinoid to mind. Do you suffer, Jannif, as you flit forever through the labyrinth of the star whale's mind?

A thought struck him for the first time: Like the childsoldiers on the plain of Yarrandel, the ship is in agony. But unlike them it cannot die.

***

He woke to dawn under the open sky. The sands had shifted; the statues had not moved at all, though some were now knee-deep in little dunes.

Dawn: like a pink-feathered pteratyger cub, speared and brought down over the gray sea. There was a kind of magic in this world; perhaps men had lived here aeons ago, perhaps it was even the urworld from which men sprang. These statues ... they must be statues, if they didn't move ... statues from a time before the Inquest, perhaps, that had stood the ravages of millennia? Impossible! How could the primitive pre-Inquestral technology have lent such verisimilitude to them?

In the morning he and Darktouch labored to saw off a piece of one, part of a garment perhaps, so as not to damage the statues proper. Their metal tools shattered on the cloth, and even the laser drill didn't budge it so much as a micron.

And Zalo watched the woman Darktouch; it was hard to take his eyes off her when the crimson-tinged shadows of the alien sun crossed her face. They rested, leaning against the hard statues. A light wind sprang up, sprinkling them with sand.

He said, "Don't you regret leaving it all behind? I mean ... yes, the Inquest has fallen. But much still stands. You could choose any world; you could be acknowledged as a hero of the revolution, you could lead some world into the great millennium of your dreams ... no? You choose the wilderness."

She said, "Oh, Zasha," calling him for the first time by his childname, "the past still clings to you. You look back and you see palaces and kingdoms and splendor. You see us as now progressing into a dark age."

"And you! You would renounce it all, the beauty along with the cruelty. You think your golden age has already begun ...

this!" He waved his arms about him. "This barren, sterile earth!"

Angry, he turned his back on her and returned to the makeshift shelter they had built beside the shuttlecraft. A crystal board, the same one he had been using in his lodgings on Alykh-hung on one wall, and he began to add more to his chart of the Seven Inquestors. If I have to edit the truth a little, he was thinking, at least I will make of all these happenings something archetypal, something universal. He worked on his chart and honed the lines of a new revision of his play, thinking of the acting troupe on Airang and wondering how long it would take in realtime to return to the tarnished streets of what had once been the Inquestor's pleasure city.

***

Around midday he said to Darktouch, who had come in, upsetting the rhythm of his composition: "All those statues have those blue bracelets in common, don't they? Maybe if you lasered a bracelet." He said it half in jest, half to get rid of the intrusion.

Darktouch left him, muttering something about one child-statue "whose bracelet seems askew."

***

An hour later he heard them shouting. And a shrill voice, a child's voice. It was a young girl, red-haired, her bracelet hanging loose ... she was kicking and biting as they brought her back to the shelter.

"Where am I?" she was shrieking. "Where's the space station, who are you people?"

"The highspeech?" Zalo said, puzzling out the meaning of her strange inflections.

At that point the girl saw Zalo; saw past him to the chart of the Seven Inquestors. Her eyes opened wide; she draped her cloak decorously about herself and knelt down before him. She was eleven or twelve, the age of a young warrior of the Dispersal. She looked familiar ... Zalo could almost put his finger on it, but . . .

"Who are you'?" he whispered.

"Please let me out of here," said the girl. "I see you are a guardian of the old truths, but ... this is the wrong planet, I think. I must not have fastened my stasis-bracelet tight enough."

"What do you mean, a guardian of old truths?"

"I mean ... " The girl stopped. She looked, long and hard, into Zalo's face.

And then she said: "Powers of powers. I must he dreaming." And she unclasped a pouch from her thigh and drew from it a deck of cards, nine or ten in all. Each bore a holosculpture of a mask that leaped up when the card was turned face-up. On the obverse of each was ... a design. Zalo saw what it was: a stylized reduction of his own chart of the Seven Inquestors.

The girl shuffled the cards, kissed then reverently, and pulled one out; she compared its image with Zalo's face. And Zalo saw himself mirrored. But an ideal self, the cicatrices only hinted at; old age had settled on his face and worn it smooth, like an ancient hill, like one of the rolling slopes of this very planet. Zalo looked at the girl, who looked at him: wonder transfixed them. Wildly he turned to Darktouch and Davaryush, who only smiled knowingly. "What kind of trick is this?" Zalo said.

"No trick, Lord Zalo," said the girl. "You know my name—"

"Who does not know it?" "And the cards?"

'The High Inquestral tarot. It is all that remains of the dawn time, the time of legends. Look: the One Mother embracing the Throne of Madness and bidding it be still at last. Look: troubled Arryk and tormented Kelver. I'm not afraid anymore, Lord Zalo. This is the dawn time. There's nothing to fear here. I understand now, I accidentally triggered the bracelet thing by tying it on wrong on Zasharron. What a stroke of luck I've found you! Now you can do it up properly for me and bundle me off to the station and I can get home, right?"

'The dawn time?" Zalo said. "Where do you come from?"

"Zasharron, you don't know Zasharron? But of course, I keep forgetting. None of this has happened yet. It's a colony world: the oldest of them actually; named after you. Oh, I should be full of awe; my parents say I talk too much. And I am out of practice in the ancient speech, since I have not been in childschool for many years. The stasis-field—"

"All right," Davaryush said. The girl stared at him, huge-eyed. "You know all our names."

The girl nodded.

"So you are from the future; from a time when this world has prospered, and has spawned a colony or two even?"

"Yes, Lord Davaryush."

"Tell me," Darktouch said, "Are your people free?"

"Free, my Lady? Why, it was you who gave us freedom. That is why we revere you as our mother."

"We're a little simple," Davaryush said, "to sophisticated people from the future like you. So why don't you tell in plain language what you're doing here, what's happened....

"Simple!" the girl cried out. "Oh, my Lord, how can you say that? But you must promise to take me back to the station and do up my bracelet properly. I wouldn't want to be stranded here."

"Well, then—"

But the child had already begun her story.

***

This is the story of how the time of legends ended.

There was an enormous cataclysm that divided the gods from men; some say it was the screaming of the star, some say it was the descent of the One Mother into the black hole of hell; some that it was the reuniting and mutual destruction of Kelver and Arryk, or the self-immolation of Siriss and Karakaël and Elloran the wise. Whatever it was, all the gods perished, save one: Davaryush, who took on mortal flesh.

And mankind fractured in the wake of the great catastrophe. No longer were they one resplendent civilization, but thousands, each unique. And though the great light of the gods had been taken from them, each labored until it had found its own light; and the light no longer flowed from one tyrannical source, but was shared equally.

The god-made-man, Davaryush, and two mortals fled to the far arm of the galaxy, with dreams of a new humanity. They came and kindled a little light on a once-barren planet. And the past survives in the Inquestral tarot, which we carry as a memorial to the past; and in fragments of the plays of Lord Zalo.

There were great secrets of science in the ancient times. Not only did men smash through the overcosm in the bellies of giant whales, but they knew also how to compress a fragment of time into a tachyon bubble and send it instantaneously through space. The children of men did not recover all the lost wisdom. But they felt, as do all men, a longing for the stars. It was said that a star died to fuel the tachyon bubbles; but the children of men, being not gods, would not kill suns. They found a new way, without the tremendous energy drain of the tachyon bubbles. Men were sent through space through the tachyon universe, with its negative time flow, in a time-stasis shield which locked the traveler into the moment of his departure, preventing time paradoxes, sealing him off until reality could recapitulate to that same moment....

The plain of statues, then, was a gigantic space station, a harbor. But its walls and its machinery had not yet been built, nor the huge town of Davarangkar beside the space harbor. But one day would come the domes and towers of a mighty city.

How had they known they would succeed? How had they picked the site of the space station? It was easy. For they had grown up seeing the passengers standing in the sand, in their millennial sleep, waiting to awaken at their destination....

And how had the earliest people known of the star travelers? There was a legend of a young girl with her stasis-bracelet askew, who had accidentally awoken in the dawn time and spoken with the ancestors....

***

"And I'm that girl!" she was shouting. "I'm the one in the legend." She could scarcely contain herself.

"Science is strange," Davaryush mused. "In our own civilization we had the technology for mass tachyon transit; but it never occurred to anyone to use it. Because above all the Inquest wanted power, exclusive power, over the Dispersal of Man. We didn't have tachyon travel for everyone because the Inquest could not bear to give up a single iota of its terrible power!"

"Our children *will* learn," Darktouch said. "Perhaps."

"I can't take this!" Zalo said. "I must take the starship now, fly back to the real world, slough off these illusions—"

And the others were laughing, roaring with laughter; their laughter echoed in the shelter, against the walls of force.

"It's a trick!" Zalo shouted.

"No trick; look at the girl! Why does she look so familiar?" Davaryush said.

The girl: standing against the chart of the seven Inquestors. Redheaded with unkempt hair; a slight, insignificant sort of girl, and yet ... didn't I have red hair once? he asked himself once more ... there were a million urchins like this one, hawking sweets and bodies in the bazaars of Airang, staring wide-eyed when he landed with his delphinoid hanging in the sky, wondering at the starstreaked night ... nothing remarkable. Until he saw his own face, ghostlike, mirrored in the wall of force, in the sheen of the chart he had been working on. "You mean I'm your ... "

The girl smiled.

"What is your name, girl?"

"Jenjen," said the girl. "My name is Jenjen, father of my fathers."

He trembled. The utterance of that name released all his pent-up grief. At last he wept. He could not stanch the tears. He raised the girl up, gazed at the face through the tearblur, until he saw behind the features that mimicked his own traces of Darktouch's face, passionate and proud ... Darktouch who had despised him, who had accused him of cruelty, of hating himself. He wept, clasping the girl who bore his lover's name in his arms. He wept the tears of the years past. And knew in his heart that when he was through with weeping he would at last be free.

***

Darkness, a terrible darkness. He had returned to the ship alone. For many hours he stalked the corridors, remembering the hiding-room and the heartroom. Presently he came to the chamber where Jannif's body rested still, after all these years; suspended in a support-pod, it still preserved a semblance of life, though Jannif's soul was lost in the labyrinthine limbo of the delphinoid's mind.

He stared at her for a long time. They had gone through so much. How can I bear to lose you? he thought. At last he kissed her closed eyes and her still-moist lips and turned away.

In the heartroom of the starship he cried softly: "My starsteed, my stallion of the night ... what is it you really feel? Can you not share it with me?"

And there came pain ... like nails being driven into his head over and over into his spine into his bones his body rolling in a barrel of nails pain beating burning blasting bursting nails driving driving into him everywhere screaming screaming until he screamed himself into silence—

YES cried the delphinoid's voice. THIS is WHAT I HAVE FELT SINCE THE MOMENT I WAS TORN OUT OF THE DARK COUNTRY. OH, THOU POOR MORTAL.

Nails nails nails nails nails—

And behind that pain, a quiet grieving. The grief of the Sunless Sound as it whispered beneath the hunters' airskiffs. The grief of songs unborn. Of torrents of light that had never burst into the thick dark sky. Grief greater than any man could bear.

Nails nails nails—

And behind that grief was pity. Pity for a being so pitiless that it could sentence this creature to eternal torment ... compassion for Zalo, for all humanity.

And Zalo said: "How can I apologize for what has happened? We are what we are. I knew, but I tried not to know. Go free now, star whale, and find peace."

***

The thick of night. Darktouch standing by the shelter under the strange thin starlight. He came to her.

He said: "I have set the windbringer free."

They were silent. The air was heavy with tension; he could not yet say, freely, "I love you," without sounding somehow inadequate.

At last he said only, "I can't believe it! That everything is coming to an end, that it's all starting over!"

"Perhaps our children will burst out into the galaxy once more. And rejoin the old worlds of the lnquestors. And heal the ancient wounds. Maybe."

She smiled at him in the alien moonlight.

"Will you teach me ... the words of your play?" she said.

"There's no audience."

She laughed. "I know of one: a captive audience at that!" Like children they raced out on floaters into the night.

They found the field populated with their frozen children,

waiting to be born. He stood among the statues. He declaimed the words of his newly composed prologue:

At the core of the curving
Of time and space, the overcosm
Coiled ....

He postured. He spoke the roles in different voices, forgetting his embarrassment. She giggled softly, then burst into outright laughter; a warm laughter full of fierce, burning pride. She repeated his words: grand words they were, but tiny in the wind that howled about them.

Then—

"Look!" she cried suddenly. Dawn was breaking. His eyes followed the crook of her arm, up into the blackness. A meteor flashed. Fireworks! The sand glittered silver for a moment; the hills glowed. The light dissipated into morning....

"It's the starship," Zalo said. "It is the past, burning up as it plunges through the atmosphere."

"Are you happy? You will never go back now."

"I think so."

"It is the end of the time of legends," she said, quoting from *The Darkling Wind.*

"The beginning of the age of humans."

The sunrise came. It was cold; dew clung to the sand; the clingfire of her dress was dimmed. They pressed closer together in front of the plain full of their unborn children.

"Oh, Zasha," Darktouch said, her lips barely moving, "have we reached the homeworld of the heart? Have we, truly, truly?"

And Zalo said, "We were wrong to dream that it was a physical place, that somewhere out there in the heavens was the perfect world. It is an illusion. If it lies anywhere, Darktouch, it lies in our own hearts; it was always there, if we but chose to see it."

"And for this we have journeyed to the edge of the galaxy?"

"It was worth it. Every painful parsec."

"Hold me close."

"You must be cold."

"It's not because of the cold."

Not just for warmth now did they cling to one another. For,

if the fall of the Inquest could be perceived as a wall that divided time, that separated all of human history into two parts, it could not be said that they had soared in triumph over the top of the wall.

No. They were about to step gingerly through a chink in it. The time had come.

But that first step was no great play, no magnificent lightweaving, no grand gesture of *makrúgh:* it was an act of love.

—Alexandria, Los Angeles, Phoenix; 1979-1984
—Bangkok, 2020

APPENDIX I
The Authorship of the Inquestor Sagas

by Professor Shnau-en-Jip

There has been a recent tendency, in academic circles, for the oft-debated "Inquestral question" to raise its hoary head once more. As always, these matters seem more subject to the dictates of fashion than to any real desire to uncover the truth. The celebrated monograph by Sminangre var Halbjuling has been unavailable for some centuries; it is therefore perhaps once again timely to trot out the few known facts about these four enigmatic texts that are among the few literary artifacts to survive the interregnum or dark age whose duration has been variously estimated at anywhere between ten and one hundred thousand years.

Even the number of texts is in dispute (see *Halbjuling*, 4:3:22). Some see in *Light on the Sound* and *The Throne of Madness* (we shall use, for convenience, the titles under which the four lnquestral texts are most frequently published) a unity of narrative such that the two must be regarded as a single literary endeavor. Others—the separatist school—would break down the books, especially the anthology-like *Utopia Hunters,* into smaller component units, in many cases assigning to the fragments different putative authors, known variously as the primary, secondary, tertiary, quaternary bards. Since there are a number of inconsistencies, both stylistic and factual, in the four books, the multiple-authorship theory has always been the more popular. Nevertheless, we cannot entirely ignore the fact that the body of tradition surrounding the four works speaks unequivocally of a single author.

But as to the identity of that author ...

We may dismiss as fanciful several highly popular theories. The theory that the author of the Inquestral texts may be identified as the historical Zalo, the playwright, can be rejected out of hand. Not only are the "excerpts" from Zalo's plays quoted in the body of the text stylistically quite different from, and, I might add, vastly inferior to, the surviving fragments attributed to Zalo the dramatist; they are not even written in the same language!

Even less plausible is the idea that the author is Jenjen: not the Jenjen who plays a leading role in the stories, of course, but a much later Jenjen, the Jenjen who appears briefly at the end and who may or may not be the "child from the future" whose expository narrative is heard from time to time during the second book of *The Darkling Wind.* This romantic fiction derives, actually, from the famous novel *Jenjen's Odyssey Through Time,* published anonymously but now known to be the work of the Queen of Arron-Sivara. It is rather charming to suggest that in the ending of the fourth book, the author "wrote herself in" to the text as a mystic clue to her identity; even more delightful is the serendipitous notion that the author was one of Zalo's descendants.

The authorship has also been variously claimed on behalf of Shen Sajit, Ton Elloran, Ton Siriss (a memoir composed shortly before her self-immolation?), and, most improbably of all, by the late Professor Nazipeshtwi, "the divine spirit of the universe, whose random ordering of the magnetic flecks within the boxes of crushed message disks, produced the books as evidence of a pangalactic purpose of whose ineluctable meanderings we should not fail to be observant."

Nazipeshtwi's intense mysticism was an ornament to the anchorite society in which he lived; his theory resonates more with his own societal context, I think, than with any physical evidence.

The multiple-author theories are, in the main, even more farfetched than those I have mentioned; a quick glance through the books suspended from my ceiling shows a total of some sixty-three such theories, each offering a plethora of subtheories and dissident disciples.

What, then, are the facts surrounding the four Inquestral texts?

They are scanty.

We know that, at the time of their composition, the Inquestral Age (if it ever existed at all) was a dim memory, a collection of dusty myths. We may infer that the texts are permeated with the value judgments of a wholly later era, and that many details of the societies, clothing, monetary systems, honorific modes of speech, and so on, have been imposed from those of a much less technologically advanced age, a period of limited star travel and of chaotically differentiated language systems, of worlds wildly isolated and wildly different from each other. The author's understanding of the vanished technology is crude; he speaks vaguely of harnessing the energy of dying stars, but fails to provide specifics that would be obvious to the dullest schoolboy. It is safe to assume that many commonplaces of the Inquestral Age (and indeed of today) were to him sublime enigmas, to be cloaked in astounding but obfuscatory language.

The language question itself is an other important problem. The "Inquestral highspeech," liberally quoted throughout the texts, survives also in many other undatable fragments. Yet the author's knowledge of High Inquestral is either very sketchy or is of a dialect in many respects different from that of all the other surviving texts. How much had the Inquestral language survived this late into the dark age? The language of the texts itself, too, is clearly a highly corrupted version of Inquestral, marred by archaizing paradigms and a pedantic but slapdash application of grammatical principles. There is no known text today that is written in the same language. Does this point to single authorship, or to a colony of speakers of a bizarre, idiosyncratic dialect of Inquestral? Only the uncovering of more texts will tell.

The final question is perhaps the most profound of all, yet perhaps the most trivial: did the Inquestral Age actually exist?

A complete examination of the archaeological evidence on various worlds is beyond the purview of this brief afterword to the present edition. Suffice it to say that the evidence is contradictory and that theorists have so far been able to see in it anything they have wanted to see. There is one glaring omission in the evidence: it has so far not been possible to prove the existence of Uran s'Varek, for no expedition to the galactic core has to this day returned. Oh, for one of those tachyon bubbles so blithely described by the author or authors of these texts!

For many scholars, the archaeological verity of the Inquestral Age has proved to be a driving obsession; it led, in at least one case, to suicide. For these, it is clearly a question of consummate importance, and their ability to enjoy the four works is diminished if they are forced to view them as fiction. Yet, in an equally real sense, such preoccupation with reality is trivial. I am sure that the author or authors would have disapproved of such literal-mindedness. Surely the most vital legacy of the Inquestral texts is not whether, in some remote dimension where the past coexists eternally with the present, the Inquestors are still storming about, playing their games of *makrúgh* and burning planets. Nay, rather, it is the fact that the author or authors have clothed their meager myths with a rich humanity, with an awareness of the human condition that renders their quaint tales relevant millennia later, even here in a milieu with which they would have had little in common, and which they could scarcely have conceived possible.

APPENDIX II

The Irinika Fragment: History and Transliteration

by Adarre, Prince of Shirasnika

The celebrated and controversial "Irinika fragment" is the only evidence we can truly point to, independent of the Inquestral sagas, of the actual existence of the High Inquest with its galaxy-spanning empire. The author of the sagas feels compelled to quote the entire fragment in full, in translation, within the body of his text, lacunae and all; he has apparently invested a bard, Irinika, who, he says, sang the entire saga of which these fragments are all that survive.

Today the fragment is enshrined in the temple museum of Irinikangkier, the capital city of this somewhat backward world; holo-reproductions are our only means of studying it.

We may wonder why the temple guardians are so assiduous in preventing galactic experts from achieving access to the actual artifact. It is time, fellow academicians, to air the suspicions that many of us have been harboring for centuries.

The lrinika fragment is a hoax!

To support my thesis, I have delved into the mysteries of lrinika; disguising myself as a youthful adept, I was able to penetrate several levels into the temple's hierarchy before I was exposed and, unfortunately, banished. My execution was stayed only by the intervention of the princess-elect ... but I digress.

Now, the planet lrinika claims to have been founded by the eponymous bard mentioned in the Inquestor saga, who "fleeing the waters of Idoresht, found her own homeworld on our fair planet" *(Irinikensang,* 1:5:iii). This is patently absurd, for lrinika is clearly the name of a planet and the author of the lnquestral sagas showed faulty etymological sense when he applied it to a woman. The suffix *-nika,* which means "planet," has always denoted the masculine gender. High lnquestral, as used in the fragment and in the sagas, has no grammatical genders, but its paradigm structures show traces of the old Aryo-Vedic gender system.

What, then, is this fragment? And why does the author of the Inquestral sagas quote it at such length? Clearly he intends to lend an air of legitimacy to the saga, and to prove conclusively to his audience that he has not once deviated from the officially sanctioned document. Why, then, is there no other writing of the sort at all, any other independently surviving text? We may rule out the songs of Sajit, for they exist only in the body of the sagas, and have never been found elsewhere.

The idea that the Inquestral author, perhaps an adept on lrinika himself, was somehow inspired by this document to create an entire imaginary universe around it, to, as it were, "fill in the blanks" or "join up the dots," is a very attractive one, and has many proponents, although my colleage Professor Shnau-en-Jip will undoubtedly disagree with me.

But the secrecy that surrounds it, and the fact that no others like it exist, combine, in my mind, to form the irrefutable theory that the document itself is an invention of the Inquestral author ... planted on Irinika for the very purpose of legitimizing his four romantic sagas ... quoted in his text so as to resemble a felicitousaccident!

You wouldn't believe the adventures I had after propounding my theory to the high priest of the temple museum at lrinika. For my evidence I shall have to turn from swashbuckling to the more sober science of linguistics, and discuss, in transliteration, the reasons why the lrinika fragment simply cannot be as old as it is claimed.

Let us take; for example, the opening lines:

tembr(?) chom ... chada(nde): per(j)e(?) ... et Engu(?ester)
dari ervikteu(?r) ch(om) Davaryu(sh) hox aiud Shtoma chadanda luchada et eryagaih kalinikan emtrezhan [next four lines indecipherable]
kang jejnaivevisk' hokh'Ton Ton Davaryush hokhte jivyten dararan sonde?

The most glaring inconsistency is *l*.5, the use of *jejnaiveviske.* The reduplicative stem with subjunctive endings suggests a causative meaning, but the author translates the word merely as "could you know" and not "could you cause to know." The use of hypercorrect, "difficult" forms just to create a more impressive tone is a feature of the archaizing tendency of the dark age. The word *Shtoma* is incorrectly in the locative, giving it an unconscionable false apposition to the phrase *chadanda luchanda,* "in the cadent lightfall."

Again, the confusion of the locative with other cases is a feature of the dark age. The use of the work *kalinika* for "utopia" is unknown anywhere else, including in the body of the sagas, where *kaloka,* the contracted form, is always used. There is reason to believe that *kalinika* is an etymologically unsound back-formation on the pattern of certain planetary names (such as lrinika). Finally, in the accusative-and-participle construction of the last line quoted, *sonde* is strictly speaking correct, but *shtende* is infinitely more stylish; only a flabby prosodist would miss out on the opportunity to end the stanza with a double-long/short rather than a single.

Analysis of any other passage in the fragment will bear out my contention that the lrinika fragment cannot be the work of a professional bard. With his lacunae and his hypothetical interpolations, the author of the lnquestral sagas has attempted to disguise his imperfect understanding of pre dark-age prosody and metric structure; but to the practiced eye, the mishemmed seams in his tapestry become readily apparent.

It is astonishing to me that Professor Shnau-en-Jip can refer to this fragment as "the most profound, far-reaching, exalted, and perfect literary artifact of all time." The author of the lnquestral sagas was imaginative, indeed occasionally brilliant. But to call this little interpolated poem anything other than pastiche, a piece of quickly-stitched-together background material designed to lend an air of authenticity to a literary creation, seems *to* me to be nothing short of madness.

Afterword
An Open-Ended Dream

This novel was published in 1985, and composed about a year earlier, at a time when I was drifting away from science fiction. It's really my last completed science fiction novel. Thereafter, my output consisted on fantasy, historical novels, horror novels, a bildungsroman ... *anything* but science fiction

From a different vantage point, the year 2020, I think it's interesting, instructive, perhaps illuminating to look at all the *what ifs,* the alternate histories and the underlying reasons ... I had not really thought about it that much until I re-read *The Darkling Wind,* a novel I had pretty much forgotten about.

I remembered the Inquestor Series as having been *big.* Huge worlds, *lots* of them, a vast array of characters, political plots, and most of all a galactic empire's collapse, very much in the tradition of, say, *Foundation,* which I had enjoyed so much as a child. I remembered many of its pieces of "hardware" from displacement plates to servocorpses, from tachyon bubbles to people bins.

Now and then I'd get messages from readers out of my past, asking when I was going to do more of the stories. But I really had no interest. I was focused, like more modernist writers, more on microcosms than macrocosms, I suppose; I thought I was taking a more inward journey, about the insides of people's heads rather than the outsides of their star systems.

Even when I finally got around to writing *Homeworld of the Heart,* the "long-awaited" (by whom, I wonder?) fifth book in the series, and was already started on the sixth, I have to admit I was relying on my four-decades-old memories.

Because I was winging it, because I remembered wrongly exactly how, when and where Sajit had grown up, I started by already writing myself into knots ... and then I had an epiphany.

There was more than one Sajit.

I had not written myself into a corner after all! Rather, the corner I had written myself into was a doorway into a wild new universe laden with pathways and possibilities.

When *Homeworld of the Heart* ends there are still quite a few apparent inconsistencies with the original books ... but I'm going to unravel every one of them ... I promise you! ... they will all be as "inevitable" as Darth Vader telling Luke "I am your father" even though Obi Wan Kenobi just told him in the last movie that Darth Vader had *killed* Luke's father....

So yes. At this exact moment I have written about 10% of the second *Sajit* sequence novel, *Stillness in Starlight.* There will almost certainly be a third.

There are other characters in the series that could have their own stories. There are planets mentioned in passing that could have entire histories written. I am not sure if that will happen, but I do plan a big novel about Varuneh, one that could stand, with *The Darkling Wind,* as the left-hand bookend to the series.

So we're talking around an eight-book series, when this is all added up.

But I want to say that only after re-reading *The Darkling Wind* thirty-five years later did I realize what the book really was, and how different my life and career would have been if the book hadn't been lost in the publishing shuffle. To cut a long story short, this book was published by Bantam at the time when the first two in the series had gone out of print from Pocket (and the Timescape line was becoming history.). The book went out of print at Bantam just before they reiussed the first two. The series was never *ever* in print at the same time, let alone from a single publisher. All chances of it catching on or achieving a wide reader base were squelched by this accident of publishing politics, which really had nothing to do with the books themselves as far as I know.

In retrospect I realize that it was this that propelled me into other fields of writing and led to my greater success in the horror field, for instance. If things had turned out differently, I'd still be in science fiction—but I had worked *so hard* on this series, poured so much of my youthful imaginative mojo into it—that I must had felt I had shot my wad.

Indeed, it took 35 years to recharge that particular battery.

So yeah, I remembered that I'd written this fun, big, fat adventure series — sort of a *Game of Thrones* in space. But after writing a fifth volume, I read *this* one, the fourth volume, for the first time in decades and it was if I was reading a book by a stranger—apart from the plot, I remembered almost nothing.

But the first thing I realized I had misremembered was what *kind* of book it was. *The Darkling Wind* is actually much more experimental than I remembered.

It's actually a metafiction, a narration that is actually being written by one of its protagonists, Zalo, while it is going on. Quotations from *The Darkling Wind* by Zalo embedded in the book actually contain pieces of other stories in the series like *The Rainbow King,* making us realize that all those stories aren't just straight narratives, but mythologizations of the events, literary artifacts *within* my own literary artifact. The series is an AI program, designed with the ability to design itself.

This means that *all* the narrative voices in the first three books became unreliable narrators because they are shown to be seen through the "novelizing" mind of one of characters in the story. It's not just an adventure with a quasi-mythic setting—it's also a book about the process of how history becomes myth.

I always knew I was influenced by Theodore Sturgeon (more of this in a minute) because the first story I remember reading as a child, *The Skills of Xanadu,* has its fingerprints *all over* this polyology. I always knew that there's a Cordwainer Smith-like feel to these books as well—the whole non-European sensibility that underlies it.

What I didn't realize until I reread this is how much an influence Chip (Samuel R.) Delany has had on this work. He is a master of narrative ambiguity. I suppose I didn't realize it at the time because when writing I'm so focused on the story itself, but when I read a novel like *Dhalgren* I am as engrossed (or *more* engrossed even) by the process as I am by the narrative.

Getting back to Sturgeon, Ted actually told me in a personal letter that he felt that in this book I was getting away from the characters and becoming more caught up in the metafiction. Reading the book now, I see what he meant.

I briefly considering sending the whole book through the typewriter one more time, and sharpening up the dialogue. In the end I've decided it's better to let sleeping pteratygers lie. Instead I'd rather spend my days diving into the universe and unearthing more stories that I know are still in there.

So here I am, sending this big old series once more into the void.

But things are different. As my old readers rediscover my work, as new readers start checking it out, I am having a much more personal relationship with my audience. The patreon thing, the social media thing—they are all miracles of my old age. I'm getting direct support for my writing from the people who are actually reading me—that is amazing.

It means I can afford to do what I couldn't do before—

I built the cathedral, you see, and the structure is all there and probably won't fall down. With the reissue of the four original books, you may now visit at your leisure and enjoy the structure pretty much as originally conceived....

But now I'm going to take a ladder and clamber up to obscure corners and carve a few gargoyles.

You may never see them, but they will be there for you to discover ... as long as I survive to finish them.

Scholarly Commentary
Towards an Inquestral Chronology

by Professor Schnau-en-Jip

With, at long last, the publication of these, the restored edition of the volumes of the Inquestor saga, it is now possible to consider the putative chronology of the events the saga describes. Having belabored the controversial "Inquestral Question" elsewhere, I will not tax my readers with another exposition of the many theories that have been advanced as to the identity of the author/authors of these sagas, which have tantalized academics for so many millennia. Nevertheless, having made it my life's work to study the four volumes of the so-called tetralogy, I have been able to compile a chart of what appear to be the main events of the Late Inquestral Age, insofar as such surmisings are possible from a work whose function must be considered literary rather than historiographic.

First, though, I should perhaps elucidate why I have referred to the Inquestral sagas as a "so-called" tetralogy. This thesis arises out of my conviction that the original author of the saga intended a five-volume saga. (See my notes to *Light on the Sound* for final proof of the single-author theory of the Inquestor sagas.) In the first place, the final "volume" is much vaster in scope than the other three; and in the second, it seems to be telling two wholly disparate stories, that of the Essondrish natives first introduced in *Utopia Hunters,* and that of the Inquestors continuing directly from *The Throne of Madness*. It would seem from this that *The Darkling Wind* is actually an editorial composite. While the tales are remarkably well blended, *The Darkling Wind* still appears to contain traces of a radically different structure. As to whether the work was actually conflated from two separate sources, as theorized by Halbjuling and Adarre, or the result of the putative bard's own second thoughts . . . this must still be considered a matter of some conjecture. Doubtless scholars will continue to exercise their thoughts over this literary conundrum until the end of time.

***

As for the Inquestral chronology:

It is sketchy. And yet I believe that what follows may be of some assistance in helping the first-time student of the Inquestor sagas to visualize, contextualize, and internalize the complex conflicts of this literary universe.

Please note that, for the purposes of this chronology, the Year 1 is taken as the year in which Davaryush was made Kingling of Gallendys, the opening event in the first of the four Inquestral sagas. Note also that lifespans are measured in realtime; time dilation must be taken into account in order to measure the biological ages of the protagonists.

20,000 years Before Davaryush (B.D.)

Discovery of Uran s'Varek; unleashing of the power of the Throne of Madness for the first time

Mother Vara
Vara's World (in preparation)

15—5,000 B.D.

Period of greatest Inquestral control

consolidation of Inquestral power
The Inquest gains control of one million worlds
(some only peripherally)
The Inquest finds and controls Gallendys
with help from the Throne of Madness

Prequel Trilogy (Vara's World - TBA)
The Web Dancer

4,000 B.D.
Power of the Inquest at its peak

3,000 B.D.
Power of the Inquest begins to wane
Boyhood of Elloran;
destruction of Elloran's homeworld

The Rememberer's Story (Part One)

2,700 B.D.
Boyhood of Sajit—creation of Tijas
Transformation of Nevéqilas into Aírang
Creation of Jatis

Homeworld of the Heart

2,400 B.D.
Adventures of Jatis on Ont
Rule of Tijas in post-Urna kingdom

Stillness in Starlight

2,000 B.D.
Elloran on Ymvyrsh, aged 12
Elloran meets Sajit
Death of Alkamathdes

The Rainbow King
Third Sajit novel (in preparation)

1,300 B.D.
Boyhood of Davaryush
Boyhood of Karakaël

922 B.D.
Elloran finds Kerrin

The Rememberer's Story (Part Two)

789 B.D.
Sajit leaves Varezhdur in search of Dei Zhendra
The Dust Sculptress

237 B.D.
Meeting of Arryk and Siriss on the planet Kailasa
The Story of Young Arryk

49 B.D.
Davaryush goes to Shtoma

Light on the Sound
The Thirteenth Utopia

DAVARINE ERA
Arrival of Davaryush on Gallendys;
Meeting of Kelver and Darktouch

Light on the Sound

2 D.E.
Kelver receives mission
to defeat the Inquest

Light on the Sound

98 D.E.
Lady Varuneh, presumed executed, finds that she has been transported to the water world Idoresht

The Throne of Madness

112 D.E.
Kelver awakens on Uran s'Varek

The Throne of Madness

113 D.E.
Lady Varuneh rescued;

The Throne of Madness

Old Sajit visits Bellares

The Comet's Story

114 D.E.
Sajit dies; Kelver challenges the Inquest to a final game of *makrúgh;* the war begins

The Throne of Madness

147 D.E.
Young Jenjen meets Elloran

Utopia Hunters

150 D.E.
Elloran searches for Sajit's missing burial place

Homeworld of the Heart; Stillness in Starlight

172 D.E.
Essondras comes under discussion as a possible war site

Utopia Hunters
The Darkling Wind

178 D.E.
Sajit's body is returned to Varezhdur

The Book of the Darkweaver

187 D.E.
Essondras is destroyed *The Darkling Wind*

189 D.E.
Zorn destroyed *The Darkling Wind*

191 D.E.
Shtoma destroyed; the Dark Ages begin

The Darkling Wind

214 D.E.
Lightfall

The Darkling Wind

347 D.E.
Zalo and Darktouch find Old Earth;
the memory of the Inquest fades

The Darkling Wind

10,000 D.E.
First known fragments of
the Inquestral sagas;
Inquestral question first raised by scholars

Allusions to as-yet-undiscovered texts are conjectural and subject to revision

An Appeal to My Readers

This novel was made possible because a few dozen people became my supporters by joining this website: www.patreon.com/spsomtow.

I'm no longer doing these books with the backing of a vast New York publishing conglomerate. It's pretty much do-it-yourself, with all the labor-intensiveness, snatching time away from money-making activities, and sloppy trying to proofread one's own copy implies.

If a few dozen more people would sign up — or a few hundred — my ability to resume my science fiction career would be much enhanced. So, please consider it.

Supporters get to read all my books chapter by chapter — in their unenhanced, inaccurately proofred and yet-to-be refined incarnations — right as they come out of my head. They get Christmas presents (though I am habitually late with them). You can join for as little a $2 a month — though hopefully you will be able to do a higher level.

And of course, do find a moment to review the book, if you are so inclined. Word of mouth is what truly propels things.

About the Author

The most well-known expatriate Thai in the world
— *International Herald Tribune*

Once referred to by the International Herald Tribune as "the most well-known expatriate Thai in the world," Somtow Sucharitkul is no longer an expatriate, since he has returned to Thailand after five decades of wandering the world. He is best known as an award winning novelist and a composer of operas.

Born in Bangkok, Somtow grew up in Europe and was educated at Eton and Cambridge. His first career was in music and in the 1970s he acquired a reputation as a revolutionary composer, the first to combine Thai and Western instruments in radical new sonorities. Conditions in the arts in the region at the time proved so traumatic for the young composer that he suffered a major burnout, emigrated to the United States, and reinvented himself as a novelist.

His earliest novels were in the science fiction field but he soon began to cross into other genres. In his 1984 novel Vampire

Junction, he injected a new literary inventiveness into the horror genre, in the words of Robert Bloch, author of *Psycho*, "skillfully combining the styles of Stephen King, William Burroughs, and the author of the Revelation to John." *Vampire Junction* was voted one of the forty all-time greatest horror books by the Horror Writers' Association, joining established classics like *Frankenstein* and *Dracula*.

In the 1990s Somtow became increasingly identified as a uniquely Asian writer with novels such as the semi-autobiographical *Jasmine Nights*. He won the World Fantasy Award, the highest accolade given in the world of fantastic literature, for his novella *The Bird Catcher*. His seventy-seven books have sold about two million copies world-wide.

After becoming a Buddhist monk for a period in 2001, Somtow decided to refocus his attention on the country of his birth, founding Bangkok's first international opera company and returning to music, where he again reinvented himself, this time as a neo Asian neo-Romantic composer. The Norwegian government commissioned his song cycle Songs Before Dawn for the 100th Anniversary of the Nobel Peace Prize, and he composed at the request of the government of Thailand his *Requiem: In Memoriam 9/11* which was dedicated to the victims of the 9/11 tragedy.

According to London's Opera magazine, "in just five years, Somtow has made Bangkok into the operatic hub of Southeast Asia." His operas on Thai themes, *Madana, Mae Naak,* and *Ayodhya,* have been well received by international critics. His opera, *The Silent Prince,* was premiered in 2010 in Houston, and, *Dan no Ura,* premiered in Thailand in the 2013 season. Since then he has composed many more stage works including the acclaimed fantasy-based opera *The Snow Dragon* (premiered in Milwaukee in 2015) and seven operas in the *DasJati* sequence which aims to put all ten of the iconic *Ten Lives of the Buddha* into music drama form.

He is increasingly in demand as a conductor specializing in opera and in the late-romantic composers like Mahler. His repertoire runs the entire gamut from Monteverdi to Wagner. His work has been especially lauded for its stylistic authenticity and its lyricism. The orchestra he founded in Bangkok, the Siam Philharmonic, has mounted the first complete Mahler cycle in the region.

He was the first recipient of Thailand's "Distinguished Silpathorn" award, given for an artist who has made and continues to make a major impact on the region's culture, from Thailand's Ministry of Culture.

In 2017 he was awarded the European Cultural Achievement Award by the Europa KulturForm, citing his building of bridges between Asian and Western cultures.

Books by S.P. Somtow

General Fiction
The Shattered Horse
Jasmine Nights
Forgetting Places
The Other City of Angels (aka *Bluebeard's Castle)*
The Stone Buddha's Tears

Dark Fantasy
The Timmy Valentine Series:
Vampire Junction
Valentine
Vanitas
Vampire Junction Special Edition
Moon Dance
Darker Angels
The Vampire's Beautiful Daughter

Science Fiction
Starship & Haiku
Mallworld
The Ultimate Mallworld
The Ultimate, Ultimate, Ultimate Mallworld
Chronicles of the High Inquest:
Light on the Sound
The Darkling Wind
The Throne of Madness
Utopia Hunters
Homeworld of the Heart
Chroniques de l'Inquisition - Volume 1 (omnibus) *Chroniques de l'Inquisition - Volume 2* (omnibus)
Inquestor Tales One: The Singing Moons
Inquestor Tales Two: A Woman Cloaked in Shadow
Inquestor Tales Three: The Child Collector
Inquestor Tales Four: The Space Between Spaces

The Aquiliad Series:
- *Aquila in the New World*
- *Aquila and the Iron Horse*
- *Aquila and the Sphinx*

Fantasy

The Riverrun Trilogy:
- *Riverrun*
- *Armorica*
- *Yestern*

The Riverrun Trilogy (omnibus)
The Fallen Country
Wizard's Apprentice
The Snow Dragon (omnibus)

Media Tie-in

The Alien Swordmaster
Symphony of Terror
The Crow - Temple of Night
Star Trek: Do Comets Dream?

Chapbooks

Fiddling for Waterbuffaloes
I Wake from a Dream of a Drowned Star City
A Lap Dance with the Lobster Lady
Compassion — Two Perspectives
The Bird Catcher

Libretti

Mae Naak
Ayodhya
Madana
Dan no Ura
Helena Citronova
The Snow Dragon
Dasjati:
- *Temiya - The Silent Prince*
- *Sama - The Faithful Son*
- *Bhuridat - The Dragon Lord*

Mahosadha - Architect of Dreams
Nemiraj - Chariot of Heaven
Prince Vessantara

Collections
My Cold Mad Father
Fire from the Wine Dark Sea
Chui Chai (Thai)
Nova (Thai)
The Pavilion of Frozen Women
Dragon's Fin Soup
Tagging the Moon
Face of Death (Thai)
Other Edens
S.P. Somtow's The Great Tales (Thai)
Terror Nova (in press)
Terror Antiqua (in press)
Alien Heresies (in press)

Essays, Poetry and Miscellanies
Opus Fifty
A Certain Slant of "I" (in press)
Sonnets about Serial Killers
Opera East
Victory in Vienna (ed.)
Three Continents (ed.)
Nirvana Express
Caravaggio x 2
The Maestro's Noctuary
Nox: Noctuary Two

www.ingramcontent.com/pod-product-compliance
Lightning Source LLC
Chambersburg PA
CBHW020531310726
48979CB00014B/2293/J
* 9 7 8 1 9 4 0 9 9 9 5 9 3 *